NO SMALL TEMPEST

NO SMALL TEMPEST

BY
EVELYN RICHARDSON

INTRODUCTION BY
ANDREW SEAMAN

Formac Publishing Company Limited
Halifax

To Laurie

© 2006 Formac Publishing Company Limited
Introduction © Andrew Seaman 2006

All rights reserved. No part of this book may be reproduced or transmitted in any form or by any means, electronic or mechanical, including photocopying, or by any information storage or retrieval system, without permission in writing from the publisher.

Formac Publishing Company Limited recognizes the support of the Province of Nova Scotia through the Department of Tourism, Culture and Heritage. We acknowledge the financial support of the Government of Canada through the Book Publishing Industry Development Program (BPIDP) for our publishing activities. We acknowledge the support of the Canada Council for the Arts for our publishing program.

Author's photo: Mamie Harmon

Library and Archives Canada Cataloguing in Publication

Richardson, Evelyn M. (Evelyn May), 1902-1976.
    No small tempest / Evelyn M. Richardson ; introduction
    by Andrew Seaman.

(Formac fiction treasures)
Reprint. First published: Ryerson, 1957.
ISBN 10: 0-88780-706-2   ISBN 13: 978-0-88780-706-0

I. Title. II. Series.

PS8535.I32N6 2006   C813'.52   C2006-904373-6

Series Editor: Gwendolyn Davies

Formac Publishing Company Limited
5502 Atlantic Street
Halifax, Nova Scotia B3H 1G4
www.formac.ca

Printed and bound in Canada

Presenting Formac Fiction Treasures
Series Editor: Gwendolyn Davies

A taste for reading popular fiction expanded in the nineteenth century with the mass marketing of books and magazines. People read rousing adventure stories aloud at night around the fireside; they bought entertaining romances to read while travelling on trains and curled up with the latest serial novel in their leisure moments. Novelists were important cultural figures, with devotees who eagerly awaited their next work.

Among the many successful popular English language novelists of the late 19th and early 20th centuries were a group of Maritimers who found in their own education, travel and sense of history, events and characters capable of entertaining readers on both sides of the Atlantic. They emerged from well-established communities that valued education and culture, for women as well as men. Faced with limited publishing opportunities in the Maritimes, successful writers sought magazine and book publishers in the major cultural centres: New York, Boston, Philadelphia, London and sometimes Montreal and Toronto. They often enjoyed much success with readers at home, but the best of these writers found large audiences across Canada and in the United States and Great Britain.

The Formac Fiction Treasures series is aimed at offering contemporary readers access to books that were successful, often huge bestsellers in their time, but which are now little known and often hard to find. The authors and titles selected are chosen first of all as enjoyable to read, and secondly for the light they shine on historical events and on attitudes and views of the culture from which they emerged. These complete original texts reflect values that are sometimes in conflict with those of today: for example, racism is often evident, and bluntly expressed. This collection of novels is offered as a step towards rediscovering a surprisingly diverse and not nearly well enough known popular cultural heritage of the Maritime provinces and of Canada.

Evelyn Richardson

INTRODUCTION

Followers of the story of Dan Redmond and Mercy Nickerson, who first appeared in *Desired Haven*, will be delighted to find that *No Small Tempest* takes up the life of their daughter Adria in the same setting, the island of New Erin. Readers who have not yet discovered *Desired Haven* — republished in this series by Formac in 2005 — will also be able to appreciate this sequel, as it has an intact plot of its own, and the main characters are newly minted. Little of the previous plot is given away in reminiscences here, so those who read *No Small Tempest* first will still be able to appreciate *Desired Haven*, but for the full effect, it's best to read the novels in the proper sequence.

Evelyn Richardson won the Governor General's Award for non-fiction in 1945 with an autobiographical account of her life as the wife of the lighthouse keeper of Bon Portage Island at the southern tip of Nova Scotia. *We Keep a Light* remains her best-known book and was republished in England and the United States as *We Bought an Island*. The story tells how the family's resourceful spirit helped them overcome the difficulties of life in an isolated situation. It contains some beautiful landscape description, but is rather reserved in its portraiture of family members.

The two novels that Evelyn subsequently wrote develop character much more fully, and are built around engaging plots. *Desired Haven* also won critical acclaim, receiving the Ryerson Fiction Award. *The University of Toronto*

Quarterly greeted it as one of the most interesting novels of 1953, and Desmond Pacey, writing in the *Queens Quarterly*, praised the book, finding the characterizations interesting, credible and well rounded.

No Small Tempest, however, went almost unnoticed by the critics, winning only a single notice at the time of its publication. Even the *Dalhousie Review* missed it. Yet the characterization is at least as good as that in *Desired Haven*. Indeed, it is so superior to the work of many popular novelists of the time as to be commendable. Evelyn's writing focuses on the culture of her region, and this results in a richness and depth in the treatment of character that is often missing in the work of her contemporaries.

Evelyn knew the region intimately. Born in 1902, she spent all but a dozen of her 72 years in the southwest corner of Nova Scotia, 35 of them on the island of Bon Portage. There, along with husband Morrill Richardson, she brought up and educated her three children. Eventually she and Morrill retired to the mainland, where Evelyn wrote books and articles on local history and tales of the sea. She also wrote a children's book and a wartime story, as well as a number of shorter works.

No Small Tempest is more specifically a love story than *Desired Haven*, but one that is sensitively written and that introduces the reader to a wealth of cultural background peculiar to the Nova Scotia "South Shore" of the late nineteenth century. The novel has a fresh and interesting plot. Perhaps it is a little sentimental in spots, but it remains unpretentious.

One aspect of Richardson's writing is unusual for her time: sexual relations are a major theme, and are treated quite candidly. There is nothing here that would shock a twenty-first- century reader: today Richardson's candidness seems refreshing and realistic. She is determined to explore the lives of her characters comprehensively, and she does not shy away from the fact that sexual interests, passions, weaknesses and strategies are major factors in human motivation.

No Small Tempest takes its title from a biblical passage in which the apostle Paul tells of enduring a storm at sea. The heroine, Adria, finds the passage when she opens the bible for comfort during the hurricane that ends *Desired Haven* and begins this story. Adria, now in her early teens, is the daughter of Mercy and Dan Redmond, the central figures in the first novel. *No Small Tempest* opens the day before the storm, when Adria meets Isles Kendrick while berry-picking on her island home. Isles is the nephew of the general store keeper and shipping agent in Prince's Cove, the nearest village on the mainland. He and his widowed mother have come to help out with the house and store after the death of his aunt, and Isles has taken the day to explore New Erin. This is the beginning of a long friendship that, perhaps too predictably, ends in romance — though not until many trials have been endured. Isles is a tall, serious fellow, somewhat reticent, who dreams of a life at sea and chafes under the necessity of running his uncle's store and caring for his mother. However, he is far too gentle and good-hearted to rebel.

Captain Dave Malone is the other major character in the novel, the third corner of a love triangle involving Adria and Isles. A sharp contrast to his cousin Isles, Dave is a good-humoured, gregarious adventurer and something of a womanizer. He is a fine and responsible captain who earns the respect of his men, but he is apt to act precipitously in his private life. He possesses little sense of shame, but is adept at spinning a good story to cover his tracks when he feels the truth would be to his disadvantage.

Modern day readers are perhaps more comfortable with romance in film than in book form, and in many respects this novel can best be read with the conventions of popular romantic films in mind. In fact, it has a good cinematic plot, with a lot of action spread over a broad scope of time.

The setting has all the appeal of an exotic outport in the last days of sail. The paddle-wheel packet steamship out of Yarmouth plies its regular trips up and down the coast but is viewed by the islanders as a noisy curiosity — no threat to the graceful and superbly seaworthy schooners that are still the backbone of fishing and trade. The island itself, with its cove and wharves, is not so very different from some modern South Shore communities, and many sailing vessels of the coastal fishery are still in existence, including several magnificent schooners now used in the tourist industry.

Some of the story's action takes place aboard such schooners. Captain Dave Malone, for example, saves his ship from wrecking on Sable Island after he is warned of a storm in a nightmare. Another dramatic scene features a fight on the deck of Malone's schooner, a fight that alters the fate of several characters.

Other great scenes include such events as the annual "tea meeting" in the local temperance hall, where the entire community gathers to socialize and buy and sell baked goods and crafts to raise funds. This particular occasion involves romantic intrigue, deception, gossip and even a fight outside the hall. And the court scene in Barrington, the climax of the plot, provides both local colour and high drama.

Our three major characters are supported by a wonderfully diverse cast. There is Dan Redmond, who assembled his house out of the abandoned cottages on the island — every time he needed more space, he dragged home another cottage and

INTRODUCTION

annexed it to the main house. Adria's mother, Mercy Redmond, plays a small role in *No Small Tempest*, but her strength of character and shrewd observation of human nature emerge clearly, particularly in a confrontation with Thankful Newhall.

Thankful is well named in an ironic, Dickensian way. She was imported to the island as schoolteacher to the Redmond children in *Desired Haven*, but is not well liked. She is a cruel disciplinarian, and hides a rather loose moral character under the disguise of rigid propriety. Adria once finds her spying with a telescope on the young men swimming naked off the wharf. Thankful tries to worm her way into the family by seducing one of Adria's brothers. She is also a vicious gossip, and out of jealousy and for revenge she puts her talents to work to destroy Adria's reputation. Richardson's dialogue in these gossip scenes is priceless.

Nabby Nowlan, the village witch, is still with us in *No Small Tempest*. However, her illegitimate son Waitstill plays a bigger role. He appears in the earlier part of the novel as the hired boy on New Erin, a friend of Adria's who treats her with innocent worship. Waitstill isn't bright, but he has some real talents, and is treated fondly by Adria. He grows to be a huge fellow, and joins the crew of Malone's schooner when he is old enough. Waitstill's fate is tragic. He suffers severe brain damage, and after being nursed back to some semblance of physical health by Nabby, becomes a veritable Frankenstein's monster within the community. His life and the lives of Captain Malone and Adria are strangely intertwined.

Of the minor characters, Obie Knowles, the loquacious ship's cook and neighbour from *Desired Haven*, is also still with us. Obie's fondness for embroidering a good story becomes entangled with Thankful's gossip to produce a witch's brew that lands Adria in serious trouble, but not without some very humorous consequences as well. His daughter, Arabella ("Airy Bella" as he pronounces it) has grown into a surprisingly beautiful girl with a lively sexual appetite. She is not treated in any depth, but has an important role in the plot as she becomes involved in an affair with one of the main characters. And then there is Isles' mother, Priscilla (Cilla), a lively, intelligent, good-humoured and wise older woman, an old school friend of Mercy's. She and Mercy are the kind of women who form the backbone of the community — and are so familiar in our rural villages, contrasting sharply with the likes of Thankful.

Despite these well-drawn characters and the novel's other qualities, Claude Bissell, in his roundup of Canadian Fiction for 1957 in the *University of Toronto Quarterly*, found it disappointing, claiming that it has all the faults of a popular sequel. He attacked the book's characterization and its regionalism. He also accused it of heavy sentiment, and an awkward pretentiousness. Bissell may have supposed that Richardson was exploiting the sexual theme for popular appeal, but perhaps the conclusion to be drawn from his harsh criticism is that women who wrote love stories were simply not to be taken seriously by the critical establishment of the 1950s.

No Small Tempest is not without flaws, and two criticisms can be levelled quite fairly at the novel. The first is that Richardson uses rather too much omniscient narration to fill in the blanks in the lengthy time span. This is not due to a lack of ability where creating good drama is concerned, but to a lack of experience, and perhaps to the lack of a certain instinct for sustaining the dramatic effect over the long haul. The second is that the exigencies of the plot occasionally get in the way of credible dialogue. Dave's proposal of marriage is not entirely convincing, and the dialogue in the final love scenes is a little saccharine and

INTRODUCTION xiii

stilted. Yet some of the dialogue, such as Obie's testimony in court, and like Thankful's gossip, is quite brilliant.

In 1955 Richardson gave a talk entitled "No Ivory in Light Towers" at a Canadian Authors' Association convention in which she discussed her life as a writer. In the talk she mentioned the wealth of dramatic material, both current and historical, that her life in southwest Nova Scotia had provided. The focus of *No Small Tempest* is somewhat different from *Desired Haven* with regard to this material. Where her first novel explores a variety of themes — from witchcraft and smuggling to folklore and history — this novel concentrates more on society and personal relationships. Perhaps this gives it more the flavour of a romance than a historical novel, but the local colour and authenticity are also there. It is full of little details of South Shore life in the late nineteenth century, and it has a serious theme too.

The novel's conclusion is not simply the resolution of a love triangle. It invites reflection on the responsibility of all the characters for the events that have occurred, happy and tragic alike. This may be a romance in the nineteenth-century tradition, but it is set within a vivid sense of time and place, and played out by sympathetic characters of considerable depth.

Readers who enjoyed *Desired Haven* will enjoy *No Small Tempest* too.

Andrew Seaman, 2006

DR. ANDREW SEAMAN, a member of the English Department at Saint Mary's University, has taught courses on the literature of the Maritime provinces for many years. He has a particular interest in literature reflecting the history and culture of Nova Scotia, and has published articles on Charles Bruce, Ernest Buckler, Thomas Raddall and Frank Parker Day.

And when neither sun nor stars in many days appeared and no small tempest lay on us . . .

—Acts 27: 20

ONE

On that September morning in 1865, island-bred Adria Redmond woke to the certainty of coming storm. She told herself wistfully that it might clear the air, and she had in mind more than the thick atmosphere pressing upon her counterpane. To twelve-year-old Adria a storm meant tumultuous grandeur of clouds and sea followed by cleansed air, washed sky and lightened spirits; a rising wind could stir her as the flood stirs a grounded boat, but this morning she felt no exhilaration. She lay still, thinking back over the summer. Never had her world held so much beauty and wonder, so many people to love, so much love to give them. The dawns had glowed with more delicate loveliness than the dawns of other years and the sunsets had blazed across the harbour in greater glory. Now clouds were gathering over New Erin as constraint and unhappiness deepened among its inhabitants.

After breakfast the humid morning became a queerly taut one of fretted nerves and distrait grownups absorbed in an impenetrable waiting. Adria soon asked, "Mamma, before the storm breaks may I go foxberrying?" Her tight voice betrayed her awareness of the kitchen's undercurrents and her desire to be away from them.

No matter how busy or weary, Mercy Redmond had time and understanding for her children. She drew her daughter close and brushed the tendrils from the troubled forehead. At her mother's touch Adria felt her tight perplexities loosen and drop to be stepped out of, like an unbuttoned petticoat, and it was with a lightened heart that she left the house, pewter berry-pitcher in hand.

New Erin, her island home, lay quiescent as if determinedly snatching rest before an expected ordeal. The air above it was both lifeless and filled with distant, inaudible vibrations from the wind and sea now rushing to assault this rampart of southwestern Nova Scotia.

The small lighthouse on the westernmost point dozed with daytime's blank windows, indifferently beckoning a few listless sails to the shelter of Redmond's Harbour. Behind the squat tower the shorn mowing-field spread to encircle barns and sheds and the rambling white house. All these turned their backs upon the outer bay to watch the harbour where, a hundred yards from the front door of the house, the grey spiles of two wharves penned the quivering water of a narrow dock. Beyond the homestead the wedge-shaped point broadened abruptly into a circular island (of some six hundred acres) with a shoreline bitten haphazardly, like a child's cookie, by the ocean. On the seaward side the rough pasture land rose gradually; on the harbour side it climbed quickly, dipped and mounted again, forming Nigh Hill and Further, where cattle were feeding on the slopes and sheep had found the blue shadows under the spruces of the inner shoulders.

By the time Adria had reached the depression between the hills, her clothes were clinging to her damply, and she brought up a wilted apron corner to wipe her face. The hillside's mossy hummocks were covered by crimson foxberries and their glossy leaves, each cluster so like pieces of enamelled jewellery that Adria tried several against her white apron yoke before denuding the slender stalks. Kneeling amid the vivid berries she decided that the hollow, like a big green butterbowl tilting shoreward, was really her favourite spot of all New Erin. Her sunbonnet dangled in its customary neglect and bleached wisps from taffy-coloured braids tangled in her black lashes. She brushed them away with the back of her hand and hitched along to another spot of berries. As she moved, her dress drew tight across her budding breasts and a button rolled, tickling, down her back. *Serena's right. It's high time the blue gingham went into the rag-barrel.* She knew that she clung to last summer's dress as part of her carefree and vanishing childhood, and her eyes grew softly vague as her berry-wise fingers went about their business and left her mind free to recall last summer's Adria, who had fitted loosely into the new blue gingham. Not only had her body burgeoned into unfamiliarity; she often had a nightmarish feeling of being caught halfway through the open doorway between childhood and young womanhood and of hearing Gramma Damie's impatient, "Well, milady, come in or go out," while she found herself unable to do either.

A gull drifting past carried her eyes across the glassy half-mile of Redmond's Harbour and to the wooded shore of Narrah Isle, which in the strange thick air appeared to have been pulled closer and out of shape. The mainland village of Prince's Cove lay partly hidden behind the little island but Adria could see, above and beyond Narrah's spruce-tops, the scattered homes lining the nearer slope of Meeting-house Hill and the twisting tan road which straightened respectfully before the Meeting-house and then vanished. Outlined against the sky the church had a dignity befitting its place in the community, where to be a stranger to its doors was to be a stranger indeed.

Adria had never been to her father's church in St. Joseph's; it was too far away and the people there were French; but when she visited her grandparents in the Cove, she had gone with them to preaching-meeting. She enjoyed settling herself, stiff in starched muslin, between Grammy's rustling black silk and Grampy's tickling serge, and she lifted her voice joyfully in the opening hymn. It was conceded that Mr. Stouten (tall and thin, in contradiction of his name) had great staying powers, but he was apt to "pay off" from his text until no amount of wriggling could ease young bodies, though older folk might forget the hard pews in stolen naps. But Adria absorbed the atmosphere of sanctity and hushed devotion, while it was a joy to grasp, out of the preacher's inexhaustible flow, phrases and sentences uplifting and stirring by sheer beauty of sound. Now, alone on the hillside, she recalled lines from a treasuring memory, "From the rising of the morning till the stars appeared," "ready to pardon, gracious and merciful." Withdrawing her eyes and her memories from the white Meeting-house, Adria murmured, "the great winds of the Lord," as a blue-flag cluster rasped forebodingly.

Her love lent enchantment to every inch of her island home, but an unprejudiced eye would have noted that the hillsides were bespattered with rocks of every size and shape, and that the sod was stretched to breaking over hummocks which betrayed a hidden fellow to each stone in sight. As she followed the red berries, Adria came to a group of mounds that differed slightly from the surrounding ones, though the grass grew as lushly between them and berries clustered as thickly upon them. The eastern end of each was marked by an upright slab of the ubiquitous granite, and the foot by a smaller piece. There were ten of these parallel mounds, not counting the two that lay slightly apart and had the pitifully short space between the upended stones.

Though Adria never tired of tales concerning the island's first settlers, she could not deny some jealousy of those who, before the Redmonds, had trod the cowpaths through spruce and alders, and known the broken shoreline. This feeling stopped short at the group of graves where some of those predecessors lay, forever at home on New Erin with the surf's muted roar drifting across them. To the Redmond children the unfenced graveyard was merely a reminder of long ago, like the open cellar-holes and crumbling stonewalls dotting the island. Yet sometimes the two tiny graves aroused in Adria a pity, too sweet and faint to be sadness. She was stabbed now by an unnamed sorrow, as if the past broke through time with reverberations of the losses and pain endured on the hill, or as if the future sent back a reversed echo of the grief it holds for everyone. Even as she put her head down upon her cradled arms, that poignancy fled, but the present's distresses came crowding in upon her and girlhood's releasing tears fell upon a small grave.

The solitude of her hollow was never invaded by more than an inquisitive heifer or a nibbling sheep, and here Adria had wept away many real and imaginary hurts. Again the warm air wrapped her close, the ground cradled her and the sea whispered, Hush now, hush. Her tears soon stopped and she lay with empty mind and relaxed muscles.

Then, abruptly, her body tensed. Slowly she turned her head and, through lashes still beaded with tears, looked up to see, frighteningly close, a tall figure outlined against the sky. Her mother's reiterated warning rang clearly, "You must never wander beyond sight of the house and if you meet a Strange Man you must say 'Good day' politely *and hurry home*." These words had always held harsher import than the injunctions regarding dry shoes and clean aprons, and had tied Adria's childish tongue in her encounters with friendly seamen ashore from anchored vessels. As she sprang to her feet now, every muscle was tensed to run or struggle.

Relief flooded her. This was not a Strange Man, only a strange boy. Man or boy, the tall intruder was smiling at her, thwacking his knee with a rolled cap and looking as silly as she felt. He said, "I'm sorry if I frightened you. I wasn't expecting anyone to be here. You . . . You scared me, too." He had a man's deep voice, but it was still husky with recent change from boyhood's treble and his desire to reassure her gave it an appealing gentleness. His blue eyes were friendly and a crease in his right cheek, too long to be a dimple, deepened as he smiled. Adria thought his nose too large for his thin face but she liked his firm lips and cleft chin.

He had a well-scrubbed look and his shock of golden hair had only recently escaped discipline, while his trousers and white linen shirt were finer than Prince's Cove everyday wear. Adria was suddenly conscious of her ragged braids and the shortcomings of last year's dress. She flushed as she pulled her skirts into place and hid her berry-stained hands beneath her apron. The two young things stood staring at each other, ill at ease. The girl first found words. "I'm Adria. Redmond."

"I'm Isles. Kendrick. I rowed over from the Cove." He pointed to his skiff, beached at the foot of Nigh Hill. Adria had been too wrapped in her own thoughts to see or hear his arrival.

The partly filled pitcher gave Isles a conversational opening. "My mother declares no other berries have the flavour of island ones, though I tell her that's just because she used to pick them here when she was a child." His young voice held man's tolerance for a feminine whim.

"Here? You mean on New Erin?" He could have said nothing surer to rout Adria's reserve. She dropped to a low stone and, with eagerness lighting her eyes and curving her mouth, commanded, "Tell me all about her!"

In an age which preferred dimpling rose-buds, Adria's mouth was considered too generous, despite its curves and well tucked in corners, but her long eyes under their black lashes were never criticized, being grey as fog and clear as the sea beneath it, but warm while sea and fog are cold. Hers was still a little girl's soft and changing face yet it held sure promise of beauty; heartbreak and happiness were to shape and set it but never to erase completely the responsive smile and open gaze.

This is a nice friendly little girl. Pretty, too. Isles felt a puzzling urge to smooth back the unruly hair. Instead, he dropped upon a rock and tried to recall his mother's stories. "She was Priscilla Ryder. And she always calls this 'Ryders' Island'."

Adria nodded. "That used to be its name."

"She lived at a spot called 'Sand Cove'." He was beginning to remember. "But she was only ten when her father died."

Adria's eyes went searching. Which one of those anonymous stones marked the resting-place of this boy's grandfather? Isles sat erect. "Are these *graves?* Is this the Ryder burying-ground? You were crying, but these mounds. . . ."

"Nobody's been buried here since the Redmonds came," she assured him. How explain when she herself did not know what had caused her tears? To dismiss the embarrassing memory of them she asked, "What happened to your mother then?"

"Her uncle and aunt in Prince's Cove brought her up after her mother married a Hines' Harbour man. She says she sat with Mrs. Redmond in school and that I must bring her for a visit some day." He added proudly, "Mother's a good sailor. She's been with my father to China and India and Australia."

"Then Redmond's Harbour won't scare her," Adria laughed. "Mamma will be glad to see her for not many Cove women will cross water. Of course," she hastened to add, "we'd like you and your Papa to come, too. Will you be visiting long in the Cove?"

"Mother and I live there now. We came from Halifax last week. My father went down with his ship—off Java—before I was born." Adria made a soft sound of sympathy and he continued, "This spring Uncle Theodore wrote that Aunt Sarah had died and would Mother come keep house for him. He said he wanted me to learn the business since it would be mine some day. Mother felt we should come because the old folks had been good to her. And I . . . Well, I must earn my living, now that I'm through school."

Mr. Ryder's grand-nephew! It was hard to connect this slim friendly boy with the heavy, sharp-eyed merchant who was the Cove's most prosperous citizen. To think that Isles would some day own the general store, the busy wharf and — more exciting — the schooner *Fearless*. Adria's imagination needed no push into deep water, the merest nudge served to launch it. Isles would captain his own vessels, lofty full-rigged ships; she would watch them making harbour and . . . .

Her companion broke into her daydreams. "I want to see the hilltop view," he said and climbed the few remaining feet with Adria close behind him. He turned to the open sea as surely as a compass needle swings north, and Adria knew he had no eyes for the sloping flank of Nigh Hill nor the shallow pond reflecting its grassy dyke. He did not hear the sibilance of the little breeze that had found the treetops behind him, nor smell the rankness of disturbed kelp at shoreline. Adria, too, forgot the signs of coming storm as with far-gazing eyes this new friend opened his heart to her. "I always hoped I'd go to sea. Command ships, like my father. But Mother. . . Mother is frail, and I'm all she has."

Adria's quick sympathy went out to him. *He loves his mother but he hates being cooped up in his uncle's shop.* She thought of her own mother, questioning seamen for news of Patrick, the brother Adria scarcely remembered; and of Gramma Damie's face whenever a storm struck. It was hard to be the one left waiting. Yet Adria knew how a schooner, stretching for the open sea, could draw her in its wake and leave only her body rooted to the land; how much stronger the pull must be on a boy held by his mother's love and a sense of duty.

To bring her friend back from the skyline, Adria offered, "Did you know your mother's old home makes Papa's office, the spare-room and Mamma's bedroom?" She laughed at his puzzlement and the success of her ruse, laid a tanned hand upon his arm and turned him towards the house. "Papa and Mamma came to the Ryder house on the point, but there were eight other cottages scattered over the island so whenever Papa wanted more room he just moved another house and joined it on." Irregular roofs, ells and jogs bore this out. Adria continued, "Serena—she's our cook—she says she hates a house that doesn't know which way it's going. But I love it! Though when I was little I used to get lost in it and they'd find me crying. It's still scary in the dark because the Secret Cellar . . ." She stopped short. She *never* mentioned the Secret Cellar and its part in the island's present troubles. But Isles' face showed he had already heard "talk" about her father's liquor smuggling in defiance of the neighbourhood's strong Temperance sentiments. Her distressed silence was broken by a metallic clangour from the house. "That's Serena," Adria explained, "whanging with her poker on the old cauldron near the door. Calling me home. Serena hasn't a *mite* of patience. I'd better hurry."

"Me, too!" Then Isles added rather shyly, "I'm still a stranger in Prince's Cove, but already I feel at home on your island."

Adria could not answer for happiness. This nice boy sensed New Erin's welcome. Of course, he belonged to it, in a way, because of his mother. "I'll walk with you to your skiff," she offered, and side by side like old friends, they turned down the hill.

TWO

THE instant Adria stepped into the kitchen the knot in her chest tightened as if it had never been eased by the hours on Nigh Hill. The air of constraint and waiting hung undiminished over everything and although the coming gale was mentioned it had become a symbol. The storm's centre continued to lurk below the murky horizon, but it sent heralding combers that swept in with increasingly heavy thunder and raked the shore with mounting violence.

With the first of the wind came real worries. Mamma went to her room and Kiah, the faithful hired man, put off into the storm's threat to fetch the doctor. The afternoon dragged while the gale strengthened and the sky darkened. At suppertime the boys left to drive the sheep to safety and Grampy Sam, milk-buckets in hand, went to the barn. Serena, her thin face and voice expressionless, charged Adria with the kitchen's care and disappeared into Mamma's bedroom. Papa wandered out into the storm and back again, uselessly, unseeingly. The house, though it groaned and cried out, bravely withstood the savage beating but, as darkness fell, all outside seemed abandoned to the screaming wind and the evil riding down on New Erin. Loneliness became the core of the storm and Adria was lost in it. In her own need for companionship she remembered that Gramma Damie was alone in the bedroom off the dining-room and helpless from her twisted ankle. With Grampy so long absent, she might need some one to look in on her. Adria lit her small bedroom lamp and stepped into the dining-room where the wind was pushing the rain around the window-frame in bubbling rage. From the bedroom doorway she saw that her grandmother was dozing. Grammy asleep could not bolster

Adria's courage and she turned away, shielding her lamp. The feeble light fell upon a brown Bible lying on the bureau—Adria's own Bible, recently lent to her grandparents, because theirs had been burned with their home.

A gust slammed against the house and the lamp flame flattened and faded; when it was again erect, Adria picked up the book and returned to the lonely kitchen. She sat down by the table, remembering that on any occasion one had only to open the Bible to find a personal message for enlightenment and strength. She had never tested this, but Mamma and Grammy and Serena had proved it many times. She turned back a section and peered at the revealed page. The Acts. Her eyes widened, for there at the bottom of a column, was her own name, Adria! She was flooded by confidence in a God who, in the midst of the present tumult in His created world of land and water, could yet be bothered with the opening of a girl's Bible. She found, as she read, that Adria seemed the name of a place and not a person, but this page was surely meant for her, for here was storm and shipwreck. She turned up the lamp's wick and bent closer, forgetting the wind and the beaten house, forgetting her search for a message, absorbed in the apostle Paul's account. "And when the ship was caught and could not bear up into the wind, we let her drive." "The next day they lightened ship." How familiar it all sounded. Finally there they were, poor men, unable even to take a sight and reckon their position. "And when neither sun nor stars in many days appeared and no small tempest lay on us . . ." Adria ceased reading, caught in the words' poetry. She said them over twice and then again, so that they would always be hers. But did they hold the message for this wearisome, frightening night? They had not calmed the wind nor stilled the surf, as she had half expected. Yes, she decided and felt her spirits rise bravely, if briefly. *It means I shouldn't be afraid. Paul lived through his storm and I will, too, in God's care.*

Around midnight, at the height of the hurricane, her father found her huddled at the table, a forlorn little girl, striving to keep awake. As he tucked her in on the kitchen couch, Adria felt him bend and kiss her tenderly, and loved him more than ever. Then the sounds of the storm blended into one sound, were caught indistinctly and then completely lost, as sleep claimed her.

THREE

A GLORIOUS OCTOBER sun smiled at Adria through the kitchen panes as she wiped the breakfast dishes and it told her, This is no day to spend making beds and scrubbing floors. It aroused a hot yearning for Nigh Hill's wide views and freedom from the kitchen's demands. She stole an exploratory sidewise glance at Gramma Damie who was bent over the dishpan beside her, one knee resting upon a stool to ease the bandaged ankle, and sight of the valiant figure routed all temptation to desert. Actually, the early hours, after the night's renewal of body and courage, were not the really difficult ones. Bedtime brought utter fatigue and rebellion because the day had again denied time for the shores and woodpaths, or for books and piano. However, the busy days were taking on familiarity, repetition brought skill to new tasks, while Adria's young strength and wavering spirit increased to meet the demands upon them. Each night she believed tomorrow would bring one of the carefree hours she had known before The Storm.

Other disastrous gales were to have their designations but for New Erin the one just past was to remain The Storm. It had battered the island cruelly, smashing its dyke and wharves and leaving the dock a tangle of broken timbers. That first morning, as the rising sun revealed wholesale destruction, Papa had told Adria gently that her baby sister had not lived, but that Mamma had been spared to them. A world that still held Mamma could not be completely strange, but it was more than desolate when search showed that Grampy had perished trying to save his *Didamia*. Adria knew, without having been told, that her father had been "ruined" by The Storm; that his vessels and cargoes had been lost and he had been forced to mortgage New Erin. Yet, out of disaster had come some good; liquor smuggling on the island was over.

"Thyah! That's done once more." Gramma Damie wiped the dishpan with a dextrous flip of her cloth. She reached for her cane, pushed the bolstering stool tidily under the sideboard and hobbled to her rocker.

Adria glanced across the wide room to where her mother sat by the window, away from possible draughts. She ached to see the pitifully thin slow hands busily knitting — added reproaches to her earlier impulse towards truancy. Mercy sighed as Serena shaped dough into smooth bread-loaves. "Saturday morning, and so much to be done. If only I could be about."

"We don't mind," Adria assured her stoutly. "Just to have you in the kitchen again—why, it's like having the captain back at the wheel!" *We're not much of a crew. A tomboy and a crippled grandmother. Serena's the only able seaman.* She felt this nautical imagery lent colour to the situation and, as she washed off the sideboard, she might have been scrubbing a deck. They were fighting head winds, too, for to hold his trade her father must speedily make repairs and this meant workmen to be fed.

Through the window unattainable Nigh Hill shouldered the eastern sky, reminding Adria of her meeting with Isles Kendrick, which had taken on the faraway dreamy quality of all events preceding The Storm. Then, as if her memory had drawn him, Isles was rounding the house corner. *I knew this was going to be a special day!* With him was a bonneted little lady who must be his mother. Isles glimpsed Adria at the window and raised a hand in a gay salute. He was just as she had remembered him, tall and strong-looking but a little awkward, friendly but shy. "Mamma," Adria turned with a glowing face. "Here's Isles and his mother come visiting like he promised." At Mercy's blank look she asked, "Didn't I ever tell you about *Isles*?" There was no time to do so now as she whisked off her apron and hurried to welcome the guests.

Priscilla Kendrick saw in the doorway a thin girlish face with grey eyes catching the sea's sparkle and a wide mouth smiling welcome. She did not wait for her son's introduction. "You're Adria," she said and kissed the girl warmly while Isles smiled delightedly down upon them both.

Isles had spoken truly when he said, "Mother is frail." But her hollowed blue eyes were merry and her pale lips were full and smiling. With her high forehead and indeterminate nose, Isles' mother could not be called pretty, but Adria felt no disappointment—like Isles, Mrs. Kendrick was somehow just right. She was saying, "You can't imagine how I've been longing and plotting to get on this island! This morning seemed made for sailing so I asked Uncle Theodore to give Isles time off. If you don't put us in a boat and set us adrift, we plan to stay over Sunday." She indicated the small satchel she carried and the basket on Isles' arm.

Adria led her guests proudly to her mother. The two women embraced as if only weeks, and not long years, had passed since they shared a school desk. Priscilla apologized, "I wanted to come to you during your troubles but, dear me, I've been laid low myself."

At the first opening Adria introduced Isles. He saw a tall, sweet-faced woman with fair braids above a wide brow. Her eyes, though darkly shadowed by recent illness, were grey and warm as Adria's were, and when she smiled at him he knew he was going to love Adria's mother. She took both his hands in her thin ones and gazed up into his face. "Yes, you have a Kendrick look. But your eyes—they are Priscilla Ryder's own blue ones."

At Adria's agonized "Mamma!" she dropped his hands and smiled across at her friend as if excusing the young's repudiation of all debts to preceding generations; but she reprimanded her daughter with a glance. Adria was sorry. "But you sounded like Grammy pointing out my big Nickerson mouth and my Crowell ears!"

Isles hadn't minded the kindly scrutiny and comment. When a Cove oldster peered into his face and accepted him with, "Ayah, ye favour yer Paw. I mind Isaac had jest sech another beaky nose an' stubborn set to his chin," Isles was elated. Adria couldn't know the good feeling such comparisons gave a boy who had never seen his father, but he grinned down at her to show all was well, as she dragged him to another rocker and her bird-like little grandmother.

The kitchen was the largest Isles had ever seen but its low ceiling, boarded walls and softwood floor followed the Cove pattern, as did the boxed-in stairway, the handmade benches and stools. It was an open-armed sort of room and he felt at home in it immediately.

A huge stove, dazzling testimony to the powers of blacklead and elbow grease, filled the jog under the stairway. Before it a bony woman, with iron-grey in hair and eyes, was adding salt pork to a huge bean-crock. This was Serena Swim, both slave and mistress of the black monster before her. She turned and scoured Isles with a look, then jerked her head towards a barrel-chair. "If Adria is done showin' ye off, ye might as well set." He heard Adria's sigh of relief; apparently he had been welcomed by the household's most exacting member.

His mother was speaking. "Isles, please lift my basket to the table." She explained to Mercy, "I didn't know just what would be welcome, but I thought a houseful of men and boys would eat up 'most anything." With a white blue-veined hand, but a capable one withal, she lifted the snowy basket covering and unpacked the contents to exclamations of appreciation, which were augmented on the arrival of Adria's brothers.

Handsome black-haired Will, with his father's figure and air of breeding, was nearer Isles' own sixteen years, but Charlie, with the mop of bronze curls and the freckles, was the one the newcomer preferred.

Another youth entered, his arm piled high with firewood. Isles noted first the powerful frame, and the muscles straining the homespun shirt. *Mother should look at this chap, if she thinks I'm big and strong for my age!* Soft brown eyes, fixed on Adria, and a good-natured grin gave the boy's slack features a certain appeal, though his dark curls denied any acquaintance with a comb and his heavy jaw showed black need of a razor. Isles recognized this boy as hired help, despite Adria's warm greeting. "Waitstill," she said in a voice bright with pleasure in her guests, "This is Isles Kendrick. I met him on Nigh Hill the day of The Storm." With her hand upon Isles' arm she led him to the other and her attitude said plainly, I bring my friend to my friend.

To Isles' utter astonishment, the eyes he had thought gentle if a bit empty, became hostile black slits above the piled wood. "If it'd been me catched him, I'd larnt him t'keep off other people's prop'ty."

Adria stamped her foot. "Waitstill Nolan! Isles is *company.*" She drew Isles back to the group about the basket, saying like a mother excusing her fractious child, "I don't know what gets into Waitstill sometimes." There was a tumbling crash as Waitstill flung wood into its box and disappeared through the open doorway.

Isles' discomfiture at this encounter soon fled under the eager friendliness of Will and Charlie and he left the house with them, impressed as carpenter's apprentice at the icehouse under construction.

When the men came to dinner, Isles was happy to see his mother as busily engaged as if she had always known the Redmonds' cupboards and sideboard. She charmed Waitstill with a little joke, giving his name the Cove's slur, "Waits'l? Some relation to the Mains'ls and Fores'ls?" The boy's guffaw was as hearty as if he had not heard many turns of the same jest. "I remember you, Hezekiah," she told the tall man with the drooping mustache in the homely weathered face. "You're not a bit fatter than when you mended my slate for me." Kiah blushed, delighted at the recognition.

Dan Redmond greeted Mrs. Kendrick with great courtesy. "Your visit is doing Mercy good," he assured her. But, despite bright words for his guests, he was weary and discouraged. Recent events had made him acutely conscious of the cleavage between himself and his neighbours; he was set apart, through no wish of his own, by his early life and education, by his religion, by his prosperity and possessions — shaken though these now were — and by the part his illicit liquor traffic had played in them. He was thinking that Mercy and this pleasant friend had skipped ropes together, could claim near or distant relationship with every Cove family; his childhood companions were in a far country and (apart from his children) he had no kin in all this land.

Sensitiveness to his mood may have prompted Priscilla to speak of Dublin and the Liffy and the neighbouring mountains. "My husband's ship once lay in the harbour making repairs and we spent every possible moment exploring the city and countryside." Her voice was sweetly husky, never raised and seldom quickened, but running along like a little brook in no particular hurry. She knew Queenstown and how Skibbereen and Mizzen Head looked, falling astern. The Redmond boys listened enthralled to the little woman, dainty as a fairy godmother, who went on to speak of foreign cities as a Cove woman might mention Grannie's Head or Barrington.

The two carpenters were the last to enter the kitchen. Bradford Sears was as tall and thin and sparing of words as Obediah Knowles was short and stout and loquacious; but both had sailed with Captain Sam and both felt at home on New Erin. Because this was the end of the week and the carpenters eager to start homeward, the men ate first. Adria noted that Isles, urged by Serena's persuasive pressure at his elbow, matched serving for serving with Will and Charlie. When the room had emptied of men and boys, the women ate.

Having her "sipping-cup" of tea, Priscilla smiled at Adria beside her. "I'm an islander, too. I was born at the Sand Cove."

"Isles told me. And I know the cellar-hole. The stone steps are still there. And right in the middle of the open cellar a spruce tree is growing."

"Now, I must see that. Next summer, when your mother is stronger, let's all go on a picnic there." If she had not already won Adria this would have done so — this assurance that good times would come again, and that Isles and his mother would be part of them. Behind the lights and shadows in the grey eyes turned to hers, Priscilla glimpsed a fine young spirit, intelligent, loving and vulnerable. She put an arm tenderly about the girl. "I wish you and your brothers would adopt me. My half-sister in Hines' Harbour has a family but they've never seen me, and I have no one to call me 'Aunt Cilla'."

Adria's smile was radiant. "And Mamma can be Isles' Aunt Mercy."

The New Erin household kept the Cove Sabbath (from even unto even) and Saturday afternoon was dedicated to ushering it in. There was much lugging of water and filling of kettles as the women, one after another, excused themselves and returned looking scrubbed and sanctified. The kitchen basked in peace and leisure while the beans baked in their slow oven and the brownbread kettle danced a gay jig in its container of boiling water. Conversation took a desultory and intimate tone. Mercy and Priscilla laughed over girlish escapades while Adria listened entranced to the "Do you remember's." Not until her elders became involved in tortuous family relationships did her interest wander. She stole away for her bath and returned to hear her mother asking, "How is your Uncle Theodore keeping?"

"Not too well. His dropsy grows worse as fall comes on. But he says his mind is at ease, for Isles is taking hold beyond his fondest hopes. Isles was homesick and lonely at first but he's quick to make friends and he's more contented now." Priscilla sent Adria a smile. "A daughter is a great comfort but it's a blessing Isles was a boy. I'll soon be utterly dependent upon him, for the years have eaten what Isaac left me. I sometimes fear that Isles longs for the sea as his father before him. The Lord forgive me for a selfish woman, but I cannot let him go."

Mercy, looking at the transparent face to which the morning's outing had brought no colour said, "Isles is a good son. He won't leave you."

Damie roused from a doze and fixed her eyes upon the visitor. "Has the' been much scandalizin'? About the smugglin' and all? After me comin' out so strong on Temp'rance?" Having dealt in gossip herself, she knew its propensities towards growth and distortion.

Priscilla could meet her tacit plea for denial. "I do believe The Storm blew all else out of mind. And trouble makes friends."

"It's true what ye say," Serena agreed. "I was flabbergasted at how many folks came to help at the worst, or who sent oven-supplies."

"Still we would have been lost without Serena," Mercy paid quick tribute. "And I have cause for pride in my children. Adria has been a great comfort, and the boys are working like men." She sighed, "Though I wish Will had more of Charlie's steadiness."

The conversation was interrupted by the rattling latch and Isles' appearance in the doorway. "Mrs. Redmond," he pleaded, "Kiah says that if Adria will go along and show me what to do, I can tend the light. May she come, please?"

Adria sprang up eagerly, then remembered that suppertime was near. Don't ask me to give up lighting-time with Isles, her big eyes begged her mother.

Mercy smiled. "Adria will be a good teacher. I think her first real walk was to the lighthouse with Kiah." To her daughter she said gently, "Wear your warm shawl, dear."

Aunt Cilla added, "No need to hurry back. Serena and I will manage supper."

FOUR

Adria had felt herself one of the kitchen's women, but as she stepped outdoors, Isles saw again the girl of Nigh Hill. When she winced at the sight of the broken wharves and the strewn shores, and put out a repudiating hand, he clasped it quickly. He indicated the long walls he had helped board-in that morning. "Your father will soon have a bigger and stronger icehouse than the old. Then he can set about repairing Long Wharf and other damage. And look there," pointing to several schooners anchored in the harbour and the pink tied up at the wharf-end. "New Erin's hills will always break the wind, and the sail-loft still has gear to sell." He gave her hand a playful tug and grinned down at her. "But let's get the lamps lit." She dropped his fingers and edged through the V gate onto the lighthouse path.

The fitful breeze played with the little curls about Adria's temples but lacked energy to stir her shawl or skirt, the sky held summer's soft tints rather than fall's clear austerity, and a roseate bank on the southern horizon told of warm weather's fog. The two walked silently, halting once to gaze across Clam Cove and the broken dyke where sheep were browsing, their pond reflections moving with them. But Isles must always be watching the ocean. "See that rakish barquentine off Pilot Point? She'd be a quick-stepper in a breeze," he said.

Adria shook her head admiringly. "You have eyes like Waitstill's. Papa took him from the schoolroom because, for all Miss Newhall's switch, he could never learn A from B, but he can tell a vessel's rig when I can only make out a blur."

Nearer than the barquentine and under a loop of black smoke, the Yarmouth packet was hurrying home with churning side-wheels. Isles and Adria agreed steamers were ugly and clumsy-looking. Their eyes went to the snowy upper course of a full-rigged ship, floating cloud-like above the skyline. "We can see her better from the lantern," Adria said, and they hastened their steps. However, before entering the tower Isles must go to the bank's edge and inspect the fog-bell on its gallows-like frame. "Fog can blot out the light but sound pushes its way across the water somehow," Adria explained. "I used to go with Kiah to ring the bell when he'd hear a fisherman's conch-shell, or when the *Katie* was off in the fog." Isles could picture the small Adria listening for the flap of a sail or the creak of tholepin between the bell's muffled tones.

The heavy lighthouse door opened into a room, not more than fifteen feet square, whose slanting, beamed walls were unfinished and unbroken except for two small windows and a few shelves holding cleaning equipment and spare lamps. Casks along one wall held kerosene and Adria must have noticed Isles' distaste for the smell of oil-permeated wood. "Kiah doesn't like kerosene either," she confided. "He mistrusts new-fangled things, but he admits it gives a clearer flame than the old fish-oil or lard, and he brags that Papa was the first hereabouts to use it." She was gathering scissors and various cloths from their nails, and she handed Isles a spouted oilcan. "In case Kiah didn't fill the lamps. He usually prepares everything at sunrise when he puts the lights out, but he's dreadfully busy and like he says, 'Seems one pair o' hands can do only so much'."

Isles already appreciated Kiah's devotion to the Redmonds, and he could imagine the hired man reproaching his freckled work-worn hands for their inability to accomplish more.

A flight of open wooden steps led upward. Isles mounted, lifted the metal door at the top and leaned down to assist Adria, but she was swiftly and adeptly beside him in the lantern and lowering the trap-door. "So noan of us won't try to walk on air," she mimicked Kiah. "Air. Air," bounced hollowly back and forth between the metal walls and roof, while Isles looked eagerly about the small six-sided room in which they now stood. The upper half of each wall was a large window, joined to its neighbours by a heavy metal frame. Under five of the windows ran a zinc-lined trough, and a square central table held five brass lamps with attached reflectors. (The window facing the house needed no light.) After the lamp-bowls were filled Adria fell to trimming wicks, and set Isles at polishing brass reflectors. "I'm the one for the chimneys, though," she said, demonstrating with her slender fingers. Then, holding up a red globe to catch the sun, "Look through it." Isles saw an unbelievable, crimson sky and sea. Adria told him, "Kiah used to save the cracked chimneys for my playhouse. I could change my world by looking through the ruby glass. Magic, you know. I was a great silly for make-believe." She laughed at the childish Adria, and the lantern walls gave back a soft peal.

In their troughs, each below its window, lamps, chimneys and reflectors soon shone and mirrored one another in diminishing and confusing images. When the sun brushed the horizon, Adria reached beneath the central table and from a metal container took a lucifer, a piece of sandpaper and a wooden spill. She gladly relinquished the lucifer to Isles who drew it sharply across the sandpaper. As it burst into flame Adria stole its blaze with her long-burning spill and, while Isles deposited the smoldering match in the table's bowl of water, lifted a red chimney and gave fire to the waiting wick. When all the lamps were burning she watched the flames for a moment, though they were scarcely discernible in the sunset's strength. Then her eyes sought Isles'. Isn't lighting-up fun? Didn't I do my part well? they begged.

"Miss Grace Darling." Isles made her a mock bow. He added at once, "I'd never been in a lighthouse before and I wouldn't have missed this. Your father did a noble thing when he established his light; many and many a seaman must have blessed him." He glanced over the sweep of water served by the little lamps then, with quick hands upon her shoulders, swung Adria about. The ship they had sighted was coming up the bay, with all canvas spread. Across the water sunset streams of carmine, saffron, amethyst and apple-green blended, or ran separately in exquisite bands. With the lightest of upper airs helping the flood tide which bore her, the ship appeared to move not from pressure of wind on canvas but as if drawn by invisible threads in a steady unslackening hand. Coloured ripples and the dainty white-edged bow curl moved with her. Her yardarms and stays were golden, her upper courses rose, while lilac shadows washed down the lower sails and deepened to purple on her deck. Adria's heart lifted and sang, but this was beauty beyond words.

She and Isles came back from enchantment at the trap-door's lifting rattle and the appearance of Waitstill's untidy black head. "I run from the barn the minute I sighted her," he panted as he gained the lantern. "Golly, Adree, ain't she purty?" Adria kept her face averted, but Isles believed she minded this interruption, as he did.

Adria minded it. She had given up protesting, but she hated Waitstill to call her "Adree." Just now, after the silent delight shared with Isles, she almost hated Waitstill's clumsy bulk and his noisy breathing. "Do be quiet," she said crossly, and then felt crosser because at her displeasure his grin vanished and over his shallow eyes flickered the shadow of baffled and repulsed affection, and the unquenchable loneliness that always touched her heart. Contritely, she attempted to make amends. "I wish I had Papa's spyglass so I could read her name and port o' call."

"Why, Adree," Waitstill's good-nature was quickly restored. "I can tell ye, 'thout no spyglass. She's the *Clara Caie*, out o' Yarmouth. On her maiden v'yage." He grinned proudly—not often was he the one to impart information.

"How do you *know*? I believe you're just making that up!"

Waitstill only grinned the broader. "I've heard tell all about her. But what is she puttin' in here fer? No storm's acomin'." He scanned the bay and whistled. "Fog, though."

Adria saw that seaward of New Erin the sunset colours were already blotted up by the fog that had been out-waiting the sun to smother the bay. She wanted to reach and pull the ship beyond that wet clutch. Already the sails' hues were fading; the water that had been opalescent satin was now rough grey homespun with a crimson overthread. Almost as if she sensed a pursuing foe, the gliding ship was gaining speed; her sails were rounding before the growing air and her wash came swelling through the smooth water to foam among the rocks below the lantern windows.

Isles had remained silent. He could feel the ship under his feet, hear the promises whispered to sails and rigging by the coming breeze, almost taste the kiss of harbour water along her sides. The work with the laughing Redmond boys, the good pull of muscles against lifted timbers, Adria's sweet companionship—all that had made this a happy day—went stale at the sight of square sails. Perhaps he only fancied an attempt to exclude him as Waitstill moved closer to Adria and said, "She'd be a grand ship for our v'yage. A proper *White Wings*."

"Yes," Adria replied shortly. She wished Waitstill wouldn't drag up that old make-believe and the name *White Wings*, which had seemed poetic when she chose it. Her brothers had long outgrown the game of appropriating (in imagination) any likely craft and manning it by a New Erin crew; but childish Waitstill could still lose himself in the magic Adria kept alive for him. Unwillingly she took up the old pretense, and almost immediately found herself explaining to Isles' back, "It's only a game . . . and I've always been captain, because I thought it up. Waitstill's always been first mate. But you . . . You could be . . ."

"Don't you be a little goose," Isles replied sharply, out of his strong discontent. "You know a girl could never be master of a ship, any more than Waitstill could be first mate." At the stark truth, he saw the stars leave the grey eyes and the curved lips close tightly to hide their trembling, but before he could even put out a hand in repentance, Waitstill broke in angrily, "Listen, you. Any more o' yer slack lip an' I'll *show* ye if Adree can't be cap'n."

Adria was amazed that such trouble could grow out of harmless make-believe, but she knew her influence with Waitstill. "Hush," she told him. "Let's watch the *Clara Caie* round the point."

But Waitstill had swung away with an angry mutter and the trap-door slammed down behind him.

Isles turned with an apology on his lips, but Adria's own hurt and bewilderment demanded expression. "You think I'm silly, pretending like that with Waitstill," she said forthrightly. "I know I'm only a girl. And don't you suppose Waitstill realizes that he can't be mate on any ship but a make-believe one?" Loyalty forebade more, but compassion and a plea for understanding were in her words, "It isn't easy to be a Waitstill."

"It isn't easy to be anybody, little Adria," Isles told her in a tight voice. "You and Waitstill. . . You admit yourself. . . But me! I *could* be master of such a ship." He gestured without taking his eyes from hers. "I have it in me," he said simply. But Isles was not one to dwell upon his own hurts. "I'm ashamed for speaking as I did," he said humbly. "I'll go as cabin-boy."

She was contrite in turn. "I should have remembered how you feel about ships. But I forget to be sorry for you. You seem grown-up and . . . sure, somehow." He smiled at that, but their intimacy was gone and they turned to separate windows.

The ship's hull was hidden and her upper courses were

advancing eerily alone. Then the fog swirled forward and upward to swallow the mast-tips, and onward to blanket harbour and island. Outside the lantern all the world was fog and, although the red lamps gained brilliance, a damp chill was already penetrating the metal walls. Adria and Isles were two youngsters tired from the day's excursions and excitements. Adria drew her shawl about her and said meekly, "Perhaps we'd better go home now."

From midstairs she looked up to admonish, "Be careful to hold the door till you're well down. Sometimes it slips and Kiah says it could stun a man or break his neck."

Once outdoors, their ears caught muffled shouts through the seaward fog, the sound of shearing water and the dance of reef-points. Finally came the rattle of chains and an anchor's splash, then the ship might never have been.

When they started towards the house Adria held her head high as she did when pride must cover hurt, and there might have been tears upon her lashes and there might have been only fog-drops. Isles tried to undo the harm of his earlier words. "I wouldn't want to hurt you, ever. You're so little and brave and sweet. All day I was thinking how hard you worked about the house and knowing you must feel caught there sometimes, just as I feel in the shop. I remembered the morning on Nigh Hill and wished we could have it back again." He reached over and took her hand once more, and some of his warmth and kindness flowed from his covering palm into her fog-chilled fingers and into her sore heart. Presently he asked, "Why does Waitstill hate me? This morning we were all wrestling a bit and when I pinned Will or Charlie down he glowered as if he wanted to step in and flatten me properly. It's queer, because I rather like him." Then, "Who *is* Waitstill? Besides the Redmonds' hired boy?"

Adria faced him earnestly. Strange to have to explain Waitstill, for so long an accepted part of New Erin. "You must have heard of Nabby Nolan, the witch? Waitstill is *her* boy." Having declared the worst, Adria waited for Isles' reaction.

"I've heard about Nabby," he answered matter-of-factly.

"She's a hateful, wicked woman! She put a spell on Grampy Sam."

The childish curve of her cheek, the tremor in her voice, filled Isles with a swelling protectiveness that amazed him. There was no derision in his tone. "Do you believe that? That she could bring harm upon your grandfather?"

"Why-y-y, yes." Under her fog-weighted lashes her raised eyes were black and wondering. "Don't you?"

He shook his head, tightening his hold on her hand.

"But I was at the launching. I heard her put the curse of fire and water . . ."

"Oh Adria! Every witch, or old woman who likes to pretend she's a witch, always pronounces that curse. Or they do in books; I've read it a dozen times."

"But the fire did destroy . . ."

"Let me tell you this: I was visiting Uncle Theodore then and walked past Grannie's Head that evening. I met a tramp, smoking a pipe, and watched him turn towards your grandfather's barn. After the fire there was talk of running Nabby Nolan out on a fence rail, and Uncle Theodore asked me to tell the men what I had seen."

"Were *you* the one who saw the tramp?" That was somehow convincing. "But the schooner. Nabby said, 'She'll never wet her jib, but she'll drown every man aboard her,' and she laughed horribly when she said it." Adria shuddered. "The *Didamia's* sails weren't even bent, and Grampy Sam was the only man on her." Adria stopped and there was now no doubt between fog and tears. After an awkward moment Isles drew her head against his foggy coat. She groped for a handkerchief, "You'll think I'm an awful cry-baby."

"I guess girls cry more than boys." Then Isles remembered his own solace. "Do you like books? That's how I escape sometimes. After I go to bed, because Uncle Theodore thinks novels are one of the devil's tools, like cards and liquor." He added in an embarrassed rush, "I brought you a book today. Mother has it in her satchel. *The Old Curiosity Shop;* I thought a girl would like that."

What a wonderful present! Another book of her own. Adria was already comforted.

Isles continued, "If you like, I'll bring you my books to read."

"You're 'specially good to me," she said, drawing away from his coat.

"Why not?" He smiled down at her and his voice had its deep man's tone. "I want to look after you, so that when you grow up you'll go voyaging with *me* and with no one else."

FIVE

LATER, alone in the middle-room, Adria pulled the little blue rocker towards the hearth and squeezed herself sidewise between its round arms. Long before she was born Grampy had made the small chair for a toddling Catherine and fashioned its straight-legged mate (on the opposite side of the fireplace) for Patrick. Catherine was married now and had the finest of furniture; Patrick—nobody knew much about Patrick since he ran away to sea. Catherine, then Tamsin, and finally Adria had rocked their dolls in the blue chair while Patrick, Will and Charlie had in turn been outgrowing the red one.

Adria had built the evening fire and as she bent forward to add a stick, the tight blue rocker moved with her like a grotesquely slipped bustle. She sat back again and watched the fire gain colour as the twilight deepened. She was seldom alone like this at the fireplace, for the middle-room (joining the kitchen ell and the "company" wing) was the heart of the home. Its red carpet had well-worn paths, its furniture was somewhat battered, the ponderous mahogany table had been marred when salvaged from a wreck and nobody scolded if an apronful of shells and pretty pebbles was dumped upon it nor winced if boys crashed against it. Beside the table's usual baskets and piles of sewing was a crudely shaped piece of pine and an open knife, evidence that Waitstill was still trying to pass on to Charlie the skill by which his seemingly clumsy hands carved delicate chains and miniature ships. The Boston rocker beside the table was where mother sewed in the evenings while Papa settled himself with a volume from the shelves of books—books which helped to set the Redmonds apart in a district where a Bible and an almanac constituted most household libraries.

Miss Newhall, the teacher, and Serena (once her kitchen was

tidied for the night) joined the family in the middle-room, leaving Kiah and Waitstill, and such hired men as seasonal projects employed, to gather about the kitchen stove and spin their yarns. When crew members came ashore from vessels in the harbour, Kiah acted as host to them while their captains visited in the middle-room. Memory gave back to Adria the sour vessel smell and the rasp of brine-roughened clothes rather than the faces of these guests. She had always felt there was something beautiful and queenly about her mother as she shared her home, and something fine and chivalrous about the rough men as they accepted the sharing.

Though it would be selfish to begrudge the warmth of a family fireplace, Adria much preferred the evenings without such visitors, when she and her brothers could crowd close to their parents and demand a song or a story. Mamma had a wealth of old ballads, and family tales about the Nickersons of Grannie's Head and the Ryders who had settled New Erin. Of how the last Ryder had been moving to the main, abandoning the island cottages and cleared fields to wind and fog, to hard-hack and stunted spruces, while across the ocean on another island, a young man was being drawn to its shores, though he was unaware of its existence.

Adria knew well the story of young Dan Redmond who had crossed the Atlantic and called his island New Erin for Old Erin's sake. Often, when the wind screamed and the surf thundered, she would rouse from a fire-lit page and coax, "Tell us, Papa, how you found Mamma and New Erin." Then, on his rich voice, Papa would carry them all to Dublin city and a lonely boy, to a long voyage, a shipwreck, a rescue and a lovely lady at perils' end. No book on the lined shelves held a story to compare. "And so," Papa always concluded satisfyingly as he smiled at Mamma, softly aglow in the firelight, "I won me a wife and bought me an island where we lived happily ever after."

Yes, the middle-room was a great place for stories and dreams, holding as it did the intermingling imprints of the Redmonds and Ryders, the lingering essence of transient sea-farers, and ghostly personalities from the past who pressed gently but unmistakably about the fire on a stormy night—or in the half-dark where Adria sat alone. Yet it could never become haunted, being too much frequented to suit any ghost. Doors led into it from the hall, the office, the dining-room, Mamma's bedroom, the front and back yards, so that there was never any knowing which door might open or who might come through it. She who lifted the hall-door latch at that moment was the person Adria least wished to see.

Thankful Newhall was much given to migraines and had spent the day in her room. The firelight showed that her brown serge had been exactly adjusted, while her hair still bore the comb's furrows and her face the shine of recent washing. Obviously she was prepared to impress the Redmonds' guests. She entered with a mincing step but seeing only Adria moved more freely as she thrust a spill from the mantel into the fire and went to the table lamp. When she bent forward the full swell of bosom and thigh contradicted her pursed lips and cold eyes, as if a spendthrift's body had been given a miser's head. She seated herself with a prim tucking in of skirts and a hungry look towards her unfinished motto ("Blessed be the Pure in Heart"), forbidden on this Sabbath eve. She had cause for pride in her exquisite needlework and she knew that her shapely hands were her most feminine feature, never showing to better advantage than when she plied a needle.

For five years Thankful Newhall had been with the Redmond family but not of it. In Adria's first memories of the schoolroom (the chamber above the middle-room) kind Uncle Philip, her mother's foster brother, had been teacher. Of the Redmond children, Adria best loved her books, her mind leapt most swiftly to meet new truths. She had been prepared to love the new teacher, and to win her praise, but the child's outgoing heart had been repulsed by Miss Newhall's cold stare and biting tongue. No doubt before the young Thankful had taken up her duties on New Erin she had been warned of Dan Redmond's Catholicism (a strange phenomenon in a district of unbroken Protestantism) and she had never ceased to be on her guard nor to show her concern for the misguided. But it was not only on religious matters that Thankful remained as prickly as a sea-urchin.

She had been absent during The Storm, and on her return Dan Redmond had explained that the schoolroom would be closed, for Adria must help her ill mother and the boys would be working with him. "Just now I cannot pay your wages," he told her frankly, "but I will give you a recommendation. . ."

"Oh, no indeed, Mr. Redmond! I could never consider leaving you in your hour of adversity. I will turn my hand to any task, no matter how far beneath me. And without recompense." She had left an amused and exasperated recipient of loyalty to watch her virtuous back through the office door. Since then she had capably taken over much of the family sewing; she had straightened out Dan's confused bookkeeping and written business letters in her fine angling hand. None of the Redmonds voiced the ungrateful thought that, despite the press of work, they would be happier without her help.

This evening Miss Newhall gave no sign that she noticed the girl by the hearth and Adria could not decide whether this was a time for the rule, "Children should speak when spoken to," or whether she would be considered rude for lack of greeting. She set herself against the ill-ease she had always felt in her teacher's presence, but she became aware of the cramping rocker and her misshapen ridiculous appearance. As she squirmed free and rose to find another chair, Miss Newhall's thin voice broke the silence, "It's a good thing you live on an island, where folks can't see all that goes on. There'd be talk enough, on the main." She peered across the circle of lamplight while Adria waited, inwardly recoiling from some unknown, but certainly approaching, unpleasantness. "A young lady, almost, alone in the lighthouse with a strange boy." Thankful flicked her sharp tongue across her upper lip.

Adria was indignant. "Isles isn't strange! I met him on Nigh Hill the day of The Storm and we talked for hours."

"Is that so? I don't know *what* people would say if they knew you'd been out on the hills with him, too." Her tone said much more than her words and she darted a sly glance at the girl's sensitive face.

Adria had known only her mother's great charity and her father's easy tolerance; this was her introduction to the ferment in evil minds, the yeast that starts gossip working to distort lives and break hearts. As yet she was too innocent to grasp all Miss Newhall's implications, and had no words to repudiate what she sensed, but the tone and look shamed as well as bewildered her. Yet what cause had she for shame? Miss Newhall liked evil; she looked for it. Adria cried scornfully, "Were you watching us with Papa's spyglass this sundown?"

A startled face drew back from the light. "Spyglass! What do you mean, Miss Flip?"

The girl knew she had scored. Knew, too, clearly and coldly, that Miss Newhall's surface fastidiousness covered a nasty mind, as her schoolroom discipline had covered cruelty. "Oh, I've seen you," Adria said airily, though her heart was pounding, "watching from behind the curtains in the upper hall." *If looks could kill I'd be a corpse on the carpet.*

"The i-dee-ah! Your imagination runs away with you. Your parents have said so, many times. No one would believe such a thing if you told it."

"They'd believe this."

June's first warm day had brought permission to throw off bundlesome woollens and Adria was hurrying to her bedroom, her feet sinking noiselessly into the stair carpet. The railing hid most of the square upper hall with its heavy furniture and drapes, but as she turned the top step she glimpsed a huddled figure at the northern window. Her heart skipped in alarm before she recognized her teacher. But what was Miss Newhall doing there in the hall's close warm air on such a glorious day? And with Papa's spyglass? She always boasted that her far vision compensated for her near-sightedness. What held her so enthralled?

Adria crept down to the lower hall and, curiosity-driven, to the window beneath Miss Newhall's. No vessels were in harbour, no sail or flashing oars heralded coming visitors, Narrah's shore was deserted. Will and Charlie and Waitstill, ready for spring's first swim, were romping on Short Wharf. Their milk-white bodies gleaming, they poised on the edge then plummeted, straight as gulls after herring, into the dock. Their heads bobbed up, seal sleek. At the ladder there was much pulling and pushing before all three boys ran to dive again. Their antics were fun to watch, but plain enough without any spyglass. All at once Adria knew a nausea like the beginning of seasickness. *That* was why Thankful Newhall's tongue was so busy about her lips. But how silly. Adria had always known that boys were made different from girls. Even without brothers, anyone should know. But why did Miss Newhall care? You'd never find Mamma or Serena spying at bare-naked boys. This had something to do with the way men laughed when they called Miss Newhall an old maid, and why Will said worse things about her behind her back.

Adria slipped away unnoticed, but the incident clung to her mind and spoiled several days.

She had not expected the repressed memory to leap into the open on angry words, nor to see fear of betrayal as well as venom in Miss Newhall's flushed face. Pity stirred; the sense of triumph ebbed, leaving her limp and aghast, for she had been taught respect and obedience to her teacher. She wanted to run from the room but a new pride would not let her retreat. Although the words exchanged and the birth of enmity had taken but a few minutes, it seemed she had been facing Miss Newhall for a long time, and the approaching sound of her parents' voices was never more welcome.

SIX

By morning, in one of autumn's swift changes, the fog had fled. A piping north wind tumbled white clouds across the deep blue sky and frolicked with the dancing harbour chop. Its keen northern edge had been blunted by passage over warm coastal waters, but it retained enough bite to tingle the skin and invigorate the blood of those who stepped out into it. In the middle-room a semicircle of women in subdued Sunday dress had drawn their chairs close to the fire and settled down to enjoy the day of rest, but the morning's sparkle and briskness had found their way into the kitchen and Adria, "tidying-up," was singing—for the first time since The Storm.

> Safe within the lifeboat, sailor,
> Cling to sin no more.
> Leave that poor old stranded wreck
> And pull for the shore.

This could be a rollicking tune, but it was a Sunday School favourite and permissible on the Lord's Day.

Serena returned from feeding the hens and, as she hung up her shawl and stepped to the stove to warm her reddened hands, announced the season's first ice skim on the well-bucket. She wore her Sabbath raiment (a black bombazine dress, a snowy linen apron with generous ties and a knitted lace border and, to protect both, an apron of everyday calico), as much part of Sunday as the relaxed atmosphere.

If Adria had not lifted her head to answer Serena, she might not have noticed the stealthily opening door, nor the head edging around it. A head with crisp tawny hair and sideburns under a visored cap, with skin copper-tinted by a hotter sun than New Erin's, and a pair of swiftly darting blue eyes. A pirate! Adria thought wildly, though pirates belonged only in books. Last evening's ship had been a pirate craft stealing in under fog's cover. She stood pinned to the floor in terror. The intruder's dark blue eyes gleamed wickedly as they fell upon Serena's hunched back and there was menace in the finger laid across his lips, enjoining silence upon Adria. He slid through the doorway and in two noiseless strides was behind the defenceless, unaware Serena. Adria, aroused to action at last, seized the broom and stepped forward. Two strong brown hands flashed swiftly at the waist of the black bombazine. Adria halted, nonplused, while the cotton apron, and then the Sunday linen, slipped to a heap on the floor.

Serena swung about and, in ludicrous succession, her gaunt face registered shock, anger, disbelief, joy, and its customary imposed blankness. Then, while Adria gaped, she reached up and soundly boxed the ears of the tall pirate, who did nothing but laugh and dodge and hug her. "So ye figgered I'd forgotten yer tricks," she said crossly, though her eyes were blurred and her thin lips quivered, "but well I mind the' was never no keepin' my apron-strings tied with Patrick Redmond around."

Patrick? This was no runaway boy, but a tall, broadshouldered man with — Adria now saw — the dress and bearing of a ship's officer. He was saying, "Not little Adria!" in an incredulous tone. His arms were iron hard, his body solid as a wharf-spile as he lifted her and drew her face down against his rough one. "Do you remember me at all?" he asked and his blue eyes, dark as the October sea, were wistful as they probed hers.

"A little. You used to rock me in the barrel-chair and sing to me," she answered happily.

"So I did. But I left you playing with your dolly, and here you are nearly as tall as Serena. Pretty as a picture, too."

The astonishment and joy in the kitchen were as nothing compared to what swept the middle-room as Patrick went to his mother's arms and then to Gramma Damie's. When the happy tears were dried he acknowledged introductions to Mrs. Kendrick and Miss Newhall, but the latter's utmost gentility was wasted on him. "The New Erin teacher? Then where is Uncle Philip?" he demanded.

Mercy made a helpless gesture. "There have been many changes. You have been gone so long. So long."

Priscilla rose and with a look brought the reluctant Thankful also to her feet. "You'll excuse us while we visit with Serena."

Mercy's first inquiry was, "Have you seen your father and brothers?"

"They met me at the wharf. Also Kiah and the fine-looking lad with the yellow hair—Isles. And what's-his-name, the hired boy. I had my men row them all out to inspect my ship." Pride coloured his words.

Mercy asked swiftly, "*Your* men? You're mate on that fine new ship?"

"I'm her master."

"Patrick," she whispered, and it was enough.

Patrick had not been prepared for the marks which illness and the years had left upon his mother, but he found the tenderness in her eyes and voice unchanged. Despite her pride for him, he knew she would have welcomed him as warmly had he returned a seaman before the mast. He could not gauge so surely what lay under his father's congratulations on the new command, for the years had not breached the barrier between father and son. But he was back in the middle-room, of which he had dreamed on many a howling night, and it still held the essence of home, although it was smaller and shabbier than he had remembered. He realized that everything about New Erin had shrunk and, quite apart from The Storm's damage, was more drab than his mind's eye had loved to picture.

He was not reproached for his desertion and long silence; nor did he attempt to explain or excuse them. His mother asked avidly for news to cover the seafaring years and he gave it briefly, stressing only his unremitting determination to learn and rise. His last voyage had given him chance to prove himself when, three days out of Calcutta, the master of the *Gloria*, Baltimore, had sickened of a fever and died, leaving Patrick, his first officer, to deliver ship and cargo. A command under the *Gloria's* line could then have been his, but he had scarcely set foot ashore when he had been approached by Mr. Killam of Yarmouth (in Baltimore on shipping business and proud of the fellow Nova Scotian whom the waterfront was lauding) who was seeking an enterprising skipper for his new *Clara Caie*. Yarmouth had seemed next door to home, and Patrick had stipulated that if he took command at once, he would put into New Erin, outward bound.

"When I left home I swore I wouldn't come back until I called myself 'Captain Redmond'." So the determined jaw must have looked many times on the climb to after-deck. "But now," his face softened, "I wish I had been less stubborn."

Adria had been doing mental addition and subtraction. She asked her mother hesitantly, "Is Patrick really old enough? To be captain?"

"He's gone twenty-three, not the youngest master I've known." There were more important matters. "Have you married, son?"

"No. But I have learned how mistaken a hot-headed youngster can be. The girl I loved would not renounce her faith and I could not adopt it." His tone closed any further discussion, and this was the sole reference he made to the hurt which had driven him from home, but Mercy welcomed the implication of old wounds healed though newer ones might throb.

Patrick continued, "I could have reached out my arms to hug the island, last sundown, and from the bay nothing seemed changed. Then the fog shut in. I left word to be called when it cleared and I was on deck at dawn. I thought I'd made a wrong landfall. Short Wharf gone. Buildings missing. The shoreline altered. The fields sere—why, I'd bragged all over the world how they kept green into December! But when I looked across at Grannie's Head and saw no big grey house. . ."

Grammy interrupted piteously, "That ain't the heart-breakin' part."

He crossed to her and put his strong arm about the flaccid body. "I know," he said tightly. "Father told me. And that was when I understood how much I had lost by my foolish pride. As if life and death would stand still for Patrick Redmond. Even last year, if I'd come home, Grampy Sam would have been here to greet me." He bent over and she clung to him briefly. "You'm like him," she whispered. "You've heired his build and his ways. Go set ye down, so I can feast my eyes on ye."

There was much to tell him. Catherine and her husband had recently moved to the States. "We haven't heard just where they are settled," Mercy explained, but her voice hinted distress at the lack of communication, and made her son aware that many times she must have said, hiding her hurt, "We've had no word from Patrick."

Tamsin was in Boston and would soon be marrying Philip, who was teaching there. Patrick couldn't picture roguish Tamsin grown up and married—especially to sober Uncle Philip. "But I shall look them up, when I'm next in a New England port," he promised, rising to stand against the fireplace, and to gaze about the room.

Behind him a log cracked with a sharp report, breaking his brief absorption. He moved to the table. "Who's reading *The Old Curiosity Shop*? You, Adria? I still read *Pickwick Papers* when I need to laugh. If you like to read I'll send you some new books from England." He was impressed by his young sister's unfolding intelligence. *She has the Nickerson gumption.*

"You're bound for England?" Adria asked eagerly.

"Timber for Liverpool, where we're to pick up iron and mixed goods for the East. We'll be shuttling back and forth—South America, Hamburg, Bombay . . . The *Clara Caie* will have no trouble finding cargoes." The pride in his ship was good to hear.

It must have been augmented as his father and brothers returned to the room, elated from their inspection. After some talk of rigging and fittings, charts and logs and speeds, Patrick grew restless. "I must have a yarn with Kiah," he said. "And I want to walk around the island once more. Alone," he hastily forestalled his brothers' eagerness to join him. He drew out a fine watch. "I'll be back in an hour. I want to see the pool where I shot my first ducks; the Sand Beach where I learned to swim —every rock and tree on the island will seem like old friends."

Leaving her mother and grandmother happily absorbed in the homecoming, Adria slipped into the kitchen. Aunt Cilla turned to with a right good will and even Miss Newhall lent a hand in the tremendous preparations for the mid-afternoon meal for, as Serena pointed out, 'twasn't every Sunday the Probable Son came home. When the dining table was gleaming with linen and silver and the best china, and laden with her brother's every "favourite dish," Adria returned to the middle-room.

"Patrick is talking with his father in the office," her mother said. Both men threw off whatever they might have been discussing, as Dan gently helped his wife to her feet and Patrick handed his grandmother her cane. "Bear your weight on my arm, little Grammy," he told her, and she hobbled proudly beside him into the dining-room.

Dinner was a prolonged and pleasant meal, and talk continued about the table long after Serena's coaxing brought nothing but satiated refusals. Kiah, looking bound and choked in his black Sunday suit and string tie, was the first to push back his chair, muttering that he must "see to things." He returned almost immediately to say that the *Clara Caie* had her boat over. Patrick hastily consulted his watch. Parting was upon them.

From a kitchen window Adria watched the *Clara Caie's* rounded sails go down the lead-blue bay, under a cold hard sky. The wonderful day was over, but life would be happier for them all because of it. Four distant figures on the seaward shore were her brothers with Isles and Waitstill—watching the ship out of sight. She wondered what effect the visit of the successful older brother would have upon the younger ones. Will might develop Patrick's driving ambition. Adria loved Charlie dearly (as small children he and she had been inseparable; together they had opposed Will's older-brother tyranny and plotted to outwit Miss Newhall), but Charlie would walk no after-deck at twenty-three, nor would he wish to, for the open sea did not draw him. *He'll be here to look after us all, as long as we need him.* And this was comforting.

Adria gave no thought to what Patrick and the splendid ship might mean to Waitstill. On Christmas morning she was stricken with remorse when Waitstill brought her a meticulously carved and fitted model of the *Clara Caie*. Kiah had helped with the intricate rigging and Serena, late at nights, had sewed the linen courses, complete to sky-sails and flying jibs. At Waitstill's request Charlie had lettered a name across the stern—not the expected *Clara Caie, Yarmouth,* but *White Wings, New Erin.* Adria choked as she told the happy Waitstill, "It's the most beautiful present I ever had. I'll keep it always."

SEVEN

THE changes wrought by the next five years were gradual and unspectacular. Confounding Prince's Cove prophecies, Confederation did not bring immediate wrack and ruin. Instead, Nova Scotia's shipping towns entered an era of unprecedented prosperity, blissfully unable to recognize a mortal enemy in the steam-driven hulls which would replace their windships. New England ports each year lured more of the coast's ambitious young, but the growing American fleets increased the demand for bait and ice from the western harbours. New Erin shared in this trade and regained much of its losses, although things were no longer done on the large scale that had once marked the island.

In the home, while life was setting into its new pattern, Adria continued to develop skill in her work and pride in the family's dependence upon her. Although the piano soon jangled under her stiff fingers and was left untouched in the closed music-room, she rescued some minutes each day for her books and lost herself briefly in their world of words and knowledge. She lightened the kitchen with her morning songs, she laughed at Charlie's jokes and kept Waitstill in good humour. Mostly she was content, but she was being pushed too rapidly across girlhood's heights and depressions onto the adult level of responsibility, and there were times when she was swept by a yearning for an unknown something, rightfully hers, which life was denying her. Then she must leave the house and tramp the outer shore until its greater restlessness had eased her own. When she returned to the kitchen, tired but restored, neither Serena, nor Damie, nor Mercy betrayed a knowledge of her absence—perhaps each had known her own brief rebellions.

Through the years the Kendricks proved true friends. Isles

was claimed by the boys the minute he landed, but Priscilla was the closest to a girl companion that Adria knew, and perhaps every woman keeps some girlishness for a chosen one — a daughter or young friend. On fine evenings they strolled the near shores, sharing the surf or the tide's gentle rushes and ripples. They brought Mercy bouquets of beach-flowers (pink bindweed, silver cinquefoil, beach-peas and sea-lavender) though Serena awaited their slightest wilting to seize upon them and toss them out. Now and then Priscilla would declare that Adria needed an off-island visit, and the family would rally loyally to see that she got away. It was on these mainland visits that her friendship with Isles had grown. Their young minds explored and settled world affairs, in the way of young minds. They chatted of anything and everything: the books they shared, the news in the *Nova Scotian,* or trivial family concerns. They laughed together at Isles' humourous anecdotes about Cove "characters" who added much spice to his days, or discussed new business ventures. Isles confided his discovery that even a village shop provided opportunities for service. He tried to handle the best "buys" for women whose every penny must be made to count; he could carry over an honest man when a poor season meant tightened belts for all under his roof; he could tear up a bill for a widow whose man would never come back to pay it. Isles was fine and good and Adria was proud to have his friendship.

On a marvellous June morning Adria stood at Aunt Cilla's gate, filled with excitement and a sense of freedom which had been growing since she boarded the *Katie* and her responsibilities had begun to slip astern with the wake. She refolded the boat-cloak upon her arm and turned to scan the road from Ryder's wharf. Will should hurry with her satchel; she didn't want to waste a minute of these precious two days. She glanced behind her at the Kendricks' neat white house on its knoll, and the path winding down through the front yard to the picket fence. Aunt Cila would not see her until she appeared at the back door, for this was a surprise visit.

The tight basque of Adria's blue challis, severely buttoned to her slender throat, disclosed that the five years which had added inches to her height had also slimmed her waist and given compensating curves to hip and bosom. An early wildrose bud in her neck-brooch pointed up her clear colour which, in turn, set off her black lashes and long grey eyes. She removed her brimmed bonnet, protection against the glare from sun and sea, and uncovered lustrous hair, darkened to chestnut and confined in a fashionable snood. In a gesture retained from childhood, she brushed away a vagrant curl with the back of her hand, then, remembering the maturity of almost eighteen, she tucked it carefully under the snood-band.

Aunt Cilla's gateway afforded an excellent view of the placid cove of which the full tide had made a brimming saucer. The air was soft as only June air can be, less salty than New Erin's, richer with perfumes from gardens and fields. Her surroundings were enchanting, but Adria noted that the sun was overhead and recognized her growing emptiness as hunger for the noon meal.

Where had Will got to? Surely so early in the day, and on such a day, he had not stopped to have a drink behind some crony's fish-shed! A familiar uneasiness about her brother diluted her impatience, but she pushed it away, telling herself she had earned this respite from family worries.

On her left was the blank red side of Ryder's shop. It was Isles' shop now, for Uncle Theodore had died two years ago, and Isles had apparently become reconciled to life ashore. Actually the shop was much under the care of a red-headed young clerk, Rhuanna's Vol, the soul of loyalty and honest endeavour but cursed, Isles declared, with a propensity for muddling the simplest undertaking. Lately, to assist Vol, a Miss Deborah Goodwin spent each afternoon behind the dry-goods counter, and feminine customers placed great faith in her advice, Aunt Cilla said. Isles would fetch Will if he knew Adria was waiting, but he had not been on the wharf when the *Katie* tied up, and she shrank from facing the shop's possible customers. Will and Charlie were completely at home in the Cove but Adria felt that the village considered her an outsider. She did not know that its people seldom made the first overtures, nor suspect that her beauty and "Redmond air" could scarcely recommend her to girls who found Isles Kendrick attractive, nor to parents considering him as a possible son-in-law. Isles might envy youthful seamen swaggering down the wharf to a waiting schooner, but many mothers envied Priscilla whose son was safe on dry land and owned a home and shop, a wharf and vessel.

Just as Adria decided against waiting longer, sure that Will had forgotten all about her, her ear caught muffled hoofbeats. They came from her right where the road, on its way to Hines' Harbour, meandered past Aunt Cilla's fence then swung abruptly around a point of spruces and was lost to view. Horses were few along the shore and to island ears hoofbeats held the charm of the unusual. While Adria listened for the grating of wheels, a dust cloud whirled at the bend of the road and, settling upon the spruces, disclosed a ponderous-footed horse with a rider bouncing to its ungainly trot. Adria stepped back to escape the choking dust, then saw with astonishment that the horse was being pulled up before her while the rider looked at the Kendrick house as if he had found the place sought-for. He rode not with a horseman's skill —even Adria recognized — but with the grace of a splendid young body and with delight in powerful, well-controlled muscles. As his hand went up to remove his seaman's cap, a blue tattoo showed on his wrist and, free of the cap, damp black curls fell across a brow startlingly white above a bronzed face. The rather loose mouth laughed above a dark shaven chin, and hidden eyes danced through narrowed lashes.

Upon halting, the steed slumped into the dispirited attitude of the old farm-horse it was, and the rider forgot his mount for the girl standing against the picket fence. He could appreciate the delicately curved figure, the vibrant hair, the large grey eyes, and the restrained smile for the horse with its makeshift saddle of canvas and its rope bridle. He made his voice engagingly boyish, though at twenty-five he had come a long way from boyhood. "I'm looking for Mrs. Priscilla Kendrick's house. I'm her nephew, Dave Malone from Hines' Harbour."

Aunt Cilla's nephew! Adria's smile broke through and she stepped towards the newcomer, her red lips parted. "I'm . . . Aunt Cilla . . ." She started to explain her presence at the roadside.

The young man slid towards her across the broad back of his nag and, before she could raise a hand or take a backward step, leaned down and kissed her—not roughly, but fully—upon her soft and untouched lips. Then smoothly and effortlessly, he righted himself and said soberly, "I'm proud to meet you, Aunt Cilla. Though from Maw's tell, I'd expected you to be a bit older." He laughed silently and his screened eyes said enchanting and impudent things.

Adria's lip trembled and her face crimsoned in distress. She put an innocent hand up to her mouth as if she might touch the shape and texture of a kiss. Dave Malone saw she was not going to pass his audacity off as a joke, nor was she going to pretend shrill anger to hide secret relish, as other girls had done. He dismounted and Adria noted that his height matched Isles' six feet, that his shoulders were nearly as wide as Waitstill's. "I'm sorry," he said in a suitably contrite tone. "But you looked so sweet astanding there—like a little wildrose yourself . . ." He put out a hand towards the bud, but dropped it as she shrank back. He continued, a trifle less confidently, "I won't play any more tricks, since you don't like 'em. Don't be scared of me. I was only teasing."

Adria had known only her brothers' undemonstrative affection and Isles' warm courtesy; she was completely at a loss with this brash young man. To add to her confusion her lips were still tingling from the pressure lately upon them and her heart pounding fit to burst her bodice. She had been stirred by her first kiss, and her young heart rushed to meet romance.

The cocksure Dave Malone was now excusing his dusty homespun pants and open grey shirt. "I just took a notion to see my aunt, so I 'borrowed' my neighbour's horse without changing my clothes. I never expected to meet a pretty girl here. I never expected to meet *such* a pretty girl anywheres."

Adria blushed again. Accepting the evidence of the front hall's big mirror, she had sometimes judged herself comely, even if too thin and big-mouthed, but a dimly lit mirror and a knowledgable young man were not to be compared for assurance in such matters. Finding her voice, she told him who she was. "Mrs. Kendrick is really my mother's friend, but I call her 'Aunt Cilla'. I was waiting for my brother . . ." She had forgotten Will's dereliction.

"Perhaps you'll introduce me to my aunt. She's never seen me and, for all I know, she may turn me from her door." His eyes were wide now. Dark hazel eyes, strongly flecked with brown, and pleading for her support.

Adria's laughter was merry. "Aunt Cilla wouldn't turn even a tramp away." She pointed out the barn-gate and watched him lead his horse away, noticing that he limped slightly. The girl who puzzled her mother by her blindness to what lay in Isles' clear gaze, found herself eager for more of the admiration and challenge in the screened eyes of Isles' cousin—that rude prankster who went about kissing strangers and pretending he mistook them for elderly aunts!

Priscilla greeted her nephew warmly enough, but she asked family news in a guarded way that reminded Adria of hints that Aunt Cilla's widowed mother had married beneath her, and that the Ryders had had little to do with the second family. But, looking at Dave Malone, she decided that the past feeling must have been due to each village's belief that its inhabitants were naturally superior to those who had the poor taste to live elsewhere. Adria, quite at home in the Kendrick kitchen, was setting the table when Isles came whistling up the path and put her satchel inside the door. "Will left it with me. He wouldn't stop for dinner," he explained. He moved towards her eagerly but, seeing a stranger, merely took her hand and at his mother's word, turned to meet his half-cousin. The two men measured each other carefully then seated themselves and fell to talking. *Isles has a pleasant way.* Adria heard him put his guest at ease. *And a good face. Not altogether handsome. Certainly not as exciting as . . . some. But dear and familiar.*

During dinner Dave gave vivid accounts of his brothers, Peter and Jonathan, and their four younger sisters. Dave's father wrestled a living from a rocky farm, a woodlot and the inshore fishing-grounds. "Us three boys got berths on fishing-vessels as soon as we could see over a dory's side. We considered the old man too free with a rope-end." Most men laughed (however ruefully) at childhood's chastisements, recognizing their justice or inevitability, but Dave's voice held a cold vindictiveness that momentarily chilled Adria.

"Where are your brothers?" Priscilla asked.

"On the Banks. They're skippers. Of Gloucester vessels. I sail from Marblehead, but we run afoul of each other now and then, and we're all home, more or less, during the winters."

Adria knew the Bankers' timetable. Not until November or December did the crews return to Nova Scotia. She interposed, "How is it you are home now?"

"Didn't you notice my hobble? The doctors said I must rest my right leg if I didn't want to be lame the rest of my life." He reached under the table to rub his leg as if mention of his injury had aroused pain. "On this spring's voyage the *Admiral* and her skipper were both smashed up bad. The captain's days at sea are done and when my leg is limber again I'm to be master of the refitted *Admiral*," he told them.

Not until Cove men were home and exchanging yarns did Isles learn of Dave's courage and stamina in rescuing his injured captain and bringing the battered *Admiral* to port under jury-rig. But if none of his listeners guessed what had gone into gaining it, all were congratulatory on his new command.

When Isles excused himself he suggested, "You might like to watch the trap-boats come in this afternoon, Dave." Isles had been one of the first to buy the new and capacious trap-seines, and Ryder's wharf was a busy spot when the boats returned, gunwale deep with mackerel.

"I'll be there," Dave answered easily. But while Priscilla had her afternoon nap, he joined Adria on the front steps. The tide deserted the cove, leaving untidy green skeins of eelgrass and tipping skiffs at crazy angles, but the two young people saw only each other, while the sweet June afternoon made every exchanged word as stirring as a caress. Adria told Dave how The Storm had changed her life. He seemed not to appreciate what it had meant to be denied the years at a finishing school (the music and books and plays and the taste of the world which Tamsin had known); his sisters had been glad to put away their Fourth Readers and bid the schoolhouse good-bye. He understood better what the mainland visits meant to her. She told him earnestly, "Your aunt is a second mother to me. And Isles is like a brother."

Dave judged she was dissembling, as girls would. She couldn't be blind to Isles' adoration, as plain to be seen as the man himself. However, he would not be the one to point that out. "Tell me more," he demanded, "Your voice . . ."

"People say I have some of my father's Irish accent."

"Not that. It seems to be saying more than the words you utter and it makes me ashamed of my own rough speech."

Custom had attuned Adria's ear to the seaman's vernacular, often more picturesque than grammatical, and she assured him she heard no fault. "Except when you tell such barefaced fibs—about aunts, and all." She felt the hot colour rise to defeat her attempt at teasing, and to remind her that Dave was eight years her senior. *I don't want him to think I'm saucy. Or free.*

"I'd tell just such another this minute, if you wouldn't h'ist sails and away." His look was daring but he could admire her delicacy and reserve; Dave was ever superficially adaptable to moods and surroundings. "You're different from any girl I ever knew," he told her, and was glad she had no way of guessing just how different. She led the talk to his adventures at sea and thrilled to his mature and steady tones, scarcely the same voice as had told of "borrowing" his neighbour's horse like a prankish boy.

"A Banker's life is hard and dangerous, but it's much freer than life on the square-riggers where a man's very soul can be at the mercy of a bullying mate." He pictured the separate world that each fishing vessel became, and the forecastle comradeship after the crew had shaken down together. He told of fair and spanking breezes and the lee rail awash, of cloudless days on silken waters, when the assembled fleets rode the wide ocean like gulls in a harbour; the sudden snow-squalls and the blinding fogs which meant death for dorymen astray from their vessel; the wild storms that drove the schooners into deeper, safer water beyond the Bank's edge, and away from the fish; the nights when a bountiful catch was dressed down by torchlight, while darkness pressed close about the workers, and the flaring flames were reflected from glistening oilskins and shimmering fish, leaving the rest of the world in deepest night save where, across the black water, torches of other vessels shone like lighted lamps in home windows. Adria, who had never before glimpsed what drew men to the fishing fleets, forgot her former opinion that the workaday schooners lacked the romance of deep-water ships.

Unbelievably soon Isles was turning in at the gate and Aunt Cilla, from the back-steps, was announcing supper. Adria sprang to her feet guiltily. After her eagerness to visit the Kendricks, she had scarcely thought of them all afternoon! She searched Aunt Cilla's face, but it was unreservedly affectionate as she took Adria's hand and drew her through the doorway, leaving the conversing men to follow.

EIGHT

ONCE again Adria was visiting the Kendricks, but now November's early twilight wrapped the outside world and lay thickly folded in room corners. Adria came lightly down the front stairs and paused with a hand on the newel-post to gaze into the sitting-room. Through the isinglass windows of the round heat stove the fire was escaping in thin bands to dance among the wallpaper's gilt scrolls and over the mahogany grapes on chair-backs, and to settle on the conch-shell at the door. Aunt Cilla's sitting-room was smaller, squarer and tidier than the Redmonds' middle-room but it had the same homeliness. Yet, since her arrival yesterday, Adria had felt something was lacking. Not love and warmth of welcome, certainly. It might be the excitement which Dave Malone had brought to her June visit.

That admission introduced another. More than his new and hastily taken friendship for Will had brought Dave to New Erin several times during the past months, although to the family he consistently ignored Will's sister. She had not liked the hint of furtiveness in his seeking her out alone, but she conceded it had added zest to otherwise ordinary meetings. The evoked secrecy, the significant inflections of his voice and the quick pressure of his hand on hers, never failed to stir her pulses. Because Dave was Aunt Cilla's nephew she had accepted him at once, then fashioned her own Dave Malone out of his single kiss at meeting and her unacknowledged longings. But missing him now smacked of disloyalty to her friends and Adria put thoughts of Dave aside as she stepped into the sitting-room.

Aunt Cilla was seated before the front window but she was not watching the road, nor the darkening gust-whipped cove; her head was bent above a small chest in her lap, and her pale hands lay folded upon it. To dispel a sense of intrusion Adria gaily announced, "Here I am, 'ready for the fray' as Serena says," and came to stand by the window, inviting inspection.

She glowed with that exquisiteness dispensed to girls on the threshold of womanhood. Priscilla recognized its poignancy as she watched the firelight play on the smooth cheek and the curls above the white brow. "You're lovely, child, lovely. The green silk fits perfectly and the white lace sets it off. Your eyes have a way of taking colour from what you wear and tonight they're dark and green as a fir-branch. Isles will be proud of you." Priscilla laughed tenderly. "You'll remember your first tea-meeting for there'll be more cracked hearts than dishes tonight in the Hall!"

Adria rejoiced at this praise but she said, "I wish you were coming with me. I dread being thrown among so many strangers," and was fleetingly tempted to ask if she might stay at home.

"After my last week in bed, the doctor says I'm to keep quiet, though I feel well. You will have Isles. There's nothing like a beau at your side, you'll find, to bolster your confidence."

Isles will take good care of me. But he isn't really a beau. Even Miss Newhall could make nothing out of our friendship. "Where *is* Isles?" Adria's impatience was partly pretence and partly excitement. "I thought only women were supposed to be slow getting dressed."

"You'll learn better, my dear," Priscilla assured her calmly. "But Isles should soon be down. I have something to give him before he leaves." She smoothed the box cover. "I had planned to wait until next week on his twenty-first birthday; but you will be back home then. This is a special occasion; I want him to have it tonight."

"What's this I'm to have tonight?" Isles' long legs twinkled behind the bannisters as he descended.

"Come on, slowpoke," Adria urged him, "People have been passing along the road with baskets and bundles for hours and hours!"

"Let me see if you pass inspection, as Adria did," his mother said and Isles strutted across the room with assumed vanity, bringing with him the good masculine scent of bay rum. Adria thought she had never seen him look so nearly handsome. His blue serge set off the white shirt-front and black cravat, his abundant fair hair gleamed from brushing, his freshly-shaven cheeks were clear and smooth as a small boy's. Her glance, though Isles did not see it, was warm with affection and admiration.

Priscilla took her son's hands, explaining to Adria, "Isles has his father's long slender hands. 'Gentleman's hands' Isaac used to call them scornfully, but they had fought canvas and iced rigging and known salt spray in their raw cuts." She reached into the opened chest and drew out a thick gleaming disk on a gold chain. "I want you to wear your father's watch tonight."

Isles sobered instantly. "You always said I should have it only when you considered me man enough to wear it. Thank you, mother." He took the proffered gift from her open hand.

"Your father would want you to wear it tonight, I'm sure." Then, "I'd like Adria to see the inscription."

Isles opened the case and slanted the golden surface of the inner back to catch the window's light, while Adria bent her head to read the fine engraving:

> PRESENTED BY
> THE CITY OF BRISTOL
> TO CAPT. I. A. KENDRICK
> OF THE *Hyperion*
> FOR HIS GALLANT RESCUE OF
> CREW AND PASSENGERS
> FROM THE DISABLED
> BRISTOL BARQUE
> *Isles Ashford*
> 26TH NOV. 1848

To Adria's questions Priscilla answered, "When there is more time I'll tell you about the rescue and the presentation dinner. Tonight the important thing is that Isles wears his father's watch."

"And is Isles named for the barque?"

"Yes. If our baby was a boy I wanted to name him for his father, but Isaac wouldn't hear of it. Along this shore we like Biblical names, but some places find them old-fashioned. Just before Isaac sailed I said, half-joking, 'I'll call the baby after the *Isles Ashford.*' And my husband said, 'Do that. Then he'll bear my initials at least.'" Priscilla put the dear past aside. "Wear your watch, son," she said warmly, and when he had slipped it into his pocket, she helped him adjust the chain across his brocaded waistcoat. Isles bent and kissed her and, as he straightened, her empty hands fell resignedly upon the open box.

Adria's mother and grandmother kept similar small chests and, in them, just such treasures. A faint fragrance of spices from far shores, a hint of shipboard and salt seas, rose from the souvenirs. Adria broke the silence, "I wish I could travel as you did. If I'd been a boy I'd have sailed . . ."

"The Lord knew what He was about when He made you a woman," Priscilla chided. "As for me, if Isaac hadn't happened to be a shipmaster and I hadn't been so fond of him that I couldn't bear him out of my sight, I never would have set foot upon a deck."

Adria marvelled at love's compulsion. "But you had great adventures, like the mutiny . . . Tell me, did you . . . ?"

"Mother! Adria!" Isles expostulated. "No more of your 'yarns'. We're bound for a tea-meeting, remember?" His smile denied real impatience but he stepped into the hall and returned with Adria's green cloak, her fur tippet and muff and the matching hat, which was really no more than a band to perch upon her piled hair. Isles shook his head at its absurdity as he held her cloak. Shrugging into his topcoat he told his mother, "Don't wait up for us if you get tired."

"I'll wait." Priscilla smiled back at him. "I'll want to hear all your news." She watched the young people down the path, Adria's hand lightly upon Isles' arm, her face turned to his as he bent to catch her words, or her smile. They made a picture she long remembered and her face was tender as she closed the little teakwood box.

The outdoor air bit as they stepped into it but it raised Adria's already elated spirits. She turned at the gate and waved to Priscilla. "I like your house, Isles, so compact and trim on its knoll."

Isles pulled her arm more securely through his. "It comes to life when you're in it. Do you ever think you'd like to live on the mainland in a house like ours?"

His voice had a new timbre and, as his hand closed over hers, its vibrancy flowed sweetly along her arm. Since he had arrived at New Erin yesterday to fetch her, Isles had shown purposefulness in all he did and said. Aunt Cilla's affection had altered. Without acknowledging the import of either, Adria had unconsciously set herself against the undercurrents in her friends' attitudes. For, even now as the disturbing tremor in Isles' touch raced to her heart, part of her mind was wondering if Dave Malone would be at the tea-meeting and, when Isles dropped her arm to fasten the gate, her eyes searched the bend of the road for a lithe figure on a jogging nag. She answered Isles, "I've never pictured leaving home. It's hard for Mamma and Serena to manage when I'm away for even a few days."

"I know." Isles sounded troubled as he took her arm again. "Life seems to have caught both you and me." He continued as if he had been over the arguments many times, "I can see that this may be the place I am supposed to fill and I try to content myself in it. But you. You shouldn't give all your youth and all your love to parents and brothers. I keep hoping that Will or Charlie may marry and bring home a wife to release you." Adria started at the idea but, before she could assure Isles she had seen no sign of matrimonial intentions from either brother, he went on, "Surely you want to have your own home someday?"

The gusty wind and the deepening night pressed them close together and left the rest of the world remote as the pale stars peering through the scud. Adria was moved to put all her dreams and longings into words for Isles' understanding, to embrace his concern for her, to feel the present communion of spirits expand and blossom into ecstacy, as she knew it might. Her heart was delicately poised between awakening love and continuing friendship, but perhaps it had already received the deciding fingertouch. They had passed the dark windows of Ryder's shop and could see, half-way up Meeting-house Hill, the outline of the Temperance Hall, with its orange windows and the chimney's swirling smoke. This was no time or place for long confidences. She said, "Marry? I hadn't thought much about it. Down to earth thinking, not dreaming. But I'm past eighteen and I wouldn't want to be an old maid like Miss Newhall. *That* I know."

She turned her face to escape the dust from a miniature whirlwind and found herself looking at the Cove's reminder of the sea's tyranny. "Though old maids are spared a lot." She gestured towards the neat new cottage, starkly uninhabited. Shadows gave its blank windows the look of weeping eyes. They might well weep, Adria thought, for the young skipper who had not come home, and for his bride-to-be who had never set foot inside the carved front door. After her betrothed was drowned, Alethea Sears had gone into a rapid decline and now, stories declared, came back from the grave to flit—a drifting, ethereal whiteness—through the empty rooms, and to show a pale flickering candle at the windows. "But a haunted house should look terrifying," Adria said, "this looks only pitiful."

Isles drew her still closer, hunching his shoulder against the gusty wind, but the moment of promising intimacy was over. As they approached the Hall he called her attention to the carriages with raised shafts on either side of the entrance; to the lanterns hanging on the open-faced horse shelter; to the row of small boats beached on the near shore, and the figures passing through the light as the Hall door opened and closed. "The Sewing Circle is having a good turn-out. The new carpet for the church aisles is as good as laid."

"Isn't that splendid?" But Adria was not really interested. She had glimpsed a pair of shoulders that for a second looked familiar, and her ears were closed to the pleading in Isles' tone. Stubbornness against her true feeling would not let her recognize what Isles hoped from this evening. *Tonight I don't want anyone depending upon me for happiness.* Deep inside, something cried out at the hurt to her dear friend and to her better self, but she was swept by the sudden headiness and magnetic sense of danger that was Dave Malone's effect upon her. As they turned into the Hall yard, she pulled carefully away from Isles' cherishing hand. In spite of herself, her eyes went surreptitiously questing among the grouped men for a black head, and her ears strained for the sound of a lazy voice.

NINE

NOVEMBER, with its short dull days was a relaxed and sociable month in the coastal villages. The inshore boats no longer ventured forth and their crews, whose summer sojourns ashore had been mere matters of snatched sleep and replenished dinner-buckets, now ignored wind and tide. Crews from the Grand Bankers were home to spend the winter with their families. Wharves, roads and shops swarmed with stalwart youths and men in their prime, reversing the summer's preponderance of boys and greybeards. All were happily possessive of wives and sweethearts (now blooming, with their men once more beside them) and basked in domesticity, unable to believe that before spring they would again be in the grip of sea-fever.

In November the winter's wood-chopping and hauling were abeyant, while indoors, fall housecleaning was completed, winter wardrobes readied, and stoves not yet proved insatiable. There was a pause between seasonal demands. Singing schools nightly burst into solfeggios, while many a shipmaster proved himself as handy with a tuning-fork as with a belaying pin. At the Sabbath-night preaching and at midweek prayer-meeting every pew was filled and it was an unusual and unlucky girl who lacked an escort home. The good women of the Sewing Circles and Ladies' Aids, observing all these propitious signs, drew long breaths of considered satisfaction and announced the date of the annual Tea-meeting.

During the week preceding Adria's visit the Prince's Cove women had been in a frenzy of cooking and sewing. The weather was holding fair, but November's freakishness was well-known and the success of the meeting depended upon the attendance from neighbouring villages. Many would be drawn by the reputation of Prince's Cove cooks and the lavish tables set on such occasions, more would come to meet friends and relatives and to catch up on news and gossip. Women would want to compare new bonnets and dresses, for no man worth his salt came back from "across" without presents of stylish garments, or lengths of dress material from an American store. Younger folk would come for the oldest and most irresistible reason of all. Yes, the adjacent settlements would patronize the Prince's Cove tea-meeting, and next week Prince's Cove would attend that put on by the Cape White Sewing Circle. Before winter shut in solid, each Temperance Hall, or transformed schoolhouse, would have held a similar merry mixing of the population for miles around.

The motto for public buildings seemed to be, "the nobler its purpose, the plainer its lines," and the Temperance Hall of Prince's Cove, erected by Christian and idealistic endeavour, perforce resembled an enlarged fish-shed. Yet, as Adria and Isles turned from the road and crossed the few feet of trampled front yard, happy excitement seemed to seep, with the muted buzz of conversations, through the closed door and windows and to lend the air of a great and dazzling occasion. As the young couple approached, the group of men before the lantern-lit door broke up and moved aside, with warm greetings for Isles and polite hat-raisings for his companion.

Adria did not recognize many of the bronzed men, but all seemed friendly and something in their gaze made her lift her head a little, made her feel well worth looking at. She was conscious of Isles, carefully beside her, and grateful to have him there, but she was losing her earlier misgivings at meeting many strangers. A man stepped forward and under the lanterns his red face and redder whiskers had a setting-sun-in-fiery-clouds effect. "Good evening, Captain Stoddart." With a smile Adria held out her hand to the skipper of Isles' schooner *Fearless*.

The captain took it warmly. He spoke in the low-pitched, soft tones characteristic of seamen ashore, as if without the powerful background noises of sea and ship his voice rang too loud in his own ears. "When are ye makin' that v'yage with me, Miss Adria. T'morrah morn be a good time? We set sail early." This was an old joke between them—whenever she could be spared from home, Captain Stoddart had promised her passage on the *Fearless* for a visit to Tamsin in Boston.

Isles, watching Adria's unaffected smile and shining eyes, was proudly conscious of the younger men's envious glances, though he spoke to Captain Stoddart. "You still plan to leave on the morning's ebb?"

"Ayah. We sh'd be out the bay by sunup. I wanted t' tell ye, though, we may be a man shy. Vol's Paw won't be fit fer sea this fortn't, Dr. Whitehouse says. An' men jest back from a v'yage is mostly loath to ship out again so soon. Fur as that goes, we can make out if we have to." Captain Stoddart's full face denied concern.

"No, I wouldn't want you short-handed with the possibility of a winter storm. But neither should we wait. Wonson and Pew have telegraphed they want the mackerel as soon as possible. Let it be known there's a little extra pay in the berth." Isles spoke decisively and Adria began to understand why older men, like Captain Stoddart, were content to remain in the employ of Ryders', though that now meant young Isles Kendrick.

Several older men moved forward to inquire of her parents' health—everyone appeared to know who she was. A tall gentleman in well-cut broadcloth and stovepipe hat enjoined her, "Tell your father that he is missed. In days agone he and a boatload from New Erin were among the early arrivals at these gatherings, and he always bought supper for a tableful of young'uns whose people couldn't pay."

"'Taint only fer the money he spent that he's missed," a thin-voiced little man behind the first speaker added. "Grand company, yer Paw allus was, at such times. A fine-lookin' man too, and one to give an air to any gatherin'."

Adria felt regret that her father now lacked both the means and inclination to play the part of local gentry. She told the men, "My brothers planned to come tonight but the wind is too high. This is my first tea-meeting, but my mother and grandmother have told me about the good times *they* used to have." She noted that the murmur of voices had stopped and everyone was listening to the Redmond girl. "I'm glad I came," she ended in confusion.

The nearer ones smiled and nodded. "Mistah Isles will take good care of ye," another soft voice assured her. The evening was a great success before she had even entered the Hall, Adria thought happily. With her hand again on Isles' arm, she moved forward.

The small dimly lit entry was crammed full of wriggling boys with soap-polished faces and water-slicked hair. The confining best clothes and new boots did not prevent the aiming of covert pokes and kicks, nor brief and inconclusive scuffles. "Gudgeons," Isles told Adria, but in a voice that every boy could hear, and grins broke out on upturned faces — the squirming youngsters did resemble a school of the darting little fish. As a way opened before the two grown-ups and closed behind them, Adria felt herself included in the liking and respect which followed Isles. He pushed open the inner door and they moved into a burst of laughter and talk and—after the entry's faint illumination—into a blaze of light.

For an instant all talk seemed to cease and all eyes to turn upon the newcomers. Adria knew quick panic, a terrible distrust of petticoat strings and a conviction of wind-caused blowsiness, but Isles led her proudly across the room and seated her carefully on a bench along the far wall. While he found a peg for his greatcoat, Adria clasped her hands inside her muff and looked about her.

The long bare walls were lined with lanterns, suspended from strategically placed spikes, and their glow was aided by a few hanging lamps dropped from ceiling beams, but more effectual were the rows of borrowed house-lamps lining the two long white-linened tables. Cutlery and plates at each set place, and crowded bowls of pickles and preserves, all gave back the lamp-light in a most cheerful and inviting manner.

Tonight the raised platform at the hall's far end remained in shadow, its curtains fluttering unnoticed in the draughts from the opening door. Attention was on the opposite end of the room and its scantier curtains which bulged as matronly bodies pushed against them and billowed inward with the breeze of hurried passages, for behind them were the stove and cupboards and counters used by the women. After the crisp air outside, the smells escaping the curtains made Adria's nostrils twitch. From behind the curtains came also the buzz of many excited, responsibility-laden voices, the rattle of dishes as baskets were unpacked and the contents sorted upon waiting plates and platters.

The benches near the door held groups of conversing men, variably clad in "shore" vestments, and the scraps of their talk drifting across to Adria concerned shipmates and vessels. In their best black dresses and mantles, elderly women—retired from behind-curtains activity — welcomed visiting ladies, who pretended not to notice the Sewing Circle's occasional and inevitable mishaps; next week, or some week soon after, Prince's Cove visitors would turn an unequally unseeing eye upon *their* equally obvious difficulties.

Bustling about were the Circle's solid nucleus of middle-aged matrons, plainly experienced and with no small children to hamper their efficiency—their daughters were working beside them and their sons ogling other young helpers. Younger women must keep one eye upon their offspring, must dart out now and then to grab a misbehaving young'un and set it upon a bench with a thud that threatened alike tender posterior and sturdy plank. The marriageable maidens were aware of masculine eyes, and their movements were studied rather than competent. All workers shared cheeks flushed from the close heat behind the curtains, and a slow wilting of starched tea-aprons. Girls, too young for beaux and too flighty to be trusted with good food and best dishes, clustered in the shadowy corners to giggle.

To Adria the hall was noisy and rather confusing, but Isles soon returned to her side. With him was a young woman. "This is Miss Goodwin, my life-saver in the shop. Miss Debbie, this is Adria. I've told you about her."

"Indeed he has! I'm happy to meet you." But she didn't look happy. Adria took the soft, outstretched hand. Softness was the most apparent characteristic of Miss Debbie's face and figure, but the yielding exterior must have covered a firm core. When a fall from a yardarm had left her father a cripple, he had been appointed Customs Officer to spare him the gall of charity, but it had been his motherless youngster, Deborah, who had learned to keep the records and make out the Clearance Papers for the shipping that used Redmond's Harbour or Prince's Cove. Until she began to clerk in Isles Kendrick's shop she had taken in sewing to fill any moments salvaged from keeping house and caring for her partially helpless father. She had been doing this so capably and for so long that she was counted among the village spinsters, though she was barely twenty-three. Adria thought her brown eyes gentle and appealing as they watched Isles. He was saying, "I'll leave you to get acquainted. I must speak to Captain Stoddart again." His smile included both, but it rested upon Adria.

As Debbie sat down beside her, Adria wondered how one went about getting acquainted. Before she could test a method she felt the bench give under added weight and turned to see Obie Knowles' flushed face at her shoulder. He bent across Adria to nod to Miss Debbie, making himself at home on a bench presumably reserved for ladies. "Don't mind me. When manners was handed out, I must 'a' been away cranberryin'." He rubbed his cupped palms over his knees in appreciation of this witticism. Now there was no need to do more than listen—not too closely—while Little Obie discoursed on all present. "But how's yer Maw, Adria?" he finally inquired, turning his faded blue eyes behind their lashless lids full upon her. "Ye know," he confided, "I courted her onct. Like enough she's told ye." He smoothed his pant knees again, proudly recalling the figure he must have cut in Mercy Nickerson's eyes. "But she up an' wed yer Paw. Ef she regretted it I must omit she never let on t'me." His tone commended her rectitude even while it deplored her lack of judgment.

"She wouldn't," Adria assured him demurely, but glancing aside lest her twitching mouth betray her, she met the brown eyes beside her. She looked hastily away from the shared mirth, but she and Debbie were already acquainted.

Debbie took over. "How are all your family, Obie? I see Mis' Cynthie is busy as usual." Adria recognized the hustling fair woman with round steel-rimmed glasses, determined mouth and the air of command.

"Ayah." Obie's response was not enthusiastic. "An' Tillie." Adria followed his pointing finger to a thin woman with a high flush on her hollow cheeks. "As purty as ary woman here, Tillie is. Got her a good-lookin' man, too, though Nathan ain't much of an earner." Nathan was a stocky strutting man with quick black eyes and a luxuriant black mustache which he fingered lovingly. "An' thyah, third from the left on that end bench, with all them purty black ringlets, that's my Airy Bellah." Adria thought Arabella, who might be ten or twelve, had a bold and saucy manner but she could say truthfully, "Her curls are beautiful and her eyes very black and bright."

"She'll be the purtiest girl in the Cove. I *don't* know but the purtiest along the whole shore," the fond Grampy prophesied.

"One of the prettiest, surely," Debbie assured him.

Before Adria could add a word her heart lurched at a voice and a laugh from the doorway. Above those surrounding them, Isles' fair head and his cousin's black one showed. "Dave did come," Adria breathed and Miss Debbie looked at her swiftly in troubled surprise.

Once Dave's gaze found Adria he was quickly before her, hat in hand, declaring plain as words before everybody why he was attending a Cove tea-meeting. Cynthie Obie, rushing towards the curtained recess, paused at the sight and lifted her apron to wipe her glasses. Assured she was seeing aright, she looked at Isles, who had been engaged by Mr. Stouten. The minister had just arrived and Isles could not break off a greeting rudely, as his cousin had done. Nonetheless he saw more surely than other onlookers how possessively Dave bent above Adria. Saw the glow on her upturned face, and her sweet wide smile. He had hoped, walking home, to find words to tell her what he had tried to show her all the years of his young manhood. Now his heart fell. *She has never looked at me as she is looking at Dave. Never blushed and watched her hands to hide what her face might betray.*

The hush preparatory to the call for "first tables" had fallen over the hall as Isles crossed the room. When he seated Adria he tried not to mind that Dave manoeuvred into the place on her other side, nor that his cousin soon had that portion of the table in laughter, while Isles himself sat miserably quiet and desperately alone.

Adria tried to divide her attention between Isles and his cousin, but Isles' voice was lost under the meaningful and disquieting shadings in Dave's. She turned uncomfortably from Isles' look to watch the glinting hazel eyes break through their obscuring lashes and gaze, suddenly and soberly, deep into her own. When those eyes fixed upon her mouth, she felt again the pressure of warm lips in that preposterous kiss at meeting, and Dave's knee pressed against hers disturbingly, even while his eyes were looking most innocently into hers.

A woman's voice, agitated but diffident, came from behind them. "Mistah Isles, I wouldn't ask ye. But seems you'm the first man through yer supper. Leastways ye ain't touched a mouthful sence I been awatchin' ye. I wonder if I might ask a favour." There was a vocal wringing of hands in her breathlessness.

"Anything at all, Mis' Lucy John," Isles assured her.

"It's my cream crock. I pushed it well under the wagon in the corner of the shed, so as it wouldn't get upsot. An' didn't I come in an' fergit about it! Now it seems we'm about t'run shy o' cream, and I was awonderin' . . ."

Isles rose. "Just tell me where I'll find it." He excused himself and left the table.

Unreasonably, Adria now wanted him back beside her. She felt uncomfortable at Dave's covert touch, at his foot seeking hers, and moved, as imperceptibly as possible, into Isles' vacated seat. But Dave did not mean to let her retreat. He leaned over and his voice was pitched so low that she must bend her head to hear it, and his breath was warm upon her ear. "There's something I *must* talk to you about. Come for a drive with me."

"Drive? Didn't you ride that same horse . . . ?" She saw she had hurt his pride. He wouldn't have ridden bareback in his fine black trousers and braided coat, yet she had been picturing him as on that June day.

"I hired the smartest rig in MacDonald's livery stable!" Adria looked properly impressed. "I planned on taking you out in it. I want to talk to you and what I have to say won't wait." He gave his words a portentous cast, which his face bore out, and Adria felt that, although he might exaggerate to influence her, there was a true urgency in them.

From habit, Adria's first reaction was to respond to any plea for help but she asked, "Don't you want to talk this — whatever it is — over with Isles? Haven't you noticed how even the older men consult him?"

"This is none of Isles' affairs. If you can't help me, no one can." The tense, almost whispered, words were drawing attention.

"If you think Isles won't mind my leaving . . ." She could not suspect the local estimation of the proposed insult to her escort, yet she sensed the inherent disloyalty in an absence with Dave.

"I'll explain to Isles later. We won't be long. I left the horse harnessed and the buggy ready; I can have him between shafts in no time." Without further persuasion he went towards his coat.

Adria rose, torn between misgivings and a confused desire to please Dave. She spoke a few words to Deborah, got her cloak and muff and joined him. As they threaded their way across the hall Dave greeted several acquaintances with great unconcern, but Adria felt many eyes like pricking needles upon her back. She stopped in confusion when she saw that he was leading her, not to the front entrance but to a small side-door against the curtained platform. She had not noticed it; how had Dave discovered this unused exit? Before he had even spoken to her tonight, had he laid his plans to steal away with her, unknown to Isles? She wished herself back at the table, but to return now would take more courage than to go on. Dave's hand was compelling upon her arm; she walked through the little door as if she had no will of her own and with her head lifted proudly to hide her qualms.

The cream crock had been well stowed and the borrowed lantern none too revealing. Some time passed before Isles re-entered the Hall to be met by Mis' Lucy John who seized her crock, thanked him, and disappeared. Almost he had known he would find Adria gone. And Dave. He didn't need Deborah's soft voice, "Miss Redmond said to tell you she had gone for a short drive and would be back immediately." Her sympathy strove for covering words, "Such a lovely evening for a drive. . ."

Windy, and cold as Greenland. But it would be "a lovely evening" driving beside Adria.

Debbie's gentle voice trailed off before the blaze of anger in Isles' face. *I suppose I should feel glad that he's cross at her. But I do like his Adria.*

Isles turned to leave the crowded Hall but in the entry he met a strong surge of roughly pushing bodies. These were the young rowdies of Pilot Point, and their truculent air served notice that they were looking for trouble.

No one in Prince's Cove held with the notion that all men were created equal; they were too familiar with nature's blatant disparities, and generations of families, living side by side, had left open records of heredity's heavy thumb on the balance-scale. Incessantly a shifting and readjustment went on in even the smallest settlements; honest, thrifty parents strove to marry their offspring into similar families while the lazy and not-too-honest tended to mate with their like. Early in the Cove's history its less desirable inhabitants had coalesced on Pilot Point, part of the village and yet distinct from it. The men were known as dauntless fishermen, hardier than most; they were also known as drinkers and brawlers when ashore. More than once they had turned a tea-meeting into a free-for-all and left the hall wrecked.

Isles had only one thought, to get out into the covering night where no one could read from his face how he was taking his girl's desertion. He couldn't blame Dave for wanting Adria — how could he help it? Nor Adria for losing her heart to his handsome, charming cousin. He blamed himself for delusion and procrastination, but for the moment he hated Dave. His hatred was in the way he breasted the wave of young men entering the Hall. He caught one chap with his shoulder and spun him about. "Pardon," he muttered but his tone and his eyes were savage.

"Look where you'm agoin'," the young man said as savagely, "Or I'll put a kink in your mainsheet."

Isles laughed scornfully.

"Be ye lookin' fer a fight?" The Pilot Pointer was plainly hoping he was.

"Fight?" said Isles, measuring the other insultingly. "Why if I blew on you, you'd fall over." He knew the other's slimness hid a wiry strength; he heard his own words, ugly and boasting, but his self-derision was a bitter and evil thing, like his anger.

"Come on, then," said the Pilot Pointer, turning and lurching towards the outer door. "Come on around back, till I comb ye out."

Like a wave caught and turned, the group swung about and carried the willing Isles with it, out the door and around the corner and to the Hall's black shadow where a bleak wind came off the cove, unbroken. Neither man felt the wind though they were soon stripped to their shirts. There in the darkness they grappled. When an arm was free they slugged with it, when a leg was free they kicked, though Isles' lighter boots lacked the weight and iron-hard edges of his opponent's sea-boots. Isles did not attempt the other's biting tactics, but later he remembered with shame his gouging fingers seeking an eye, and the savage satisfaction when his fist met his antagonist's nose. The unseen ring of men around them closed and moved back as the struggle continued, a ring that became solider as Prince's Cove men joined the Pilot Pointers. The fight did not spread among the onlookers, partly because there was no telling which champion was faring best and neither appealed for help, and partly because no one knew what had started the battle. As suddenly as they had clashed, and with as little reason, the combatants disengaged and drew apart, panting and spitting. There were the sounds of the Pilot Pointer sniffling blood and the wiping application of a sleeve. When Isles moved towards his coat his right foot dragged unevenly across the frozen ground.

His leg was shooting red hot needles up the length of it, but he was cleansed of his rage and, to his surprise, not a whit ashamed of having been engaged in a brawl. He turned to tell his unseen opponent that no ill-will remained on his part, but the other was ahead of him, "Ef I'd 'a' knowed," he said, "what kind o' fighters shopkeepers really was, I'd never 'a' harkened t' Dave Malone."

"What had Dave Malone to do with it?"

"He asked me t' keep ye busy whilst he took yer girl for a drive."

"He needn't have bothered you." Isles was glad his voice betrayed nothing. "Miss Redmond is free to go driving with whoever she likes." Getting into his coat he said, through rapidly swelling lips, "It was a good fight. We'll try again some time, after I can stand on my leg, and your nose is healed. I hope it's broken."

"Well, seems t' be," the other assured him, equally without rancour. "Ef 'tisn't, I can't blame *you*." He hawked mightily and spat, then, with a knot of his companions, was swallowed up in the night. Isles never heard his name and never knowingly saw again the young man upon whom he had wreaked much black bitterness.

TEN

THE wind made riotous snatches at the buggy, but Adria was warm under the bear-robe, and the hoofbeats upon the frozen road had a pleasant rhythm. When a sudden lurch threw her against Dave his arm swiftly encircled her. For a moment she stiffened against such intimacy, then she turned to snuggle against his coat's rough fabric, feeling delightfully small and helpless against the bulk of his body and in the possessiveness of his arm. They drove for a time in silence, while Dave's arm tightened about her to ease each jolt from the rough road. Then, with a grating of wheels, the buggy turned into the mouth of a woodroad and left the thwarted wind to keen through the treetops above it. The woodroad was smooth, grass-grown and unrutted since last winter, and Dave looped the reins about the whip-holder, leaving the horse to amble or halt as it pleased.

Adria drew herself away and straightened her hat. Somewhere among the trees a little brook was babbling as it rushed through the night but, like the soughing wind, it added to the surrounding silence, and left her keenly conscious of her heart's expectant pounding, for she felt in Dave a return of the urgency which had impelled her to follow him from the tea-meeting. His head was now close above hers and his voice was strained. "I'm not going to back and fill about this. I brought you here to ask you to marry me."

She was truly stunned. There should be an interval after the awakening of love, for dreaming and the translating of dreams into reality. She had not yet named Dave's attraction for her, nor attempted to discover how much his actual self resembled the picture she had drawn out of her inexperience and romanticism.

When she could not speak Dave went on, "I never wanted to marry any other girl. That day I saw you at Aunt Cilla's gate I knew you were what I'd been waiting for." Still she could not answer although memory of that meeting was melting her frozen surprise. He was too wise to touch her yet, but he let desperation edge his voice, "I need you. You don't know how much. Perhaps you *can't* know, brought up on an island, what temptations a man comes up against. How much he needs a good woman, to keep him on a straight course." His voice softened in confession, "I haven't done all I might, Adria, and I've done some things I shouldn't have." Apart from thinking this admission frank and showing a praiseworthy repentance, Adria took no real meaning from it; often she felt guilty at her own sins of omission and commission. Though his hands were still, his words, ragged with emotion, reached for her. "But if you'll marry me, I swear I'll be true to you till the day I die." He waited when her hands in their muff went up against his breast to halt his embrace.

What shall I say? Adria tried to ask herself if Dave was what she wanted in a husband. Marriage was forever, and there should be no misgivings. But confusion and belated self-questioning make an open net, and more than a net is needed to stem a tide. She felt herself being swept along in a delicious and enervating flood.

A more self-centred girl might have noticed that Dave's concern was for his own needs, but the past years had accustomed Adria to giving. Here was a plea from a man for her woman's strength (a plea few girls have ever resisted) and from a practised supplicant. She found words at last. "But I've only seen you a few times; I scarcely know you."

"We knew all we needed to know of each other by the end of that first afternoon."

She believed he was right, but one irrefutable fact remained. "I'm not free to marry. I can't leave New Erin while my parents need me."

He seized upon this eagerly. "Is that what's standing in our way? Let me make my home with you and your people. Most years I'm ashore for only a few months and New Erin could use another man during the winters."

Local custom would sanction such an arrangement. The family would welcome another member. The thought of Dave at home on New Erin was intoxicating. Adria drew a long breath. "I'll talk it over with my people when I go home tomorrow,'" she promised huskily.

"No. We'll decide this now, ourselves. Of course, we must have your father's consent to marry." He had regained his assurance as if, Adria thought uneasily, everything were settled and her wishes no longer mattered. "I'll speak for the licence . . . ."

Adria gasped audibly and sat more erect, but he went on casually, "This wind will moderate before dawn and I'll sail down to New Erin tomorrow. We could be married within the week."

Adria's arms were still rigid, the little muff still inflexible, against his coat. Within the week! She had barely grasped the idea of future marriage, perhaps next fall when Dave was again ashore.

"Now, don't tell me you have to sew a lot of clothes and all that guff." He pleaded, "Don't make me wait. I might not come back next fall. Think of Crowell Smith and his Alethea. You must have seen their little empty house here in the Cove."

"Yes, oh yes." She dropped the muff. Dave was right. It was only that she had been confused by his tempestuousness. *I have room in my heart for another loved one. Strength to work a little harder. I won't neglect the old for the new.* She lifted her face.

This was Adria's first real kiss, her first experience with the answering hot uprush that can be mistaken for love. Dave's lips were hard and exultant as they accepted the surrender on hers.

Close together under the bear-robe, they shaped and reshaped their plans. Until in a blissful pause Adria recalled, with an accusing clarity, Isles' face bent above hers as he hunched his shoulder to break the wind. "Dave," she said, "You must take me back now. We've left Isles alone all this time. I'm ashamed." She was deeply agitated and Dave turned the horse at her beseeching; he knew better than she how long Isles had been waiting.

Once on the mainroad they met carriages, and couples walking homeward, and when they topped Meeting-house Hill, the orange oblongs of the Hall windows were one by one turning black, while the bobbing lanterns of stragglers dispersed. Adria's first tea-meeting was truly over. She would remember it, as Aunt Cilla had foretold. Dave whipped the horse past the Hall, explaining, "I don't want the last old hens looking us over and cackling. Isles won't be waiting for us there; he'll be home. I won't go in to see him and Aunt Cilla tonight, because I must get the horse back to his stable."

He said good-night at the gate, bruising her lips with his, pressing her close to his body, making her aware for the first time of its hunger for hers. He let her go before he frightened her but his soft laughter was triumphant.

Adria heard the starting buggy wheels grind against a frozen rut as she found the back door latch. In the glow from the kitchen window she paused to assure herself she was the same person who had waved good-bye to Aunt Cilla and set off on Isles' arm — how many hours ago? A lifetime. Isles would be waiting in the kitchen. *He should be angry with me.* Her buoyant heart suddenly contracted with a sense of loss and she began to see her recent decision as it would appear to the Kendricks. Isles would stand by her—hadn't he told her only tonight that she should be thinking of marriage? But Aunt Cilla would not be pleased; for some reason she was not fond of her nephew Dave. With desperate homesickness replacing the long evening's elation, she wished herself near her understanding mother. It was a somewhat subdued Adria who slipped through the back entry and into the kitchen.

Priscilla had been dozing in her rocker. She wakened with a start and turned up the lamp wick. Her eyes went to Adria's face and, as if she read an expected message there, she smiled with special fondness. "Where is Isles?"

Adria echoed her words, "Where *is* he? I expected him here with you," and she looked helplessly about the shadowy room.

"Then who brought you home? Oh!" Her hands grasped the rocker arms. "I *thought* I heard carriage wheels! You've come to tell me Isles is . . . hurt. Are they bringing him in?" Her usually placid voice was sharp with anxiety.

"No, no, Aunt Cilla," Adria ran and put a comforting arm about the sagging shoulders. "Isles is all right, I'm sure. He'll be along shortly; they were shutting up the Hall as we came by. Dave brought me home. He couldn't stop to see you because he had a hired rig." Miserably, "I never thought of your being worried over Isles."

The wind sighed reproachfully in the chimney and the fire answered it snappishly. The lamp's faint sibilance was audible in the continuing silence. "Why didn't Dave bring Isles home, too?" Priscilla finally asked in her usual steady tones.

Adria straightened and stepped back. "Dave took me for a drive and . . ." She realized there was no excuse for her desertion of Isles.

"A drive! At this hour of the night!"

Adria glanced guiltily at the clock and saw that its scandalized hands hovered near midnight. She said contritely, "We didn't think of the time. Please don't be cross with me."

"I'm not cross. But you must remember that when you are in my home I'm responsible to your parents. Dave should know how quickly gossip starts." She could not guess, despite her experience with rumours, that Adria would long be remembered as the girl who had come to a tea-meeting with one escort and left with another, in the face and eyes of everyone, while neither beau had bought her so much as a pincushion from the fancywork table, which showed how lightly they had valued her.

Priscilla sighed, *Why do I go on so? I wouldn't have cared how late Isles kept her out. It's because my dreams are come to naught that I scold the child.* She said somewhat lamely, "I wouldn't want gossip to distress your mother."

"Mamma won't mind when she *knows*," Adria assured her. She turned her face eagerly towards her friend and the lamplight revealed the dark pools of her eyes and the winsome curves of her mouth, deepened and sweetened by a new quality. "Dave took me driving so he could ask me to marry him." She strove to transmit and share the rapture that rose again with memory. "You'll soon be my aunt, *really*."

Priscilla's face went bleak. *Aunt. That's not the name I hoped to hear.*

" . . . married right away," Adria was running on, "Just as soon as I get Papa's permission. There's no one to make a wedding on New Erin now, so we'll likely be married in the parsonage." She drew a long quivering breath. "I can't believe this is me."

"Neither can I," Priscilla answered with flat honesty. "Have you given a thought to how your mother will manage without you?"

At her tone the joy faded from Adria's face, but she explained,

"I'm not deserting the family. Dave doesn't ask that. When he's not at sea he will make his home on New Erin. We planned it all—that's what kept us so late—and I can scarcely wait to tell Mamma."

Priscilla felt a sympathetic pang for Mercy, whose disappointment would match her own. Perhaps they had been mistaken and Adria had not been meant for Isles, but there was an out-of-true feeling to this, due to more than her jealousy for her son. She sighed and said no more.

Adria glanced about restlessly. "I did think Isles would be home. I must tell him I'm sorry about leaving as I did." Priscilla was pleased that the girl showed sincere abashment. "But Dave said *he* would explain afterward and that Isles wouldn't mind. He knows how good Isles has always been to me."

Yes, Isles' devotion would raise Adria's value in Dave's eyes. Though he mightn't admit it, there was satisfaction in stealing his cousin's girl.

Adria asked yet again, "Where can Isles be?"

"Perhaps he took a girl home and has stayed a while," Priscilla suggested drily.

Adria was openly dumbfounded. To herself she denied the suggestion hotly. *Not one girl I saw tonight is fine and good enough for Isles.*

Priscilla looked again at the clock. "We won't talk more now, my dear. Take off your things, then warm yourself at the oven-door; the bedroom may be chill. Your brothers will be coming for you on the early tide and you must get some sleep."

Adria wished to put her cheek against Priscilla's and whisper that she didn't want sleep, that it could bring no dream to compare with her waking one; but something forbade her. She said meekly, "I bid you good night." But she paused at the stair door. "You'll tell Isles? About Dave and me?"

"I'll tell him. Good night."

Until movement in the spare bedroom ceased, Priscilla sat motionless in the rocker. If she prayed for guidance or strength, the prayer was silent and hidden. When she moved it was with certainty. She dressed warmly, turned the lamp low, closed the stove draughts and shut the entry door softly behind her. She was back in her chair before Isles came limping in. He felt her love and her yearning, though she spoke no word and made no sign as he flung his coat upon a chair and bent stiffly to remove his scuffed boots. Her tone denied any wish to pry but under the words, "What has kept you so late?" she was saying, Here I am, son, if you need to talk.

He answered her question, "Walking the roads and ducking into the woods to avoid meeting people." As he straightened, his mother saw his torn pant leg, his swollen lip, the crusted blood over one eye.

"Dave?" she asked.

"No. Though he had a hand in it." He told her of Mis' Lucy John's mislaid cream crock and the opportunity it had afforded his cousin. "I believe he came to the tea-meeting determined to take Adria from me." Even through his disappointments, his established protectiveness reasserted itself. "Adria?" he asked. "She's home?"

Priscilla nodded. "She's abed. And asleep, no doubt." What must be said came with difficulty. "She had news for me when she came in. Happy news, she believed, but far from happy for me—or for you." He turned his head away as if sensing what was coming. "She is going to marry Dave. Soon."

For a time he did not speak, while the clock on the shelf callously ticked away the seconds in time to his heart's sick beats. He pulled out a chair and sat down beside the table. Because for so many years they had shared everything, he told his mother what had most relentlessly driven him along the dark roads. "He'll break Adria's heart. He's not fit to marry any good girl."

"I feared that," she agreed simply. "But perhaps he loves her truly. Many a wild young man settles down when he finds the right girl. If you are thinking I should warn Adria, it would be of no use, believe me. And I don't want to turn her from me; she may need her friends. If they would wait! By next spring Dave might have found a new love, or Adria might see him in a clearer light. But he is eager to have the winter with his wife. And who can blame him?" There was always the sea's toll to be reckoned.

"Adria was meant for me. I should have swept her off her feet —I think there have been times when I could have—just as Dave has done." He laid his arm upon the table and leaned his head wearily in his hand. "I believed I shouldn't ask her to take on the cares of a husband and family until she had known some freedom. And she seemed still a girl in many ways. But I was wrong; she was ready for marriage."

Priscilla did not answer. Who could say if Adria would have met his avowed love with the same headlong response she had given Dave's? And Isles had not Dave's freedom. He carried the burden of his mother; he could not give up his business to be with Adria on New Erin.

Isles went on, "If only Dave were staying ashore and I were the one at sea! How can I bear to watch them together, or to know she is alone and perhaps needing help?" He betrayed a young and vulnerable pride, "How can I face the Cove's pitying looks?"

"You won't have to." Priscilla came to place her hand on his shoulder. "You can be at sea until this blows over." As he stared she told him, "After Adria had gone to bed I slipped across the road to see Captain Stoddart." *No need to tell Isles I had to wake the poor man and his wife from their sleep. Nor how much they understood without words and how glad they were to help.* "Vol had told me the *Fearless* was sailing short-handed. Captain Stoddart was pleased to hear you might fill a berth yourself." She gave him no chance to express doubt, but gestured towards the small chest that always stood under the stairway. "I've packed the sea-chest that went with your father on *his* first voyage." Her even voice betrayed none of her renunciation. When he made no answer, she asked hesitantly, "Did I take too much upon myself? I gave Captain Stoddart no definite word, just that we would like him to call here on his way to the *Fearless*." A wild hope sprang up that her proffered sacrifice would not be exacted from her.

Isles put his cheek upon her hand, where it rested on his shoulder. "You love me that much," he said in humble wonder. He knew she had shared his hope that Adria would still the last of his seafever and anchor him safely ashore with the two women who needed and loved him. True, a trip to Gloucester was no deep-sea voyage, but it would serve him now. "What about the shop?" he asked. The ropes of duty and obligation had not slackened.

"Rhuanna's Vol can do all the heavy work; I'll go each day to keep the books up to date and 'to straighten Vol out' as you say. Debbie might give some extra help. Go son," she urged, "It's time you met the merchants with whom you do business."

He pulled her soft cheek down against his hard young one in wordless gratitude. "You say you packed the chest? I must get into sea-clothes."

"You must bathe your lip and that cut over your eye, and let me put some anodyne on your bruised leg. Then you must have something to eat." It was a relief to minister to physical hurts. Finally she insisted that he snatch an hour's rest upon the kitchen couch and, despite his protests, he slept. She sat where she could gaze upon the rumpled fair hair, the brown upward curling lashes, the mouth that, relaxed, had retaken the boyish curves she achingly remembered. She recognized that she was sending from her the last of her boy; the son who came back would be completely man, and this night's confidences would never be duplicated. Yet, when Captain Stoddart's knock came, Priscilla aroused her son matter-of-factly; she kissed him briefly and did not cling to him; nor did she weep to see him go through the door with his sea-chest upon his shoulder. If she strained her eyes in the pre-dawn greyness watching a figure cross the wharf-head, or in following a schooner's lights through the channel, there was no one to know or feel reproached.

At breakfast Adria was amazed to learn of Isles' departure. "He never said a word to me about such a voyage!"

"He decided rather suddenly."

Adria felt bewildered. *Aunt Cilla's eyes are bleak and cold, almost as if she blames me for Isles' leaving.* "He didn't go against your wishes?"

"It was my suggestion."

What had gone on while she was in bed last night? Aunt Cilla looked as if she lacked sleep, even as if she might have been weeping, although her composure denied this. "Did you tell Isles . . . my news?"

"I told him you were marrying Dave, yes. But I'm afraid we were overly engrossed with preparations for his trip, because he forgot to leave any message for you. Probably he thought you wouldn't need to be told that he wished you happiness. Isles is your true friend."

"I know. You and Isles. I can't tell you how I . . ." Her voice caught and she turned her face to the window, pretending an absorption in the back fence.

Despite her resentment at Adria's blindness, Priscilla loved the girl only less than she loved Isles. Gently she said, "Tell me about the tea-meeting."

Adria, forgetting breakfast, tried to remember persons and incidents that might interest Priscilla. But under her chatter, she was conscious of a wrong turning taken somewhere and the impossibility of retracing her steps. Until she remembered that before night Dave would be with her on New Erin. Lost in the warm shivering bliss of physical recollection she sat staring across the cove until a coming sail impinged upon her mind and she sprang to her feet. "The *Katie* is nearly to the wharf. I must get my satchel. Don't look sad, Aunt Cilla. I'm not going far!"

Priscilla had a different conception of distance.

ELEVEN

ADRIA would have confided her news to Charlie, but she sat silent beside Will as the *Katie,* perilously heeled over under his foolhardy use of sail, sped homeward. There was a tarpaulin to cover her knees and her boat-cloak was thick — the flying spray would do her body no harm while she turned her mind inward. Will handled the tiller automatically, staring ahead. Once, glimpsing his expression, Adria was shocked out of her self-absorption into compassion for this brother caught in some net of his own knitting. She wished she had courage to ask what tormented him and if she could help, but one did not intrude upon Will's moods. Out of her own recent awakening she found it strange that with several pretty Cove girls doting on him, Will showed no interest in any of them.

No word passed between brother and sister until the wharf had been rounded and the sail let go. When Will had helped her up the ladder and handed her satchel from the boat she smiled down at him. "That was a grand trip. I like to get my face washed, coming home."

Will's head came up and his dark eyes met hers in a flash of sharing and enjoyment. "You aren't soaked, then?" he asked boyishly. "I never heed how much water flies, but I should take better care of my pretty sister." Before she could answer this overture, he had turned to furl the flapping sail.

Adria burst into the kitchen with cheeks richly glowing from wind and spray and small salty curls damp about her face. Joy came from her like a flame, and Serena turned from the stove, poker in hand, to watch her run across the kitchen and kneel quickly beside her mother's rocker. "Mamma! I have such news for you." The words tumbled out, "I'm going to be married."

"Married! Darling." Mercy's tone poured love and rejoicing over the kneeling girl, and her hands went out to cup the vivid face. She looked deep into the wide eyes before she bent and kissed her daughter. "Is Isles here?" she asked, looking towards the door as if expecting him to enter.

It puzzled Adria that her mother should ask about Isles at this time. "No. He's finally gone to sea! Oh, just to Gloucester on the *Fearless.*"

"But why now?"

"Never mind Isles. Don't you want to hear about Dave and me, and our marriage plans?"

Adria glanced over her shoulder at the clatter and saw Serena bending above the fallen poker.

"Dave?" Mercy was saying. "Dave Malone?" Then she kissed Adria again, holding her cheek close and long against her daughter's.

She thinks I'll be leaving her. Adria hastened with reassurances. "Dave knows I can't be spared and he's willing to make his home on New Erin. He'll work here during the winters and help with expenses." Her mother made no response and Adria rose to her feet. "I'll go tell Papa. He seemed to like Dave." Her voice had a pathetic tremor of uncertainty now and Mercy's heart upbraided her for having dimmed that first glow of shared happiness. Adria was pleading, "You don't think I'm being selfish? Or too . . . too precipitous? It's Dave, really, who doesn't want to wait."

Mercy could answer, "I've never known you to be selfish. If you love Dave truly, your father and I will do all we can to smooth the way for you—and for him."

As Adria hurried away, Serena and Mercy faced each other with a long defeated look. Mercy laid her sewing aside. "I'd best be the one to tell Ma, and to caution her against saying too much. We'll guard against Miss Newhall's tongue, too. Hurting Adria cannot help." With a sigh she went towards her mother's room. "And Isles away at sea! I wonder what went wrong."

When Dave arrived to claim Adria, it was impossible not to admire his virile good looks, not to approve his open adoration of his betrothed. Yet Mercy was conscious of the strong will under the pliant manner, and the lack of fine perception in this man whom her sensitive daughter had chosen.

Two weeks later Dave took his bride from the parsonage to his Hines' Harbour home, to "show her off" as he boasted. Their return ushered in a winter of laughter and high young spirits for New Erin, as Dave set himself to become one of the family —and succeeded famously.

Only Miss Newhall did not share the winter's gaiety. At Will's teasing her pale eyes swam with tears or flashed with an anger more than commensurate with the cause. The others tried to ignore these unpleasant incidents—though Adria felt Will really shouldn't taunt the woman before them all—but as the weeks went on, Miss Newhall grew increasingly snappish. Sometimes Adria caught Dave eyeing Thankful Newhall as if he suspected the hidden nature under the layer of propriety, but when Adria attempted to probe this attitude he merely laughed and rumpled her hair. "Don't worry your head about her," he said, "There's lots of Thankies in the world, but only one Adria." There was no talking things out with Dave.

Adria rejoiced that Dave fitted so readily into the household, more easily than she would have done in his home, for she had not been at ease with his large hearty mother, who could not have been less like Priscilla, her half-sister. Neil Malone, the father, was a silent man, though kindly-spoken the few times he addressed her. Dave's brothers and sisters were married and in their own homes nearby. Peter had screened eyes like Dave and Dave's deep silent laughter; Jonathan was engrossed in his wife and baby son; the girls were handsome, high-spirited replicas of their mother. Despite her efforts to join in the noisy fun of family gatherings, Adria had felt out of place, and been glad to start back for New Erin.

The winter proved moderate. Before March the last heavy ice was gone from the harbour and as it disappeared Dave's plans for departure took shape. New England firms customarily sent vessels in ballast, with bulkheads removed and holds lined with temporary berths, to transport crew members for the Bankers. This year Isles and Captain Stoddart had decided they might better have the fares, and had fitted the *Fearless* for a cargo of men and a quick run across the Bay. Before the sailing date ninety men from the shore villages had engaged passage. Her decks were crowded as the *Fearless* lay to off the lighthouse, and Dave was rowed aboard. Adria had kissed him good-bye on the wharf, where a chill wind stirred the slush ice among the spiles, but Dave was already gone from her, his mind pre-empted by the *Admiral* and a new season's contingencies. She went to the lighthouse to see the *Fearless* go down the bay and she stood straight and tall knowing that, if Dave looked back at all, he could not fail to recognize her dark cloak against the white tower. She watched the schooner climb the long fluid hills and drop down behind them, until its sails were lost behind Pilot Point. If the fair wind held the *Fearless* need spend only one night at sea; tomorrow evening should find her tied up in Gloucester. As Adria turned from the empty horizon she consoled herself with Dave's promise that within a fortnight he would be anchoring overnight in Redmond's Harbour, on his way to the Banks.

She woke through the night to a rising wind and the spiteful hiss of snow against her window. She turned to snuggle closer to Dave and came fully awake. Her husband was at sea in this wild northeaster, and she could only lie awake and pray as she flinched at each mounting squall. In the morning her window was heavily frosted and ridges of snow lay half-way up the panes. For three days winter clutched the island fiercely while surf ran high.

Two weeks of fair weather passed without sight of the *Admiral* or word of the *Fearless*. The coast was wrapped in dreadful waiting, for every village had men on the Prince's Cove schooner. A Captain Jorgenson, forced into Redmond's to repair a splintered boom, had a distressing lack of news. Three days before, when he had left Marblehead, the *Fearless* was still unreported and believed lost in the northeast gale which had swept everything before it. The *Admiral's* owners were seeking men to replace Captain Malone and his Nova Scotian crewmembers, for their vessel must sail. Dan gave his daughter this report as gently as he could. All that day no one met her eyes nor looked closely into her face. The family withdrew in spirit, leaving her alone to find herself, but holding their love and compassion within reach, should she need to grasp it.

As sundown neared she said only, "I'll tend the light tonight, Kiah," and put on her cloak. The clear air held the first tantalizing hints of spring, but the path was hard beneath her feet and, inside the lantern, the windows bore frost ferns, while her breath hung white above the lamps. Without consciousness of time she stood staring down on the darkening bay, wondering at her inability to grasp what the day's news might mean. Still feeling nothing but emptiness, she turned and descended the ladder-like stairs.

Halfway down the path she turned, out of habit, for a last inspection of the lamps. Behind the silhouetted tower, sunset had faded from the pale clear sky, but down the bay a waxing quarter moon trailed a silver veil across the restless water. Feeling returned; such a night was torture to a wife whose husband was somewhere on the ocean that stretched endlessly away. If—she let the fear take shape for the first time—if he were not in its depths. Darkness fell and the night wind stirred, and died, and stirred again as she walked the path, facing now the light's red beam and now the shadowy length of the house, until she felt herself weary enough to sleep, despite her tossing mind. Bedroom windows had lit up briefly and darkened; the household would be abed.

Adria turned through the gate and saw against the sky the "pulpit" of the kitchen ell. This outer railed platform had a stair leading up to it and a door opening into the kitchen chamber. The small platform had served the Redmond children as a look-out and Adria had often climbed the steps to discover sails unsuspected from the ground. How could she be sure now that Dave's vessel was not just over the horizon? As she climbed, the rows of moonlit shingles led her eyes to the junction of kitchen and "cooper-shop". Despite its name, barrel-making was only one of the activities carried on in the low-roofed, mud-floored addition. At its far end were the hearth and forge where Kiah did blacksmith work; on one side hung sides of leather and a cobbler's tray; across the shop, shavings perpetually curled under the bench where planes and spoke-shaves, frows and drawknives lay scattered. The cooper-shop had been a place of childish delights, but nowadays Adria entered it only when needing firewood from the pile next the kitchen door.

The "pulpit" was sheltered from the light breeze and only an occasional derisive gust slipped around the corner to whirl her skirts. In the cold moonlight the bay undulated and gleamed like white silk, diamond encrusted. Outer combers rolled free through the brightness and into the darkness beyond, but inner swells wheeled and poured into Clam Cove, their shoulders carrying moonbeams to spill among the black rocks and scroll the shore with silver.

As the night's pure splendour eased her heart, Adria yearned for Dave beside her. Then came a surprised, detached appraisal, clear and cold as the moonlight. *Dave would never lose himself with me in beauty like this. Since he left me I have been pretending a oneness that we lack—except through our bodies.* At that she was swept by memories and lonely hunger, reminding her that married love meant more than the sharing of beauty, more than minds attuned. Yet a quiet voice insisted that those things should be a part of marriage. Perhaps the fullness of all love's phases came only with the years, which blended them into a deep and all-embracing affection. The last of her detachment gave way. Suppose she and Dave were to be denied the years to make a full marriage? Suppose their life together was already ended?

The moonlit path across the bay no longer promised hope; she could not lose herself in the hypnotic breaking of waves, of water surging and receding again and ever again. The silver was slowly withdrawn from the water but the sinking moon took on colour until, as it hung impaled upon Pilot Point's black serrations, it was red as fire. It even gave the crisp air a smell of fire.

A smell of fire! Adria swung about and sniffed to catch again that pulse-quickening alarm, or to prove herself mistaken. She could smell nothing, see nothing amiss. No smoke rose from any of the house chimneys. Perhaps a breeze had stirred the ashes on the cooper-shop forge and sent an acrid whiff up the flue and across the low roof to frighten her. Had the cold blurred her eyes? The roof's far edge was wavering. Above the waverings a transparent white plume formed against the night sky. Smoke? Then at the small back-window a red line flickered. Or was it a last reflection from the setting moon? It flickered again and *behind* the dusty pane. Fire! In the cooper-shop amid the shavings, creeping to the dried wood piled against the kitchen wall.

TWELVE

ADRIA groped for the door behind her, stumbled through the close darkness of the upper chamber and boxed-in stairway. Smoke was seeping into the kitchen but she hoped the blaze was an incipient one and that she could extinguish it. When she opened the door to the cooper-shop, however, a billow of hot and acrid smoke drove her backward. Choking, she closed that door. Then she was across the room and banging at another. "Kiah! The cooper-shop's afire! *Fire!*" She heard a muffled response, then Kiah's feet hitting the floor and the stamp of a boot. "I'll rouse the others," she called to him and sped through the black rooms, guided by some instinct which avoided the heavy pieces of furniture and directed her hand to door-latches. She awakened her father on her way through the middle-room, then ran, panting, to the foot of the front stairs. One good shout (if she could gather enough wind) should waken Miss Newhall in her room across the lower hall, and rouse her brothers on the second floor. She took a deep breath and sent a call upward through the dark stairwell. "Fire! Charlie! Waits'l! Will! Fire!" Charlie's reply came faint but certain. He was awake. He would rouse Waitstill. "Will!" she screamed. This was no time for his indifferent lying abed.

A sleep-drugged answer came. Not from upstairs and the hall's length. From behind her. From the bedroom across the hall. From Thankful Newhall's room. A sick disgust for the woman, for Will lying beside her, and for their dark deceit momentarily submerged her errand. But only momentarily; the great need to avert disaster pushed all else aside. "The cooper-shop's on fire. Hurry, Will. Thankie, up with you! You can help pass buckets." Her tone was rude. She meant it to be. She turned and hurried away. She could not bear to face her brother and, in any case, it behooved them all to make haste.

Flames danced behind the greenish-black curtain of smoke belching from the cooper-shop's front door. Kiah, a slopping bucket in each hand, was running towards the flames. In the yard two lanterns dimly illuminated the area about the well-box. At the well an unfamiliar figure—Serena! Her thin body swayed with each push and pull of the windlass, and beneath a man's jacket, snatched (Adria knew) from the nearest peg, her long white nightgown flapped about incongruous sea-boots. "Here, let *me*," Adria said sternly.

"Gittin' too old for sech didos," Serena panted, stepping aside.

As Adria swung the full bucket up, her father, tucking his shirttails inside his trousers as he ran, seized it without losing stride. Then Charlie and big Waitstill were there. Thankful did not appear, but Adria and Serena passed buckets while the men fought the flames back and back to a smouldering pile of bark and wood beside the forge. In surprisingly few minutes the fire was out. Catastrophe had been averted, but its threat left them all shaken. Dan spoke with unwonted severity, "Will, when you tempered that axe this afternoon, you couldn't have extinguished your fire properly. I suppose that, as usual, your mind was not on your work. Luckily the sparks went where they did, and not into shavings. There was more smoke than fire apparently." He did not need to say, Your carelessness might have burnt the house down about our heads.

"We sh'd thank Adria. Certainly," Kiah said with gentle pride in his favourite. " 'Twas she discovered the smoke in time."

Adria remembered another evil she had discovered and kept her eyes from Will's sullen face.

Serena must have slipped away when the battle appeared won, because now, in dress and apron, she summoned them all for a cup of tea and a bite to eat. Indoors, they huddled close about the stove, for now that the heat of the struggle had deserted them, all were aware that the wind had a March edge. Adria found she could talk and laugh with the others, in a reaction from fear and urgency, as if somewhere she had gained confidence in Dave's return. Even Will appeared happy to share the safety of long-loved rooms still sheltering the family. Adria was perplexed as to what she must do. *After I've slept on it I'll decide. They can't go on. I must make Will see that he shames Mamma and all our home stands for.* Looking at her brother's still boyish face she felt accused. *I shouldn't have been put off by his surly manner. That was only to hide a guilty feeling. I should have found a way to help him.*

Mercy had not joined them in the kitchen and Damie must have had her "good" ear to the pillow, since no querulous demands for information came from her bedroom. Finally, when all were warmed and drowsy, Dan suggested they go back to bed. Will offered to watch lest another dormant spark cause trouble.

The eastern sky was greying as Adria, dragging herself sleepily towards bed, entered the middle-room. Her mother had lit a fire and she looked up now from her chair beside it. Before Adria could speak, Thankful Newhall entered purposefully through the hall door. She was nonplussed and angry to find Adria confronting her and peered questioningly at Mercy's face. Adria had pictured Thankful as primping before her mirror until every hair was plastered in place and every seam straight, while others struggled with smoke and cinders and dripping buckets. She saw instead that Thankful's hair was untidy, her eyes red and swollen. *I shouldn't be uncharitable about her appearance. Dear knows I'm no thing of beauty right now.* But she admitted that, no matter how unreasonable she might be, she could have forgiven more if Thankful had youth and beauty to match Will's.

For once Thankful was oblivious to her appearance and the impression she made, as she moved defiantly forward. "Mrs. Redmond, I have a matter to discuss with you." Mercy turned quickly at the rude tone.

"Surely it can wait. We all need rest now," Mercy replied.

"No, it can't wait. I mean to get my word in before milady starts her lies. If she hasn't already." Thankful's lips were the thinnest and bitterest of lines.

Mercy looked at the white-faced woman in amazement and then towards Adria, seeking an explanation. Adria drew a long breath. She was weary and she would have welcomed time for consideration, but Thankful's attack must be met. She told her mother, "I hadn't decided what to do about this. I hoped I could spare you worry and sorrow, perhaps by appealing to Will. But now you will have to know." As Thankful started to interrupt, Adria silenced her with a sharp gesture and continued, watching her mother who looked tired in the pallid lamplight.

"When I called Will tonight—to help put out the fire—he was not in his own room." *Oh, this is hard to say.* "He answered me from Thankie's room. He . . . He was asleep there."

The lines upon Mercy's face lengthened and deepened. "In Miss Newhall's room," she whispered, instinctive repudiation changing to reluctant acceptance before Adria's grieving eyes. Slowly Mercy turned to the sullen woman before her. "The boy's teacher. How could you do such a thing? Yes, *you.* Not Will, who is younger by many years."

Thankful lost none of her defiance. "I planned to talk to you alone, Mrs. Redmond," she said stubbornly.

Adria stepped squarely beside her mother's chair. "And *I* plan to stay right here, to spare Mamma anything I can. I have a right to hear what must concern everyone of the family."

The small eyes darted from face to face, the sharp tongue flickered over the dry lips. "Then hear this. I want Will's name for my child."

Mercy moaned softly and laid her head back upon the chair. Despite herself, Adria recoiled. She had not foreseen this. Triumph flushed Thankie's cheeks and fired her weak eyes. "I mean to be married at once," she went on, following up her advantage.

"And Will?" Mercy did not move her head from the chair back. "Is he eager for this marriage?"

Thankful glared.

Still Mercy did not look at her, but as she continued her voice grew stronger. "Will has no means to support you and must consult his father. You and I, Miss Newhall, cannot decide this matter."

"What is there to decide? If you don't see that Will does right by me, the Redmond name will stink worse than ever." Thankful's voice was growing shrill.

"It's a name too good for *you*," Adria said hotly. She turned a little sick to think that this woman's child would be a Redmond.

Mercy said, "Hush, dear," as if preoccupied, and Adria was surprised to see that the shock and pain in her mother's face had given way to a calculating look. With her eyes straight and probing upon Thankful, Mercy spoke calmly and with a new command of the situation. "I suppose you would not say what you have, without sure cause?"

Almost the insolence wilted, but, "Certainly I'm sure. And it's not surprising. Will has been mine for years. Ever since..."

"I want to hear nothing about that," Mercy's tone was icy enough to freeze the bluster. "Bring your things to my bedroom at once. You will sleep on the couch there, and Mr. Redmond can take the spare room. We shall decide about this disgrace you have brought upon yourself — and us — after a few weeks where I can watch you."

It was almost pitiful to see the boldness shrivel, to see cringing replace challenge but, as she understood how her mother had checkmated Thankful's move for an immediate marriage, Adria could summon no pity. Pity would have been no answer to the malevolence the other woman spat at her, "You are to blame for this, blab-mouth. I wish I could have foreseen what you would be when I had you in the schoolroom!" The shapely hands twisted and crooked themselves, then dropped, still tensed. "Holding yourself so much above me, because you got yourself a husband. I suppose you think Dave Malone was swept off his feet at sight of you and couldn't wait to be wed." She laughed. "He couldn't wait, true enough. You didn't know that while you were in Hines' Harbour a little man with a crooked arm came looking for Dave."

"A great many men know Dave," Adria kept her head high. "What did he want?"

"He wanted Dave's name for his daughter. She needed it as I need Will's."

"Mamma," Adria pleaded for denial, but Mercy remembered the little man's defeated look when he learned that Dave had married Adria Redmond.

She did not answer. She was staring at Thankful Newhall as if seeing her for the first time. She rose to her feet and Thankful fell back before her anger. "If I had any sympathy for you, you have killed it. Only the cruellest heart could tell this about a man who may never come back to defend his name. And tell it to his worried wife at such a time. You may worm yourself into this family but you are to remember, now and always, that I will not have evil gossip in my home. Another word, and I summon Kiah to set you ashore on the mainland."

Thankful dropped her eyes and turned towards the hall. Ignoring her, Mercy told her daughter gently, "Try to put the woman's spiteful tale from you. In any case, don't grieve about what may have happened before Dave met you. A woman is wise never to open the door on the past." She lowered herself wearily into her chair. "Please ask Will to come here. He must make a clean breast to Dan."

Adria returned to say she had heard Will and her father talking earnestly in the office and had not interrupted them. Mercy was thinking aloud. "This was at the bottom of the pretended loyalty after The Storm. I must have been blind. But how could I guess what might come of her staying?"

"Oh, Mamma! Don't blame yourself. How could *anyone* have guessed? I can't believe it now."

Sleep had been driven from Adria's mind and she moved towards the kitchen and breakfast preparations. Before the porridge was cooked Waitstill came with word that Will was gone in the dory and here was a letter for Mis' Redmond. Mercy read it and told the others merely that Will had decided to start for the West and a new life. Adria thought wryly that it was like Will to leave the family to cope with what he couldn't face. But she was glad he had escaped.

To everyone's relief, Thankful took his desertion calmly. Perhaps she had recognized that she could never hold him once her threat of disclosure had been nullified. Perhaps she knew she had lost her gambit and the game in the interview with his mother. She spent the day packing and informed Mercy she had decided to return to her foster-parents. "Away from this Popish wasp-nest."

Mercy said, "As you like. We can't force Will to marry you but we will give you a home and provide for his child."

"Child! You mock me. You knew there would be no child. Didn't you?"

"I felt you lied," Mercy admitted. "I hoped you did. That you might bear his child seemed harder than knowing you had ruined my son." She stopped Thankful's attempt at recriminations. "Mr. Redmond will pay the salary owing you and Kiah will take you and your belongings to Barrington. This much I can promise you: no word from New Erin will make it harder for you, if you decide to put your sin behind you and reshape your life."

THIRTEEN

By suppertime the impact of confusing events had faded, and the now familiar ache of anxiety had returned to Adria's heart. Sadly, she adjusted the table-setting to minimize the gaps of two empty places. She tried to dismiss the many versions of the local belief that, even as the greatest waves rolled in triads, so losses and disasters, came by threes. Had Dave, the latest comer to the household, been the first loss in this series? *But Thankful Newhall can't be counted a loss. Many's the time I've wished her off the island.* Then, although she felt heavy and stupid from want of sleep, she pretended serenity for her parents' sakes. Not until her father had entered the kitchen and she saw his smile, did she guess his message. "A Marblehead schooner, all decked out in new sails and rigging, is beating into harbour. The nameboard says *Admiral*."

Weeping and laughing she ran like a child to bury her face and cling to him, while he held her close. Happy tears soon dry and, with their traces still on her cheeks, Adria stooped beside Gramma Damie's chair to hug the round little figure, and gave Serena's hand a squeeze in passing. Weariness dropped from her; Miss Newhall was a figment of a nightmare now ended; she forgot that Will would not take his accustomed place at the table.

At last, at last Dave was in the doorway and she was in his arms, feeling the hard muscles jump under her hands as he lifted and kissed her hungrily, setting a sweet strong pulse pounding in her ears.

Not until supper chairs were pushed back did her father ask of the *Fearless*, "What happened?"

"Plenty," Dave replied easily, and he made it seem a light thing that the schooner had been storm-driven while ice built upon her until she wallowed, unmanageable as a small iceberg and in constant peril of sinking. It might have been a joke upon crew and passengers when the *Fearless* reached the fringe of the Gulf Stream—as they had prayed she might—only to have the ice drop from the hull and leave her monstrously topheavy in a running sea. The men, pounding ice for dear life's sake, knew that each lee roll might be the last; yet Dave had apparently gloried in the struggle and swung his axe with careless defiance of the reaching seas.

Adria knew that her very existence had been forgotten during those precarious hours and realized that she could have no place in the greater part of her husband's life. How can a man and woman grow to be one, she asked herself, if he lives among dangers she can scarcely conceive even on hearing them narrated?

Every listener was caught up in the account, but Waitstill's breath was as harshly audible as if he were pounding ice beside Dave. Charlie smiled at him. "Guess we'll stay ashore, eh, Waitstill?"

Waitstill surprised them all. "I d'know. Me, I guess I'd foller Capt'n Dave anywheres." Dave was gratified and gave Waitstill a close scrutiny before continuing.

Freed of ice, the *Fearless* found her rudder cranky and could not make way against the head wind. A new threat arose, for ninety-odd men need much food, and the schooner had been provisioned for a short run, but Dave could joke now over the reduced fare of hardtack and a swallow of water. Finally a Swedish four-master, sighting them, sent over a boatload of supplies and, with that turn in their ill-luck, the wind came fair. Five days later they tied up in port.

That's over and done with, Dave's manner said, as he turned the talk to his present voyage. He admitted, "After my delayed start I shouldn't have stopped here, but I had promised Adria and I feared she might fret." Fret, indeed.

Later, in their room, he belittled Adria's distress over Will's transgressions. "Why all the fuss, if Thankie's not in trouble after all? Sure I knew Will was sleeping with her. I ain't blind, for Lord's sake! But what does it matter to us?"

Adria said no more and she did not let herself remember the little man with the crooked arm. She had prayed that Dave come home safe, and here he was. Tomorrow he would be gone again, to hourly danger. Her trembling hands went up to smooth his cheeks, to draw his mouth down.

Before dawn the *Admiral* was away, leaving Adria aware that her life would henceforth be made up of empty waitings and tumultuous reunions. Yet, with the first of each behind her, she felt more capable of meeting those to follow. It turned out that for long periods she was carried along in the flow of day into day, week into week, and Dave became scarcely more real than the shipwrecked princes of her childish daydreams. July brought the sight of Bankers passing off shore on their way to American home ports, and suddenly she was aching to look again upon her husband and to feel his arms about her. Dave came ashore out of a night fog, proud that his vessel was deep-laden without the loss of a man. In the morning he was gone. He would stop again outward bound. By December he would be home for the winter.

Yet Dave had been ashore only a November week before he grew restless and Adria welcomed his suggestion that he might visit his people. With his boisterous family he could work off the excess energy and the high spirits that sometimes seemed too exuberant among older and more settled folks. He arrived back with what he obviously considered wonderful news. He had bought Crowell Smith's house in the Cove. "I've hired Obie and his son-in-law to paint inside and we can move in before Christmas."

Adria could not hide her dismay, nor her hurt that he had not consulted her in such a matter. She had already learned her vulnerability to his displeasure and her inability to move him once his mind was set, but this concerned more than them alone and she must take a stand. "You promised I shouldn't leave New Erin so long as I was needed."

His face tightened and his hazel eyes were dark and wide with amazement and resentment. "I got the house reasonable. And the Cove is a good little place to spend the winter — church and Lodge and gatherings. Isles and Aunt Cilla. Lots of neighbours. You can visit your folks all you like while I'm away, but a man wants his own home and his wife to himself — what few weeks he has ashore."

"I know." And Adria did know. "But I explained how it would have to be. And you understand and promised . . ." She wished she need not always betray her feelings under stress, but her voice would persist in failing her, her mouth would quiver, though she knew Dave had not meant this to wound her and he could not understand why she was not sharing his pleasure. She tried to explain that her own promises were never given lightly, and she had expected him to keep his.

Mercy broke into the strained silence which followed. "Perhaps you shouldn't have asked Dave for such a promise, for a wife's duty is to her husband first of all. Now that I am stronger you needn't feel bound by your word to us, nor by a sense of duty. The New Erin family is smaller; most of the time Serena and I can manage, and during the busy seasons we may find a hired girl."

Adria felt as if her mother had pulled a mat from beneath her feet and, just as she would seek physical balance in such a case, she now strove to make mental adjustments. "Crowell Smith's . . . ", she stammered, " . . . isn't that Alethea's house?" Strange that Dave, with his seaman's superstitions, should buy the house that had stood empty as if left, by communal consent, to the spirits of the ill-fated young skipper and his love.

"The roads would be lined with rotting, empty houses if nobody would live in the homes of drownded men," he told her matter-of-factly. Adria felt a heavy certainty that "Alethea's house" would repulse happiness, but she could not put such a fear into words; others than Dave would deride her notions. She must try to accept the fact that his word did not bind Dave; that in her case he had given it as a means of getting what he wanted—her surrender—and that even as he had been promising her he had known that he could, and would, force her to his way when it pleased him. He would not care how greatly this shook her faith in him. *He's not much like his cousin. I've never known Isles to break his word.*

FOURTEEN

PRINCE'S COVE soon grew accustomed to seeing the white of material curtains and the orange of earthly lamplight, instead of ghostly glimmerings, behind the windows of Alethea's house, and began to forget that the neat clapboard dwelling and been built for a young couple other that Captain David Malone and his Redmond wife. The house itself closed about the newcomers as if awaiting them. Dave bought furnishings generously, but some of Adria's old home came with her into the new, for at her parents' urgings she had chosen furniture and linens from the closed New Erin rooms. Accustomed to sprawling ells, Adria had judged Alethea's house small, but by village standards it was moderate size, having back entry and pantry, a kitchen with the usual family bedroom off it, a small dining-room and parlour. Stairs from the narrow front hall led to the unfinished chamber, which could make children's bedrooms.

The nearest neighbour was just across a narrow lane that branched from the main road, turned west along Dave's fence and lost itself in the thick spruce of the pasture-lots. Adria soon learned that the nearby yellow cottage belonged to Nathan Lumsden, Little Obie's cocky son-in-law. Tillie, whose cheeks had been too thin and too bright at the tea-meeting, had died before the following spring. Cynthie and Obie had closed up their own home and moved in with Bella and Nathan.

From the first Little Obie was a frequent and long-lingering visitor. He liked to settle his bulk in a favourite chair and talk, often about his Airy Bellah, "'most growed up now, and the purtiest thing in ten counties." When Adria hinted to her husband that she could spare Obie's company and conversation at times, Dave replied, "Did you ever listen to one of Cynthie's jawings? My heavens, Adria, let the man stay as long as he likes." Adria laughed and made Little Obie welcome. He was shipping as cook with Dave next spring, and Adria suspected that his open admiration was not unappreciated by his skipper.

While the young couple were settling in their new house, Cynthie made no friendly overtures, but furtive movements at her kitchen windows proved this was not from lack of interest. One afternoon, while Dave was out, a knock at the back door took Adria from unpacking a box of precious books. There could be no mistaking the Airy Bellah of her grandfather's boasts although in the year since Adria had seen her, the girl had attained a precocious young womanhood. She was not tall, having her father's thickset figure as well as his black hair and eyes, but under a red hood she was amazingly pretty in a bright bold way. She lacked no self-assurance as she presented a chipped cup and announced, "I'm Bella Lumsden. Grammy sent me t'borry a cup o' tater-yeast t'send some more agoin'." In the kitchen, the darting black eyes made Adria wonder if the girl had not been sent to satisfy curiosity as much as for yeast. However, Adria was pleased at the visit, since borrowing and lending would mark her acceptance as one of the Cove housewives, and she gladly filled the cup from the gurgling yeast-jug.

Bella's sharp eyes had found the box of books. "Am they novels?" she asked.

Adria mistook her tone for one of interest, or what would have been her own delight at seeing new books. "Some of them are," she answered. "Would you like to borrow them? Do you like to read?"

"Read?" (Whoever heard of doing anything so foolish, her blank tone conveyed.) "I guess I'd catch it, if I brought one o' them divil's works into Grammy's sight!" Her red mouth made an exaggerated O of shock and repudiation.

Adria could not decide between amusement and annoyance and as no other topic presented itself Bella prepared to leave. Adria wished to be friendly. "I hope the yeast proves lively enough. And do come again," she urged.

The two houses with the lane between had no other close neighbours, but Adria did not fear a lack of friends — not in the same village with Aunt Cilla and Isles. However, when she and Dave called, Isles usually excused himself to oversee work on the wharf's new ell or on the warehouse which, as Aunt Cilla proudly explained, were necessary to his expanding trade. Adria was pleased to hear that he and Captain Stoddart had bought a new schooner, the *Dauntless,* but more pleased that he had purchased a carriage mare, Sally, to take his mother driving. She did not consciously miss the old companionship with Isles; she understood that he had his business ventures and short voyages, as she had her home and husband; but she sometimes asked herself if she were the only person who saw how much Isles had changed. How quiet he had become. How wrapped up in his work.

Adria hurried to have her house in order before Christmas. She had hoped to spend the day on New Erin but the snowstorm which decked the village like a Christmas card had been preceded by severe cold; the cove was frozen across and upended icecakes lined the shores. On Christmas Eve she could not quite overcome her disappointment and her eyes were red when Dave came in during the afternoon with the happy word that Aunt Cilla and Isles had agreed to be their guests for supper and the evening.

If Adria had been in a reminiscent mood she might have recalled her fears that Alethea's house would repudiate happiness. If she had, she must have laughed at them, for joy was flooding every corner of it as, resplendent in wine-red silk (Dave's coming-home gift), she hugged Priscilla and gave her hands to Isles, before he went with Dave to stable Sally. Content was a glow about her when, after supper, she and Priscilla made final preparations for the expected visits of the "Sandy Claws."

Among the forefathers of the Cove's inhabitants were those Plymouth authorities who had denounced Christmas as a "Roman corruption" and had passed a law declaring it a crime to celebrate by "forbearing of labour, feasting, or in any other way." Nevertheless, a modified version of old English mummery had survived in the Colony and crossed from Cape Cod to Barrington. Before leaving New England it had become entangled with the Dutch homage to St. Nicholas, and by the time local pronunciations had exerted their influence, Prince's Cove youngsters (continuing the ancient rites) went Sandy Clawing. Adria knew of the custom from her mother, and she waited with delighted expectancy for the first knock.

Some callers would prefer the back, some the front door, so both kitchen and parlour were bright with lamp and candle light, and rich with the fragrance of apples and oranges brought from cold into warmth. The centre lamp on the parlour table shone softly on familiar New Erin furnishings and, on the mantle above the radiant stove, Waitstill's miniature *White Wings* spread her sails and seemed to move in the draughts of rising heat. In one corner a round table held modest presents to be exchanged in the morning. In the opposite corner stood a symmetrical fir from the back-pasture. Among its branches glittered delicately shaped and richly glowing sugar-barleys (horses and dogs, flowers and birds) and the big candy hearts which Dave had bought in Boston, and which bore printed sentiments, outlined by candy flowers in gorgeous colours and intricate designs. On long strings dangled red bags bulging with nuts and small candies, yellow apples and crimson ones, alike polished to a mirroring gloss. Across the branches ran strings of the fluffiest popcorn, mixed with the reddest of cranberries. It was a tree that would entrance any eye.

The kitchen table held bowls and plates piled high with treats for the Sandy Claws. Priscilla had added her store to Adria's cookies, doughnuts, fruit cakes and pound cakes, and plates of pulled taffy. Isles had provided candy sticks, pressed clusters of Christmas raisins, figs and dates and a barrel of apples. The new home would be certain to provide ample bounty, but Adria voiced qualms to Priscilla. "I hope my cakes and cookies will be as good as the Cove women's. You know I never cooked much at home; Serena wouldn't allow anyone messing around her bowls and board."

Priscilla laughed at her misgivings.

"And I don't want to seem different or 'stuck-up.' I don't have any trouble getting along with children—or old people. It's the ones in between who leave me tongue-tied!"

"Just be yourself, as you are with me and Isles. Once the Cove people know you . . ."

Adria said softly, "I want Dave to be proud of me. He sets great store, you know, on others' opinions. He thinks I should laugh and joke with everybody, like he does—be more like his sisters."

Surely he is not trying to change the girl who drew him by her difference from the ones he'd known! Priscilla was annoyed.

Adria glanced about her rooms and decided nothing more could be done to impress visitors. "Let's rest a bit before the Sandy Claws come, Aunt Cilla." She indicated a chair inside the parlour door. "I wonder what they are doing at home," she said wistfully as she sat down next her friend. She could not hide that the family were much in her mind on this first Christmas away from them.

"Missing you," Priscilla told her positively. "But feeling you close to them. For our loved ones are all close at Christmas. They are counting the days till you come see them again, but they are content that you are well provided for, and loved, in your new home."

Aunt Cilla could always find the rights words of comfort. The two sat silent in the festive room, hearing Isles' and Dave's deep tones from the kitchen but actually listening for other voices. Nevertheless, they started when the expected knock came. At which door had it been? It was promptly repeated and as the women hastened to the kitchen, Dave threw open the back door. He shrank back in apparent fright at what met his eyes. "Who-o-o-o, who are you?" he chattered in mock terror.

There were delighted chuckles and sniggers from the dark shadows by the doorsteps and a ragged chorus, "Sandy Claws!"

"What good wind wafts ye here?" As if they were a complete surprise.

This was momentarily baffling, then a reedy voice announced, "A Christmas breeze."

"Well, come in, come in," Dave said, "since it's Christmas brings you."

These Sandy Claws could not have seen more than ten Christmases, for their lack of height and breadth belied the wool whiskers and fierce tarred-rope moustaches of the three boys, and refuted the sweeping skirts, the high-perched hats (over stranded-rope coiffures) of the four girls. In the same way a white ring about the necks denied the boys' sooted faces and the girls' black stocking-leg masks. All held empty wooden buckets in awkward hands. The girls tended to huddle together and giggle, since this was the evening's first call. One of the boys, with do-or-die determination, pulled out a mouth-organ; another licked his lips and, giving a preparatory hitch to overlarge pants, launched stiff-legged and sweating into a sailor's hornpipe, hampered no more by borrowed garments and seaboots than by a missing sense of beat. Heavy boots and tune went their separate ways until breath gave out. The mouth-organ, after being knocked out with satisfaction and wiped upon a sleeve, joined the girls' sweet high voices in a children's favourite which Adria herself had sung,

> "Chick-a-dee-dee, chick-a-dee-dee
> And merrily singing his chick-a-dee-dee."

The big seaboots thumped an accompaniment, off beat but vigourously.

When this was finished Dave solemnly complimented all the performers, then turned to the smallest boy, who had taken no part. "What are you going to do, to get your bucket filled?"

"Nawthin'."

"Can't you sing?"

"Naw."

One of the girls, in the patient voice of an older sister, explained, "I've tried t'larn him. But he can't carry a tune and he can't remember words."

Dave's shoulders were shaking with silent laughter and, behind their lashes, his eyes were dancing. "Wouldn't you like to learn a song for the next house?"

This was a departure from the accepted routine. The pale eyes were doubtful and Adria noticed that the black faces turned in one accord towards their known friend, Mistah Isles. His kindness was unfailing; his good-nature less overwhelming than Cap'n Malone's, whose teasing laugh puzzled them. Isles nodded, smiling directly into the questioning eyes. Reassured, the black faces turned in unison back to Dave who informed the smallest Claws, "I'll learn you one. It's called, The Lost Sheep on the Mountain, and it's sad but purty."

"It's gotta be short. And it's gotta be easy," Big Sister warned.

"It is," Dave assured her. To the little boy, "Don't forget the name, now—The Lost Sheep on the Mountain." Every ear was plainly alert. "It goes like this." In his powerful sea voice Dave bleated nasally, "Baa-a-a-ah!"

Even the grown-ups jumped. One little girl shrieked and dropped her bucket from a nerveless hand. But the unexpected blat was so much like a wandering old ewe's that, after the first start, the girls collapsed, hysterical, into one another's arms, while the boys hooted and pounded their comrades' back. It was hard to say which was being more entertained, the laughing adults or the enchanted youngsters.

The success of this first call was spurring the Sandy Claws on to others. Dave signalled Adria that this was the time to pass around the "treats" while he and Isles attended to the waiting pails. "Easy does it, Dave," Isles finally laughed. "There's another gang at the front door now and this goes on for hours." The grateful Sandy Claws slipped out into the back entry where, judging from the excited whispers and squeals, they paused to count their "haul" by touch.

In the kitchen, striving to still her laughter and straighten her face, Adria's gaze met Isles' in the spontaneously shared enjoyment that had marked former days. "Hurry, Isles, and let the others in," she said, forgetting all that separated them from that earlier sharing, and her hands were like a caress along his sleeve as she urged him towards the front door. "Weren't those youngsters cunning? I wish I were twelve again; I'd go Sandy Clawing tonight." She greeted the newcomers gaily, her cheeks flushed, her grey eyes luminous under their dark arched brows.

Isles, catching her profile against the lamplight, felt the old pain stab his breast. There she was, poignantly beautiful—the girl he had loved through the years—and warmly happy as his cousin's wife. He wrenched his eyes away. There was Dave, with his white brow gleaming under black hair, with rich colour in his weather-darkened cheeks and red lips smiling. Sometimes Isles wondered just what lay behind the veiled eyes, yet when Dave opened them wide and met his they were frank and friendly. Certainly, they should have nothing to hide for Dave had settled down into an exemplary husband. Isles himself was the one who should veil his eyes and his love for another man's wife. He should not have accepted Dave's invitation, despite his mother's urgings. *On Christmas Eve, of all nights, I should have kept my selfishness at home.* Apparently no one else noticed the falseness of his laugh, the tightness of his jaw. As the evening wore on and somewhat older and more experienced Sandy Claws appeared there was no flaw in his genial manner or in his apparent enjoyment.

Some of the later groups made it known that their "spoils" would go to widows with children too small to be out, or to lonely old people. Then more substantial gifts were in order— flour, sugar, tea and oatmeal—as well as the special treats. These groups well repaid the bounty they received. A quartet rendered, beautifully, new songs heard in New York or Boston. Others sang old favourites and, though none of these were carols or seasonal songs, imparted to them much of the Christmas joy and spirituality. A ridiculously costumed group, with a rare gift for farce, acted their song, "Strike up the Band, Here Comes a Sailor," while Isles and Dave rolled helplessly upon the couch and Adria wiped away mirthful tears.

The pauses between straggling groups lengthened and when a belated couple informed their host, "We're the last on the road," Isles thought that one more Sandy Claws would have been too many.

He went to the door with Dave and Adria to call goodnights after the departing pair. The three stood for a moment in the night's crispness, catching across the snowy fields another "Merry Christmas" shouted from some other open doorway which, like theirs, would be laying an orange band across a white yard. The snow had added the last desired holiday touch, softening roofs and fence-posts, capping the tide-line rocks. The softwoods along the fence drooped their whitened branches, and under its shell of ice and snow the roadside brook was tinkling like a music-box. Adria said softly, "This is perfect beauty," and stood lost in it with her shoulder against Isles' arm and all her loveliness finding its way to his sore heart.

Dave seized one of her hands to pull her inside. Laughing, she slid the other hand into Isles' warm palm and between the two men walked to stand for a moment before the shining tree. She yawned helplessly and apologized, "I'm sleepy from laughing! I never dreamt Sandy Claws could be so much fun. Dave, they loved your nonsense. So did I!" She rubbed her cheek softly against his sleeve in an affectionate gesture, and Dave bent to kiss the nape of her neck, where the little curls lay close.

Isles dropped her hand swiftly and he sounded weary as he said, "Come, Mother, we must be leaving. Get your cloak on while I bring the sleigh around to the front door."

This was not the first time Adria had noted a puzzling harsh edge to Isles' deep voice. Tonight she caught the resemblance to the smothered protest and pain from a pebbled undertow. But what struggle under the surface gave that roughness to Isles' tone? It was gone as he called, "Goodnight and Merry Christmas," above the sleighbells.

FIFTEEN

ON NEW YEAR'S DAY winter initiated a long and continuous demonstration of what it could do with a plentitude of snow. Although a path could scarcely be cleared to schoolhouse or church before a new storm filled it, nothing disrupted the nightly masculine discussions about the shop stove, and Dave ploughed through the deepest drifts with a careless employment of his long limbs and superb physical energy. Adria was content to sit at home, sewing or reading while the stove glowed and the snow rustled against the windows, but she had a sense of unreality, cut off as she was from both island and village life.

It pleased her that Dave was quickly accepted by the Cove. He had had the respect due a Marblehead captain, now he was winning friendliness and liking. His easy smile and teasing eyes charmed matrons and spinsters alike—but in the most innocent way—while he ignored the pretty and fluttering young things. No one could accuse the present Dave Malone of having an eye for the women.

Unfortunately the winter's severity prevented the usual feminine gatherings so that Adria met her neighbours only after Sunday service, and then briefly. Dave's friendship must spread itself out, like the tide over the flats, wide and sparkling; Adria's affections ran in a narrower deeper channel. She did not need many companions, but she welcomed Deborah Goodwin's friendship. Deborah and her father lived on Meeting-house Hill and Adria waved from her window as Deborah floundered doggedly through the drifts, to and from Isles' shop. It was a happy occasion when the bundled figure first turned off the road and made its way to Adria's back door. Immediately it was as if the two young women had known each other always. Deborah rejoiced in the books Bella had scorned and shared her few worn volumes with Adria; they exchanged patchwork and crochet patterns, secrets and Cove news. The sole flaw in this new comradeship was that Deborah and Dave did not prove congenial, and the soft brown eyes showed no response to Captain Malone's pleasantries, teasing, or cold disregard.

The stormy winter had promised to be long, but incredibly soon Dave was growing restless and Adria had begun to count the dwindling days before he must leave for Mablehead. Overnight, it seemed, the village emptied of men. This year New Erin felt the seasonal drain, for Waitstill joined Dave's crew. The Redmonds were loath to see him leave but they accepted his decision. Kiah made his sea chest, which Waitstill embellished with carved scrolls and curlicues; Mercy gave his garments final care and stitches, while Dan contributed new sea clothes from his stock. Waitstill was like a child preparing for a first party, yet when the time came for him to leave the only real home he had known, his courage nearly failed him. "I'll be back by-and-by, so the's no cause fer me t' blubber," he told them in a choked voice as he stumbled out of the kitchen.

In Prince's Cove, the little house and the double bed were terribly empty for a few days and nights, and then they might never have known Dave. They remembered him when the outward bound *Admiral* put in overnight, but then Adria stripped the bed and closed the house and left in the *Katie*, with Charlie whistling at the tiller.

The spring and summer on New Erin made a dreamlike interlude broken by Dave's two overnight visits, like sudden awakenings followed by sleep's erasures. Mid-October brought an ephemeral snow which ostensibly announced Dave's imminent return, though he could not be expected for another month. Adria suddenly felt the little house yearning for her and was impelled to return to the Cove. Yet when Charlie landed her at Ryders' wharf, the sun was brilliant, and the village had its manless summer look. From the road, the house was again Alethea's, yet once inside, Adria knew with surety it was time she came home to it.

She brewed Charlie a cup of tea before he left. "I hate to go back without you," he told her. "New Erin is not the same when you're away." His young face was long and sober.

Again she felt resentment at Dave's callously broken promise. "I'm truly sorry. This isn't what I planned, or wanted." She drew his head down and gave him an unaccustomed kiss, striving to put into it her affection, her remorse at her dereliction and her admiration for his assumption of duties and his steadfastness in carrying them. He understood. He rubbed her cheek with his, took his hands from her shoulders and left quickly.

Before morning a fall storm was driving across the cove, tossing the anchored boats and pushing the tide high among the dying marsh reeds. Adria knew again the anxiety that each storm now brought as surely as rain rode the east wind and slashed at her windows. She prayed for Dave, for Waitstill, for all husbands and sons and fathers at sea. During the night the wind dropped and dawn brought clearing skies; the succeeding days of glorious weather drove worry before them as the crisp winds drove the clouds.

A week had passed and Adria, as she sat sewing in the afternoon sunlight, was thinking she had been silly to leave New Erin on a whim. A knock at the back door was completely unexpected. "Isles!" She had no thoughts but how good it was to see him. "Come in, do."

He thanked her gravely. "But you mustn't ask me in." To her indignant gaze he explained, "You mustn't ask any man in while Dave's away." He shrugged a shoulder towards the house across the lane, but his eyes held hers; he meant the advice.

"Why shouldn't I ask you in? Dave's cousin and my friend for years?" She saw the movement of Cynthia's curtains. "Isles, do you get the feeling that some people watch only for mistakes and failings?"

"Perhaps," he admitted, but swiftly dismissed the subject. "I couldn't stay now, even if the Cove approved."

He went on gravely, "I came with good news for you." And repeated, "*Good* news for *you*. Dave is safe. So are all the crew of the *Admiral*—Waitstill and Obie and the others who sailed under Dave. And with them all but one of the *Sapphire's* crew." He paused to let her absorb this, while his long fingers tightened upon the cap in his hand. "But there is terrible news for many Cove families. We got only the dying tail of Friday's storm. It hit the Banks in its full fury."

Adria put out a hand to grasp the door-frame. Isles repeated, "Dave is safe. He'll be home before morning. The *Admiral* made Barrington Bay at noon and Dave sent a messenger to me at once. He believes the *Colfax* and the *Raven* from the Cove, the *Melissa* from Cape White, his brother's *Hunter* and God alone knows how many other American vessels are lost. Bad news travels fast and none too straight, so I came to tell you what I knew while Vol harnesses Sally. Then I'll help Mr. Stouten take word to the bereft families."

Isles is brave. Though I'd never thought of sympathy and true kindness as taking courage, I can see that they will this afternoon.

"I thank God that Dave has been spared." Isles laid his hand upon hers as he turned away. "Your fingers are like ice; go inside and get warm." *She would despise me if she knew how my heart behaved at the first mistaken belief that Dave was lost.*

Adria saw that he was moving across the yard towards the yellow house. "Didn't you say that Obie . . .?"

He turned his head. "Nathan shipped on the *Colfax*."

She went down the steps towards him. "But Isles! Can't I help? A woman — to comfort Bella?"

"Of course. She'll need your kindness. I was thinking only of sparing you."

The *Admiral* anchored in the cove by the light of the waning moon, noiselessly; the Cove members of her crew rowed heavily ashore and made their way silently (as if ashamed because they had been spared while so many had been taken) across the fields and along the paths of the black-windowed, mourning village.

The instant Adria saw him at the door, all she had ever felt for her handsome young husband, intensified a hundredfold, swept over her and she ran to his arms in an agony of love and thankfulness. When she looked into his face she saw the harsh lines and the shadows of fatigue and grief. His shoulders drooped and even their breadth seemed diminished under their load. She brought clean clothes to replace his torn and salt-encrusted ones. She set favourite food before her silent husband, who ate little. His eyes were wide and defenceless, empty of the almost frightening hunger for her that had marked other homecomings. The husbands and fathers and sons who had not come home, the widows and orphans and bereft parents who were enduring this night, were between him and his wife.

Not until they were in bed and the lamp blown out, did he turn to her, and then his need was for someone to listen, there in the covering darkness. As if he were her child and not her husband, she drew his head upon her arm and stroked his hair and his cheek, while he talked.

The weather on the Banks had been holding fine and fish were plentiful; Friday night Dave left the deck confident of an early full fare. Almost at once he dreamt. (No need to explain to Adria a seaman's faith in a warning "vision in the night"). A band of white horses came trampling and plunging down upon him, and the foam from their curled lips was hot and wet upon his face and hands as, transfixed and helpless, he awaited their death-dealing hooves. He came awake, sweating and shaking from the shattering beat of his heart. He went at once on deck, but the planks were motionless beneath his feet; the glimmering sea was flat and about him the fleets' riding-lights twinkled steady as the stars. Two vessels away to starboard lay the *Hunter*, Peter Malone master, and aboard was Jonathan, shipped as seaman with his brother while his own schooner lay on the repair slip. The *Admiral's* look-out leaned motionless upon the starboard bow; Dave did not speak to him but went below and turned in. Again the white horses thundered down to override him. "But this time you were there beside me, and I saw that you carried a white bridle. You thrust it into my hand and vanished while the noise of the hooves died away, the foam flecks dried and disappeared. I dreamt it all once more and then I slept."

The sea at dawn lay like satin and the air was mild as summer's but Dave's dream stayed with him. At noon the riding-sail caught his eye. "It was plenty good to last out the trip, but the thought struck me, Could Adria's white bridle be the new suit of storm-sails we had in the locker? The white horses, anyone would know, meant breaking seas. Something made me call Obie, who had his line over the side and was pulling in fish.[1] Though he muttered and looked like a thunder cloud, we broke out the new sails."

Then unreasoning fear took charge. Dave sounded the horn to call in the dories and when the men came up over the side they were grumbling and slatting gear. "I made them nest and lash their dories and hoist the new sails. 'We're heading for deep water' I told them, and they looked as if I had taken leave of my senses, and I couldn't blame them. Sails limp as dish-rags and

[1] With the dories away, the captain and cook stayed aboard and fished from the schooner's deck.

we preparing to leave good fishing when another day or two would fill the holds. I pretended 'twas the look of the sky, but there was nothing wrong with it, far as I could *see*. Then old Jared Osborne spoke up. 'Stow yer slack lip, ye fools,' he said, 'and thank the Lord for a smart skipper. Can't ye *smell* it acomin'? Or am yer noses all red-leaded putty like they 'pear t'be?' That made me feel better, and on the heels of his words a puff of sulky air riffled the water and shivered the loose sails."

Taking advantage of every air of wind, Dave started to work clear of the anchored fleet. He ran close by the *Hunter* and hailed Peter. "Strange," he said, staring into the night above them while Adria, hearing the pain in his voice, drew him yet closer. "Strange that Jonathan should have shipped with Peter on that voyage. The first time, for Maw was always dead set against more than one of the family on a vessel. I didn't see Jonathan, of course, he was out in his dory, but Peter came to the rail. I swung to him, beckoning him to follow me into deep water and I pointed to the west where, sure enough, a smur was making. His laugh came to me across the water as if we were standing on the same deck, and he mocked me."

When the first squall came sweeping over the vessels, Dave looked back to see dories hurrying for their schooners and sail making on some spars. Well ahead of the others, the *Admiral* sped for deep water and there fought for her life. "Your sails was all that brought us through."

Mine? But Adria said no word. She listened—Dave must have known how closely by the thumping of her heart beneath his head.

"We rode out the worst storm I ever hope to endure. I doubt any man lives through two such."

Next day the gale had passed and when he had regained control of his vessel, Dave put her about and went back to search for the *Hunter*. "That's how I sighted the *Sapphire*, awash and down by the bow. I thought at first we'd have to watch helpless as the seas took her, but somehow we got the crew off and aboard the *Admiral*." He lay silent for some minutes. "I cruised about another day, but I knew that the *Hunter* was gone. The *Sapphire* had passed her, dismasted and drifting to leeward. The captain told me he could make out two big men aft, as if they fought the wheel." Again he fell silent, defeated.

Peter and Jonathan would be the two biggest men aboard.

Adria suggested without much true hope, "Mightn't they still be afloat? Mightn't another schooner have rescued the *Hunter's* crew, as you did the *Sapphire's*?"

"The *Sapphire* barely cleared Sable Island—that cursèd deathtrap!" Like an obituary were the next words, "When last sighted, the *Hunter* was between her and the bar." Dave's tone was more heart-scalding than any tears could be and all of Adria's sympathy went to him in a pulsing flood.

Then, grief having been somewhat assuaged by its sharing, his body stirred. But after he fell asleep Dave moaned piteously at intervals, until Adria drew his head again upon her breast. *This is true marriage—tenderness and dependence upon each other.*

Despite the weight upon arm and breast, she slept.

SIXTEEN

A WEEK later the repaired *Admiral* left, but hope had died that other vessels might limp home. On Dave's return he visited his parents briefly and came home depressed. "Let's close the house and spend this winter on New Erin," he suggested and Adria was pleased that Dave, too, considered the island a refuge.

Once on New Erin, however, Adria felt the new communion with Dave slipping from her, despite her efforts to cherish it. But before long there was a different bond between them. The morning she woke to sure knowledge, Adria was both exalted and stilled, as at a holy revelation. Dave's joy would match her own, but just for a time she would treasure the wonder alone. The night came soon when she crept into Dave's arms. She had to whisper her news twice before he grasped it. Abruptly he held her off to search her face in the bedlamp's dim light. "The devil you say!" It might not have been displeasure in his voice, perhaps not even dismay; it was not awe or rejoicing. His next words hid whatever it might have been. "I'm sorry. I never meant..."

Adria was dazed. *Sorry? Sorry for this great gift. Where is the unity I believed we had reached?*

"Don't blame me too much," he said half-coaxingly, half-resentfully.

How try to explain? She wept a little and he comforted her, lovingly and patiently enough, but quite obviously with the idea that this was one of the unreasonable manifestations of her condition. As her tears dried Adria remembered that she had smiled fondly at Dave's early declarations that he didn't want her dragged down by babies on her skirts and in her arms, didn't want her beauty spoiled. *But that was before I knew.* Perhaps a man couldn't understand the glory and humility of an annunciation.

In the morning it was Dave who was happy and excited at the prospect of a child. "So long as you aren't put out at me," he told her, "I can afford a family. As skipper my lays from the *Admiral* are good ones." They agreed that since this child was part of October's homecoming and the ensuing fullness of love, that he should be named Jonathan Peter in memory of the lost brothers.

There would have been no possibility of keeping such a secret from three women and, indeed, Adria shared it proudly, welcoming the understanding of her grandmother and mother who had relayed life to her, as she would now pass it on. Their sympathy eased the mornings when nausea overcame her, for Dave ignored all the discomforts of pregnancy as if they were feminine foibles unworthy of a man's concern. Adria was glad he would be away before her figure thickened greatly, that he would not see her during those awkward months when her beauty would be spoiled, as he feared. Yet, once he was gone, Adria began to dream of a boy with his father's black head and tangled lashes about hazel eyes.

His fair-haired daughter (Mary for Dave's mother, Ellen for Mercy Ellen) was born in the room where Adria herself had entered the world, and Serena's hands first held her, just as they had first held her mother.

Cynthie Obie and Bella came to relieve Serena in the kitchen. Cynthie's eyes stayed cold and hard behind their glasses and, since she chased a speck of dirt as relentlessly in Mercy's home as in her own, she led the New Erin men a desperate dance. What interest was left from the battle for cleanliness went to pretty, lazy Bella, who rolled her black eyes and swung her hips at Charlie, in vain.

Cynthie was much sought as midwife, but Adria was content with Serena's familiar and crotchety ways. One morning, glancing up from Mary Ellen's fuzzy head cradled upon her arm, Adria was astounded to see Serena's iron-grey eyes blurred and her thin mouth working. "I had a little girl like that onct," she said in shame-faced explanation. Serena with a baby at her breast!

"She only lived a few days."

Adria made a sound of sympathy and her arm tensed under the tiny body upon it.

"I s'pose I didn't have strength nor heart t'give it," Serena mused. "Frettin' myself t'death about the good-fer-nawthin' father." She seized the basin and towel and hustled them from the room, as if they had been blabbing what was best kept quiet.

Adria tried to remember what she had heard of the rascal who, already wed, had pretended to marry the young Serena, and was filled with pity for the woman who had lost both husband and child. Life must have been empty indeed. But when she voiced this thought Serena surprised her by saying, "I've been blest. Every Redmond young'un was like my own. Though I never wanted t'let on."

Dave proved properly enchanted with his daughter whose eyes soon turned to hazel under tangled lashes that lay soft upon her cheeks as she slept. Yet after the little family had moved to the Cove, Adria learned that Dave wanted no part of the baby when she was fretful, and resented the demands that left less of Adria's attention for him.

More disturbingly, he began to send out dart-like remarks that hit Redmond foibles and failings with uncanny marksmanship. Adria bit her tongue lest she reply in kind, shamed by his betrayal of petty jealousy. And jealousy appeared the only explanation for his persuading Waitstill to spend the winter in his mother's shanty on Grannie's Head, and not among his New Erin friends. Homesick Waitstill often wandered into Adria's kitchen and sat awkwardly content, smiling open-mouthed admiration of Cap'n Dave.

That spring after Dave was gone, the house did not cast off his presence. When Mary Ellen drew down her mouth to cry or opened her eyes wide, there was Dave again. A flood of memories would crest with his recalled kiss and leave Adria hungry for him. Only the mental abrasions were gone, and she could set about repudiating small doubts and rebuilding her love for his return.

By the following winter two years had passed since the October disaster and the Cove appeared more normal. The patient women of the shore villages, with screens close behind their eyes, made outward pretence that life was the same. In two years younger sons had grown enough to fill, as it were, the berths of their drowned brothers and they must have their sociable winter ashore. Tea-meetings were courageously planned, and endured, in halls which gave back echoes from sea-stopped voices. Young Sandy Claws made their rounds to hearty welcomes—children must have Christmas. Older groups came to the fortunate homes with larger receptacles, expecting and receiving extra bounty, because of the many fatherless families dependent upon their neighbours for even a meagre Christmas. Adria baked for weeks ahead and piled the buckets high with an eager hand and grateful heart; was not her husband beside her, her child safe in its cot?

The winter flew by; on the first of March the *Fearless* was rubbing against Ryder's wharf, ready to set sail on the afternoon ebb. Isles was checking details with the captain when a stranger approached him. "Mr. Wilson of Barrington asked me to give you this telegram as I drove through. He said you would deliver it."

As the man hurried back to his rig at the wharf-head, Isles glanced at the entrusted message. "It's for Dave," he told Captain Stoddart, "I'll take this to him, and be back before you sail."

He would not otherwise have intruded upon Dave's last hour before sailing, but a telegram in itself bespoke urgency. He admitted that he welcomed an excuse to call, since once Dave was gone, visits to his home must cease. *But I'm not altogether a hypocrite. Dave has proved a good companion and I count myself his friend. If there's both bliss and misery in being near Adria, they harm no one but me.*

Dave was not alone with his family, Isles saw as his cousin took the telegram and urged him into the kitchen. Waitstill's huge frame crowded the square armchair beside the door. His brown eyes still went to Adria, but his black thatch of curls was bent towards Mary Ellen who, astride one immense seabooted foot, was riding a cockhorse to Banbury Cross, with ringlets lifting and hands tightly clutching Waitstill's huge thumbs. The big man's smile vanished as Isles appeared and, once more, Isles wondered at Waitstill's continuing dislike. After all, it was the admired Dave who had won Adria from them both.

Dave read his telegram. "I'm to meet the owners in Boston instead of Marblehead. A brand new schooner, *Ocean Spray*, is waiting for me there. He had been mentally engrossed with the coming season's dangers and rewards; now with knowledge of a new vessel to command, his love for his wife and child seemed a puny thing beside his passion for the sea.

Adria spoke in a rush of proud congratulation, though he appeared scarcely to hear her. The light from the window flashed on her knitting needles as they swiftly rounded the toe of a black sock. She explained, as if to cover her husband's indifference, "These are for shore wear. Mary Ellen was croupy and a care last week, or I shouldn't be so late finishing them." Isles thought she preferred busy hands as parting neared. Watching her fingers, he saw her reach upward and knew that a gleaming hair was being knit along with the black yarn, for since the first cruise from the Cove, its women had been knitting such strands into their men's socks.

Waitstill asked, "What fer do ye do that? With yer hair, Adree?"

"It will bring the sock's wearer back to me," she explained with bent head. Dave continued to pack and when Adria said, "There it's done!" she sounded wistful.

Waitstill squirmed. Mary Ellen, tired of her lagging steed, slipped off his foot and crept to Isles' lap. "They'm right good-lookin' socks," the big man offered then. "I wisht Maw'd make some like 'em. But she claims 'tis a poor foot can't shape its own heel."

Adria laughed and Isles glanced with new respect at Waitstill. His words hadn't been by chance, he was deliberately trying to take Adria's mind off all that might prove stronger than a knitted hair.

"Dave," she was saying, "those socks that are too large for you. I believe they'll fit Waitstill." She went into the bedroom and returned with a pair of heavy grey socks—well-shaped as to heel—and laid them across Waitstill's wide lap. "There's a hair of mine in the toe of each, and they'll bring you back safe," she told him affectionately. Waitstill disclaimed any casting of hints, but stuffed the socks happily into a capacious pocket.

"Here are yours, dear." Adria put the fine black pair on the open sea-chest. Dave's response was indistinct and as he averted his head from his wife the marring streak of selfishness showed fleetingly across his vital face. Isles glimpsed the sulky mouth and the white indentations along the nostrils. *Why the man begrudges the gift to Waitstill! Yet if he felt the urge he'd give his coat to any tramp that came along. Is it because he wants to be considered the generous one? Surely he can't resent Adria's kindness to the man who was part of New Erin.*

When Adria had set out tempting dishes for the "mug-up," Dave insisted his cousin have a cup of tea. Now he was the merry host, talkative and hospitable, affectionate towards his wife, condescending to the flattered Waitstill. But once Waitstill had pushed back his chair, Isles rose. "Time for you and me to hoist sails and leave Captain Malone and his wife to say their farewells."

Waitstill stooped and picked up the packed chest as if it were no heavier than Adria's tea-caddy. "I jest dropped in t'help the cap'n aboard with his gear," he told Adria and went swiftly through the doorway. All knew this apparent lack of courtesy was no such thing; it brings ill-luck for a seaman to bid, or be bidden, good-bye.

SEVENTEEN

JUNE flowed down the folded hills, danced the length of Sydney Harbour and wandered, in lost little airs and flower scents, among the grey buildings of Sydney town. A handsome carriage, outstanding among the many equipages enticed from coachhouses by the afternoon sunlight, rolled smoothly along a street whose shops became chandlers' establishments as it slipped down to the waterfront. Three men, desultorily talking on a corner, turned their heads as the carriage neared, flashing its paint and varnish. The horse was a splendid bay and its pace a song, but the men's eyes slid over it to the woman holding the reins. She drove with an insolent air, indifferent to the fact that no gentlemen bowed to her and no ladies nodded, though bowing and nodding went on all about her. Under a provocative bonnet, auburn curls fell to her shoulders, and her face glowed, white as skimmed milk, against the richness of her hair and the ripeness of her mouth. No one would mistake her for a lady, but few would deny her beauty. In her carriage behind her glistening horse, she was superb and knew it.

When nearly opposite the three watchers, a loose cobblestone caused her horse to break the perfection of his step and then to stumble. The youngest and tallest of the men moved forward a swift, perhaps involuntary, pace. The woman's strong hand and full voice at once steadied her nervous animal and the carriage rolled smoothly on. But the driver's dark eyes had locked with bold hazel ones in a seaman's face; the toss of her head betrayed awareness that she had impressed the man just passed, as she impressed most men.

David Malone gazed after her with racing pulses. "Why didn't you tell me you had women like that in Sydney, Mr.

MacKay?" he demanded of the dry-faced, thin-lipped little man beside him, and a hot light flickered behind his eyes.

"We have only the one like that," the other returned soberly, "even in Sydney."

"One will do me. Where does she hang out? How does a man get to know her?"

"If there's any sense in him, he doesn't be trying," was the sour admonition.

"I'll know her before I sail," Dave boasted stubbornly, confident that the woman had been as aware of him as he of her.

"Remember, Cap'n . . ." the rotund man on his other hand began.

"Keep your oar out of this, Obie." The tone was incisive.

"It's a long time ye'll be making Marblehead, then," MacKay said dryly. "For that's Flossie Todd and, though many a man has been taken by some such idea as yours, she's been Big Tom Angus McLean's piece for two years now. He's jealous as a bridegroom. And Flossie knows which side her bread is buttered on. She never looks at another man, they tell me, particularly when Big Tom Angus is in town." He laughed at the other's interruption. "And could ye be giving her a turnout like that ye just saw? And that dress and bonnet, brought over special from France, the women do tell." He spat upon the worn sidewalk. "Big Tom Angus . . ."

"That old tub of blubber!" The slim young captain laid his hand across his own waist, flat and hard as a plank. "Didn't you mark the come-on look she gave me?" Flossie Todd might have blushed at the boasts which followed; Dave's companions did not. "I'm not sailing before, Mr. MacKay. And that don't mean you can take your time on that bowsprit." He strode away in the direction the carriage had taken, male arrogance in every footfall and every swing of his arms.

The crew of the *Ocean Spray* knew that a shattered bowsprit alone had brought them into Sydney. Now, with its successor pointing the way home, they must lie in the dock awaiting their captain's whim. Little Obie had provided the explanation for the delay, and after the first ribald comments, older steadier men were strongly disapproving. Other vessels would have reported the *Ocean Spray* slightly damaged, and at home worry would grow. The crew lolled restlessly about the wharf or vessel's deck, whittling and spitting their disgust and impatience into the dirty harbour water. Even the most disapproving made some little allowance, however, for they all knew that their skipper's weakness was not strong drink, though he liked a glass; nor bullying his crew; nor carrying sail beyond reason. No, his weakness had always been women and he had never hid it. But, if he had to be a fool just now, why not pick a woman who would not keep them all dangling in port? They chafed at the delay, but they accepted it, with grumbling and ill grace, as they would have accepted head winds and other hindrances to a run home.

Dave's aberration hit Waitstill differently. What had long been recognized by the rest of the crew had been hidden from him in his blind respect for his captain. He could laugh at the foc's'l yarns and jokes about other men and he bore with his usual wide and empty grin the crew's twitting about his own fear of women. Scared! Nobody knew as well as he how truly scared he was! He'd run a mile or jump off the wharf, just like they said, if a bad woman was after him. He had known no women but his bitter-tongued, quick-handed mother, kind Mis' Redmond, Serena of the sharp words and the generous second helpings, laughing Tamsin and little Adree, who had been the pet of the hired boy starved for family affection, and later the friend of the childish young giant. None of these feminine personalities could be fitted into the men's coarse jokes. As for Adree, he wouldn't allow himself even to think about her when others were about, much less when such talk was going. Only after the off-watch were all quiet in their bunks, could he take out his memories and thumb them over like a bright book. Then he could believe again in the *White Wings* and Adree and himself sailing, sailing, under fair skies on a smiling sea. Didn't Adree keep his model of the *White Wings* on her mantel-shelf? Hadn't she shown it to him on his first visit to her new home, opening her parlour to him? Sometimes, when alone, he lifted the cover of his chest and laid his huge cracked hand upon the long pair of grey socks that lay atop his scanty store of garments. So shapely they were, so evenly knit! How they would cling to a man's feet, how warm they would feel in damp seaboots. Holding them under the smoky light he would believe he could catch a glimmer of the red-brown hair knit into the toe. Adree's own hair. He remembered how her childish curls used to tickle when they fell across his face, or twine about his fingers when he found an excuse to lay his clumsy hand upon them. Adree's hair would bring him safe home! He never considered wearing the socks to replace his ragged ones, or for extra protection on the cold night-watches. They filled a different need. Had he been one o' them knights little Adree used to tell about, he would have ridden into combat with a long sock of heavy grey yarn on his flagstaff, or what-ye-call-it.

The socks were another bond with his skipper and idol. They both had samples of Adria's loving handwork and a hair from her head to keep them from under falling blocks and out of the reach of those sudden seas that sweep aboard and snatch a man in passing. Naturally the spell in the captain's would be stronger, made by his own wife. Besides being a skipper to follow through hell and high water, Waitstill considered Dave a fitting husband for Adria and a proper father for Mary Ellen. His feeling for Cap'n Malone had become interwoven with the long-borne love for the Redmonds; it was part of goodness and kindly affection, and a man's respect for a better one.

Thus Waitstill alone of the crew showed himself confused and sullen at the captain's dallying and, at times, his morose stare pierced even Captain Malone's preoccupation with his campaign. From the men's comments, Waitstill gathered this was no new course the captain was sailing, yet he had been as sure of Dave's love for Adria as of his own fidelity if ever any good woman should love him. He had no words to relieve the heavy bulk of his disillusionment; oppressed by its weight he moped about and responded to remarks by threatening gestures. The crew began to tell one another that something had come over Waitstill.

Four days of perfect sailing weather went by while the *Ocean Spray* chafed and tugged at her lines and the men lounged discontentedly about the deck or sought their own diversions ashore. Then late in the afternoon, Captain Malone appeared from the after-cabin in his shore-going clothes, good black broadcloth, white shirt and softly knotted tie, wide felt hat and polished leather boots. His hair shone, his narrowed eyes danced, his teeth flashed, his cheeks were smooth from recent shaving and the colour was rich across them. Waitstill had never seen him so strikingly handsome; his jaw dropped in admiration before he remembered that all this was for no good.

Dave was not unaware of the picture he made. He paused

at the schooner's side, with his hand upon a stay, preparatory to swinging to the bulwark and the wharf; he turned to his crew, and his smile asked them to share his elation; it was vaunting, comradely and a trifle apologetic, as if tacitly acknowledging he had imposed upon them; but it also held a reminder of his position and their impotence. "Well, b'ys," he said, "we sail when the tide turns at sunup."

There were appreciative murmurs and a few sly grins. Someone boldly urged that he be back on the vessel before the morning tide, or the *Ocean Spray* would sail without him. Waitstill stood somewhat behind the others, his face scowling and his mouth agape in his effort to accept what his eyes and ears told him.

Dave turned to complete the step onto the rail, but a splinter caught his trouser leg and, as he stepped back to release it, a line of his red underwear and fine black sock was disclosed.

What happened next left the crew forever perplexed. As Dave bent over his snagged trouser leg, there was a heavy movement from abaft the mast and two men went reeling aside as Waitstill shouldered past them. His eyes were blazing in his white face, but his hands were loose at his sides and his voice was quiet. Quiet, but it carried to the hushed men though it made no sense. "No, Cap'n," he said, "not in them socks."

Dave straightened and looked across the narrow strip of deck. His face was no longer open and smiling; he could look ugly when his bow was crossed. "Who's to stop me? Not Waits'l Twiddle—" As Waitstill moved closer, Dave dropped his voice to a savage low key. "What about the socks that lays in your chest? My wife. And the hired man. A fo'c's'l hand." This false accusation would excuse his own behaviour and his anger at interference.

For a moment Waitstill's mouth hung slack, and his breath rasped harshly. Then, with a roar like a goaded animal, he bore down upon Dave with flailing arms. Though their captain was a big man the rooted crew suddenly realized how much bigger the angry Waitstill was. Dave was unprepared for this berserk rage, but he had not won command of vessel and men by standing paralyzed before the unexpected. He stepped swiftly aside and forward, dodging Waitstill's murderous lunge, and he sent his hard fist to meet the other's chin. There was a snap like a cracking spar. Waitstill's black head went back, his arms spun once or twice, and his head hit the deck with a sickening thud. He lay still.

No one moved or seemed to draw a breath. The captain's face was as bloodless as that of the man sprawled at his feet. He knelt and thrust a hand beneath the coarse jacket. He rose and faced his crew. "Make all ready to sail. See to it, Zeb. I'm going for a doctor."

The fog was a chill dank curtain across doors and windows. It crept endlessly in over the cove, relentless and deceptive as the sea which gave it birth. Adria put wood on the fire and sat down the teapot, though the thought of food and another lonely meal distressed her. Dave must surely be lost out there in the cruel sea and fog. To think that once she had wished herself a boy that she might give herself to the sea's beauty and mighty moods! Mary Ellen whimpered from the cradle and her mother moved quickly to soothe her. When the child was again asleep, Adria stepped outdoors to listen. But there was only the slurring wash from the near shore and the diffused restless tone from the outer reefs. She accepted the absence of any hopeful sound and returned to the kitchen; yet she was not surprised when, a minute later, a shadow passed the pantry window and steps sounded upon the back platform.

At the door Dave crushed her to him. She did not feel the fog upon his face nor the dampness of his pea-jacket; she did not shrink, as she always shrank despite herself, from the smell of fish and bilge that seemed to permeate vessel clothes. He told her, "I thought we'd never reach here, though we crowded all sail from Sydney." When she only clung to him he asked, "Aren't you glad to have your old man home?" He held her off and looked at her searchingly. She couldn't possibly have heard anything about Waitstill, or the Sydney delay.

She was pale and drawn; her grey eyes were enormous and black in their deep hollows, her warm mouth was quivering and not from his kisses. "You can't know how glad! All spring Mary Ellen has been ailing so that Dr. Whitehouse advised against taking her on New Erin. Just after the *Three Sisters* brought word you were homeward bound, she became worse. Much worse. So very ill. For over a week I didn't know. I didn't know. Only two days ago Dr. Whitehouse told me she would get better. Aunt Cilla and Debbie and Cynthie—they've been good. But Mary Ellen cried for Papa. And I'd waken, calling your name. I had such need of you, Dave. And you in trouble at sea!"

At sea. He sent a frantic backward glance through his memories. *Suppose my baby had died whilst I dallied in Sydney?* Superstition and remorse shook him. *This will be a lesson to me.*

Vol had gone but Isles was finishing the ledger before locking up for the night. When the bell above the door tinkled, Isles stepped out from the office, thrusting the pen behind his ear and tossing the hair from his forehead. The doorway framed Little Obie's round face like a moon whose shadows have run together. Unlike the secretive moon, however, Obie was plainly bursting with news.

Relief made Isles abrupt. "So the *Ocean Spray* is in at last! What kept you, man?"

"Kep' me?" Obie was briefly nonplussed. He hadn't meant to begin his story this way. "I s'pose ye didn't sight us roundin' Narrah? Ye didn't mark we had a dory out?"

"The fog hasn't lifted all day," Isles pointed out, "And it's thick."

"So 'tis," Obie agreed, "Thick as mud an' jest as coarse." He snapped his cap over his knee and sent droplets flying. "But we did have a dory out. We landed Waits'l on the outer side o' Grannie's Head."

"Isles asked the question expected of him. "Why couldn't Waitstill walk home like the rest of you?"

"Waitstill won't be doin' no walkin' fer a long spell," Obie said unctuously. "We had t'carry him to his Maw's."

Isles was surprised at the depth of his regret that an accident had befallen Waitstill, since the big man had never shown him anything but resentment. "The storm?" But the *Three Sisters* of Barrington had reported only slight damage to Dave's vessel, and no injuries to the crew.

Obie settled himself in a chair beside the cold stove and by his own system of wide tacks revealed the story of the snapped bowsprit and the Sydney repairs, of Dave's infatuation and annoying delay. He finally reached the captain's appearance on deck. "Handsome as the divil. If the divil *is* good-lookin' and I s'pose he must be."

"I think likely," Isles agreed with twisted lips, picturing a devil with laughing eyes, a boyish charm and the sea's own lure about him.

"The skipper was 'most to the side when Waits'l spoke up. *What* do ye think he said?" Isles shook his head hopelessly. "'Not in them socks' was the words he uttered. Wasn't that as loony as ever ye heared? What would socks have t'do with it, I sh'd like t'know? In the fo'c's'l, runnin' home, we chowdered it over, but noan of us could fathom it out."

Remembering the scene in Adria's kitchen, Isles had an inkling denied the crew.

"Then the cap'n said somethin' we couldn't hear, an' Waits'l made for him with a roar, like a bull let loose. The Cap'n's fist met Waits'l's chin, crack! Waits'l fell, all in one piece like a tree. I hope I never hear again the sound of his head hittin' the deck."

Isles' hands gripped the counter's edge as he forgot, in the dreadful climax, the cook's meanderings to reach it. "You said you carried Waitstill ashore. Dave killed him?"

"T'tell the story an' tell it true, we thought so. An' we stood huddled like a bunch of old ewes. But Cap'n Malone rubbed his knuckles on his pants an' took charge. 'Git Waits'l to his bunk, b'ys.' He knowed, and' we knowed, that it would go easier with him, in case of an inquiry, if we could swear Waits'l died in his bunk. 'Ye all saw I was forced t'hit him,' he said. 'Twas true. 'You'm not t'blame, cap'n,' I said, and others mumbled agreement. But we all kep' lookin' the other way from Waits'l's eyes, rolled back in his head, an' the line o'blood that trickled from his nose an' across his cheek into a little puddle on the deck.'

"The doctor come an' he said Waits'l wasn't like t'die. Anyways, what do them city doctors care about one fisherman more or less? An' we was glad t'be makin' a wake fer home."

Obie thinks more could have been done for the injured man. But Isles did not interrupt.

"He laid like a log in his bunk all the way. Now an' then I poured a little gruel into him, what didn't run out the corners of his mouth. An' he'd swaller water by times. He never spoke one solitary word from the minute he fell till I seen him laid on the bed in his Maw's house. I s'pose she'll do what's needful fer him."

"Dave sent for Dr. Whitehouse?"

"Not as I know of. I guess we was all too glad t'git Waits'l ashore an' hurry to our own homes."

"I'll harness Sally and take word to the doctor now," Isles said curtly. "I'll have to close the shop." He hurried Obie through the door. Then, as he turned away, "Dave plans to sail for Marblehead in the morning, I presume?"

"Fur as I know. He's in a great hurry now, seems." Obie sounded almost embarrassed as he said, "Amongst us for'rd hands we been talkin' o' passin' the cap around. Waits'l will be long abed and the's only his old Maw. We all like the way you take hold in time o' trouble. If we raised some money, would ye look after it fer Waits'l?"

"I'll be glad to," Isles assured him in a warmer tone. "Captain Malone probably planned something of the sort, but he will find other worries at home tonight. His little girl has been terribly ill."

"I know how 'tis," Obie soothed him, not really listening, and rolled off into the fog to recount to other ignorant ears what had happened to Waitstill Nolan.

EIGHTEEN

A WEEK later Isles, overseeing the loading of the *Dauntless,* caught a glimpse of Adria passing the wharf-head, basket on arm. As small children often do, Mary Ellen had made a quick recovery and could now be left in Cynthie Obie's care on occasion. *It's good for Adria to be out again, and Mother loves to have her come.* Yet something about the size of her basket, about her steady walk (as if she faced a distance) and the shawl over her summery dress, did not fit a call upon her Aunt Cilla. She visited few other Cove homes; where else could she be going? When the answer came to him he beckoned the mate, "Keep things going as they are. I'll not be long," he said.

Adria had had a good start and she had stepped along briskly. When Isles turned through the Grannie's Head gate, her light dress and bonnet were disappearing over the ridge that hid Nabby Nolan's cottage. He hurried his step. On his last visit Waitstill could do no more than mumble incoherently, but by now Nabby might know what lay behind her son's injury.

Adria would have felt easier had she known Isles was close behind her. It had seemed right and natural to pack a basket and visit the stricken Waitstill, but as she turned down Grannie's Head she felt a growing uncertainty of her wisdom. She paused at the site of her grandparents' house, where all that remained were the chimney and fireplace, crumbling into the cellar. The remembered past was close and poignant, but Adria saw that wildflowers bloomed above the cellar walls, and the lilacs which had bracketed the front door were bent under their purple clusters. Life's beauty could cover its scars. Across the harbour lay New Erin with its memories of blundering, kindly Waitstill. She moved forward, no longer doubting her courage to face the woman whom the Cove sedulously avoided.

A path wandered down the rocky slope, between bayberry

and blue-flag, and disappeared around the end of Nabby's shanty. Adria had expected to be repelled by the witch's home; instead she was conscious only of its pathetic solitude and exposure. Some night soon the wind would flatten it in a rage and the swollen tide would scatter its grey timbers and broken boards. Above it circling gulls lamented its coming fate.

Adria followed the path around the shanty's corner — and stood entranced. Between two rocky ledges lay an indented beach of small stones, rounded and polished by a million tides until they shone like grey satin. The shoreline was carpeted with purple beach-peas and silver-green sea lavender. The happy peeping of nesting shorebirds came from the fringing blue-flags, and yellow-birds darted among a point of alders. To think that all this loveliness lay unsuspected behind the rocky headland!

Adria did not hear the opening door behind her but she turned. She had not seen Nabby Nolan for many years, and, although local tales should have prepared her, she could not repress a start at the woman confronting her. Nabby would have been taller than her visitor but she was bent like a swamp spruce. Adria saw first a heaped head of hair, still strongly marked with black streaks (like dirty foam at tide line). Of the piercing eyes beneath the snarled hair, one was green and one brown; both were faded but their glare was the most intimidating thing about Nabby, for the sharp nose and shrunken toothless mouth were little different from those of other old women. Apart from looking as if they had been thrown on from a distance and with no careful aim, her clothes were good, making Adria recall that most of Waitstill's wages always went to his mother. A crooked hand held the door in a pointedly inhospitable manner but Adria was under the spell of the beauty before her and she said impulsively, "This is a lovely spot! Your beach is prettier than any on New Erin."

"New Erin, eh?" Nabby said in a rusty voice.

"I'm Adria Redmond, Adria Malone now. Waitstill must speak of me and of my husband, Captain Malone."

Adria jumped at the shrill cackle. "Speak of ye! He speaks o' nawthin' else. 'Tis Adree an' Dave, and Adree and a pair o' socks, an' Dave shouldn't go. . . He speaks of ye until I could screech. And I do." She peered sharply to see if a sudden screech might not frighten this guest.

Adria said merely, "No doubt that makes you feel better."
Nabby tried a new tack. "You'm one o' the Nickerson breed.
They've allus meant trouble for me an' mine. I sh'd think ye'd be
ashamed t'look me in the face."

Adria was taken aback, not by the vicious tone, but by this
reversal of what she had always understood. Gramma Damie
declared, "Gypsy Bess an' her brood! An evil day when they
'lighted on Grannie's Head, t'be a millstone about the Nickerson necks." Adria was struck by some resemblance between the
two women for, although Nabby was nearer Mercy's age, she
was old, old, and set in her opinions like Grammy. The resemblance was reassuring; she had learned to discount much of
Gramma Damie's scolding. She said firmly, "I didn't come to
look you in the face. I came to see Waitstill — if you'll let me,
please — at any rate to leave a few things I cooked for him.
Things he used to like when he was on New Erin."

The sharp eyes didn't flinch nor the hard face soften but
something behind both reminded Adria that she and Nabby
had motherhood in common. "My child has been sick too. For
a time I feared I would lose her. She's only a baby and Waitstill's a grown man; but I think of you as I pray for my child
and I pray for yours, too."

"Prayers! A lot they amount to! Better start t'pray for that
husband o' yourn. Better to have prayed his arm might rot at
the shoulder before ever it struck my son. Before he coaxed
Waits'l aboard a vessel. A witch's curse on him . . ." The eyes
were growing wilder and the cracked voice rose. Despite her
determination not to be intimidated by Waitstill's queer mother,
Adria stepped back.

There was a movement behind her and Isles came around
the shanty. He was breathing fast as if he had hurried, but on
seeing Adria he stopped and was at once easy-going, imperturbable. Her heart, which had begun to race, quieted at his smile
and nod. "Good day, Nabby," he said politely, but the look he
bent on her was severe and his voice held warning. "I hope you
haven't been frightening Mrs. Malone with your nonsense."

To Adria's surprise the old woman turned to him with something like a smile.

"Adria," he scolded, "why didn't you let me know you planned
to visit Waitstill? I'd have sent Vol along to carry your basket."

"Or sagged it yerself!" Nabby darted glances from one to the other. She laughed slyly at a joke dredged up from a fathomless depth, and continued to laugh while Isles' face reddened, though he was watching Adria as if to assure himself she had received no hurt. Adria now had no doubt that the woman was mad, and wondered if she should be locked up lest she harm her sick son. Abruptly, and still tittering, Nabby turned, flung the door wide and gestured for them to enter.

Isles ducked beneath the lintel and his fair hair almost brushed the low ceiling's rough boards. The shanty's interior was true to Cove accounts of its dirt and squalor — there was even a stone gin bottle lying among the hearth's ashes, to bear out the tales of Nabby's drinking — but the bed on which Waitstill lay was covered by clean summer blankets and its corner was comparatively neat. Adria cared little for Nabby's housekeeping, or lack of it. When she saw what lay on the bed she gasped and put out her hand for Isles'.

Waitstill's huge frame was only a skeleton. Above the sunken, black-bearded cheeks the brown eyes were dull with a terrible vacancy. This abandoned hulk was not Waitstill. She was stricken by the knowledge that Dave's blow, however justified it must have been, had killed Waitstill, that only his poor body had come home. She dropped her basket upon a bench and, weeping, turned to Isles. Above her head, Isles sent another warning look to the old women and then drew her head down upon his chest. "I know, I know," he said gently. "I could have cried myself when I first saw Waitstill. I thought what it must have meant to his mother when the dory brought him to her. Dr. Whitehouse says that only his mother's care has brought him through. And he *is* better." He patted Adria's shoulder and turned her towards Nabby, dropping his arms.

"Yes," Nabby said, "he's better. He takes gruel now, and gulls' eggs, soft-cooked. Strengthenin', they be." She addressed Adria with pride, "You'm too young t'recall. But yer Grammy'll tell ye I nursed Waits'l's Paw back t'life from a blow on the head."

Adria gestured towards the basket. "I didn't know Waitstill was so dreadfully ill. Perhaps what I brought won't do for him. But you can eat it. I thought . . ." She looked towards the table where food was piled in disorder, and her hesitation betrayed her former fear that Waitstill and his nurse might be wanting food.

"Mistah Isles is t'thank for that," Nabby dismissed the pile with a careless nod. "An' fer the new blankets. 'Tain't *his* first visit if it be yourn." So Isles had cared this much about his cousin's crew man — or for her childhood friend. When she turned to him he hastily explained that Waitstill's shipmates intended to pay something towards the food.

Nabby was watching them and burst again into her annoying cackle. " 'Pears t'me Dave Malone was barkin' up the wrong tree. He! He!"

"We must be going," Isles interposed, "I'll walk up the ridge with you, Adria, but I'll take the short-cut along the shore. I left the *Dauntless* loading."

"That's right," Nabby whispered slyly, "Don't let nobody see ye," and went into laughter again.

"Come, Adria," Isles said, and anxiety sharpened his tone.

It penetrated the silence wrapping Waitstill. "Adree," he whispered and his eyes seemed searching.

Adria turned and made a few running steps towards him. "Here I am," she said and sank beside the low bed. He raised a hand feebly and she took it in hers. His eyes made a great effort to focus and he summoned his voice. "Dave hadn't ort t' . . . them socks," he said before blankness wiped his face and his nerveless hand fell. Adria and Isles went through the open door, out into the sunshine. Silently, Nabby Nolan watched them go, her face now as blank as that of her son.

Once clear of the house, Isles paused until Adria had wiped her eyes and tucked away her handkerchief. "Promise me," he begged, "that you won't visit Waitstill again. Let Vol deliver your baskets, as he does Mother's. You saw how deranged Nabby is, and I must warn you that she blames Dave bitterly for Waitstill's state."

"Dave says Waitstill attacked him, or was about to." Adria sought reassurance, for this was almost unbelievable.

"Little Obie said the same," Isles told her, "But it's no use trying to explain to Nabby; I've tried. She blames your grandfather and your father for stealing Waitstill from her, years ago, and now she blames Dave for luring him into the fishing. Waitstill's father was lost overboard from a vessel, they tell me, perhaps it's all tied together in her jumbled mind."

"But Waitstill loved the Redmonds, and he worshipped Dave!"

Isles reverted to his warning, "You must never go back there.

Dr. Whitehouse says Waitstill's brain is injured to a considerable extent, and as he regains strength he may have spells of violence. I hate to think of his mother alone with him. I couldn't bear to think of you there."

"I promise, Isles. I do. Since I can't help by going."

They walked on. "Did you notice Waitstill mentioned those socks I gave him? Isn't it sad that he should treasure them—a pair that Dave wouldn't wear—and that he remembers them, sick as he is?"

"Sad, yes. But I think it was your consideration of him and the affection behind the gift that counted with Waitstill."

After a silence, "Tell me honestly, Isles, did you feel that Dave . . . that he resented my giving Waitstill his socks? I guess everyone has notions; I find some of Dave's difficult to understand. It keeps coming back to me that Dave was put out that afternoon. Surely he wouldn't have welcomed a chance to . . . to strike Waitstill . . . to hit back at me through him? Oh, don't listen to me! I'm wicked to let myself think such a thing about my husband."

"The crew agreed that their skipper did the only possible thing." Isles did not voice his own suspicion that the very vehemence in their protestations hid an indefinable misgiving.

Adria turned on the ridge and looked across at New Erin. "Home," she said. Then, wistfully, "I'm not at home in Prince's Cove. Do you think people feel that and resent it?" For the first time Isles realized that Adria sensed the slowness of the close-knit Cove families to include an outsider. Adria went on, "I've tried for Dave's sake to put down roots here; but right now I am merely waiting until he has called on his outward trip, and then I shall take Mary Ellen and go home to New Erin for peace and healing." Her grey eyes were clouded and colour stained her face as Isles' quick glance searched it. She had not meant to reveal her growing fear that much was wrong and missing between her and Dave. "Though why I should need healing, I don't know!" She tried to laugh off her words as one of her old exaggerations. "I'm tired, of course, from the baby's illness, and worry over Dave's absence."

Isles answered her gravely, "You need New Erin. Pretend now and then that you are a little girl again. Pick berries in the sheltered hollow some warm morning and think of a boy who found you there once, long ago." He laid his hand —

Isles' long, sensitive hand — lightly upon her arm and looked for a moment down into her eyes with an intensity that made Adria's waver. He smiled sadly before he turned upon his heel and strode down the hill.

Adria walked homeward and though the full basket no longer dragged on her arm a less tangible weight slowed her steps. Poor Waitstill! When she recalled Isles' bidding to remember the boy on Nigh Hill, she sighed again, "Poor Isles." She came to herself with a start and shook off the spell of nearly maudlin pity. As if Isles needed commiseration!

Prince's Cove housewives peering from behind curtains, saw young Mrs. Malone hurrying homeward, her head proudly erect. Some envied her the pretty clothes her captain husband brought from the States, some her youth and her beauty; no one thought of her as a lonely girl with a sore and troubled heart.

NINETEEN

It was a cheerless fall. Early October's crisp winds fled before a series of rain-dumping easterlies, and the sun fled with them. October's rains became November's sleet and snow; children's noses ran perpetually and old people hugged the fire. Priscilla Kendrick was put to bed with a choking cough that left her white-faced and blue-lipped. Dr. Whitehouse warned Isles gruffly that he'd better pray hard for a spell of clear dry air, his mother's heart wouldn't stand too much of this.

Neighbours rallied as always in time of sickness. Rhuanna, Vol's little mother, left her menfolk — with their hearty consent — to fend for themselves and installed herself as fulltime housekeeper for the Kendricks. Other women took turns, day and night, in the sickroom, or appeared with covered dishes at the back door. Isles felt humbled before the outpouring of kindnesses, and proud that his mother was held in great affection.

The desire to show their goodwill towards Mis' Kendrick swept the village like a benign epidemic — neighbour caught it from neighbour. Like an epidemic it ran its course, and as the weeks dragged other illnesses made their demands upon the village until only a faithful few shared the sickroom vigils. Isles seldom left the house since he alone knew how to hold his mother when the cough was at its worst. To help care for Aunt Cilla, Adria often engaged Cynthie and Bella to stay with Mary Ellen for a few hours, and on a drizzly afternoon (following days of alternating hope and fear for her friend) she knocked softly at the Kendricks' kitchen door. The tremulous smile on Rhuanna's little mouth denied her brimming eyes, and she pulled Adria through the door with surprising vigour. "Happy day! Dr. Whitehouse has just been! He says her heart is stronger and her cough easier. Mistah Isles an' me, we thought so but we didn't dast say it out loud. But ye can see for yerself. Put yer cloak and bonnet off, do." She led Adria across the hall and, even before she reached the open bedroom door, Adria knew that Priscilla's breathing was indeed easier.

Isles came to his feet from the chair beside his mother's bed. Now that the crisis was past he looked gaunt and desperately weary. "My dear," Adria said, shocked at his appearance, "tonight you must go to bed and get some real rest. Rhuanna and I could watch." At her side Rhuanna nodded assent. Adria continued, "I'll just run home and make arrangements for Bella and Cynthie to sleep at my house and care for Mary Ellen. After supper I'll be back to nurse Aunt Cilla tonight." She smiled at Isles, who had made no comment. "Surely you trust me not to leave her, and to call you the instant you're needed."

"I'd trust you with anything, Adria." Even his voice was weary, and she recognized again the undertow of pain.

Once Priscilla had been settled for the night Isles went gratefully to bed. Rhuanna snatched a nap on the kitchen couch, leaving the doors open between so that Adria might summon her with a word and Priscilla, propped on heaped pillows, dozed most of the time. The night crawled on and the house slept with faint nocturnal stirrings and thin protests at the wind's nudgings, while coalesced fog fell like rain-drops on the window. The shaded lamp was turned low and the room sealed as tightly as possible against the damp outside air; Adria became achingly drowsy and welcomed the infrequent need to fluff the pillows or administer medicine. During the dark hour before dawn there was a flurry of wind, a wind with a clearer voice and a push for a different house-corner. Adria crept to the window. The stars were out and Cape Sable's light was flashing. The weather had changed at last! No doubt it had been the first of this lightening air which had brought relief to Aunt Cilla. When she tiptoed to the bedside table, Isles' watch said five o'clock. Her heart jumped at a knock on the back door and with maternal alarm she whispered, "Bella! Something has happened to Mary Ellen." She heard Rhuanna stir and move sleepily towards the door, while she held her breath.

I'm imagining things! But no, that was Dave's voice. She turned but, remembering her promise not to leave the sickroom, stopped, her eyes upon the invalid and every sense straining towards the kitchen. From the doorway Rhuanna whispered, "The *Fearless* is anchored at Redmond's. Your man wouldn't wait for daylight, so him and some others rowed ashore." Rhuanna shook her head at Dave's impatience. "I'll keep an eye on Mis' Kendrick whilst you greet yer husband."

Thankfulness for Dave's safe return was uppermost in Adria's heart as she went to the kitchen. In his arms she murmured, "Dave, oh Dave," while her hands brushed the salt-rough fabric of his sleeve. "I thought it would be next week, at least, before the *Fearless* got in." She laid her head against his chest in grateful acceptance of unexpected good fortune. Only then she sensed that Dave's arms, though they had closed about her, were holding her with constraint.

"Plain to see you wasn't expecting me," he said coldly. "Perhaps even if you'd known I'd be in, you would have been away from home. If not on New Erin, then out to the neighbours. Any old woman ahead of your husband, eh?"

"Neighbour! Old woman!" (That Dave should hurt her immediately when she had hoped . . .) "Aunt Cilla. She has been desperately ill. Only last night she took a turn for the better. You know that when there's sickness *you* have always done more than your share of sitting up nights."

This reminder of his role as sympathetic helper mollified him and his voice lost some of its sulkiness. "Just the same, it's a shock when a man comes home to his wife and is greeted by a phiz like Cynthie Obie's. Have you ever beheld Cynthie in nightgown and curl-rags?" He held her off and looked into her face.

He sounded so aggrieved and Adria had such a clear picture of Cynthie in night garb that her laugh bubbled up irrepressibly. She tried to silence it against Dave's coat and suddenly his resentment dissolved in shaking laughter, even as his arms tightened, at last, about her. They whispered and kissed briefly and then Adria urged him go home. "Tell Cynthie and Bella they can go; make up the fire and have a mug of tea – you know where to find the breadbox and cookie crock. Rhuanna and I will fix Aunt Cilla for the morning then I'll hurry home – to you." She half-drew, half-pushed him towards the door. Her whispered admonition was a promise. "Mind now, don't wake the baby until I get home." She lifted her face for his kiss and her closed lashes threw black shadows down her cheeks. He kissed her lids gently, ashamed of his earlier ill-temper.

Cynthie was halfway back between the warm bedclothes when she was struck by the knowledge that if Captain Malone was home, Obie Knowles was home, too. Home and, like enough, trying this very minute to break into his tightly secured house. She leaned across the bed and shook the figure on the far side. "Bella. Wake up now. Ye hear me?"

"Ayah," Bella mumbled. She turned from the light as her grandmother lit the bedlamp. Her black curls under the slipped night-cap looked so sleep-sodden that Cynthie hated to shake her, but she did. "Cap'n Malone is home."

"Whyah?" Bella asked brightly, to show she was wide awake, though her eyes might be shut. "I don't see him."

"Ninny! He *was* here. Rattlin' the door fit t'wake the dead. I sent him t'fetch his wife. An' they'll be back any minute. So get up, slugabed. Haste now!" Cynthie gave the girl a poke as she struggled into her own clothes. "Yer Grampy's home too, doubtless, so I'll go let him in. Now, Bella, you git dressed and soon as ever Cap'n Malone and his wife are back, you come direct home. Mind." She wished the girl wasn't one to coddle her body so; but there! she was a pretty thing and young. Bella was a handful, but Cynthie's puckered heart belonged to her orphaned grandchild; her hard eyes softened behind the adjusted spectacles as she looked down upon her.

Bella, yawning and groaning, rolled over to the front of the bed and got her feet out upon the mat. "That's right," Cynthie commended her, "Hurry home t'greet your Grampy. He won't believe he's ashore if he finds you ain't in the house."

Bella listened to the door latch drop and to a few echoing steps that must be her grandmother's crossing the yard. She shivered and rolled back into bed, pulling the quilts about her until only the tip of a black curl and a nightcap string showed.

In the sickroom, Priscilla stirred. Adria lifted her gently and held the water-glass to her lips. Priscilla sipped and fell back weakly. Her eyes were clear and her voice distinct. "Was that Dave I heard?"

"Yes. The *Fearless* is in. Dave was rejoiced to know you are better. He'll come to see you soon."

"You sent him home alone? To an empty house." Aunt Cilla sounded worried.

"Cynthie and Bella are there, with Mary Ellen. I promised Isles not to leave you."

"You shouldn't stay." Priscilla paused to gather strength and her breathing was quickened as she insisted, "Hasten home. Seamen. Famished for their wives." There was knowledge and tolerance and memory in her words.

Adria blushed and patted the thin white hand, but Priscilla insisted, "Go, child." Her urgency conveyed itself to Adria who could not quite dismiss it as a sick whim. *Dave IS touchy; he may still be sulking and feeling ill-used because of my absence.* She put Priscilla's hand down gently and summoned Rhuanna. "Aunt Cilla wants me to hurry home to that nephew of hers." She smiled at the limp figure in the bed. "Please call Isles."

When Adria slipped outdoors, night's black bowl still covered the village, though the sun was prying up the eastern rim and, the wharf spiles and boat masts were etched against the pale sky. After weeks of chill dampness the dry north wind was tonic to nostrils and lungs; the weariness of the night's vigil disappeared. Her heart was singing, eager to discard all doubts, and her feet were winged along the muddy road to home and Dave.

From the yard she saw a glimmer behind the Knowles' curtains and, as she turned up her own steps, the kitchen door across the lane opened briefly and outlined Bella as she slipped through.

Dave was not in the kitchen. "He was tired," she murmured, accusing herself. A low-turned lamp guttered softly; the stove held coals which, replenished, snapped and crackled. She stood close to the grateful heat, chilled but glowing, weary but beyond weariness. She laid aside her wraps and moved across the room. "Dave," she said softly at the bedroom door. There was no answer but the sound of regular breathing from their bed. She opened the door and went in. The light from the kitchen showed that he slept, as she had often seen him sleep, half on his stomach, half on his side. He lay completely relaxed and he did not stir as she pulled at his shoulder. She drew the covers over him carefully while her excitement and anticipation, which had been tightly wound, let go like a snapped spring and left her limp. *Aunt Cilla needn't have sent me flying home. All Dave wanted was sleep.* She was shocked at herself. *Surely I don't begrudge a tired man his rest!* But she did not stoop to kiss him, nor did she slip in beside the sprawled figure. On the kitchen couch she pulled the comforter about her shoulders and told herself she would nap until the baby wakened. Instead she lay staring while her mind reviewed the night's incidents and her body cried out to her husband who lay beyond reach (barred off by sleep and his repudiation of her warm promise), only a few feet away. Dave might be punishing her for not being at home to welcome him. She tried to push the suspicion away, but her mind had long before accepted a cruel streak in Dave's love. *What is wrong with us? With our marriage? Did Mamma ever find Papa a stranger? Why was Aunt Cilla worried for Dave, just off his vessel? Did she go to sea to save her husband for her own love? Did she ever have cause for worry?* She turned restlessly and reminded herself that her own parents and Isles' had apparently overcome any difficulties that had faced them and gained the security of a true marriage. So would she. She would build a home whose foundation and sheltering roof were the love of the man and woman inside it. She accepted the fact that she and not Dave must dig the cellar and cap the roof of such an edifice, and felt a resurgence of faith and inner strength. Concrete plans and fuzzy-edged dreams had scarcely begun to merge when Mary Ellen's sweet piping announced the beginning of the day—Dave's first day home.

Whether or not the disappointing homecoming was to blame, the winter did not draw them closer, although Dave was kinder in a casual maner and easier to live with. They shared delight in Mary Ellen's endearing ways; they visited Aunt Cilla and Isles; they attended Meeting and the Cove's few social gatherings where they made a handsome couple and where Dave was his most charming, flattered by the attention and respect shown him. It should have been a happy winter. Adria wondered if she had expected the impossible, if there was nothing in any marriage beyond what she and Dave possessed, but an instinctive knowledge of love's possibilities repudiated that conjecture. What separated them was not so much an obstruction as a gap which, she saw, had always been there but which now, instead of closing as she might have expected, was widening. Occasionally they leapt it and in transient intimacy believed it did not exist or had been permanently bridged; but Adria feared the time when it should have grown too wide for her to cross; when she would no longer be able to reach a hand to aid Dave in his swift and heedless passage.

Dave spent much time with other Cove men and often on

a sunny day walked back along the woodroad; he said he liked to swing an axe and chat with the choppers, that another winter he would cut firewood from his own woodlot and pay Obie to haul it.

Before dawn the empty ox-sleds went up the lane with lanterns bobbing, and disappeared behind the spruce and firs. At dusk the loaded sleds made their last trip home and Mary Ellen liked to stand on a chair by the window to watch the steaming oxen and the driver plodding beside his slow team. She would summon her mother, "Come — see — come — see." It was by obeying her command that Adria became aware of Bella's walks up the woodroad — rather, that the girl hurried home from it before the first sled appeared, cutting obliquely across the pasture. The wooded road must be a fairyland when shadows lay purple on the snow under the trees, but Adria could not imagine Bella drawn by beauty. There were many men in the winter woods — not only the cutters but trappers who stayed overnight in the small camps. Lazy Bella's sudden penchant for long walks disturbed Adria. The girl was foolish and spoilt, yet she was only a child in judgment, with none but simple, doting grandparents to guide her. It would be a shame if she lost her good·name by slyly meeting some boy whom Obie had forbidden to come courting—some lad as irresponsible as herself. When Adria had noted several furtive returns, she broached her fears to Dave. He had finished his supper and lit his pipe; the cosy kitchen seemed the perfect setting for sharing doubts as well as contentment. She concluded, "Bella seems more grown-up this winter. And so pretty too; despite her bold look. Cynthie worries about her; and she *could* come to harm with so many men along the woodroad now."

Dave let her finish, his face and his curtained eyes revealing nothing. She was astounded then at his biting scorn. "So you're a 'curtain-twitcher' yourself! After all you've said against Cynthie's spying!" He tamped his pipe angrily. "I suppose you've blabbed this all over the Cove — to your precious Debbie and all."

"Dave," she pleaded for fairness. "You know I don't want to 'make talk' about Bella; I want to prevent it. I thought as Obie's skipper and neighbour you might drop him a hint. I've mentioned this to no one else, but you are my husband; I should be able to speak my fears to you without being considered a gossip." She bent over her sewing, more hurt than she wished him to guess. "Perhaps no Prince's Cove man would harm a child, and an orphan. I wish I hadn't mentioned my worry. Let's forget I did."

Again she must have said the wrong thing, for Dave's tone was harsh. "Don't fret over that little strumpet."

"Dave Malone! You're not to speak that way about the girl." More calmly, she continued, "All last fall Bella seemed fond of me. She avoids me now, but if I have a chance I shall advise her not to go in the woods alone. A young girl can't know what construction might be put on her actions."

"You'd best keep your oar out of things that don't concern you," Dave answered sullenly, getting to his feet and reaching for his coat. "The less you see of Bella and Cynthie Obie the better. And if I hear scandal about the girl, I'll know my wife started it." He slammed the door behind him.

Not until the *Fearless* had sailed with her spring cargo of fishermen and Adria was preparing to leave for New Erin, did her concern for Bella reassert itself. Her earlier fears now appeared trivial and unworthy, for Bella never left the house and Cynthie let it be known her granddaughter was suffering from a slow fever. Neighbours, remembering Tillie's fatal lung trouble, shook their heads pityingly. Moreover, Cynthie gave callers a grudging welcome and kept Bella out of sight, so that people feared poor Cynthie's troubles were bringing out a queer streak.

On New Erin Adria caught no echo of the talk that buzzed throughout the Cove that spring and summer, though she did hear that Cynthie and Bella had moved back to Obie's neighbourless house near Grannie's Head. The talk had simmered down and Adria had other concerns when she returned in the fall, for when Dave came home his black-haired son, Jonathan Peter, lay on the pillow beside a white but triumphant mother, and Rhuanna moved quietly between kitchen and bedroom. Yet, when Adria was up again, the blank windows across the lane had a hostile glare and she would have welcomed the fluttering curtains and Cynthie's half-hidden outline, and Obie's rambling discourses in the Malone kitchen.

If Dave was a trifle subdued that winter, Jonathan Peter was not, and Adria was less engrossed in probing the finer aspects of marriage than in filling the children's demands. Dave appeared satisfied to have it so. After all, they were six years **married**.

TWENTY

THE SAGGING sky dropped May rain which the wind seized and flung across the fields and buildings of New Erin. The house yard was comparatively sheltered, but flying runnels from the lintel forced the man outside the kitchen door to turn up his sodden coat collar. Here, with the storm's clamour broken, his ear caught memory-enchanted sounds: the drip of rain on weathered shingles, the merry gushing of a gutter and — not quite a sound — the thirsty greensward's swift absorption of the downpour. Behind these was the diffused and steady roar of inswinging surf and the plaintive cries of sandpipers. Once days like this had drawn him to fathom every puddle and to turn his open mouth to the tasteless rain. He did not like to count how many years ago.

Those inside the house would not have escaped the years' mutations. *But they will find me most changed of all.* Though he had actually paused but a moment, he felt the accusation of wasted time and lifted his hand as if to knock. Wincing, he let it fall stiffly back against his side, then with his left hand he rapped smartly and lifted the latch.

The kitchen's warmth rushed to meet him, carressing his wet cheeks and cold hands, penetrating his sodden clothes. With the warmth came the kitchen smell, impossible ever to forget, impossible to describe. It held the fragrances of crusty bread, spiced molasses cake, baked beans and kettle brown-bread (of course! This was Saturday night). And, ah yes! the sweet bayberry perfume from the dried leaves in his mother's aprondrawer. All were there in the first breath he drew as he stepped inside the door.

He saw that the family were at supper about the long table. He did not sort out individuals but, as if on a collective face, he saw surprise and bewilderment give way to recognition, then to something that might be shocked, pity quickly veiled. Above the scraping of chairs pushed back came the glad cries, "Patrick!" His mother reached him first, going to his arms and raising her face for his kiss, oblivious of dripping coat and wet cheeks. She must have seen that his right arm hung stiffly but she said only, "Come to the fire. You shouldn't be out in such weather." He might have been coming in from the remembered puddles.

Then his father was shaking his hand, and the grinning young man who must be Charlie was pounding him on the shoulder. The beautiful woman with the fine eyes and generously curving smile was Adria. She was backing her mother's efforts to get him next the stove and out of his coat. Across the table Kiah and Serena beamed at him. With her silver mug a small girl in a high-chair banged out her joyful approval of all the happy excitement. "That is your niece, Mary Ellen," Adrian explained and moving proudly to the cradle where an infant lay, with a round black head turned aside on the pillow, "Your nephew, Jonathan Peter."

Patrick, smiling down upon the sleeping boy with a bachelor's awkward homage, wondered fleetingly what sort of man his sister's husband might be; his mother's letter announcing the marriage had given him the impression of misgivings.

He refused offers of a change of clothes, reminding his mother that a seaman was enured to dampness and that his own garments would soon dry. "I'll get my sea-chest and portmanteau from the warehouse, once the rain stops." This time he had not been rowed ashore from his anchored ship. "I came through on the coach from Halifax. In Prince's Cove Mr. Isles Kendrick insisted upon giving me dinner and when I wouldn't consider waiting out the rain, brought me across — in as neat a little sloop as I'd want."

Charlie nodded, "The new *Lady Fair*."

"That was typical of Isles' kindness," Adria assured him, and the warmth in her tone and the tenderness about her mouth held Patrick's glance, until he remembered that Adria was married, and not to the likeable Isles Kendrick.

He bent to straighten a pant-leg — and to hide his face. "I lost the *Clara Caie* in March," he told them, and the loss was still raw and open in his voice. The soft murmur of commiseration was not an interruption. He straightened casually, but the harsh lines about his mouth had deepened and now that the rain-lashed colour had left his cheeks, his face was pale as well as thin. He plainly drove himself to continue, "Somehow I miscalculated and put her on the Buck Rocks off Cornwall. She went to pieces almost at once. One man was drowned. I smashed my right arm trying to get a line ashore." He lifted the stiff arm. "I must rest it for a few months."

Mercy looked at him closely. *The arm will heal but we must mend the hurt to his pride. And his grief for the loss of the ship that has been his life for twelve years.*

Serena knew a cure. "Ye need a bite t'eat." She indicated the steaming plate of beans and brown bread set at his old place.

"I'm to have a new ship next spring," he told them, and already it was easier to talk about it. "In the meantime there was nothing I wanted so much as a visit on New Erin."

"There is nothing we could want so much as to have you," his father told him, reseating himself as the others slid into their places.

Adria was remembering Patrick's first homecoming. There'd be no mistaking this thin, quiet man for a buccaneer, nor for the proud young master of his first ship. She glanced about the table as if with her brother's eyes. *What differences he must be noting in us!*

Patrick was pleased to see that his mother looked stronger and younger than on his last visit. His father had aged but he retained the straight-backed erectness, the air of the courteous host which his son remembered, though only his family and his servants were present. Patrick had always considered Serena and Kiah as old people; they looked little older now. Gramma Damie was like one of the wrinkled russet apples he used to find behind the barrels in the spring — with a still sound core. Charlie had grown from a gangling boy into a man, but the greatest change was in Adria. On his last visit she had been a pretty child; now beautiful was the only word for her. Her beauty came as much from her regard for her children and her parents, and from some inner generosity, as from her exquisite colouring, long grey eyes with black lashes, and heavy chestnut hair.

During the next weeks no one asked for details of Patrick's injured arm or the loss of his ship. The time would come when he would want to talk; he would be with the family for almost a year, and they could wait. Meanwhile there could be no doubt of Patrick's joy at being home. Adria sat down beside him on the front steps one evening when a summer sunset coloured the harbour and only the whisper of water and the twittering of swooping swallows broke the stillness. "I wonder I could ever have left this," he told her. "In most places an angry boy might slam the door behind him and start down the road, determined to run away and so vindicate himself; but when darkness lowers he had only to turn about and the road leads home. Where boys take to the sea, the road back is often lost for good, or not found for many years."

Adria knew of the mistake that had driven him from home. He added, "I kept bitterness in my heart for a long time. It hardened me to sea life and made me harsh as I climbed to the afterdeck. But whenever an older man was kind to me I turned to him as if to my father. I fell in love with the daughter of one of those kind men. She was of my father's faith and I thought for a time it would be my faith, too. I learned that an inborn belief can be as unyielding as New Erin granite. I shipped out on an East Indiaman and fought the thing through. Not until I had worked out tolerance for others' beliefs, and strengthened my conviction that a person must not compromise with his own, did I understand my parents." He said in a lighter tone, "When I got back to port my girl was married, and my heart did not break. Then there was the *Clara Caie*. You've heard of men who love only their ships?"

"You're not meant to be one of them," Adria denied quickly. "I'll find you a wife." And wished that she might.

Patrick spent little time in reminiscing, for he and Charlie were full of plans to enlarge New Erin's trade. Without Adria's understanding how it came about, Isles had entered into the plans and enlarged their scope. The large Halifax to Yarmouth packets, which handled freight and passengers from intermediate ports, were unable to serve many shallow and reef-barred harbours. Isles' schooners would collect the exportable fish from these small ports, and New Erin's Long Wharf would provide sizable shipments for the packets. In the same way, it would clear goods shipped in. The *Dauntless* would run to the eastward; Charlie in the *Lady Fair* would go westward as far as St. Joseph's. Here Captain Arthur d'Entremont had retired to a fish business and was pleased to join the enterprise headed by his friend Dan Redmond.

Long Wharf again became fenced by boat masts; Cove men rowed "on" to work by the day. Long tiers of briny barrels formed until there was scarcely room to walk between them, and the fish-flakes spread from shore to barn. The vessels, coming into place at the wharf with a rattle of mast-hoops and a flogging of points, fascinated Mary Ellen as they had her mother. The island's activity and contentment reminded Adria of the years before The Storm. But now she was the grown daughter of the house; Mary Ellen, golden and quick as a sunbeam, was New Erin's joy, trudging on untiring legs after the menfolk, losing their tools, upsetting their milk-buckets and nail-boxes, begging Kiah for pickabacks and clutching his scraggly moustaches as he tossed her high. Dark-haired, placid Jonathan was still his mother's boy entirely, and his warm plump arms about her neck were sweet beyond words. The children, and Adria's love for them, were part of New Erin's resurgent life.

Charlie had not been sailing to the western harbours for long when he confided to Adria that Captain d'Entremont's daughter, Arthenese, had his heart. Adria vaguely recalled childhood visits from a gentle girl with black eyes and quick dimples. "Don't say anything to the others," Charlie begged. "I can't ask Arthenese to come make her home with three elderly women who cannot understand her language. I believe Captain d'Entremont would take me into his business, since he has no sons. But there's New Erin."

Adria assured him things would work out. Smiling, she asked, "Arthenese doesn't speak English? I know you have little French. How do you understand each other?"

"We're learning a little of each, and we manage." He blushed. "When her hand is in mine, and I can see her eyes, we have no need for words."

"I was only teasing," she told him fondly, "and your Arthenese sounds like a darling."

Adria was grieved to hear that Debbie's father had suffered a stroke and died soon after. Later, she heard that Debbie was making her home with the Kendricks, so as to give more time to the shop and provide company for Mrs. Kendrick. It was strange to think of Deborah in the house that had been her own second home.

She heard, too, that Bella had returned in restored health

from a long visit with an aunt "up Yarmouth way" and had, almost immediately, married a widower on Pilot Point. *All that vital prettiness must be wasted in such a marriage. And Obie had such fine dreams for his Airy Bellah.*

Actually Cove affairs and Alethea's house seemed part of a world which would not concern her until Dave's return in December. She had pushed to the back of her mind all misgivings as to her marriage. Loyalty and pride forbade her confiding in anyone — what was there to confide? A dissatisfaction, a frustration, which might disappear with Dave's homecoming. She would cope with it when the time came.

The time came unexpectedly soon. Surprise was her only emotion at the sight of Dave in the doorway. He had come home to the Cove and, though he pretended to hide it, he was displeased that Adria had not been there to welcome him. "But Dave," she remonstrated, drawing away from his arms after the first kiss, "you must have known I would be here. How could I expect you so early?" Then, in real concern, "What sent you home? Not storm and tragedy again?"

In a wind the *Ocean Spray* had dragged and fouled another vessel so that both had been forced back to port for repairs. Dave had taken the Boston packet to Yarmouth and come to the Cove by coach. He had family news for the Redmonds. Stopping at his mother's in Hines' Harbour, he had learned that Hazelitt and Catherine Morris were back in their big home there and, as one of the family, he had called. Hazelitt, he said, had grown excessively heavy and had recently suffered a stroke which left one side paralyzed. However, his wife was a solicitous nurse and rumour had it that Haze had returned with money to last him the rest of his days. Dave was wasting no sympathy on him. Catherine had sent her love to all on New Erin and regretted that she could not leave her husband to visit them. "She wants to see her father on a business matter. Something about an old debt."

Dan Redmond's face lightened wondrously at this news. He asked many questions about his oldest daughter and began plans to visit her and bring her home briefly — husband or no. "That will be a happy reunion indeed. Can't you stay, Dave, so that Adria and the children may share in it?"

Dave insisted he must get back to Prince's Cove. He hoped to find a winter berth to make up for the scant returns from the

Ocean Spray's latest and unfortunate trip. Patrick's suggestion that he work with the new freighting firm was rebuffed. Adria sensed a wariness and a measuring between Patrick and Dave and she sighed, contrasting the easy friendship that had sprung up between her brother and Isles.

Patrick watched Adria's eyes lose their glow, saw her mouth firm in resignation, her manner lose its assurance. It angered him to see her anxiety to placate Dave who apparently took her grace and beauty for granted. He found much of New Erin's comfort and happiness left in the boat which took Adria and her children to Prince's Cove.

TWENTY-ONE

DAVE had gone to Hines' Harbour to engage a berth on the *Voyager,* leaving Adria puzzled and hurt. Surely after several prosperous voyages Dave should be able to weather a poor one. She wondered if life ashore with her could now mean so little that he preferred the perilous winter fishing. Would he not miss the children, at least?

Jonathan was deep in his afternoon nap, and Mary Ellen contentedly busy in her playhouse under the spruce-tree. This might be the last day in the playhouse until spring for, although there were bursts of sunshine, the morning's calm had been followed by vicious gusts and one brief squall had left snow pellets dancing on grass and doorsteps.

A knock was followed by the appearance of Little Obie's face around the entry door. He held out a large fish. "Here's a fresh-caught pollock. Thought it might go well for supper."

Adria thanked him and inquired politely after Cynthie and Bella, wondering what had brought her one-time neighbour calling after his long absence. She brought her knife and cutting board and set about cleaning the fish, so that Obie might "visit" with her as she worked, and know his gift had been welcome. His usual flow of words seemed strangely scanty until he blurted, "Ye know where yer husban's at?"

"You wanted to see Dave? That's too bad. He's gone to Hines' Harbour to see about a winter berth on the *Voyager.*"

Obie's laugh was as sharp and unexpected as a firecracker. "I'm agoin' t'tell ye. I don't look fer no thanks, but its fer yer own good. I ain't sayin' Dave's never been t'Hines' Harbour this fall; I ain't denyin' it's possible. But it's precious few times he's got past the turn-off t'Pilot P'int."

"You mean he goes that way to see Waitstill?"

"I mean no sech a thing." Obie was snappish. "Ye knowed Airy Bellah was married to Zack Crowell an' livin' down on the P'int. Zack ain't got much, but my poor Airy Bellah can't be choosy now. I mean," he said at last, "yer husband's gone t'see her."

"Arabella?" Adria was more perplexed.

"Ye knowed, didn't ye? Or suspicioned? Cynthie claimed ye did from the first, but was too proud t'let on." His pale eyes sought hers in shame and trouble.

"Knew what?"

"That yer husband was the one t'blame fer Airy Bellah's trouble; that he's been payin' fer the keep o' the child, up Yarmouth way."

Obie talked on. He knew Adria listened although she kept her head bent and her hands fumbled with the pollack, "I ain't been much of a man. I shipped under Cap'n Malone after I suspicioned who was to blame, because I didn't dast face up to him fer all he's so pleasant-spoken. But I'm no longer beholden t'Dave Malone; I got me a berth on a Lockeport schooner. The trouble is, he's back at his old game while Zack's away t'the east'r'd." His voice was weary and defeated.

Adria's first sympathy for the fat little grandfather was swept away by her own pain. "Why come to me?" she asked.

Obie had given little thought to what this revelation might do to her, but when she raised her head he flinched from the starkness of her face. He said, "I figgered you sh'd be the one t'put an oar in. You could bring Dave up all stan'in', if ye'd a mind to. Lots o' wives has done so." Knowing Cynthie's shrewish dominance, he misjudged Adria's influence over Dave. "An' before Airy Bellah gits herself inta any more trouble."

It's Bella who matters. What about me? And suddenly she could no longer endure Obie's pleading gaze and his endless words. She wanted to put her hands before her eyes; she wanted to thrust her fingers into her ears; instead, striving for control, she picked up the scaly knife as if to resume her work. But, when Obie began to speak, she turned towards him and heard herself say in a strange high voice, "Talking won't help. So stop it. *Stop it.* And please go now." To his aimless expostulation she gestured towards the door with the hand holding the knife and her voice broke on a shrill, "*Go!*"

She saw his eyes fixed on the blade as he slithered from his chair and hurried through the door. Catching a nervous backward glance she whispered, in a spasm of hysterical laughter, "He thinks I was going to use the knife on him! He'll spread word that I've lost my mind." Laughter turned to bitterness, "And people will feel sorry for charming Captain Malone who has a crazy wife." For some minutes she huddled, shivering, next the stove. There was no refusal to accept Obie's story. *But what can I do about it? What can I do?* She could not take Dave back into a yearning, forgiving heart, as she had done following Miss Newhall's disclosure that first winter of her marriage. For her heart felt no yearning, no forgiveness. Love that had been struggling to endure, now died. Her breast ached and knotted with its passing, yet she knew she had only to endure this last pain, because Dave's ability to wound her would cease with her love. To remove herself beyond his voice or the touch of his hand seemed ultimately desirable. *I'll take the children and go to New Erin where I'm needed and loved.* But they were Dave's children, too, and he would never give them up.

She saw two figures pass the window and recognized, with amazement, Aunt Cilla and Isles. She forced a semblance of welcome into her "Come in," but Priscilla stopped short at sight of her face. Isles looked about the room, "I hoped Dave would be home. Where is he?"

"With Bella. So Little Obie says."

"Obie came here to tell you that? The . . ." Anger clamped Isles' lips.

"Don't blame Obie. It's time someone told me," she said wearily.

Isles led her gently to the couch and seated himself beside her. While Priscilla watched in silent compassion he turned her face to his shoulder. "I have worse to tell you. You know I would bear the pain for you, if I could. But I can't put off the telling. Remember you are my brave Adria."

She stirred when the portent of his words reached her but he pressed her face back against his shoulder. "I have bad news from Hines' Harbour. You knew of your father's plans to visit Catherine?"

She nodded.

"He and Patrick must have misjudged this morning's calm. You've noticed the gusty wind?"

"Yes. Oh yes."

"The *Lady Fair* made the harbour mouth and because she was a new boat, some men watched her come about for the channel. They saw the squall lashing the waters astern and the snow that followed. Nobody knows what went wrong, but when the squall was over the *Lady Fair* was bottom up." He paused but Adria said nothing, made no move. "The men had a dory off and on its way almost as quickly as I can tell it, but the harbour is a long one. They were too late for all but Patrick."

"Papa?"

"Gone. And Kiah."

"Kiah, too? Faithful Kiah." Her words were toneless. "Patrick, you say. Patrick or his body?"

"Patrick is alive. At your sister's, under the doctor's care. Mrs. Morris sent a messenger to me at the shop. Patrick's head was injured but your sister believes he will be all right."

Adria wept, clinging to Isles and giving herself utterly to grief — a cleansing grief that washed away corroding shame and bitterness. When she could stifle her sobs she asked, "Does Mamma know? And Charlie?"

"No. I want you to come with me to break the news." *Can I really be glad that she knows Dave has failed her and she must lean on me?*

"It will kill Mamma."

"No." Priscilla spoke. "It will not kill her so long as she has one of Dan's children to live for. And you will be the greatest comfort to her. I've come to look after your house and children until you are free to come back."

"You mustn't! The work and care might be too much for you, Aunt Cilla."

"Rhuanna is coming to help. You needn't worry about us here. And, my dear, you mustn't tarry now. Darkness is coming and the weather may worsen." Priscilla spoke in her usual even tones but aching sympathy was in her eyes and in the touch of her thin hands as she helped Adria into the heavy boat-cloak and buttoned its warm hood.

Jonathan cried on seeing his mother dressed to leave him and Mary Ellen, having seen Uncle Isles and Aunt Cilla arrive, rushed in to stand in stricken silence. Adria kissed them and shut her ears to Jonathan's sobs, knowing Aunt Cilla would soon charm him.

As she and Isles turned down the wharf Adria heard the slap

of waves against its timbers and saw that gusts still clippped the crests of the running chop, although the wind was obviously going down with the sun.

Isles borrowed the nearest boat. She was scale-encrusted and proved a sloppy sailer, but her keel bit deep, her broad side lay solidly upon the chop and her patched sail rounded stiffly. Isles sat to windward and broke most of the spray from Adria, turning often to see how she fared. The water that reddened his cheeks and ran down his face did not wash the encouraging smile from his lips nor the compassion from his eyes. Once Adria wondered dully why she had never noticed how handsome Isles looked in sea-clothes, for the yellow oilskins set off his fair skin and clear eyes. But handsomeness was of no importance. She recalled her mother's words, on some forgotten occasion, "There's nothing so strong as gentleness, nor so gentle as true strength," but her eyes were still blind to what lay behind Isles' strength and gentleness.

Isles said little but gave his attention to sail and tiller. Each long tack was at once a welcome respite and a frustrating delay from the task ahead. When at last the boat slid along the inner side of Long Wharf and the sail flapped wearily after its straining trip, darkness was thickening over the shore. From the lighthouse, black against the tumbled sunset, the red lamps sent their beams. Along the path came Charlie's slight figure, hastening to meet the unrecognized boat he had sighted from the lantern. Once upon the wharf, Adria took Isles' arm, but before they had forced their heavy feet into the first step, she turned to lay her head briefly against the cold wet oilskin covering his breast. "No one else in the world, Isles . . ." She stopped for words. "Thank God for you," she said simply and moved towards the house. Not once since she had left the children had she thought of Dave; nor did she think of him now.

TWENTY-TWO

DAVE, who arrived the following afternoon, brought the first real comfort to Mercy. Her grief appealed to the tenderest in him and, after he had leaned over to kiss her, he sat down beside her and took her hand in his. Adria could almost believe that he was mindful of nothing but Mercy's distress, until she noted how adroitly he worked in an excuse for his absence, forestalling any criticism or questions. He said he had been sure Isles would receive Catherine's message and break the news to Adria, therefore he had gone at once to the Morris home to offer help and to find out the truth about the tragedy, for rumours were many and contradictory. He had shared the night vigil beside Patrick and this morning, when his brother-in-law had been pronounced out of danger, he had questioned the rescuers.

"Am I tiring you? Would you rather not hear?" he stopped to ask solicitously. Mercy nodded for him to continue and her hand tightened upon his.

"Kiah never came to the surface, apparently. Perhaps he was caught down, perhaps struck by the boom or tiller. Patrick was half stunned and has a nasty cut across his head." He hastened to reassure her. "The doctor — summoned from Yarmouth and one of the best — is certain the cut will heal cleanly and give no trouble, but for fear of concussion he has ordered a week's rest in bed." Dave laid his other hand, strong and brown, over the passive white one in his palm. He took a few seconds to frame what he wished to make plain without adding to the widow's grief. "Everyone agreed that Mr. Redmond gave his life to save his son. Men saw two heads come up within a few feet of each other, but the keel of the *Lady Fair* was already beyond their reach, downwind. One head moved through the water towards the other. Then there was only one head.

Then none. Then there was seemingly only one, but its shape gave hope that one man had dived and saved another. Your husband must have been a powerful swimmer."

"He was," Mercy whispered. She turned her head away but she listened.

"Later his cloak was picked up, afloat. He must have got out of it and probably out of his seaboots. When the boat reached him he was supporting Patrick. The men feared it was a lifeless body he held, but as the father grasped the gunwale with one hand, the young man opened his eyes."

Along the shore much weight was given the words of dying people and a meaning read into the simplest (part of the universal effort to catch a glimpse beyond the door which opens to all in time, but which vouchsafes a full view only to the entering one). Dan's last words would be as long remembered as his courage and sacrifice. He had smiled upon the son in the curve of his arm and said distinctly, out of stiff blue lips, "You were always my good boy, Patrick." ("Why did your mother weep so broken-heartedly at that, Adria, when she had been shedding no tears?" Dave asked later. She could not tell him; she had no memory of the child, Patrick, pleading for his father's withheld commendation.)

Dave continued despite Mercy's tears, "The men told me that Patrick seemed to rouse at that; he smiled back at his father as the rescuers reached to drag him into the boat. Then, as if his work was done when he saw Patrick safe, Mr. Redmond loosened his hold upon the gunwale. He vanished before their eyes without a sound or a ripple.

"I felt like swearing at them when they told me that," Dave said, "but I've known the same mistake to be made before. It's natural to grab the one who seems furthest gone, while the man who has kept up until the boat arrives has exhausted the last of his strength and gives up when the fight is over."

Mercy dried her tears. "Dan found his son at the last; and Patrick his father. I can never thank you enough, Dave, for what you've told me this day."

Adria wondered at Dave's felicity in alleviating her mother's sorrow. Did he, remembering the loss of his brothers, know true and sensitive sympathy, or was he losing himself in a favourable role, as he had played the part of true lover and devoted husband? *What a horrible, suspicious person I have become, to doubt his sincerity at such a time.* And, as the days dragged by, Adria admitted that Dave had never shown to better advantage, that the household derived much help from his sympathy and unobtrusive assumption of duties. Only to his wife's grief could he bring no comfort.

Mercy was not one to hug sorrow to her; by the end of the week her unselfish spirit was ready to take up her share of life's burden again. The time was come when Adria must stop avoiding Dave, must decide what was to be done with the broken marriage ties that snarled their feet. Dave must have reached the same conclusion for one morning, as she came from her mother's bedroom, she found him standing, tall and determined, beside the middle-room hearth. "We should be making plans about going home," he began carefully, "I'll inquire for a capable woman to help your Maw until she's stronger."

"We can't talk here," Adria told him and led the way to the deserted music-room where she pulled up the blinds to let in the sun. She knew herself to be stony-faced and hard-eyed and wished she might be otherwise, but tenderness had bled to death with her love as she had stood, fish-knife in hand, and listened to Little Obie. She told Dave directly, "I'm not going back to the Cove this winter."

He had not expected this. His brows lowered and his eyes came out from behind their lashes. "Not going back? Remember, a man has the say about where his children shall live."

"You have others than mine," she told him.

He tried to bluster that grief had touched her mind.

She stood straight as he and told him Little Obie's disclosures.

"Well, what did you expect?" he demanded angrily, immediately attempting to foist the blame upon her. "You send a man home alone to his bed — and there's another woman in it!"

"Bella was scarcely a woman."

He was irked by that. "No woman! She knew what was what. But you were to blame as much as her. Or me. You make no allowances for a man."

"Was I to blame for the Hines' Harbour girl whose father has a crooked arm? Did you ever wonder how I felt when I learned you'd married me to cheat another girl?"

"What old gossip peddled ye that?" He tried for scorn but his face showed guilt. *I never knew she suspicioned!* This gave him hope. *She forgave that, put it behind her and never threw it up to me till now. If I play my cards right this will blow over, too.* The prospect of losing Adria was suddenly bleak, impossible. *I'll give up Bella, if I can't keep Adria any other way.* He pretended abashment. "I told you before we married that I was weak that way. The truth is I could never leave women alone since I've been big enough t'flip a petticoat. And you ain't always helped me."

Again he was accusing her and Adria, looking into her secret heart, confessed sadly, *I was partly to blame. I was never the dominating wife he needed to keep him straight. Perhaps I didn't care enough, after all.* She told him, "I'd have thought the value you set on your neighbours' good opinion would have kept you straight in your home port."

"I must say you plan to give Prince's Cove a tasty morsel to chew on now," he said caustically. Then, rapidly changing to the boyish penitent that always won her, "Take me back and let me prove to you . . ."

Her decision had unconsciously been made, awaiting this juncture. She lifted her head and looked full into his eyes, where tiny embers of angry shame burned behind the narrowed lids, "Stay with me on New Erin this winter. Mamma needs me, the children love it here and the business requires another man, even if Patrick soon returns and we can hire someone to replace Kiah." (As if anyone could replace Kiah!) "By the time you sail in the spring we should have reached some agreement. At least, here I shall not be putting you in temptation's way."

"Women's hearts are all hard," he complained, "If a man tries to get close he only bruises himself." Actually Dave capitulated with surprising speed. Now that Adria no longer cared, he put new value upon her approval. "But noan of this sleeping in your Maw's room," he stipulated stubbornly.

She glanced about her. "When you give up Bella I'll do my part. We'll put a stove in here and have a sitting-room to ourselves when we wish, and the bedroom off it." *What other hope is there for either of us?* But the thought of Bella brought physical distaste and a sense of violation; she would need all her strength and courage to keep her promise.

For a time Adria felt she had lost all her youthful hope and faith, lost her sanguine outlook, her open grasping mind, her pleasure in little things — a tumbling cloud along the mainland hills, a white sail catching wind and sun, birdsong and the tide's murmur. Only her capacity for work and service remained and she drove herself hard. During the first grievous days Dave was another shadow among the shadows of lost ones, scarcely so real as the overwhelming memories evoked by Kiah's barn-coat on its nail, or her father's bookmark between the pages of a volume. She now saw Dave with none of love's softening illusions but rather with a sharpened perception for flaws and a blindness to his better qualities, but she told herself there was no help in what Kiah had called "pressing a thorn to the heart" and gradually acceptance and serenity rose from the deep roots of inheritance and character.

Patrick came home bandaged and pale. He was shaken and humbled at his father's sacrifice, grateful for Catherine's loving care. He delivered a letter from his sister and Mercy smiled tenderly when she had read it. "Catherine sends me the money that should have been your father's all these years. I'm glad she meant to recompense him; that would have made him happy." Yet she cared so little for the money itself that Adria must gather the scattered notes and give them to Patrick for safe keeping. She suggested the time might come when Catherine's repayment would serve Mercy well. Patrick agreed and that evening at his father's desk he told Adria, "Before I leave in the spring I shall settle things so that Mother will always have her home and enough to keep her."

Trade slackened as usual during the winter and Patrick spent hours bringing his father's books up to date and settling business matters, often after long discussions with Isles. For with Dave and Patrick both home, Isles came often to take part in a gunning expedition, or to sit about the fire with the family. Characteristically, it was Isles who found the solution to the overwork again imposed upon Adria. A welcome solution it proved when Rhuanna and Vol moved in with Priscilla, and Deborah, out of friendship and the goodness of her heart, gave up her pleasant life with the Kendricks and came to New Erin for the winter. In a few days she might always have been one of the household. She spoiled Charlie equally with Mary Ellen and Jonathan, cajoled Damie and Serena and gave Mercy much of the love her own mother had not lived to receive. Only with Patrick was she silent and withdrawn. *I do believe she's scared of him!* Adria was amused that Patrick's surface severity should deceive her friend. She was more amused to see Patrick's efforts to overcome the timidity in the soft brown eyes. *He may know how to handle a crew but, plain to see, he has no skill with Deborah.* "You don't like Patrick," she commented once.

"I do. Indeed I do." Warm colour rushed over Debbie's face. Then, in puzzled, diffident tone, "But he isn't much like Isles, is he?"

Adria laughed fondly. "Why should he be like Isles? You know there's no one just like Isles."

Winter moved down upon the household, and its members settled into the accustomed ways of meeting and checkmating it. Despite its gaps, the circle about the evening fireplace took on a comforting familiarity, and Mercy's face regained tranquility as Patrick real aloud or related his adventures. Debbie's needle idled and her eyes never left the narrator's face. Adria suspected that Patrick made everything sound more intriguing just to impress Deborah, for she always looked terrified at the exciting moments and swore she wouldn't go to sea for all the gold of the Indies.

The children, with their gaiety and mischief, forbade dwelling in the past. Seldom a man sat down without a child upon his knee and Dave's love for them was open and touching. Damie, matching their childishness, made room for their chairs and toys in her warm corner next the stove where she sat contented with her patchwork.

Though Damie in her corner seemed shut off from the rest of the household she was still aware, as she proved one afternoon when she and Adria had the kitchen to themselves. "A pity a man and woman couldn't have the rough edges and useless corners trimmed off at the start, so as to jine in a neat an' wearable block," she offered. Adria murmured agreement, pretending not to know what her grandmother had in mind. Damie admitted, "The years most gen'rally clips 'em t'fit. A great waste o' time and good calico sometimes; many stitches t'be picked out and resewed."

Even Grammy sees that Dave and I form no smooth pattern. Adria could not share her elders' faith in time's healing, and righting of wrongs. Time dulled the stabbing blades of grief, true, but it did so by blunting and tarnishing many edges one would have kept sharp and bright.

Time had merrier turns, Adria was glad to admit when, one sunset, Patrick coaxed Deborah to walk with him to "light up", and returned with her hand in his. They might both have caught some of the lamps' glow, except that theirs beamed from a deeper, richer flame. But surely some of the ruby chimneys' "magic" had rubbed off on Deborah, whose soft face was transfigured. Later, when she and Adria were chatting over this new development, Adria hinted that the lighthouse lantern, overlooking the sunset-coloured bay, might be a romantic spot for a proposal of marriage. Deborah blushed and lifted brown eyes, "It wasn't that way, at all," she confessed. "Captain Redmond— Patrick—was that nervous he started to speak the minute we were inside the door. I was surprised—who'd ever expect . . . ? His voice boomed so loud and sounded so fierce echoing back and forth in that cold, empty room. Adria, you've no idea! I was still a little in fear of him and I tried to run behind the oil casks." She laughed and lifted a gore of her skirt. "Smell," she insisted, and the reek of kerosene still came strongly from the cloth. "I don't suppose many couples plight their troth across a kerosene cask. I never heard or read of any, did you? And wasn't I the silly to be afraid of Patrick?" That was no longer of consequence. As far as Deborah was concerned all that now mattered was Patrick, and no amount of teasing by others could change her singleness of interest.

All at once spring began its advances and retreats in the annual and involved dance with storm and fog. A restored and confident Patrick went to Yarmouth to see his employer and his new ship. He returned exuberant. Mr. Stouten married him to Deborah in the New Erin parlour, with his mother's smile upon them both; and Debbie, who avowedly hated the sea, blithely packed to share the after-cabin of Patrick's *Silver Moon*.

Her brother's brief absence in Yarmouth had emphasized Adria's concern for those on New Erin after his departure. Dave would soon leave for the Banks. Who could Charlie find to help him? The new freighting project was too necessary to the district, too potentially profitable, to be lightly relinquished. Patrick, too, had been taking thought. He told Adria, "I can't stay home, much as I love New Erin and all of you. I would come to hate what kept me from blue water, and be of no use to anybody." That evening he summoned the family and opened a discussion.

Dave surprised everyone — none more than Adria — by casually suggesting that he give up fishing and become a partner in the freighting enterprise. "If Charlie's willing I'll buy his share and take over his position here. Some of my Prince's Cove crew will join me on New Erin. Then Charlie can go to his little French girl and still work with us." Charlie flushed at Dave's tone, but his eyes brightened at this possible solution to his problems.

Patrick was crisp. "You and Charlie can make any arrangements you wish — subject to Isles' approval, since he is part owner in the business. Father's share goes to Mother; mine is already in Charlie's name. Though Mother is to have a home here always, the island and all its buildings are Adria's to pass to her children."

Dave clearly caught the implications in this entailment, but Patrick continued smoothly, explaining to the surprised faces, "The island and property are mine to dispose of. When I came home after The Storm I gave Father money to transfer the existing mortgage to my name. This spring I paid him the rest of the island's value. All papers are with Mr. Robertson in Barrington. What assets Father had at his death will, naturally, be divided according to law. That will take time, since Will and Tamsin are not in this country. Meanwhile, if Mother needs money Mr. Robertson will get in touch with Mr. Killam. If Charlie isn't at home, Adria can see to such matters; she has a clear head."

Adria tried to thank him, but astonishment and gratitude bound her tongue.

"What I've done," Patrick went on, "I consider payment towards the years that Adria and Charlie bore the brunt at home, during the sicknesses and discouragements, while I was chasing over the world, unknowing and uncaring, and gathering considerable money as I roamed."

Adria felt the lifting of a load. No matter what course Dave now followed she and the children would have a home. What she did for him henceforth she would do freely, as a gift, not as the duty of a dependent wife. His decision to stay ashore puzzled her, but she summoned her excitement and determination for a new undertaking. She would miss Charlie and Patrick and Debbie, but this might prove the way for her and Dave to build a partnership, after all.

TWENTY-THREE

For a time husband and wife grew closer as they shared the demands and rewards of New Erin and, the only members of their generation now on the island, turned to each other for companionship. Adria found much to commend in Dave's handling of the business; it was unfortunate that one of his plans did not work out. Daily workers about the vessels and wharves were readily obtained, but no one wanted Kiah's place as hired man and, one after another, capable foremen left the island as schooners began to sail past to the fishing-grounds. The same discontent began to work in Dave. He enjoyed the excitement of the packet's calls: her churning sidewheels and the groaning ropes as the men warped her into the wharf-end; the bustle of loading the waiting barrels and bales aboard. He liked greeting the sloops and schooners with their contributions of freight, and the meetings with old shipmates among their crews. But the dancing harbour waters were not the offshore grounds, and the unfamiliar demands of cattle and land made him impatient and short-tempered.

Though staying ashore had been his own idea, he began to blame Adria for keeping him, and she resented that. Soon they ground at each other like rocks caught in the undertow of their fundamental differences. Dave found increasingly frequent excuses which took him to the Cove or Hines' Harbour and often, on his return, Adria smelt liquor on his breath. Her childhood fear of drunken men and her old shame for New Erin's liquor traffic increased her distress and added another abrasive to the thinning ties between them. A sense of personal grievance will mar finer emotions; Adria retired into a cold silence or answered Dave shortly and sharply.

In retaliation, Dave scoffed at all she cherished and belittled her opinions, arraying himself against her in any possible difference of belief. He returned from the Cove one afternoon with a new gibe, "Guess who I met today on the road? Will's old flame, Thankie Newhall. She's the new teacher at the Cove school."

"Teacher! I wonder if she should be in charge of children. It's too late, I suppose, to drop a hint to the Trustees?" Adria was truly concerned at young minds being entrusted to such a teacher.

"I'd keep my mouth shut if I was you," Dave said, tightlipped with sudden displeasures. "There's many worse. Only the Redmond pride... Wouldn't do for Will to marry hired help." Such an about face! Adria suspected that he and Thankie had been sympathizing with each other against the Redmonds.

Dave was not the least disturbed about Thankful's potentialities as a teacher, but he was troubled because she had let him know (how craftily and with what false repudiations, Adria could imagine) that the Cove was criticizing him for Waitstill Nolan's plight. Not for the blow struck in Sydney—that was still considered just and unavoidable—but for present neglect. Waitstill walked the road and the shore-paths, an object of mingled fear and ridicule, and no one but Isles Kendrick was lifting a hand to help him. Dave had apparently silenced his conscience long ago, but he now had no defence against public censure. Adria was unprepared for his rebuttal a week later.

When she glimpsed Waitstill's shambling bulk behind Dave at the door, she shrank back before she heard her mother's involuntary gasp, or felt Jonathan's clutch upon her skirts. Dave announced, "I've decided to give Waits'l a home. I need a man for the rough work and he was always content here; he won't be hauling his anchor at the first sight of a vessel." Dave was combining a gesture of appeasement to Cove opinion with the riddance of onerous chores.

Serena banged the stove-lids with almost forgotten eloquence. "Men!" she said, putting into the word all her irritation at masculine stupidity and contrariness.

Dave taunted Adria, "The Redmonds always set great store by Waits'l Twiddle."

True, they had "set store" on Waitstill, accepting his defects and approving his praiseworthy qualities. Adria would have welcomed the loyal slow-witted Waitstill of other days; but not even her visit to his bedside had prepared her for this travesty of a man. She cried out angrily, "What can you be thinking of? There is no place here for him now."

The uncouth creature moved a huge hand fumblingly over his dirty beard. Did he recognize her? She blamed herself for rejecting him within his hearing. *My tongue is grown too quick and sharp.* But she was filled with anger — not blazing, but cold and searing as frosty metal. *I can't forgive Dave this. How could he bring such a . . . such a thing . . . into my home? Around my children? But this may win the Cove's approval. What does Dave care about me?*

Waitstill learned to perform most of his once familiar duties and, rather surprisingly, could soon be trusted to care for the light. He cowered from Dave's commands, often with an arm thrown about his head in a defensive attitude that Captain Sam would have recognized as the one learned in his ill-used boyhood, but he obeyed his former skipper without question. At orders from Mercy or Adria he grew perverse and surly. He snarled and shook his fist at the children and Adria was in perpetual terror lest he hit them, for his blow could smash life from the dainty Mary Ellen or the chubby little Jonathan. Dave laughed at her fears. "Waits'l? He's got no more spunk than a kitten. Just take a stick and show him you're boss."

Mercy sewed and knitted for Waitstill, as of old, but he went ill-clad by choice — hid his socks in a manger or behind barrels and wore hay stuffed into his leather "jacks." To Adria, the pitiful scarecrow came to represent the wreckage of her dreams and all the humiliations and disappointments of her marriage. Her foredoomed hopes of a fresh start with Dave had died without her being aware.

She realized that the Cove as a whole was undoubtedly applauding Dave's magnanimity, however belated; that it was well pleased to be rid of Waitstill's presence; that she would be called hard-hearted to begrudge her husband's generosity. The men who worked on New Erin or called with freight, noticed that Mrs. Redmond was sharp and severe with Waitstill (not detecting fear in the edge of her voice) and that she often took up a small stick to enforce her commands. They noted that Waitstill cringed at the stick's movement and they laughed together, because a blow from such a weapon would no more than tickle his tough skin. Some of these men, secure in numbers and with a primitive cruelty for the weak, teased the imbecile giant and taunted him in his clumsy rages. In time they accepted the sight of him gulping down raw herring from their barrels, or munching upon a handful of cracked corn dredged up from a dirty pocket.

These same men, visiting the house, noticed that Adria grew thinner, that her large eyes had a haunting quality not often seen in a young wife and mother, and that she seldom said more than a polite greeting, for Adria had crawled like a hermit crab into a shell of silence and endurance. She realized that the men never brought to her their cuts and small injuries, or their family news, as they did to Mercy, and it distressed her that her own troubles had closed, rather than opened, her heart to the burdens of others. Isles often stepped into the kitchen to chat with Damie and Mercy, when business brought him to the island. He spoke to Adria with unchanging friendliness, but now and then she caught his eyes upon her with a sad and puzzled look. Then, hearing her scolding voice with Isles' ears, she would send up a forlorn little prayer. She asked for help to bear more cheerfully the strain of Waitstill's presence and Dave's absences, her fears for the future whenever her husband returned with his handsome face loosened by liquor and a mean spirit peering from the wide eyes.

TWENTY-FOUR

ADRIA sang as she moved between sideboard and oven. Tomorrow night the children would be hanging their stockings by the middle-room fireplace. Dave had gone to the main for Christmas treats; he would be home before suppertime and Isles would be with him to spend the holiday. When the children had been tucked in bed there would be the fun of unpacking and hiding the many parcels, and tomorrow would see the tree in its place. For a few days she and Dave would lose themselves in their children's joy. Jonathan was too young to remember or understand, but Mary Ellen's delight in the coming of Santa was something to lift the heart of any parent.

Snug in coats and mufflers the children were playing in the sunshine within sight of the window, contentedly rowing a fish-tub with barrel-stave oars. The eastern door stood ajar and the morning's freshness swirled in to mingle with the smell of spices and molasses and baking ham. At dawn the crystal air had been brittle with frost, but now the sunlight was warm across the sideboard, while the surf on the outer shore flung its spray with all the lighthearted abandon of summer. On Clam Cove squattering sea-ducks, too heavy with periwinkles to rise without the help of a breeze, settled down to doze on the placid, mother-of-pearl surface. Adria knew such December days were the last gifts of the dying year, and doubly precious.

With the loosened curls about her stove-flushed cheeks she wore again the look of the girlish Adria, who had dreamed of change and new experiences as the good that each tomorrow might bring her. Well, there had been changes aplenty since then and the kitchen behind her was incredibly empty, with both her mother and Serena gone from their accustomed places.

Mercy's absence had been long-planned. Last summer Tamsin

had written of a Boston surgeon whose operations brought recovery from such trouble as Mercy's, and had pleaded that her mother combine a visit with a chance to regain her health. Adria had added her urging, but it had been Aunt Cilla who had clinched the argument. Isles had proposed that his mother spend the winter in Boston with friends and relatives; that she and Aunt Mercy travel together with Captain Stoddart on the *Dauntless,* and early in November the two friends had set sail in a spirit of high adventure.

In contrast, Serena's absence was still new and strange. This time yesterday she had been kneading bread at the sideboard. If she had noticed the sloop heading in from Cape White, she had not commented on it; but when the thin, middle-aged stranger with the worried eyes had appeared at the door, she turned as if she had already sensed the import of his errand. "This is Miah Swim," she told Adria, "my man's foster brother."

"It's about Bartlett that I come," Miah said in the quietest of voices.

"I cal'ated."

"Bartlett's t'home."

"On Cape White? Can't never be." Plainly this was not the news Serena had expected. "Last I heard of him, he was in California."

Adria wondered how Serena had kept informed of his whereabouts.

"So he was," the mild voice agreed. "But he shipped back east on a Boston barque, and then t'Yarmouth. Come on foot from the coachroad, through the slush an' mud o' last Wednesday's storm, and reached Maw's after dark, more dead than alive. He's abed and the doctor's been to him." Miah paused and wrung the stocking-cap in his hands. "Trouble is, there ain't nobody in the old home now but Maw and she's ailin'."

Serena nodded, grim-lipped, while her hands shaped the bread dough. "Eighty-odd, she must be."

"She *can't* do fer him. The truth is noan o' the Swims can. I can't ask my wife to take in a sick man — there ain't space fer an extry mouse in our little rooms, what with all our young'uns." His puzzled eyes begged pardon for inhospitality.

"'Course not, Miah. Don't talk foolish," Serena said impatiently. "What seems t'ail Bartlett?"

"They do say it's an inward growth." Pity was in the quiet

tone. "He keeps asking for *you,* says he expected t'find ye still at Maw's. After all these years! An' the trick he played ye!" But even in condemnation, Miah was soft-spoken. "I told him I'd take a message to ye, but I never held out no hopes t'him."

"He wants me t'come look after him?" Serena put the white cloth over her bread and set it to rise.

"I cal'ate so. But nobody won't blame ye, if ye refuse. Only fer Maw's sake, really, did I come."

Serena took a long, long look through the kitchen window, over the familiar fields and hillslopes. At the sink she washed the dough from her hands and reached behind her for her apron strings. "Well, what's 'llotted can't be blotted," she said. " 'Twon't take me long t'throw a few things into a bag."

Adria gasped. *Serena can't be thinking of going to care for the man!* Before she could speak, Miah had drawn a deep breath of relief and risen to his feet. "Bartlett kep' askin' me t'go fer his wife." He could scarcely believe his errand had worked out so well.

"Wife!" Like Miah, Adria jumped at Serena's mirthless hoot. Then the dour face lightened and the iron-grey eyes under the thin tight wings of hair changed. "Yes," she said wearily, "I took him like a wife would — fer better and fer worse. Till Death do part. 'Twas him an' not me that made the false vows." She turned and explained to Adria, "An' Maw Swim was sweet charity itself t'me in my trouble."

Miah bobbed apologetically and left the kitchen.

Adria spoke gently, "I wish you would spare yourself the long hard nursing of a dying man — if what Miah says of a growth is true. This Bartlett has no right to call on you." When Serena did not answer she went on, "He deceived you, and left you to make out the best you could!" For Serena's sake she felt hot indignation at the old wrongs.

Serena rolled her apron into a tight wad. "A woman keeps her marriage vows, Adria, no matter how hard 'tis," she said flatly and stubbornly, then raised her eyes in a revealing flash of admiration and understanding, "Like you'm adoin'."

Adria's tears blurred the lines of the thin plain face, so long familiar, so much a part of New Erin, into a softer, sweeter image of what Serena might have been. Swiftly she reached out and pulled the bony aging figure to her soft young breast. She held it as close as Serena's rigid embarrassment would allow, and kissed the gaunt cheek. "Go then," she said, "and God bless you. But come back the minute you are free." Though she released Serena she was still reluctant to part with her. "Can't you stay until after Christmas? To see Jonathan and Mary Ellen with their presents? Three days can't make much difference, after all these years."

Serena answered with an odd patience, "Three days followed by a fortnight's ice. What then?" Adria silently admitted the possibilities of winter weather. "No, I'll jest pack my nightgowns an' clean aperns an' what not, an' borry some o' yer Maw's herbs an' simples. She's never begrudge 'em, if she knew." She gazed around the kitchen and looked fondly upon her stove. " 'Twill seem queer, right enough, me in another kitchen, and this one with neither me nor Mercy in it." That had been her farewell; she had not turned to wave as she followed Miah and her carpet-bag towards the wharf.

As she worked about the stove, yesterday's tenderness remained with Adria and coloured her memories of Serena's prodigious Christmas bakings when the Redmond children had all been home. Her mind went out to her brothers and sisters: Patrick at sea with Debbie, Catherine in her big house with her ailing husband, Tamsin and Philip and their three boys (with Grandma to augment their joy), Will—a continent away—married well and starting a shipping business in Vancouver, and Charlie whose frequent visits would be curtailed by winter's approach and his coming marriage to pretty little Arthenese. She prayed they would all be merry and think of her as she would be remembering them on Christmas morning. Adria Malone, the only child left in the old home, would be happy on that day. There were the children and Grandma Damie to please, Dave and Isles to share the holiday meals and spirit.

And Waitstill. She saw him lurching and stumbling along the boardwalk to the barn. He had been aimlessly wandering all morning and Adria uneasily remembered his hapitual responsiveness to a change in the weather. She glanced at the sky but, thought it now held clouds they did not hide the sun. The years had made their cruellest changes in Waitstill, and the disjointed movements, the blank eyes and sagging mouth were more disturbing because they had not quite erased the kindly boy she remembered. She recalled the exquisite *White Wings,* his gift to her that Christmas after The Storm, and his pride in seeing it upon her mantel in Alethea's house. *What can I do to give Christmas some meaning for Waitstill?*

Gramma Damie claimed she didn't hold with Christmas, but recently Adria had noted small scarlet mittens, with the white snowflake design, taking shape. They would be given with excuses but the children would seize them joyously. *Just as Grammy will love the box of special candies I have for her.* Damie was still abed, declaring the beautiful morning to be nothing but a weather-breeder, for her ankle was apainin' and athrobbin' in such a fashion as could only presage a bad easterly. "Mark me well," she had warned Adria earlier,

> "Last night the sun went pale t'bed,
> The moon in halos hid her head."

Adria herself had noticed that the gibbous moon had an orange ring which enlarged and diffused itself, and that smoke had rolled along the field like the blown bladders once kicked by her young brothers. Before dawn the threat of storm had been in the sea's rote, but at daybreak the sky had been rosy, and smoke from mainland chimneys had risen straight and round and white as birch-trees, catching the glow. This morning's self-pampering was unusual on Damie's part. Since Mercy's departure she had been hobbling about with renewed briskness, washing dishes and peeling potatoes, seeding raisins and pitting dates for Christmas cakes and puddings, — rejuvenated by the sense of being needed.

With a glance at the hurrying clock, Adria put the last cookies in the oven. As she straightened she detected smoke escaping from around the stove covers — Serena's infallible sign of a changing wind — and went to close the door against the draft. She saw that the sunlight had thinned and paled, while the enormous sky that had everywhere rounded over the flat ocean and coast was shrinking down upon them; the puffs of wind, though light, held a raw chill, and under them the bay had become slate coloured. The sound of wavelets lipping the wharves replaced the earlier stillness.

She had not seen Waitstill's approach. Mary Ellen's scream was like a knife through her breast. She flew into the yard to see Waitstill's snarling face bent above Mary Ellen and his dirty hand grasping her little arm, lifting her from her feet. On the child's drained face specks of dirt from her play stood out like ragged freckles. Her eyes met her mother's in a pitiful appeal, but some instinct kept her quiet after that first terrified scream. Adria felt her own face blanch to match her daughter's. There was no time to form a plan. A glance assured her that Jonathan sat sober and silent in this makeshift boat, safe enough for the time being. She forced her voice to calmness; better, she smothered all fear and shrinking, lest they shade it, and forced it into the tones of the girl whom Waitstill had obeyed and loved. If she could sound like the old Adria, she might awaken something of the old Waitstill before this slobbering madman dashed her child to bits.

"Has she been pestering you, Waitstill? I've told her she mustn't. I know you are busy. You have a lot of work to do. And you are so good-natured. So easy-going. We all take advantage of you, I know." The words were crazy but she made her tone soothing and sympathetic.

The fierce eyes turned upon her reluctantly but as if they must in order to understand this voice from the past. Did the cruel grip loosen a little? Mary Ellen was on her feet again, and she was keeping her eyes upon her mother's face, obeying the continuing necessity for silence and immobility. Waitstill spoke sullenly, but his words were unusually connected and plain. "Hit me with a stick. I was goin' by. Everybody hittin' at me. Hit me an' laffed at me. Like her Paw. Hittin' an' laffin' an . . ." His voice thickened to a sullen rumble.

"She was very naughty. But she is not like her Pa. She is like me. Like Adree." Adria explained carefully, watching him closely. "Don't you remember how good you used to be to Adree? And to Will and Charlie? You never got cross with them. Well, you shouldn't get cross with Mary Ellen."

The eyes filmed as if in an effort to recollect, and the loose mouth tightened as if it might be preparing to smile. Adria decided to risk all before the frightened children spoil her effort by some sudden move or cry. She stepped forward and took Mary Ellen's arm. Waitstill's hand loosened and dropped as if he had forgotten it. Adria pushed the little girl before her, scooped up the big-eyed Jonathan, then made herself turn and smile at Waitstill. "Please pile the wood into the cooper-shop, that's a good boy. Captain Malone will soon be home."

(*Remind him of Dave, whom he fears.*) "He'll be pleased to see all the wood you've piled."

When the door was closed behind her she collapsed upon the nearest chair and pressed her head back against the wall. She fought a rising dizziness, and thankful tears coursed down her face unheeded. Mary Ellen stood, more stricken by her mother's present behaviour than by Waitstill's anger, then burst into shrieks of released terror. Adria soothed her.

The gingerbread men, so carefully shaped, were burnt black in the oven; from Damie's room came an irascible thumping of a cane, a signal for needed assistance, or information. Jonathan, frightened by the emotional displays about him, began to whimper. *How am I to forestall another fit of temper by Waitstill? It would be no use to bar the door. That would only anger him when he discovered it, and would not stop him.* Resentment against Dave for his imposition of this burden burned high.

Yet after the children had been fed and put to nap, Adria set a place for Waitstill and called him from the doorway. He had forgotten to pile the wood, as Adria had expected, but he had also forgotten his anger at Mary Ellen. He emptied his piled plate of fish and potatoes then dipped his hand into the bowl of porkscraps and wolfed the lot. Adria made none of her customary remonstrances at his grotesque appetite. *Nothing matters, if only he does not turn against me or the children. And soon (Oh God, let it be soon!) Dave and Isles will be here.* After dinner she urged and coaxed Waitstill back to the woodpile.

She carried a dinner to Damie who, sensing Adria's perturbation but not knowing its source, wished petulantly that the misery in her ankle would let up so she could help in the kitchen. Adria assured her things were going fine. "You're a great weather prophet, Grammy," she smiled. "I couldn't believe you this morning, 'twas so fine. But it's clouded over now and looks like wind or snow coming."

Damie was mollified, since her aches had had the prophesied effect upon the weather.

As Adria washed the dishes the first huge, tranquil flakes began to descend in leisurely circles. She had no doubt this would be one of the quiet, quiet snows of early winter, that would wrap roofs and fences and pasture spruces in soft white and give peace and beauty to shore and island alike. Even when the gentle flakes began a faster circling and the wind, trying doors and windows, found several ill-closing and rattling, she told herself the storm, if storm it might be, was still far off. Once Dave and Isles were on the island, the snow and wind would not matter, would, in fact, add to their coziness as they sat about the fireplace and talked. How welcome some of Isles' good talk would be! She went about her preparations for company, but the sparkle was gone from her anticipation as it was gone from the day. As she laid the middle-room fire, chill little drafts crept along the floor, and the wind began to howl in the chimney. The chill of the disused room struck through her gown, for she dressed in keeping with the morning's mildness. She hurried to the kitchen and its warm stove.

The short winter daylight was perishing in the storm and the kitchen was dim. The wood-box behind the stove was almost empty. She leaned well over it and began to straighten with the last small sticks in her hands. She had not seen Waitstill in the dark shadow between the stairway and the stove-back, nor had his usual tumultuous breathing warned her. The movement of his big body was as if the wall pushed forward. Before she could move, his arm went around her waist and his fumbling hand cupped her breast. His unclean bearded face drew down beside hers, "Little Adree," he mouthed.

I mustn't faint. She bit her lip hard and the darkness receded. *It was a mistake to remind him of the old days.* Her body reacted instinctively. She flung herself back and away, and felt the stove's heat strike through her clothes. Waitstill cried out, an animal cry of pain, and withdrew his arm. He began licking at his bare wrist, where a red welt was appearing, and Adria realized it must have been pressed against the hot stove. He stumbled, muttering, into the yard, leaving the door wide behind him.

As she closed it, soft white blots of snow struck and clung to her dress, but she scarcely noticed. Her legs had no substance in them, she could only cling to the door frame, fighting nausea. No fear or dread she had ever known compared to what now washed across her. Drops of moisture formed on her upper lip. "Father in Heaven," she whispered, "Not that. Not what I read behind those brute eyes. And send Dave home soon. Soon." Terror rose even to her mouth, so that she tasted its gall and spat it from her.

The kitchen had darkened and lamplight would be necessary to work by, although it was barely four o'clock. On the warm kitchen windows snow was forming an opaque curtain, but from a cold window overlooking the harbour she might glimpse the arrival of help. Disappointingly, the broad-beamed old *Katie* was nowhere in sight on the few yards of harbour now visible through the snow. For a time she stood staring out, shivering with more than cold. *What shall I do if Waitstill returns to the kitchen while I am still alone? Did the affection he bore me always hide desire? Has it turned now to a loathesome thing in the man's injured mind? How can I defend myself against him? Those huge hands could crush me as easily as they could Mary Ellen.* Fear for her children sent her hurrying back, lest they finish their naps and, wandering sleepily, meet Waitstill instead of their mother.

The kitchen was still empty. As she moved past the sideboard, she saw the row of knives that ran in a leathern strip across the cupboard's end. *I'll keep near the knives. Perhaps if he comes at me I might be able to snatch one and stop him.* (Afterward she told herself she had meant merely to threaten him with it, to turn his mind as the burn had done.) *But suppose he finds me at the woodbox again?* She must keep the fire against the increasing cold. She reached and took a sharp fish-knife from its band and, in a daze of unreality, walked with it to the wood-box. She thrust it down between wall and box, hidden but within reach as she tended the stove. Later, she wondered how she had ever hoped to defend herself against the strength of the deranged Waitstill, and realized how narrow was the chance that he would move against her within reach of it. But at the time, as she filled the box from the cooper-shop's emergency pile, it was comforting to put out her hand and touch the knife-handle.

The children wakened and she prepared their bowls of bread and milk, and gave them some of the Christmas cookies; it scarcely seemed worthwhile to save their spiciness, Christmas had receded into such an impossible distance. The wind mounted and the snow thickened. Dave would not be home tonight. She fought down panic and, with hope dead, found courage. *I've known for several hours, really, that I must face tonight alone.*

When Waitstill finally appeared, she set his place at the table-end, near the mellow light of the lamp, and he ate heartily while the kitchen ell moaned and creaked in protest at the stiffening wind. He had apparently forgotten even the burn upon his wrist. When he pushed back his chair, she approached him and, swallowing hard on her fear and abhorrence, said in a stern flat voice, "Here are the matches. Go light the lamps. Be careful—be more than careful—tonight. Suppose a vessel should be seeking harbour from the storm. Think of the poor men aboard. Do take care. Then come back to the kitchen. So I will know all is well. Do you hear, Waitstill? Come right back to the house."

He gave no sign of understanding, but he took the matches she laid before him and, disregarding her order to put a heavy coat over his ragged clothes, strode out into the storm.

Adria had not dared mention to him the again empty woodbox. She dressed in a thick "storm skirt", heavy boots and her hooded boat-cloak. She filled the box from the sheltered side of the yard pile, and then brought more wood and put it under the stair-jog, for the wind would suck much fuel up the pipe on such a night, and she meant to tend the fire till morning. The wind was increasing and tightening with cold; the soft flakes had been replaced by a fine hard powder that rasped across the windows, but the short struggles from woodpile to door offered relief from the house's tense fears, and some of Adria's childish response rose to the storm's challenge. Once the last armload was in, she took off her heavy clothes, drew Damie's rocker next the stove and took her children upon her lap.

Then, reluctant as she was to face his return, Waitstill's continued absence began to worry her. It was his habit to betake himself early to his rough bed above the cooper-shop, sleeping all through the long winter darkness. She prayed habit would hold against the restlessness now filling the huge body and tormenting the numbed brain. If so, her mind nagged, he should have returned from the lighthouse long ago.

I must make sure the lamps are lit. That MUST be done. Suppose Waitstill returned while she was out. Suppose Mary Ellen again aroused his malignant temper. How could she bear to leave her children, and on such a night? They were not yet sleepy enough to be trusted to stay in bed. She put them down gently and found them toys. She went to Damie's window and peered out, hoping to glimpse a reassuring red gleam but she could see only swirling snow. She turned to the bed. "Grammy," she pleaded, "I need your help. I sent Waitstill to light up, but he hasn't come back. I'll *have* to go to the lighthouse—at least get near enough to make sure the lamps are lit. Could you dress and come out to mind the children?"

"Don't see why not," Damie answered, struggling up from the depths of her feather-bed. "Truth t'tell, my aches is slackened off since the storm struck. Pass me my cane."

When she had seen her grandmother installed in her rocker, Adria dressed again for the storm and lit the ship's lantern that hung beside the door. "Grammy," she said, "if Waitstill comes tell him Adree wants to see him at the lighthouse." *Better me alone with him in the wild night than him here with the children.* "But don't argue with him. He might be in an ugly mood." She looked around the kitchen. *Dear God, these helpless ones are in Thy hands.* Though she ached to kiss the children she knew she must not distress them by emphasizing her departure — already Jonathan's puckered lower lip betrayed his apprehensions. "Mind Grammy, dears," she told them, "until Mamma comes back," and stepped out into the whirling snow.

TWENTY-FIVE

THE storm had worsened immeasurably since her last foray to the woodpile. Adria stood for a moment in the broken shelter offered by the house, while beyond her the wind fled, whimpering like some questing beast, down the length of the point and out across the storm-hidden bay; yet, even as it fled, it turned back upon her in angry gusts, screaming and snarling and leaping at her clothes. When she stepped out on the open path to the lighthouse, the wind struck her fully. It whipped her skirts, snatched her cloak, licked at the lantern, whirled snow into her face as if to stop her breath, and pushed her sidewise in cruel rough sport. Though snow was piling in the lee of the larger rocks, the path along the point's flat crest was blown clear. She spread her cloak to protect the smoking lantern and swung the light to this side and that, peering to see if Waitstill had lost his footing on the snow-coated grass, and was lying helpless; but the blinding flakes limited her view to a few feet. Once she imagined she saw him lurching out of the darkness before her and she stopped, relief sweeping aside her fear of him. It proved merely a trick of the driving snow and it left her weakened and dismayed for an instant.

She was nearing the narrow end of the point and spray mingled with the snow on her lips; during momentary lifts in the squalls she could see vicious white cockscombs on the nearest running chop. Every few steps she turned her back to the wind and caught her breath to send a strong call out across the sibilant snowy gusts. Nothing came back to her but the wind's derisive howl until, under its mocking, she made out the deeper tones of the surf along the outer reefs. The wind, coming off the land, had raised no billows; this was a soft voice, grieving hopelessly for her trouble and for all disasters cloaked by such nights as this. It reminded her that storm-clutched ships might be depending upon Redmond's beacon to make harbour. She forgot her snow-weighted, clogging skirts and hastened towards the lighthouse.

She was almost upon it before she discerned the red glow behind the snow-clotted windward panes. The seaward windows proved comparatively clear. "Thank God," she said, and drew a calmer breath. Since the lamps were lit, Waitstill must have been to the lighthouse. Had he heard a vessel and gone to ring the warning bell? She moved to the back of the tower, but the bell hung snow-muffled.

Some sense assured her the lighthouse was empty but, since she had come so far, she decided to make sure all was well inside. She fought the door open and squeezed through before it swung shut with a force which shook the plank flooring. There was no one in the lower room, where her rapid breathing left clouds of steam, faintly golden in the lantern-light. The tower hummed and creaked in the wind and the cold. She sat her lantern down, laid her snow-thickened mittens beside it and began to mount the narrow open steps, while above her gusts blasted against the upper tower and sucked air away through the lighthouse ventilator, lifting and dropping the metal trap-door with vicious bangs and clatters. Her hand met a sticky spot that left a dark stain. Two steps above, her fingers found another. She suspected before she lifted the trap-door and thrust her hand upward into the lamps' glow, that what she had felt was blood. *I knew Waitstill was hurt.*

The small upper room was as empty as the one below, but its five lamps burned brightly and evenly while the air felt warm upon her face and the chimneys were hot to the touch. *The lamps have been burning for some little time.* She lifted a lamp from its trough and scanned the floor, but found no bloodstains. *He was not harmed when he trimmed and lit the lamps. It was when he started down the steps that an angry gust sent the heavy door crashing upon him. I hope it caught his hand, not his head. But where is he? Why didn't he come to the kitchen with his hurt?*

She carefully lowered the door as she descended, and before she took each downward step she swung her sodden skirts clear, lest they trip her and leave her helpless at the foot of the stairs. Safe on the floor she hastened to retie her muffler and adjust her hood, then forced her hands into her cold mittens and picked up the lantern. When she had succeeded in pushing open the heavy door, the wind leaped in at her with a long harrowing shriek of triumph as if it had feared she might have eluded it by seeking refuge. It flattened the lantern flame to the point of extinction and she swung about, sheltering the wick until it flickered into life again. Shielding its precious light with her body and cloak, she stepped out and gave the door to the slamming hands of the storm, then fastened the latch. Each movement must be planned and slowly executed against the bewildering, nullifying beating of the wind. She bent and searched for footprints or drops of blood, but a drift was building against the tower and hiding the ground, while sharp-edged crystals whirled up into her eyes, blinding her and forcing her to narrow her lids to the merest slits.

Now that she faced towards home the pitiless wind drove full against her, lifting her hood, chilling her teeth to aching as she bared them in an effort to grasp each smarting breath. She bent forward and struggled on. When she turned to get her direction from the lighthouse beam, it was already lost. But the clamour of the sea on either hand (angry on the harbour and windward side, mournful from the outer shore) would guide her. Occasionally she recognized a rock, either as one that bordered the path and proved she was going straight, or as one that showed she had wandered. Her digressions increased the few hundred yards she must cover and as she had done earlier, she stopped frequently and turned to gain a snow-free breath and to call down the wind, "Wai-ai-ait-s'l!" But her voice fell dully to the ground a few feet from where she stood, or was snatched away on a shapeless roar. She expected, and heard, no answering hail, but more than once she lifted her lantern, because some shapeless rock resembled a sitting or recumbent figure.

The wind was no longer a single howling beast. The night had been taken over by a pack, which ranged and warred across the fields and shores, whooping or groaning, exulting or shrieking in agony as they were in turn hunter and hunted, victor or victim. A vortex of screaming wind and whirling snow perpetually encircled her, though she struggled to break through it. Yet she had gone but a few feet from the tower when she was conscious that her strong young body was responding adequately to the demands upon it. The first chill of apprehension, as much as of cold, gave way to a glorious pounding warmth. She turned her face and hunched it upon her shoulder and found she was breathing easily. She no longer drove herself in frantic search, nor in fear lest the light fail some trusting ship. She stopped, content to hold her ground, when the most vicious squalls struck, and moved forward when they were past. Dragging her skirts through the deepening snow she headed towards the house, although she no longer attempted to keep to the path.

She almost stumbled over a whitening mound. For a long second she stood staring downward, unable to believe that here at her feet was what she had sought. The mound moved and groaned. She stepped towards the sound and saw Waitstill lying with his back to the wind, his legs drawn up and one huge arm flung across his head at a familiar, protective angle. She set her lantern down and reached stiffly to lift the arm. "Waitstill," she pleaded, "Waitstill." Only compassion and fear for his safety was in her hoarse whisper; her repugnance and recent terror were completely erased.

The arm yielded without bending and the eyes opened to look vaguely into her face. Across the brow and down the lower cheek were black streaks like yarn ravellings. Blood. The falling door had struck his head. "Let me help you up." Kneeling, she pulled at the rigid body.

"I hurt my head. I fell," he moaned. His eyes focused upon her face. "Adree," he said in happy wonder. "Then, "Don't tug. I'm down fer good."

She couldn't accept this truth. She attempted once more to move him, but succeeded only in getting his head upon her lap and making a windbreak of her body. "Try to get on your feet. I can help you to the house. Only try. It's so cold here in the wind."

"Warm," he murmured and closed his eyes. He opened them and said, "Little Adree," and "White Wings."

"Get up and come with me now. We'll still go sailing on the *White Wings*," she promised desperately. Her tears were scalding on her icy cheeks and her heart was bursting with pity. His body was heavier than any log; she could not budge it. He still breathed but his eyes had closed under snowed lashes and the flakes did not melt as they met his face. She bent still closer to shield him and felt herself yielding to drowsiness. Numbness had replaced the aching cold. She no longer heard the howling wind nor the hard, short battering of the seas along the nearby shore. She had found Waitstill; effort was no longer required of her. She could rest.

It was an imagined echo of her children's voices which brought her awake. She struggled painfully to her feet. Waitstill's head lay motionless after it rolled from her lap. He did not answer or open his eyes to her last despairing cries. She could not move his heavy arm to shelter his head again. "I'll come back," she promised him, though she knew he could not hear. Foolishly, she somehow got out of her cloak and muffled it about his head and shoulder, weighing one edge securely with the outflung arm. She could not bend her hand to grasp the lantern-bail, so she left the flickering light, but she heard the wind catch and roll the metal frame along a bare stretch as she turned her reluctant, shivering body into the unbroken wind. "It's only a few yards to the house now," she gasped, mistakenly judging the distance covered.

Her face ached, for the slanting lines of snow seemed solid as glass slivers. The wind burned her throat as it choked her. There was now no rush of warm blood to strengthen her; the cold penetrated to her very marrow. She stumbled forward, though she must stop every few steps and turn into the wind again, for only by facing its worst could she reach the house. She pitched forward and caught herself, fell and floundered through a drift and regained her feet. Found herself against the solid earth of the front terrace. Knew the front door when she fell against it, and knocked up the latch with her feelingless hands. Got the door open. And shut. Clumped her way along the walls with legs like cordwood, with the snow-balls on her skirt hems impeding every step. So many doors. Such contrary-minded latches. Excruciating sensation was returning to portions of her shivering body. When the kitchen door yielded she almost fell against the wall of warm air that rose before her.

But there, her smarting eyes reassured her, were Mary Ellen and Jonathan. Safe. And Grammy, sitting with petticoats hoisted to feel the fire's full benefit on her little broomstick legs.

At sight of Adria, Damie strove to rise. "I took ye fer a ghost," she said accusingly. Her voice assumed authority. "Don't come nigh the fire. The's cold water at the sink. Get yer face an' hands into it. Quick as ye can. And yer feet." She found a basin, hobbled to the sink and filled it, helped to strip off the sodden, snow-encrusted boots and stockings. She sent Mary Ellen scurrying to find shawls and comforters and she piled them layers deep upon Adria's shoulders and knees. She filled a cup with hot tea and forced it, scalding hot, upon Adria, then followed it by a second and a third. The children watched the urgent ministrations, frightened beyond whimpers or questions.

"An' Waits'l?" Damie finally asked, with a glance at the white window and an ear to the wind, which had long since reached a monotonous intensity.

Drearily, acknowledging defeat, Adria answered in her grandmother's own phraseology, "He is in Eternity."

By morning the storm had moved on, leaving drifts that ridged the island and shone whitely from the mainland. Adria, dozing in Damie's rocker before the stove, came wide awake at the first light. She rose to feed the fire and every bone and muscle in her body protested. She hovered about the stove, shaking and weak from the night's ordeal, and tried to force her mind to consider this new day's demands: the cattle that needed feed and milking; the lighthouse lamps which, if not extinguished, would sputter and smoke as their oil supply dwindled; and what lay under the snow along the lighthouse path. Wearily she put the porridge and bacon to cook and opened the door to fling out the tea-leaves, indifferent to their stain upon a pristine drift. The worn-out wind was dying and sunshine webbed the harbour but she hastily closed the door and huddled against the stove, as if a frozen core within her would never melt. Damie and the children slept late. When she had given them breakfast, she sat close to the heat and drank a cup of tea.

Two figures passed the window. Dave, at last! And — her heart leaped at the impossible hope — Waitstill! She ran to the door and flung it open. For an instant she stood in stupid amazement. "Isles," she said. "I'd forgotten. You were coming to spend Christmas." *Christmas!* Isles was staring at her bedraggled gown and dishevelled hair; she had been too exhausted to think of her appearance. She didn't care. She flung herself against him, sobbing. She was unconsious of Little Obie's avid eyes.

"Now, now," Isles soothed her. "What's all this?" His blue eyes checked the children at play and Gramma Damie in her chair. "Where's Waitstill?"

She shuddered. "That's it. Waitstill. He's dead. He must be. And I hid a knife." She gestured in self-accusation towards the wood-box. "Against Waitstill. How could I? But I didn't mean to use it."

Isles spoke sharply. "Tell me where he is."

Last night's exertions had left Damie dazed. "Lost," she quavered from her rocker beside the stove, "Never sighted after leavin' port."

Adria understood that her own words were making little more sense. She drew away from Isles' arm and spoke calmly, "Come in to the fire, Isles, and Mr. Knowles." She found them chairs and seated herself. "I left Waitstill lying in the snow beside the path." Clasping her hands until the knuckles stood out white, she told them of her search and its conclusion. Aware now of Obie's presence, she made no mention of Waitstill's frightening behaviour throughout the day, nor of her terrified attempt to arm herself against him, and Obie, awaiting explanation of the knife, remembered later that she had omitted it from her considered account. She stopped to welcome Rhuanna's Vol, who entered the kitchen hesitantly and stood listening in an embarrassment of sympathy as she went on to tell how she had put her cloak about Waitstill in a vain effort to shield him from the storm ("I thought I could go back to him with more covers, once I got warm"), and of how she had fought her way to the house and the waiting ones there. "I couldn't face the night and storm again." Her tortured eyes pleaded for understanding of her weakness and cowardice. "But I kept the fire and all night I listened. Waitstill was always so strong, you know, and never minded the cold. You remember, Isles," she appealed to him, "how he always went with coat and shirt-neck open all winter."

Isles nodded, watching her exhausted face.

"I'd think I heard his step, thumping and uneven as it's been of late, but it always turned out to be a loose board rattling somewhere, or the taunting wind. When morning came I gave up the last hope. But I couldn't force myself to go look. I couldn't. I said, 'I'll let Waitstill sleep on, under his soft white blanket, in a peace and comfort he has not had since his illness.' And I knew," her voice caught, "I knew I couldn't move him. I couldn't last night."

Isles was gravely consoling. "There would have been no point in your going to Waitstill this morning — or again last night. He must have been beyond your help when you found him." *But*

Dave and I, strong men . . . He explained that he had been ready to set out for New Erin before the storm struck, but he had waited for Dave, who didn't come. "He borrowed Sally to go see his mother, but he expected to be back early. I don't know what delayed him. Obie had been to Barrington, was caught in the storm and stopped at our house overnight, but by the time he got to Prince's Cove the weather was too bad for us to attempt a crossing. This morning Vol and Obie and I started at daybreak. It was a long hard row." He rose and stood gazing down at Adria, and it was a wonder that Obie did not read more than friendliness and compassion in his look. "We'll go," he said, "and see what must be done."

He saw her flinch and his tone brought her eyes up to meet his. "You are overtired and distraught. With great cause. But believe that death came as a friend to Waitstill, that it was kinder than life has been this past while. We'll remember him, Adria, as he was in those days when he adored you, and barked at me like a watchdog whenever I came near you. We'll remember the young Waitstill, strong and willing in the service of the Redmonds, and thank God that the injured mind will now be healed." He laid his hand upon her shoulder, fighting back the wish to take her into his arms again and comfort her, and careful lest his touch disclose the strength of that desire.

Isles followed Obie out into the bright sunshine, but he turned at the corner and came back to the door. "I'll come, if possible, for the children's Christmas." Following his gaze she saw that he had managed to deposit, unnoticed, several packages on the table. "But I'm the one to go to Barrington for the Coroner, if what we fear is so. Dave will stay with his family."

Yes, blast him. Isles savagely kicked his way through the snow, remembering yesterday's agonized hours as he waited for his cousin to appear, while the sky lowered and the storm neared, diminishing with every minute the chances to reach New Erin. Remembering the long night when every squall pounded home to his heart the threat it posed for the women and children alone with the unpredictable Waitstill. Wherever Dave had been, he would have a plausible excuse for his delay; to all appearances he would be suitably grieved over Waitstill's fate. *And no one will blame him. No one but me.* He noticed the scowl with which Obie watched for the sloop's belated return. *And, perhaps, Airy Bellah's grandfather.*

TWENTY-SIX

STRANGE how many lives have been shaped by a shift in the wind, or sunshine when rain was needed.

If the Cove men could have busied themselves in the woods as usual, chopping and hauling in the frosty, balsam-scented air (that clears away suspicions and envy as it cleanses lungs and blood); if the women had not grown irritable and fault-seeking from having their men and children so much indoors and underfoot; then Adria might still have made an endurable life, out of her love for the children and New Erin. But the winter stayed wet and mild. There was soft snow in abundance but it lacked the frozen bottom necessary for hauling so that idle oxen ate their heads off in the barns while fuel piles dwindled with no promise of replenishment, and trees stood untouched in the woodlots.

The impassably muddy roads prevented inter-village visiting. Discontented men congregated about the fish-sheds' rusty, potbellied little stoves where Waitstill's death and the attendant circumstances made ideal subjects for lazy minds and eager tongues. When the known facts and probable conjectures had been exhausted, there were comparisons to be made with similar —and dissimilar—tragedies. Mention of Waitstill led to reminiscences of Joe Twiddle (his briefly known father), to Nabby Nolan's witchery and to grandfathers' tales of the mysterious Gypsy Bess. Consciences, twinging from badgerings of the slow-witted Waitstill, or from neglect of an injured shipmate, eagerly embraced mankind's long and sinister tendency to seek a scapegoat.

Nabby Nolan would not serve this time since, as Waitstill's mother, she was now an object of conventional sympathy.

Although Dave had been welcomed to the Cove with unusual cordiality, it was natural to be dubious and suspicious of anyone who had come from "away," and who was not part of the interlaced village relationships. Several times censure sailed close to Captain Malone, but yawed off. Although Waitstill's behaviour that afternoon in Sydney remained a puzzle, everyone still conceded that the captain could not have stayed his blow. And what wrong could be seen in a man visiting his old mother at Christmas time? Though Captain Malone might have been lax in watching weather signs, or he could have been back on New Erin ahead of the blizzard. Who could denounce too vehemently a man who publicly condemned himself, or who could doubt a man of the captain's reputation when he swore that, had he suspected trouble on the island, he would have borrowed a dory and rowed home that night — or gone down in the attempt?

Those few who had attended Waitstill's burial in the New Erin graveyard agreed that Captain Malone's deportment on that occasion had been proper and touching. He had referred to a captain's feeling for one of his "hands," and recalled Waitstill's devotion to him. And during Mr. Stouten's assurances of resurrection, Captain Malone had been seen to raise his handkerchief to his eyes.

But Mrs. Malone, now. Hard to tell what *she* might have been feeling. Standing stiff and white-faced, apart from her husband, with an unseeing look in her eyes. She had pulled her black cloak about her, but she had wiped away no tears though, when you came to think of it, Waitstill had been more to the Redmonds through the years than ever he was to Captain Malone. And to the Nickersons before Dan Redmond set foot upon this shore. The Nickersons of Grannie's Head, when you went back to Waitstill's Ma and Grammy, had been some to blame for them, in the first place, with their pampering of foreigners. Then Mrs. Malone's Ma, Mercy Nickerson, had gone and married another foreigner, and a Catholic into the bargain. Dan Redmond's fine airs and his "dry hands," his love of books and learning, his smuggling and his faith were all raised against his memory, and none among the various groups was man enough to remind his fellows of the good wages paid at Redmond's, of the generous contributions to every good local cause, of the lighthouse (built and supplied out of his own pocket) that had served them, nor of the piled plate and the warm bed awaiting any wayfarer whose craft made Redmond's Harbour.

From the Nickerson shortcomings, through Dan Redmond's, to Adria Malone's, was a short and logical path. It was often trod. Some shame or wariness kept men from gossiping in front of Isles Kendrick. He had always been the Redmonds' friend and was a cousin of Captain Malone's; there would be family feeling. They knew what he had said about Waitstill's end, in his quiet way that had great certainty about it, "Waitstill is gone, and better so. For his sake be kinder to the next poor devil who needs kindness. And show your sympathy for the living." However, it was more cossetting to recall the failings of others than to probe for your own. And who could give Nabby a load of wood when noan was being hauled? As for provisions, they were scant enough for the family, in most homes. Let Isles Kendrick send his coal and his bags of stuff as he had been doing — hadn't he a shopful? And, like enough, considering the emotion he had shown at the funeral, Dave Malone would be sending vegetables from the New Erin bins and meat from his pork and beef barrels.

They would have disbelieved Adria if she could have told them of Dave's unequivocal refusal to deliver the food she had packed for Nabby, and of his declaration that such a gesture would mark him as guilty in some way. This made no sense to Adria, but she no longer attempted to understand Dave. After Christmas he had moved into Kiah's room off the kitchen, saying that it was handier, but meaning that he no longer wanted his place beside her. This, though his sojourns on the main had ceased with Waitstill's death.

Unfortunately, Priscilla, with her sweet sanity and her tolerance (gained in the years of sea horizons, of foreign ports and ways of life beyond the Cove), and her ability to bring out the best in people, was in Boston. In her presence the Sewing Circle would not have listened greedily to the teacher, whose tongue kept time to the needle in her slim white fingers.

Even in a community that subscribed wholeheartedly to the virtue of the rod and its application, Miss Newhall's disciplinary measures were considered by many to be unduly severe, but her penmanship was a model, her deportment most ladylike, her vocabulary (to the ears of Cove housewives) impressive. As she grew convinced that the Redmonds did not intend to divulge her secret, she became increasingly bold in her attacks against them. She described, with a wealth of detail, the lawless smuggling, the drinking and general godlessness in the New Erin household and people were astounded to learn all that had been going on, unsuspected, right under their noses. Yet when Miss Newhall first confessed the sacrifice of her life's love on the altar of religion, some members of the Sewing Circle, remembering handsome young Will Redmond, may have hidden smiles as they bent above the quilting-frames. Thankful laid the thwarting of her love upon Adria. "We might have won out, Will and I, but she was so spitefully set that she turned the others against us. They were half afraid of her, I do believe, for she always had a wicked temper. And she hated me from the first time I was forced to punish her in the schoolroom."

Mrs. Stouten, a plain little body of ineffectual bustlings, was puzzled and intimidated most of the time — when not by her strong-minded husband and his lively children, then by his forbidable parishioners. Nevertheless, she interposed, "But is Mrs. Malone a Catholic? She often came to Meeting with her grandparents. Such a pretty little thing, she was too! And when she and her husband lived in the Cove . . ."

With a glance, Thankful asked the others to scorn the gullibility of the minster's wife. "Yes, indeed," she conceded. "Poor Captain Malone. He saw that she went to Meeting when he was home." She knotted her thread and pulled it into place. "But what did she do the minute he was at sea? Hurried back to her own kind. And all the good of Mr. Stouten's sermons undone in a twinkling."

There was a murmur of agreement. For some reason Mrs. Malone had been over-anxious to leave the Cove.

"No," Miss Newhall continued, "Will must become a homeless wanderer for love's sake. But when Charlie wanted to marry that pert little French girl — oh, that was fine!"

Religion apart, people began to wonder if Adria Malone was as Miss Newhall pictured her. Would she hesitate at nothing, if crossed? Would she drive a poor idiot out into such a blizzard as had raged that December night? Ill-fed and ill-clad. It was not surprising that Thankful Newhall should have broadcast such seeds, but that they should have found such welcoming soil. Not that real hatred was needed at first; merely a sprinkling of envy, a pinch of suspicion or malice served as nutriment.

By cruel mischance Mr. Stouten, as yet oblivious to the

buzzing talk, chose to preach a sermon on the Reformation. It was particularly well received, he felt. For some time he was ignorant that the trouble-brewers in his congregation had seized upon it as proof that the minister was on their side, and that they had gone home strengthened in their intolerance.

On his rare visits to the Cove, Dave Malone found his erstwhile admirers disturbingly cool, their faces set, their glances sliding. Some stepped silently aside at his approach, or passed with a muttered "Cap'n," the minimum acknowledgment to his hearty greeting. He did not understand that this was merely treatment due a member of the Redmond family, and suspected some deeper reason. It was unbearable that he be an outcast; he began a course of self-justification. He knew Adria's reputation for aloofness and the feeling that the village was slighted by her choice of New Erin while the little home in Prince's Cove stood empty. He declared his preference and added, "A man don't feel just as comfortable in his wife's home." Seamen asserted that Cap'n Malone ashore meant the waste of a good skipper, and Dave implied that he stayed to pacify his wife. He dropped hints, obscure hints, but his listeners, seeking to fathom them, came up with the explanation he had intended—that some wives drive their men into the arms of other women. Some of his listeners had reasons of their own for accepting and forwarding this excuse and Dave soon felt a thawing in the general attitude towards him. To his relief, apparently no one attached any blame to him for his absence at the time of Waitstill's death, nor for the crippled condition that had led to it; instead many people commented on the irony that Captain Malone's kindheartedness towards Waitstill had brought about the poor fellow's death. He never suggested that his wife had ill-used the helper but, "She jawed me well for bringing the likes o' Waits'l home! And I guess I deserved it, for after all I only meant to be helpful," Dave confided with an engaging ruefulness. Those simple souls who formed convictions without due knowledge or consideration of facts, began to tell their wives that Cap'n Malone hadn't been his old laughing self at all since that Christmas blizzard. Did he know more than he let on about that night's doings? He wouldn't be one to tell on his wife, but something was gnawing on his mind. As for Mrs. Malone, she acted more secret and standoffish than ever; not much like her friendly husband.

There might have been no suspicion of physical injury if

Little Obie had not brought forth his story of Adria having once threatened him with a knife, and added an account of her hysterical words in the New Erin kitchen. "I sh'd like t'know," he would declare, shaking his head in heavy bewilderment, "What was all that talk about a *knife*. 'Bout the fust thing Mis' Malone said was how she never *meant* t'use it. Oh, she shut up like a clam when she seen I was harkin'. But her words has stuck in my crop ever since. And I'll tell ye why. If she took a knife t'Waits'l, *he wasn't the fust one!*" This always caused a satisfactory alertness. ("That makes 'em sit up an' take notice" was the way Obie put it to himself). Even those who had heard the incident related many times could not help but listen as Obie told of his narrow escape. "I'd jest called t'pass the time o' day." Not even to heighten his story could Obie bring himself to divulge his errand, nor the helpless shame that had driven him to Adria as a last resort.

"I told Cynthie about it when I got home, and' she'll bear me out. I said, 'Ain't many I'm afeared of, ye must omit. Let alone wimmin. But when I seen that knife aflashin', I high-tailed it out o' thyah.' Cynthie agreed I done right. 'In sech a temper she'd 'a' been l'ble t'slit yer gullet,' my wife told me." The truth was Obie had gone home combatting failure and frustration, and had given a colourful account to diminish Cynthie's scorn at his inability to redress Airy Bellah's wrongs. By now he had forgotten which were facts and which fancies.

He was glad that with the new topic of Waitstill's death the scandal about Airy Bellah seemed forgotten. Not that he agreed with Cynthie that the flurry against Adria excused her husband. In fact he sometimes reminded her, "Mis' Malone mightn't be as much t'blame as some folks think. An' two wrongs . . ." Then the bitterness on Cynthie's lips, the scorn through the steel-rimmed glasses, the bewilderment and ache for Airy Bellah in his heart.

Despite Obie's tales, those who had served on the coroner's jury could not persuade themselves, or be persuaded, that they had seen a knife wound. Ah! But there had been a bruise at the back of the head. And frozen blood on the snow. Imagination and a now crystallizing purpose could do much with those facts.

Before the growing rumours had reached disturbing proportions Isles had left on the *Dauntless* for New England ports.

The Cove's charitable minority could offer no concrete denials to any of the suspicions now rampant; a few worried that Mrs. Malone herself might be unable to disprove the accusations, innocent though they believed her, for she alone really knew what had happened that night.

Rhuanna and her Vol were Adria's loyal champions. But Vol, with Isles absent, could not set his opinions against the groups about the shop stove. Deeply troubled, he gave his mother a summary of one evening's conversations. "They say that when Mrs. Malone lived in the Cove she used t'chase people out of her house, wavin' a long knife and threatenin' t'slit their gullets. Maw, she never chased me. I never even seen her with a long knife."

"Ner me," his mother said with tight, scandalized lips.

"Fishermen say Waits'l's ghost ha'nts the lighthouse, moanin' an' going on that it can't rest. But it don't say *why* it can't. Some thinks it's because he's buried on the hill amongst them old graves instead of in the Cove churchyard. They claim there must 'a' been a reason for putting him there."

"Well, I heared that his own mother wanted him buried on the island. I declare ye can't believe a word ye hear, 'cause no two are alike!" Rhuanna was easily muddled, but Vol was staunch and she would back his opinions. Besides, when she gave thought to them, the tales now flying didn't fit the Adria who had shared the long vigils at Mis' Kendrick's bedside with patience and pleasant competence, and who had proved a warm and friendly companion, once Rhuanna had come to know her. The women to whom she ventured this observation would not consider it, and Rhuanna could not recognize as universal their manifestation of resentment at those who do not conform to a local pattern. Like their men, these women could be extremely kind in response to a demand from one of their own, or from a stranger in physical distress; perhaps always kind when the need was understood. But they could be cruel to a plight beyond their comprehension and in cruelty, as in kindness, they were swept by mass emotion.

Mr. Stouten, by now aware of the rising tide of slander, set himself across it. He chose a text with care. "James 3: 8," he announced from the pulpit next Lord's Day morning. "But the tongue can no man tame; it is an unruly evil, full of deadly poison." A masterly sermon was beyond Mr. Stouten, but he gave a heartfelt reprimand to the men and women he had served for many years, and whom he had thought he knew; he expressed a true desire to lead them from further wrongs wrought by the tongue and, if possible, to right the harm already done. If he himself had no great gift of words, he knew the words of the Book before him. He used them humbly but he made their weight felt. "My brethren," he pleaded as he closed, "these things ought not so to be." His congregation stirred restlessly; its members did not take kindly to a sermon that hit so many of them. To those who recalled an earlier one, this sounded like treason to their cause. So far as the minister could judge, he succeeded only in turning his flock against him for, during the next weeks, pews emptied on the Sabbath, and greetings were chilly on week days. But he had spoken the Truth when it was greatly needed.

Following the mild winter, spring was cold and stormy. The men left for American ports and the Banks, but local boats were on the shore long after the usual launching date. Talk grew frenzied, demanding action. Miss Newhall, red tongue active about pale lips, wrote busily; there were always men willing to sign a petition to the Crown Attorney or the Lieutenant-Governor.

Adria had no warning. One minute, at the kitchen window, she was rejoicing that the faint green climbing up the pasture hollows announced the end of a savage March. The next she was reeling back from Dave's words, ". . . showed me an order for the exhumation of Waits'l's body. They've gone to Nigh Hill and the grave now." Dismay that was almost fear whitened his face. "There is talk of foul play."

"Foul play! Do they mean that injury four years ago, on the *Ocean Spray?*" He shook his head. She puzzled aloud, "There was no man but Waitstill on the island that night. No one was outside the house but Waitstill and . . ." The quick aversion of Dave's face stopped her in disbelieving horror.

"Only Waits'l and you." Perhaps the bluntness was kindly meant, to let her know the worst at once—where the order for exhumation might lead.

Adria was sure this was another bad dream like those which had haunted her all winter. Dave's perturbation lessened as he saw hers. "There has been dissatisfaction, the men tell me, about the Coroner's inquest, and a great deal of talk."

Straightening from the oven, Serena spoke. "Talk! A big plenty of it. And I can tell ye who's behind it. Thankie New'l, that's who." She poked the fire viciously. Serena had returned a fortnight before and resumed her reign over the New Erin stove. She said now, unhappily, "I done what I figgered was my duty, an' Bartlett appreciated it, but could I 'a' foreseen all, I'd never 'a' left ye."

It was a foggy May evening when Captain Stoddart brought the *Dauntless* into Prince's Cove.

In Ryder's shop the circle was comfortably established about the small fire when Isles came striding in. Heads turned at his entry, but only Little Obie's tongue was unabashed by the glower on the proprietor's face. "Well, Mistah Isles, an' how does it feel t' be back in Prince's Cove after furrin travels?" With smug assurance that of all places this was the most desirable, Obie patted his knee playfully and prepared to enjoy Isles' eulogy on homecoming.

Isles accompanied his words with a savage short blow on the counter. "It feels hellish!" The explosion unbent backs and stopped whittling hands. The men had learned that the usually quiet-spoken Isles could, on occasion, find a devasting invective that rang with novelty's impact even on ears familiar with more than one mate's free-swinging vocabulary. But now he added only, "I wish I'd never set foot in the place." Which was startling enough when the meaning and the tone sank in.

Obie's feelings were hurt at having his greeting flung back at him in this fashion. "I thought ye said ye was allus glad t'git back."

"I always *was*!" Isles tossed his hat towards a hook. "I used to think of the Cove as a sort of haven! In the cities I'd see men putting over smart deals, not caring if they ruined friends; fish-dealers and vessel owners sending men out in schooners well-insured but ready to open up in the first heavy sea; employers hiring women and children to work in their factories for just so much as would keep them working, not a penny more. I would think of the Cove. I would remember the friendliness shown me and my mother on many occasions, the honesty I'd found in most of its citizens, the steadfast faith in the church-goers, the helping hands when sickness and reverses struck among you. And I'd say to myself, 'We do things differently in Prince's Cove. We're better men and kinder neighbours.'" His mocking laugh made them stir uneasily, but the faces turned to him were puzzled by the hot and bitter words.

"I was thinking all that as we beat into the Cove." Isles' mouth twisted. "And what do I learn as I set foot ashore? Why, that these fine men, these kind neighbours, have turned against a woman like a school of dogfish." Few created things were more ravenous, or more despised by the fishermen, than the small sharks he named. He turned to Obie, "Somebody is going to throttle you yet for your talebearing! There was a fish and a knife on Mrs. Malone's sideboard, I recall, that day when my mother and I brought her the word of her father's drowning. I don't know what's behind your yarn but I do know that, no matter what else the Cove is, it's no place for any man who sees a threat in a woman cleaning a fish." A snigger or two met this, but Isles wanted no laughter.

"And the rest of you! Listening to Obie's guff! And to Thankful Newhall. Sucking up the drip off a tongue well honed on wormwood, ever since Will Redmond left her. Religion and cruel parents, my eye! I'm telling you the truth I got from Will. He ran away because his parents were going to *make* him marry her after he'd had her under his feet for years. Tolerant, mistaken fool that I was, I didn't speak out against this woman coming here as teacher. Because I believed in forgetting past mistakes. But she has done more harm with her lying tongue than she could ever do with her body."

Someone in the group sputtered in defence of the teacher. Isles swung to face the voice. "Yes, she seems to have a way of passing on her limited knowledge. But I've not liked the tales of her savage beatings, nor her foolish pampering of the older boys. As a trustee, I meant to see she left this school at the term's end. I never meant to put what I knew of her into words for the village to hash over. But I'm fighting words with words now."

"Poor Waits'l . . ." Sympathy was thick on the name.

"Poor Waitstill," Isles agreed. "But the Waitstill I knew, and liked, died in Sydney Harbour, on the deck of the *Ocean Spray*, not on the lighthouse field of New Erin. I know Dave and his generous gestures—but I say he did wrong ever to take Waitstill into his home. I say he did a greater wrong to leave his wife and children alone with the creature Waitstill had become. Could none of you see God's hand in what happened? Do you think it would have been better for Dave to find, after the blizzard, that the deranged man had slain the old grandmother, the little children and their mother, in a lunatic rage?"

Isles' voice lifted and tensed again, and he smacked his palm with an angry clenched fist. "Each of *you*, and the others like you—tell them all what I think of them—you added your spice to this devil's talk that's been brewing. We know there is evil, jealousy and envy and black depths in every heart. Instead of weeding it out, you've been watering it and feeding it and watching it grow until it has choked out all Christian charity.

"I'm sick, *sick* to think that while I was gone my shop has sheltered such an evil growth. That you sat about my stove . . ." He flung the unfinished sentence from his hands. "It wasn't enough that the coroner told you Waitstill's body bore no evidence of foul play. No, you must talk and guess and write your lying letters—oh, I know what fine hand penned them! You've succeeded in having an innocent woman charged with manslaughter.

"Now, damn you, and your scandalizing tongues, *get out*." He opened the door and stepped aside. "This shop is closed until Mrs. Malone is proved innocent. You can walk to Barrington and Hines' Harbour, where credit is not so free, and I'll laugh to see you trudging!"

As the astounded men filed sullenly past with averted faces, he flung after them, "I leave tomorrow morning to get the best lawyer I can find in Halifax." He slammed the door hard behind the last figure and he paid no heed to the angry mutter of voices from the doorstep.

When Vol stepped in from the office, where he had been listening with shivering appreciation, he found his employer with his head between his hands, staring at the floor. "You did right to tell me, Vol," he said. "But I should have held my anger. It's too late to change their minds and they won't forgive what I've said. They may even turn it against Mrs. Malone. *If they suspect my love and add their interpretation of that. . . . It doesn't matter: Adria's heart is going to be broken in any case.* He lifted his head. "Vol, are you any good at praying? I guess we'd better start."

TWENTY-SEVEN

ON THIS third day of the Barrington June Assize, the courthouse was packed, and the mainroad with the lanes leading from it were lined with carriages and patient, standing horses. No one could remember so large a gathering or such intense interest, but the municipality had never had a case to compare with this of Adria Malone, summoned to appear and answer to a charge of manslaughter. Outside Prince's Cove, the death of a New Erin servant during a December blizzard had evoked only passing interest; but an exhumation, a second inquest, followed by Mrs. Malone's arrest, had spread discussion in ever deepening and widening circles. Mrs. Malone's father, Dan Redmond, was warmly remembered by friends and business associates along the shore, and these unhesitatingly declared her incapable of committing such a crime. Other people were inclined to absorb the distorted rumours and to believe the worst. In the memory of the oldest citizen nothing (save religion and politics) had ever split so many friendships.

The Grand and Petit Juries had been selected and sworn on the first day of the assize. Then the Grand Jury had retired to study the mass of written evidence while Chief Justice Carmichael considered lesser cases. The disappointed spectators had dispersed and few had returned during the second day, while the Grand Jury remained closeted with their task.

This third morning brought a restless audience before the delayed rising curtain. When the doors were opened, spectators filled the space set apart for them, spilled down the courtroom stairs and along the lower hallway. It was a silent, morose gathering, but only a few faces showed vindictiveness or morbidness. Many were awed by what last winter's orgy of words had brought about. Following local tradition, not a woman was present. Scarcely had the court officials taken their places and His Lordship drawn his robe about him, when the drama began. The Grand Jury entered and stood like soldiers at attention while their foreman announced the finding of a true bill of manslaughter against Adria Malone.

Earlier clouds had rolled away and the powerful sun of late June poured down upon the muncipal courthouse. In the poorly ventilated courtroom on the upper floor the air was already warm and vitiated by many lungs, but the spectators ignored or endured discomfort.

Slowly, against a cramping sense of decorum, heads turned as the sheriff entered. Behind him came Mrs. Malone, attended by her lawyer, T. H. Fairfield, Q.C. Mr. Fairfield was rotund and rosy-cheeked above his fine white beard; his affability and fatherly manner almost hid the sharp glint behind the round spectacles. All eyes slid over him, however, and fixed themselves upon the woman accused of gross negligence and manslaughter. They scarcely noted that she was followed by her sister, Mrs. Morris, and by her husband, Captain Malone.

Even those who had heard that Mrs. Malone was good-looking expected to see evil and harsh cruelty plainly limned. They saw a thin young woman of medium height. From her pale face large grey eyes, with bruised shadows about them, looked full into many of those turned upon her; but it was obvious they saw nothing, being concerned with some inner matter. The waves of her hair were drawn back from a wide brow and a small hat topped the high braids which crossed her head. She might have been dressed for Meeting in the plain dove-grey gown with narrow lace at wrists and neck. She looked every day of her twenty-six years, yet there was about her a young defenselessness, despite her firm step and lack of visible agitation.

Isles, sitting with Captain Stoddart, found his pity replaced by admiration as he watched her take her seat near the table occupied by the two lawyers engaged to defend her. When the grave charge was read to her, she listened closely and answered to the usual question in a steady clear voice, "Not guilty." Oh my brave Adria, Isles' heart whispered.

A few jurors were challenged by both sides, but little delay was expected in securing a full panel. Adria found it hard to credit that this line of everyday men, by some majesty of the law, held the rest of her life completely in their power. She herself was helpless. In the preliminary examination before the Justices of the Peace, she could answer questions and tell her story; but the law denied her any voice in this Court. *I'm sure His Lordship would believe me if I could only tell him just what happened.* Isles had explained that the accused were kept from the witness stand for their own protection, lest smart lawyers trick them or twist their words. *But how could the prosecution do me harm, when I need only tell the truth?* She moved her hands restlessly, then folded them in her lap. *I scarcely know what to do with hands that have nothing in them.* Her fingers looked rough and coarse against the smooth foulard of her dress.

Catherine had suggested the soft grey dress and the sedate little hat. "A bit old-fashioned, which won't do any harm," she had said consideringly, "and becoming." Surprisingly, Catherine had been the first of the family to hear of Adria's impending arrest. Immediately she had engaged her husband's lawyer, Mr. Fairfield, and arranged bail. Her first visit to New Erin had shown her the crying need for hired help; on her next she was accompanied by an intelligent and capable middle-aged couple, Fred and Minnie Potter, who would stay as long as needed. Hazelitt was in the care of a nurse. "He understood I must go to you at this time, and my return will be something for him to look forward to," Catherine explained in the tones Adria used when speaking of Jonathan. After years of apparent indifference, Catherine was now throwing herself wholeheartedly into the family's battle, and she was bitter against the scandalmongers, lumping together all those who were not Adria's open partisans.

Adria, however, had a disturbing ability to see both sides of an issue. She knew that most of those who had stirred up the trouble against her had acted from small and spiteful motives, and at the last had shown themselves as vindictive and merciless as any hunting pack. *Yet, perhaps it was right that the death of a friendless imbecile should have been discussed and suspected. After all, what could most of the Cove know about the real me and what I might be capable of? To be honest, if Waitstill had attacked me or one of the children, I would have killed him to stop him, if I could. It would have been called self-defence, but killing just the same. For many weeks I prayed that something, ANYTHING, would take him from New*

Erin. I can't deny that secretly I might have rejoiced at news of his death and a load lifted. It was those few minutes there in the snow, when I glimpsed my old companion, and him dying, that melted my heart. As I admitted to the Justices of the Peace, I went primarily to light the lamps, not to search for Waitstill. But I would never have killed him in selfish anger. Never.

From the corner of her eye she could glimpse the family group on the front bench. Dave was nearest, looking straight ahead with set, shamed face. Between him and Charlie was Catherine. Her violet eyes, limpid under their curling lashes and winged brows, the perfect curve of jaw and cheek, the mobile red lips, betrayed nothing. But Charlie wore no mask. To escape the love and sympathy on his face, Adria looked away, and became aware of tension building up in the room behind her.

The jury panel had been completed and, at each of the two tables, lawyers were rustling papers. Above them, the judge's face was inscrutable. Adria's hazy idea of a court session had been gleaned from books, and she found the room itself dreary and commonplace, but Chief Justice Carmichael was all she had expected. When some of the court officials fumbled in their unaccustomed duties, he set them right in solemn measured tones, but with kindly patience. His countenance, like his voice, seemed the personification of the law's dignity, and seeing His Lordship there above them all gave Adria confidence in justice. She thought he looked wearied—perhaps by the many crimes he had heard unfold in just such smoky-walled courts as this, in just such pretty villages as Barrington, where one would expect to find simple joys and griefs and loving neighbourliness.

She heard one of the prosecuting lawyers call his first witness, "Valentine Nickerson." *Now who . . . ? Of course, Rhuanna's Vol! Even names have been twisted about and made unfamiliar.* Vol had been downcast when summoned to appear against Mrs. Malone, whose champion he was known to be. But Isles had impressed upon him that he could do only good if he told the truth as he remembered it, and stuck to what he knew.

Mr. Hastings, the prosecuting lawyer, now on his feet, was middle-aged — a stooped, hollow-cheeked man, with a clever, fine-drawn face and a gentlemanly air. His adroit questions helped Vol through his testimony with a minimum of embarrassment. Vol told how he had accompanied his employer and

Mr. Knowles to New Erin on the morning of the twenty-fourth of December. He repeated what he had heard Mrs. Malone relate of finding Waitstill and how she had finally left him, after putting her woollen cloak over him. Vol had gone with the other two men to search the field and had been the one to find the body, about twenty yards from the lighthouse, a few feet off the path. The snow, six to eight inches deep, had drifted around the body but had not completely hidden it. No, Mrs. Malone's cloak had not been over it. The left hand was outstretched, the other was lying on the breast. There was a little ice where the face lay and near it some blood. He saw other spots of blood where the snow had blown clear. No, not large spots, more like from a nose-bleed or a cut finger. Mr. Kendrick had sent him to the wharf for a fish-barrow and he had helped the two men put the body on the barrow. The body had been frozen stiff, They had carried it to the warehouse on Short Wharf and covered it with a sail. No, he hadn't heard Mrs. Malone mention a knife. He had stayed behind the others to fasten the boat, and when he entered the kitchen she had been telling about making her way through the storm to the lighthouse.

Mr. Kenton did not cross-examine. Jerome Kenton, Isles' school friend, had a clubfoot, so that he limped, poor man, even as he moved around the table. His clean-shaven face looked amazingly white compared with the red and brown of the assembled fishermen and farmers, and no one else in the room had such keen black eyes. He and Isles had spent many hours preparing notes, and arguing about the value of Dave's testimony. Isles had won and it was decided not to call him lest the prosecution make much of his absence or of the damaging blow at Sydney. As Adria's husband his testimony could be denied the prosecution. Adria guessed that Isles was not too sure of Dave under possible cross-examination, though he now appeared a model for loyal and solicitous husbands.

Adria liked Jerome Kenton — or she would like him, if her heart ever rejoined her mind. She knew that feeling would return, but she had felt herself scoured clean of all emotion since she had risen from her prayers that morning. The essential Adria was detached but observant, as the spirit is in severe illness or great grief.

She came to herself with a start. Astoundingly — for time

had lost true proportions — the judge was declaring the noon recess.

The courtroom behind her emptied. Then those on the front bench rose and with brave, encouraging smiles for her, turned down the aisle. The perfume of lilacs on the soft June air drifted in through an open window; the memory of sustaining love was to come back to her, many times, on the scent of lilacs. She watched them leave the room — Dave, outwardly unintimidated but inwardly shaken, at what had come about and not yet able to excuse his part in it. *He has no strength for me, scarcely enough to keep up his own appearance.* But Adria felt no scorn or belittlement, and she recognized Dave's share in the united concern which flowed to her from the family group.

Smoothing her gloves, Catherine swept through the doorway as if attending some splendid function, and every man paid staring homage to her beauty.

Charlie's lately recovered boyishness had again been washed from his face. *Yet no matter how much he hates this ordeal for me, his mind takes refuge in his wife and their love.* He and Arthenese had hurried to New Erin, assuring Adria they meant to stay until she was "back home." Arthenese, happily and unembarrassedly enceinte, would have shared the long days in the courtroom, but her husband would not hear of it and each evening Charlie went back to New Erin with an account of the day's proceedings. Mercy was now home, restored to health, and caring for Jonathan and Mary Ellen. Adria had been able to slip away with little fuss, but she treasured Charlie's report that Jonathan carried one of her slippers to bed with him. She wrenched her mind away from her children. When this was all over, she would dwell on them to her heart's content.

From the doorway Charlie turned to smile a message of faith and cheer across the emptied seats. Then Adria was being led to the small room off the courtroom, which had been allotted to her. As she picked at the food brought by the jailor she told herself she was grateful that she had been spared the cell at the far end of the lower hall, yet neither room nor cell had reality.

To open the afternoon session, Mr. Obediah Knowles was called and took the stand in a waddle of importance.

"Know the deceased? Ye mean Waitstill? Well, these last four years he's been a loony. He'd lost his faculties complete."

"Food? Didn't seem he *could* 'a' had enough, for I've see him eatin' raw herrin' an' beef from the pickle bar'l, and he allus carried a fistful o' middlin's in his pocket."

"Clothes? They was a disgrace. He wasn't fit fer the eyes of a human bein', let alone an Injun." A scarcely audible titter skipped lightly across the courtroom like a flat pebble across a pond, and sank under the weight of His Lordship's glare.

Mr. Hastings cleared his throat and started again.

Obie told of his visit to New Erin with Isles and Vol. "When we got inside the kitchen door, Mis' Malone told us she thought Waits'l was dead, out in the snow. She cried an' took on an' she spoke about a knife."

"She said she never *meant* t'use it."

In his inimitable way, Obie told much the same story as Vol's. To the lawyer's question he cheerfully admitted that after the body had been placed in the warehouse, he had gone to the light tower. "Jest t'poke around."

"No, I never seen no blood on the stairs, but the' was some spots on the lower floor."

Led back to his mention of a knife, he repeated what Adria had sobbed in her first wild relief at seeing help. Yes, he'd had a reason t'notice her words particular. Because Mis' Malone had once threatened *him* with a knife.

"She waved the knife at me an' p'inted t'the door. I said, 'Legs, do the body good!'"

"I mean I *went*."

Mr. Hastings prompted, "You felt yourself in some danger, then?"

"No, I never," Little Obie said, looking boldly about him.

When Mr. Kenton rose and limped forward he appeared pleased with this witness. He began his cross-examination by returning to the knife. Yes, Obie said, when he had called on Mrs. Malone in the fall of 1877 he had taken something to her. A fresh pollack. He admitted the aforementioned knife had looked like a fish-knife.

"I cal'ate I *am* familiar with fish-knives." Obie smirked. This clubfooted lawyer was clearly a numbskull deserving a condescending answer.

"She wasn't adoin' nawthin' but listenin' t'me talk, an' cleanin' the fish I'd brung her."

"No, she never 'proached me nor used threat'nin' langwidge."

The next question brought an end to his patience. "No, I *wasn't* ascairt. Don't talk foolishness; I knew Adria wouldn't hurt a fly."

His Lordship rapped sharply. The prosecution lawyers exchanged frustrated glances and, as Mr. Kenton wrapped his robe about him (almost as if he hugged himself), Obediah Knowles stepped reluctantly down from the witness stand.

The testimony of the next witnesses was grim. The Deputy Sheriff had exhumed Waitstill's body, which had been wrapped in a thick sheet and was in a nicely made casket. The two doctors had conducted the post-mortem examination. *No matter what they do with me nothing can be harder than this.* Adria lifted and fell on cold waves of nausea as the gruesome details went on and on. She kept seeing, under their knives, not the body wrenched from the grave, not the frozen corpse awaiting burial, not the grotesque giant body of the last few years — but the superb physique of the young Waitstill. Harder to forgive than her own degradation was the violation now being unfeelingly detailed.

Yet, when the doctors had stepped down and she could open her barricaded mind as she unclenched her aching hands, she decided their testimony would not prejudice her case. Both had found a burn on the wrist, slight lacerations on the hands, a full stomach and organs in normal condition at the time of death. Neither reported a knife mark. The brain and cranium had showed signs of a previous and severe injury, and a lesser contusion immediately preceding death. The latter blow had been inflicted by a blunt instrument and had been of such severity as might well cause partial unconsciousness and inability to move.

On cross-examination each admitted that the more recent contusion might have resulted from a fall upon a hard surface such as frozen ground, or rock, or from the blow inflicted by a falling door, if the head had been bent forward at the moment of contact. Again Mr. Kenton wrapped his robe about him, as he sat down.

Two of Waitstill's shipmates gave testimony concerning the blow and the fall to the deck of the *Ocean Spray.*

Then came a succession of witnesses. Some were men whom Adria recognized as among the less highly regarded of the district, but others had been on the December coroner's jury and were men whom she and Dave had formerly welcomed to their home. All seemed to tell similar rambling and irrelevant tales. Yet out of them emerged the salient points of all the talk against her, the case of the prosecution: she had been a harsh mistress who had ill-fed the family servant so that he was forced to eat raw foods found outside; she had callously left that injured servant to die in the cold and snow, making no effort to assist him; she had habitually beat him and, at the last, had hit him with a blunt instrument so as to cause his death; she had planned to kill him with a knife.

Her body became fatigued from long hours in a rigidly upright position and from the enervating heat, her heart was sad with memories of the young Waitstill, her mind sick with the ghoulish details of the postmortem, and wearied with the long chain of — so far as was apparent to her — inconsequential evidence.

Six o'clock and adjournment came at last. It was when she rose to her feet that she betrayed the first weakness her enemies had been able to detect. She swayed and clutched at her chair. But before Jerome Kenton could step to her side, she had removed her steadying hand and, white-faced, was again in command of her body. Touched by the lawyer's concern, she smiled to thank him and he stood for a moment looking into her face with pity and admiration.

Adria turned her smile to the family group waiting near the door. Except for Charlie, they would stay overnight at the Lindsay House nearby and they were dreading for her the next hours, which must be spent in custody. They could not know she was beyond caring.

The sheriff led the jury away in a squad. Mr. Fairfield told Adria that arrangements had been made for her to spend the night in the care of Tom Atwood, the jailer, but in a room at his home, not in the jail. At noon Adria had found Tom determined in his duty and, she suspected, convinced of her guilt, but he would not be unkind nor prying.

It rained during the night and next morning a cool little breeze from Barrington Bay found its way into the crowded courthouse. Now and then the pleasant sound of the river, hurrying last night's rain out to the sea, came up to Adria through the resumed flow of words, as two more men testified to her inhumanity. She had not slept and her mind tended to wander; she was amazed to find, when she came back to attention, that the prosecution had closed. Mr. Fairfield was opening the defence. *Then, there will be an end to this sometime. It does not go on for ever.* She took fresh heart.

As the queen's counsel addressed the jury, spectators forgot his paternal smile; they watched instead the hard jaw and the sharp eyes behind the spectacles, yet his manner remained fatherly as he explained: "This is a very serious and criminal charge, laid against a young woman, and in this instance one difficult to meet, as there was no one on New Erin on the night of the twenty-second December but the accused, her two small children and her aged grandmother. As you know, the mouth of the prisoner is closed by the law relating to witnesses, and Mrs. Malone can give no evidence or explanation. I point out to you that no cause of death has been proven; that the bruise on the head was not shown to have resulted fatally, and there is no evidence whatever to connect Mrs. Malone with any violence to Nolan."

He reviewed Waitstill's absence from the house and Adria's excursion to the lighthouse. "On her way back she came across the servant lying in the snow. You have seen the accused; evidence states that the deceased at the time of his death weighed over two hundred pounds. Could she have picked him up and carried him? When, after long coaxing, he made no effort to rise, she took off her cloak and attempted to cover the poor man. She went back to her small children. I ask you, what else could she do?" He trusted that when these facts and further evidence had been considered, there would be no hesitation in acquitting the accused.

Captain John Stoddart, his face and whiskers more like an angry sunset than ever, was first sworn. He had been one of the original coroner's jury, and he had attended Waitstill's funeral on New Erin. It would have been difficult to move the body to the mainland during such weather, and the deceased's only relative, his mother, had agreed to the island interment. He, with Mr. Kendrick, and Valentine Nickerson had taken the minister to the island. There had been another boat from Prince's Cove. Captain and Mrs. Malone had also attended the service at the grave.

As to the weather of twenty-third December, he remembered

it well. "I am not up in Natural Philosophy, but I judged the wind blew between forty and fifty miles an hour."

As for Mrs. Malone summoning aid: "Yes, I know the fog-bell at the lighthouse. I used it myself on a schooner for several years before Mr. Redmond bought it. It would hardly carry a quarter of a mile in such a wind."

Cross-examined, he thought a dory might have lived at sea the night of the blizzard. The thing would have been to row it to windward. He had seen more severe winter storms, but he would not have wanted to face the wind as it swept across the exposed point of New Erin.

Mr. Kenton then read two short depositions. Mrs. Didamia Nickerson, grandmother of the accused, had told of getting out of bed to mind the children while Mrs. Malone went to the light; of Mrs. Malone's delay in returning; of how, when she did return, she had been without her cloak, snow-covered and threatened with frostbite.

Adria heard the lawyer begin the second deposition. *I would have expected Nabby to be one of the fiercest against me. But Isles says that when the troublemakers went to her, she would not let them in. Yet later she welcomed Isles and gave her affidavit willingly.*

Mr. Kenton was reading, " . . . since his injury he had been childish and in an ugly temper most of the time. I could do nothing with him. He himself wished to go back to New Erin. He had always been devoted to the Redmonds and to Mrs. Malone. I gave consent to the burial on New Erin." *Isles says she spoke evilly against Dave and wanted to blame him for all that happened, but her accusations against him were ignored as having no bearing on the case.*

Dr. Whitehouse, looking tired but unimpressed, was next sworn. He appeared strangely incomplete and Adria saw he was without the scurfy and stained medicine satchel that seemed as much as part of him as the pointed pepper and salt beard. He was growing old and crotchety, people said, and he had been denounced for his laxness as coroner of the first inquest. He showed no awareness of the rampant criticism that had blown up on the same wind that spread the obloquies against Adria. His voice was unhurried as he told of his many years' service in the community, twenty-five of them as coroner. Yes, he knew the accused. "Brought her into the world. And her children.

Fine children." He recollected being called on an inquest on New Erin around last Christmas time, but the weather had been such that he could not get to the island before the twenty-eighth December. He had taken a jury with him. He had examined the body. Paid no attention to the burn. Such people as the deceased often burnt and cut themselves. Rope mark? Man about boats and wharves often showed such marks on hands and wrists. Had observed more closely the bruise on the back of the head, but had considered it not remarkable, believing it could have been caused by a fall, or by a descending trapdoor, as Mrs. Malone had suspected. Did not believe it had caused death.

Cross-examination brought out nothing new. His Lordship drew his watch and announced the noon recess.

In the small room Adria, recalling the jailer's wife's morning kindness strove to east some of the food brought her. The murmur of the river came up to her and she remembered, suddenly, that just across it "Grandsir Will" Nickerson had built his first home and his gristmill, after the emigration from Cape Cod over a hundred years ago. She pondered briefly on the continuity of the human chain but that brought her mind to what she wished to avoid. *My descendants will not be proud of me, as Grandsir Will's are of him.* Hardest to forgive was the harm now being done her children, as yet unaware of anything except that Mamma had had to leave them to visit on the main. *If . . . If it comes about that I cannot go back to them . . . If there are pointing fingers, or sly whispers, to hurt or shame them, then Dave must take them away. To the States, where they will not be known. Even if that means I shall never see them again.*

To open the afternoon session, Charlie was sworn. He testified that the Redmond children had always been cautioned against the metal trapdoor that provided egress to the lighthouse lantern. An inadvertent touch, or a gust of wind strong enough to shake the tower might send it crashing down. He had been taught to descend the stairs backwards, steadying the door with his hand until low enough on the ladder to drop it. Once, when he was about twelve, he had thought himself too large for such caution and had started down as if on ordinary steps. The door had fallen, knocking him from the stairs to the floor below. He had not suffered serious injury but his nose had bled freely.

Waitstill had received the same instructions as the Redmond children, but had tended to disregard them.

Then Isles was sworn. Adria watched him take the stand. Kind and sensitive Isles showed the strain of the past weeks; he looked pale and wrung. The blue eyes that had often reminded her of the sparkling sea now looked like winter water. As Jerome Kenton limped forward a few steps, Isles met her eyes, gave her a ghost of a reassuring smile and glanced quickly away. *He is afraid. Behind all his reassurances for the rest of us, Isles has been fearing the outcome of this trial.* Perhaps she was mistaken, for there was nothing in his manner, his face or his voice to denote apprehension. Adria saw that as he began to speak the jurors straightened and turned their heads to listen more intently, and, behind her, she could feel the close attention of the spectators focusing upon his words. She was filled with humble appreciation of how greatly Isles Kendrick's testimony would influence her fate, and realized that not only his time and his money but also the widespread respect for his personal integrity and his reputation for honesty, built up through the years, were being brought to serve her.

TWENTY-EIGHT

ADRIA was on the edge of mental exhaustion and words, even in Isles' pleasant cadences, were bruises upon her inner ear, yet she did not altogether miss Jerome Kenton's skill in tossing questions which allowed Isles to refute the points built up by the prosecution.

In time her mind wandered and her ear caught again, under Isles' matter of fact recital, the dissonance bespeaking pain. *Pain! That is the undertone that has troubled me. Oh, my dearest, who or what has pained you all these years? What sorrow have you hidden?* As in a dream, she was swept by piercingly sweet compassion and a longing to comfort him. Her dead heart leaped to life as she gave herself to the sensation of cradling Isles' fair head — between her hands, upon her breast. Of bending to meet his dear lips and feeling them warm and firm against her own. Of gazing and losing herself in those steady eyes.

The dream dissipated though its warmth remained. *Am I mad? Have these last days taken my reason?* But she knew this was lucid, beautiful sanity — at last. Her whole body was flooded by richness and wonder, as if she were awakening to a new and glorious world and for a short time this miracle of recognition was enough, and all else receded into phantasma.

She heard Isles' continuing testimony, but it no longer concerned her, except as every word declared unselfish devotion to her. "I left my clerk, Valentine Nickerson, with Mrs. Malone while Mr. Knowles and I rowed to the mainland. We met Captain Malone about half-way over. I told him what had happened and that I would get word to the coroner, which I did. On the twenty-eighth December I attended Dr. Whitehouse's inquest. The following day my cousin, Captain Malone, and I — after instructions from the Rev. Mr. Stouten — prepared the body for burial. We cut and tore the soiled and frozen clothes from the body and that is why the garments which are exhibited here, and which were produced at the second inquest, give a wrong impression. We had no idea they would ever be seen again, so tossed them aside meaning to burn them later. Mrs. Malone brought some of her husband's clothes to us, but in order to use them we would have had to break the limbs and we decided a new sheet would better serve the frozen body."

By now Adria could push aside memories of the bleak burial on Nigh Hill and the shock of the exhumation order. Actually she had touched her nadir of shame and humiliation when she had been dragged before the Justices of the Peace, who had plainly been prejudiced by the flood of rumours. All she had related to them bounded back from their closed minds as a thrown ball returns from a solid surface. For some days following that inquisition she had known defeat, and had wept for what had befallen her. She had found herself repeating drearily, "and when for many days neither sun nor stars appeared and no small tempest lay on us . . ." All other storms had been as nothing — even the first, the hurricane which had given her the message she had embraced as her own. Then one morning, on arising, she had admonished herself aloud, "What has become of my faith? St. Paul lived to tell of his shipwreck. So will I." Inexplicably she had felt a return of determination and inner fortitude, an angry refusal to submit to the false accusations, and a resurgence of trust in a just and compassionate God.

Now, in a light-headed detachment, she wondered if she herself had provided the core about which the stormy currents of suspicion and slander had been born to gain disastrous strength and speed. *Did it all start when I turned from my true love? If I hadn't married Dave, Waitstill wouldn't have followed him to sea, wouldn't have been felled to the deck, wouldn't have died in the snow. It was not the best in me that responded to Dave. I wronged my true self and cheated him. But I harmed Isles most. Now I can never make up to him the wasted years. Even if I am acquitted, there is still my husband and my duty.* Those who were watching saw her head bow, and her white eyelids lower. If any suspected she prayed, they could not guess she asked forgiveness for a promise made the wrong man, ten long years before.

When she lifted her head, Isles was stepping from the witness stand and Mr. Fairfield was preparing to address the jury for the last time. Isles' gaze met hers and she remembered too late to veil her discovered love. She saw him falter in his stride, on the verge of miraculous recognition there in the packed courtroom, and hastily drooped her eyes.

Later everyone agreed that Mr. Fairfield's conclusion had been masterly. He expressed himself glad to be at the end of a trial of more than ordinary interest and one that differed from all others he had attended, especially in the nature of the charges. "We have in the prisoner's box," he said in his most paternal tones, "a young wife and the mother of two small children, charged with the crime of killing a man, for that is what the indictment really amounts to. And this barbarous crime, it has been sought to establish, was perpetrated at the season of the year when a mother's heart is filled with melody and all the softening influences of Christmas. Her husband was absent on the mainland to purchase toys and sweets for the tiny stockings, and planning to return with his cousin as his guest for the holiday. Instead of the happy family gathering, what a sad Christmas must have been observed, for the home came under a cloud of grief for a dead servant. But there was worse in store. Before long a pall of disgrace settled over it — the malicious charge of manslaughter.

"But the jury will ask themselves as I did while evidence was being heard: is this all the foundation for the letters to the Lieutenant-Governor — of the talk and the inquisitions? Is this all there was in it? Then why, in the name of Heaven, was this trouble brought upon the woman and her family? The coroner's jury went through a strict inquiry without the slightest suspicion and, after all that has taken place, at this moment there is no one with more reliable evidence against the accused than when slander first started." He reviewed the evidence fully, castigated the scandalmongers and those who heard them acquiescently, then told the jury, "You will soon wipe off (as far as you can) the disgrace from this poor woman, but the arrows of hate and malice will be aimed at her innocent children for years to come." He dwelt upon each circumstance which had been made to do evidence against an innocent woman. He praised the magnanimity and moderation of Mr. Clark, the Crown Attorney. He ventured to declare that if Waitstill Nolan could be resurrected and brought there that day, the greatest anguish of his soul would be to find his mistress arraigned for his murder. As Mr. Fairfield closed in another burst of eloquence some jurors were blowing their noses and wiping their eyes.

Surely there could be little left for the prosecution to say, but as Mr. Clark rose and there was a stir of resettling bodies behind her, Adria heard a man whisper to his neighbour, "Smartest lawyer in the province. Tricky. He'll make 'em squirm."

Mr. Clark had a reproachful expression and a strong voice that filled the dark-walled courtroom. He regretted he could not regard the case in the same manner as the learned counsel for the defendant. Nothing would afford him greater satisfaction than to express his opinion that the jury had nothing to do but to acquit the accused, but he believed the case presented serious features which required much solemn consideration, if justice were to prevail. He must present to the jury — and the jury must pass upon — the question, did the death of Waitstill Nolan result from any unlawful act or omission of the accused?

It does sound as if he were just showing that he is performing his part. Adria felt encouraged.

But Mr. Clark reviewed the lack of any witnesses to what had occurred on the stormy night of Waitstill's death. He asked the jury to consider whether there was not evidence to conclude that the deceased received the blow, which had led to his death, from the hand of the accused. On reaching the lighthouse might she not have found the lamps unlit? Her previous treatment of the deceased made it easy to conclude that, finding he had failed to attend to the light, she had struck him with some blunt instrument and knocked him down. Her subsequent conduct, leaving her imbecile servant hatless and wretchedly clothed, to die in the cold and snow, never bringing a covering to place over him . . ." (In the hot courtroom, Adria shivered, hearing again the boom of surf and the sound of wind-driven snow, feeling again the cold thrusting through to her very heart. She wondered how many would have faced it a second time.)

" . . . lent strength to the conclusion that she herself had rendered him incapable by a blow or, with full knowledge of his desperate plight, made no effort to save his life. In her story to witnesses she told of stripping off her cloak and attempting to wrap it about the dying man. Where is that cloak? Not one of the three men who found and removed the body mentioned it. None of the jurors of the first inquest saw it, nor is it with the clothes taken off the deceased and exhibited here. Might she not have had a reason for putting it out of sight? Might it have become bloodstained or torn in the struggle, if struggle there was, and been tossed into the sea?"

Mr. Clark pointed out other facts as corroborating this theory, then asked the jury to cast aside all prejudice, to regard nothing but the evidence and render the verdict which, in their opinion, justice demanded. He flipped the corner of his gown over his arm and sat down.

Adria's head ached; both hope and fear had been drained from her. Mr. Clark had, after all, succeeded in making his specious arguments sound convincing. Was the jury as brain weary as she? Would their minds function clearly when they must make their decision, for or against her?

His Lordship was charging the jury: "You are now to exercise the most solemn duty in which men can be engaged, the highest obligation of free men. In dealing with this task you must divest your mind of prejudice and hearsay. You must remember that the accused is to be considered innocent until testimony *sworn before you and me* brings conviction to the contrary home to your minds. You have a great responsibility, for the reputation and liberty of this woman is now in your hands.

"The charge of insufficient food and clothing has been dropped by the Crown. The only consideration for you is, did this woman, wilfully or without intent, cause the death of Waitstill Nolan? Did he die by any act of hers? Unless you find the evidence sufficient to convince you of that fact, you are bound by all your obligations to acquit her. We will assume that she is innocent of all wrong till she found the deceased lying in the snow. If she did not try to assist, if she failed to do all she could for him, you must find her guilty on that part of the indictment. You know the locality better than I do. If she had no means of summoning aid from the mainland, she did all in her power to aid Nolan in his distress. Then I assert that the law of the land and the law of common sense will clear her from the blame of not doing what God and Nature did not enable her to do, and you must acquit her as a matter of course." He settled back into his dignified remoteness, and the jury retired.

NO SMALL TEMPEST

Perfect silence, pinned and compressed by emotion, lay over the courtroom. Adria tried to evaluate what these next minutes might mean to her. *Please, God, don't let it be too long. Give me strength to last out the empty waiting.* She had the terrifying sense that time had turned back upon her; that she had lived through this before and that the climax of horror was again close.

At the end of ten minutes the jury returned. When the roll was called, the foreman arose and announced a verdict of *not guilty*. If there was disagreement, or disappointment, it was lost in the many manifestations of satisfaction. His Lordship, smiling for the first time since the beginning of the sessions, said he most heartily concurred with the verdict. "A righteous one," he assured the court.

As soon as permission had been granted, Catherine's arms were about Adria. Dave bent and gently kissed her cheek, but Charlie's hug threatened to crack her ribs. Then faces became blurred as jurors and spectators crowded to congratulate her. *If everyone is so pleased, then why . . .?* Adria puzzled. But there were some who had hurried away and who would claim a miscarriage of justice to the end of their days.

Isles and Vol were waiting a turn. "Let Vol confess," Isles pleaded.

Vol said "It's about yer cloak, Mis' Malone. They asked me if 'twas on Waits'l. Well, it wasn't. But they never asked me if I knowed where 'twas and so I never said. I found it blowed against a rock near the icehouse. I shook it off and hung it in your front hall."

"That was good of you, Vol, but I seldom go into the front hall, and I hadn't noticed it there."

"But the horrid things that lawyer said! I might 'a' done a pile of harm. I jest thought a soft-hearted lady like you wouldn't want it around in case it reminded you of what was best forgot."

Adria smiled and put her hand on his. "Thank you, Vol. You've been a true friend all through this sad time."

Isles thumped him on the shoulder and turned him towards the door.

It was harder to accept Little Obie's effusive congratulations and his partially shame-faced explanations, "I knowed right along that Adria wouldn't never take no knife t'me. But, if ye remember, ye wasn't down right friendly," he chided her. "I thought I'd make it sound fierce an' . . ."

"And it made a good story!" Isles' angry sarcasm was wasted.

"Well, yes. Ye know I've often suspicioned I sh'd 'a' been one o' them what-ye m'-call-'ems and wrote books. I'd 'a' been a good hand fer it."

"You'd certainly have done less harm than by *telling* your wild yarns," Isles assured him icily. Obie turned away and they heard his voice long after he had disappeared down the stairs.

"Don't be too cross at him, Isles," Adria pleaded, glad of the excuse to put her hand upon his sleeve and feel his hard arm again. "Don't you remember Kiah saying, 'Talk runs out of Obie's mouth like water out o' the lee scuppers'?" Adria's thoughts went after Obie. *I'm glad I feel no bitterness. At least not towards Obie.* Then, awed, *He's taught me a little of what Christ meant when he said, 'Father, forgive them for they know not what they do.'*

Isles and Dave had planned for the Redmond group to spend the night with the Kendricks – all but Charlie, who would hasten to New Erin with the good news. Looking into Adria's sweet broken face, noticing the nervous movements of her pitifully thin hands, feeling her limp and spent beside him, Isles made himself a spearhead for the slow progress through the courtroom and to his carry-all, while men still pushed forward to congratulate Adria and her husband, whose smile and gay friendliness attested his rejoicing.

Though Catherine sat in front with Isles and it was Dave's arm which supported her in the back seat, Adria found the drive home a benediction. Sally jogged along proudly, as if she had had a part in the day's outcome. The scent of wild bush and flowers closed about them as they drove through the long shadows of the wooded stretches, and opalescent little coves and creeks smiled back at them where the road followed the shore. Adria, empty-minded and contentedly silent, drank in the beauty of early evening and felt its peace drive out pain. Nobody spoke much; their joy and thankfulness went too deep for words.

At Priscilla's door, Dave lifted Adria down from the seat. Before he could set her upon the ground she had collapsed in his arms. All the love of years was in Priscilla's quiet tones, "My poor girl! Bring her in to her bed, Dave."

Catherine had never heard such despair as Isles' when he turned to her. "They've killed her with their wagging tongues!" He took himself in hand. "Tell Dave I've turned back; I think Dr. Whitehouse is on his rounds somewhere between here and Barrington."

TWENTY-NINE

AFTER the morning sunshine outside, the hall was dim and Isles paused at the sitting-room doorway. His mother's chair at the front window had given place to a couch drawn up to afford a view of the road and the cove. Adria, half reclining upon heaped cushions, was watching the quiet water and a lazily tacking sloop. She had not heard him enter and he stood content to watch the curve of thin cheek, the sooty lashes against the white face and the soft curls about her temple. Illness had washed away the sorrowful, drawn look of last winter and spring; convalescence had brought back a girlishness less remindful of the woman who had fainted in her husband's arms two weeks before than of the Adria who had brightened the Kendrick sitting-room before her world had contained Dave Malone.

The marks of the past weeks were still on Isles' face but the guard he had kept so long and so assiduously was momentarily lowered. As if she sensed his gaze and all behind it, Adria turned her head and saw his open heart in his eyes and on his lips. She knew no surprise — this was to be. Response flooded her. "Sweetheart," she whispered, her love candid as his.

For a long moment neither moved; but not from any memory of their silent vows never to reveal the love that now filled the room. Slowly Isles walked towards her and, as slowly, Adria sat erect and held out her hands. He stopped in front of her, apparently amazed to find that he held a bouquet of pink roses. As he laid them in her lap the morning dew was still a film on the curling petals and their delicate perfume was the essence of early summer. But what were roses? Isles had dropped on his knees before her, while his eyes held hers. He lifted her hand, poor thin white hand, and carried it to his lips, hungrily, tenderly. She bent and put her cheek against his, murmuring his name in quiet wonder, "Isles. Isles." All that the years had made her was lost in the upsurging of the girl who had met a boy on Nigh Hill and welcomed him to New Erin and into her life.

It was that girl who lifted her head and said simply, "You're not comfortable," and indicated a seat beside her, laughing the soft and secret laugh of love. But he remained kneeling, while her heart tremulously beat out the seconds. Everything was said in long looks, like draughts of fresh water after parching days on the salt sea. Clear sweet draughts for two thirsty souls. When Isles got to his feet he picked a rose from her lap and tucked it into her braids. He let his hand rest upon the twined locks, remembering all the times he had ached to roughen her hair in desire or brush it in compassion. His hand dropped slowly from the chestnut braids and down the cool cheek to stay for a minute in the warm hollow of her neck. At the white fire in his touch, blood climbed to suffuse her face.

When he sat down beside her, he did not put his arm about her — even that might shatter the crystalline hush of their new world — but he kept her hand, palm to palm like a lingering kiss. Through her arm Adria felt his heart's hard pounding and the sweet tremor of the hand clasping hers. He asked every lover's question, "When did you know?"

"In the courtroom. While you stood in the witness box. With my fate undecided, I suddenly knew that you were the dearest thing I might lose. That you had always been, since that first day on Nigh Hill."

"I thought I saw awakening in your eyes, but I couldn't believe. This time I can believe. Can't I?" After its long deafness, her heart stirred at every modulation of his voice.

"Yes. It has been a precious secret all the days of illness. I hope I kept it hidden!" Alarm widened her gaze at the thought of what revelation might mean to them all.

He took his eyes from the gentle mobility of her mouth. If he watched he must kiss the lips into clinging surrender. "Even from me, until today," he reassured her. "I'm positive Catherine, constant attendant though she was, has gone back to her Hazelitt never suspecting I'm anything but your family friend — and Dave's cousin."

The name had to be spoken; both had known it was waiting to come between them, as it now did. They knew that Dave was the reason Isles had kissed her hand and not her lips. What more forbidding reason could there be?

She looked full into his face and her breath caught at the lines graved by the years of hopeless longing. "Can you forgive me," she asked in a hushed tone, "for what I did to you? To all three of us — Dave, too?"

"Adria," and his hand tightened about hers, "will you come away with me? Put our mistakes behind us? I have considered plans. I can care for you and the children and I would ask nothing better to do for the rest of my life. I have money ahead and my business here would sell for more — enough to keep us all while I make a fresh start. Where we are not known. Where people would see only a sweet and beautiful wife and a husband who worships her. The West is waiting . . ." His voice was taut with the bliss evoked by his words.

"Dave would not give up his children; I have no right to take them from him." She made this not a plea nor an excuse, but a fact both must accept. She added, "My mother. My grandmother. Serena. What would become of them if I left New Erin? Your mother, Isles. Your place in the community, the business you have built up, and the men whose livelihood depend upon you."

"They wouldn't count," he assured her in a voice roughened by emotion. "Nothing counts. I lost you once by acknowledging obstacles . . ."

Adria interrupted, "And Dave. Your cousin and partner. Though he doesn't know it, he too is dependent upon me. He cannot be faithful, but these past weeks have shown me that he loves me; I shall be faithful but I cannot love him, and perhaps I do him the greater wrong. My love will be yours always but I'm not a romantic girl now, my dearest, following my flighty heart and wrecking lives. I am a woman who can meet her responsibilities, with God's help."

Almost as if he had not heard, nor needed to hear, Isles said, "I've been building dreams of taking you away with me — like my boyish ones of sailing a fine ship over far seas and you safe in the after-cabin, or beside me at the rail. Yet I must have known these were only dreams even as I fashioned them. Running off would be no way out for us. There *is* no way out for us—together."

At the defeat in his face Adria turned her head aside and her lashes lowered over the glitter of tears. But the bliss of having found each other still deadened all else; the pain of renuciation would come later. Isles said, more evenly, "Forget I asked it of you. Tell your mind to let it go."

"Let it go! Oh no, I shall keep every word you've spoken. Keep them to warm my heart by. I shall need them many times." They were little enough comfort even then to a body trembling into renewed life. *Ah, what I would give to be Adria Redmond again, standing by this window, waiting to go to my first tea-meeting! How happily I would claim Isles' eager love, which I doomed to wither into resignation.*

Isles was rising. He stood looking down into her eyes and she knew he was thinking that never again could they trust themselves such looks, such words, such communion of spirit as they had shared this morning; that this was the last, as it was the first, of their expressed love. "I hear Rhuanna and her broom approaching." He tried for a light tone and smile to encourage her; his failure was heartbreaking. Then, "Charlie and Dave come for you tomorrow?" (This is good-bye, my sweet, his eyes said.)

"Yes, Charlie must take Arthenese home." (How can I let you go, her eyes answered.) Clasping her white hands tightly, she made herself pick up the threads of her life again. "They've been good to me, Isles, so good. Everyone has. Even the Cove people whom I suspected. . . All the tempting dishes and the friendly inquiries while I've been sick; the ladies' calls, as if to make up . . ."

"You forgive more easily than I do," he said bleakly, remembering.

Adria spoke slowly. "It's as if I am beginning a new life, with fears and distrust and angers left behind me. If only I can keep my faith and my compassion against the everyday pricks and irritations. . ." They heard Rhuanna's broom coming nearer. "Isles," Adria pleaded, suddenly alarmed at some thought, "you will still come to see us all on New Erin?" Her voice shook for the first time. "I think I can do anything if I can count on seeing your smile and your steady blue gaze, and hearing your voice, once in a while."

"I can't promise. Now that we both . . . My strength has its limit." The pain was back in his voice. "But you will know where to find me, if ever you should need me." He took her hands, pressed a kiss into each palm and closed her fingers over them. The warmth and tenderness of his lips stayed long after he had laid her hands down upon the roses, looked long and gravely into her eyes, then turned and was gone.

THIRTY

Vol was happy to have life again on an even keel, and he hummed to himself in a contented bumble as he bustled about the counter, his red head gaily blazing. He paid no attention to the three old men about the stove—they might have been items of hardware or dry goods, or afternoon shadows cast by the July sun. Most of the Cove was busy in the mowing-fields, for at the beginning of the week fishermen-farmers had fitted freshly-ground scythes into sheaths and set out to test muscles and blades unused since last haying season. Children and sunbonneted women wielded the spreading-forks and passed the jugs of cooling oatmeal water, while most grandsires, temporarily deserting shop and wharfsides, leaned against fences to offer advice and to compare the cut with the more bountiful crops of their youth. The old men had rejoiced as Vol had done when the shop re-opened, and soon its brief closure (and its cause) might never have interrupted their habit of gathering to sit and chew and peer into the past; they had had a fill of talk and argufying for a time. The shop and the Cove was peaceful with a relief like that which follows the inflammation, the long and painful suppuration and the final breaking and drainage of a deep-seated salt-water boil. There was no concern about possible scars.

As Isles came out of his office he nodded briefly but pleasantly to the oldsters beside the stove. He had forgotten most of his anger in the utter loneliness that followed Adria's recent departure for New Erin. *Other men have learned to live with nothing inside the shell they show the world, just as men learn to get around without an arm or a leg.* Dave's figure unexpectedly filled the doorway. *But it can't help to see another man who has all they lack.*

Dave's colour was high from the sun and the breeze and, as he pushed his cap back, his eyes opened wide behind the astoundingly thick lashes and sparkled with health and friendliness. "Good day, all," he said heartily and the old men returned his greeting, each secretly believing that thirty years ago he had been just such another handsome, upstanding seaman as Captain Malone, and had possessed just such taking ways, stopping to ask old codgers about their ailments and their families, as if there had never been a word said against anybody.

Isles inquired how Mrs. Malone had stood the boat-trip home, asked about the children and the older people on New Erin. Dave answered pleasantly but gave the impression of urgency behind the conversation. When Isles, excusing himself, gave Vol a nod which said, Serve Captain Malone, and turned towards the door and the wharf, Dave dropped all pretence of a shopping visit. "I'd like to see you about a private matter. It will take only a few minutes. You can't be *that* busy, man," he laughed at Isles' hesitation and strode towards the office. When Isles entered, worry for Adria tightening across his chest, Dave had found a chair. "If ever you saw a fool, Isles, here he sits," was his greeting.

"I'm a good judge of fools," Isles responded, "having known myself to be one for a long time. But you didn't row a mile to show me another."

Dave's narrowed eyes were sober. "Only a fool would get himself into the fix I'm in."

That doesn't sound as if Adria were ill again. The cords across Isles' chest loosened. He picked up a heavy ruler and stood slapping it slowly against his open palm as he waited. "I thought you might want to discuss further plans for our proposed lobster factory on New Erin."

Although Dave had been most enthusiastic about this new venture he waved it aside as if unworthy of attention. "It's Bella again."

Bella! Isles had heard no breath of suspicion. "Just what do you mean 'Bella again'?"

Dave looked both crestfallen and belligerent as he explained that Bella was again with child and named him as the father. "I've been sending her money to keep her quiet ever since last spring. Money! The Lord only knows what she does with it all. Now she demands five hundred dollars. Says she wants to go to the States and be quit of Zack and me both. If I don't come across, she swears she'll send her grandfather to Adria." Dave's brow and upper lip were sweat-beaded. "I haven't got that much right now. You know I've had expenses . . ." Obviously it hurt his pride to ask for money. Then ironically, but typically, he divulged galled resentment that the island and property were in Adria's name and hence useless as far as his raising money was concerned. "Can you let me have three hundred. Today?" he ended bluntly.

"Not so fast." Isles' voice was icy. "When have you been seeing Bella? I wouldn't think you could have turned around this last while without the Prince's Cove gossips entering it in their logs. Do you mean to say you were visiting Bella while Adria was being harried and . . . ?" His scorn blazed into the face only a few feet from his own.

Dave's quick temper flared and died; he must take whatever Isles chose to say today. "No. Not while Adria was in all that trouble. I haven't seen Bella since last December. Since around last Christmas."

"Last Christmas!" This was incredible. "Not the night Waitstill died?"

His first hurdle cleared, Dave was regaining confidence. "When I borrowed Sally I honestly planned to visit Maw and return in lots of time to make the island before sundown, just as I told you. But where the road turns off from Pilot Point, I thought of Bella. You wouldn't understand . . ." Something on his cousin's face made him conclude more feebly, "All men aren't alike . . ." This time an impatient gesture with the ruler stopped him and he interjected, "Blast women! And blast *me!* Why can't I learn to leave them alone?" But the other man heard the underlying complacency.

Dave has no sense of sin, or shame. Isles went back to the impossible disclosure. "You stayed that night at Zack's. But from Pilot Point you must have seen the storm making? In less than an hour you could have been back at my wharf."

The very sordidness of Dave's story gave it the ring of truth. "I hadn't made any plans about staying if Zack was home. But when I got near their house, there was the old barn, out of sight from the road and with lots of hay for Sally. Who was to know where I had driven or stopped? Bella was glad to see me, make no mistake. But there was Zack in the rocker by the stove, deaf as a coot but solid as Grannie's Head. Bella knew Zack liked his rum and she kept some hid away for when she wanted to get around him. So it was 'git him drunk, b'ys, and into his berth.' Which I did, finally. But by that time I wasn't too bright myself and Bella's thoughts weren't on the weather, but on a roll of bills I'd showed her."

Money for Adria's and the children's Christmas. Was it for this man that Adria had covered her glowing love with the grey ashes of duty?

"When I woke," Dave was continuing, "the wind was howling and snow was plastered thick on the panes, and Zack was coming to, out on the kitchen couch." Dave had set out next morning when the first light would show him the road. Even yet he could scarcely believe that no one had seen him breaking his way through the Pilot Point drifts, and that no one had doubted his false story of being delayed at his mother's. "I expect the talk about Waits'l drownded out all else."

Isles would have liked to crash his fist into the handsome, self-satisfied countenance. "You've thought that your little side-jaunt that day killed Waitstill and nearly killed Adria?" *Surely if this had been known, Adria would have been spared all but shame at her husband's unfaithfulness.* But Isles was too confused and angry to weigh the matter.

"I don't see that Waits'l was much use in the world," Dave retorted callously. "And Adria's trouble is behind her now. I mean to make up to her for all she's been through. I can tell you her little finger is worth more to me than all Bella's wheedling body! We're going to start afresh. I've promised Adria and this time I mean it. But what chance will I have to make a go of things with Bella hanging around my neck? It don't seem fair that this trouble should come up now, when I've determined to walk the straight and narrow path."

Isles could have quoted a proverb anent sowing and reaping, but forebore since his cousin was glowing with unfairly burdened virtue. Dave came back to his point, "You'll give me the money for Adria's sake, if not for mine."

Something in his tone brought Isles' head up with a snap, but Dave's eyes were screened, his face blank. Isles asked, "How do you know Bella will leave you alone after you give her this money?"

"I'll see she leaves the country. I'm sick to death of her

whining. I'll not be walking to Pilot Point in the hot sun after today, you can bet." He added, "I'll row to Grannie's Head and leave my skiff at Nickerson's old wharf to save a haul over the flats, for the tide will be out time's I get back."

Isles had turned to the small safe. *I can't buy Adria happiness; I may buy postponement of pain.* "This once," he told Dave as he counted out bills. "Not ever again will I lend you money for this sort of thing." Blue eyes locked with hazel and stared them down.

Dave's spirits rose as he left the office, having obtained what he sought. He had a courteous greeting for a matron at the dress-goods counter, a jest and a laugh for Vol, serving her. Isles wondered if some wishful distortion in himself made the heartiness ring falsely, made him see only selfishness behind the flashing smile.

On the sunlit doorsteps Dave paused and looked about him leisurely, then stepped out into the road and strode off—tall, handsome, broad shouldered and slim hipped as a youth, and facing the dusty miles with a youth's confident swing. The sun and the high clouds, the blue of sky and the deeper blue of the cove, the green and gold bands of half-mown hayfields, the fragrance of drying grass and the heavier scent of warm spruce that bordered the road, all these and the world beyond, might have been made expressly for him.

Dave Malone was still a fine figure of a man but he looked more than his thirty-five years when he reached the crest of Grannie's Head at dusk, for he walked wearily and his shoulders were thrust forward against the greyness now rolling in. The fog was heavy and wet to the lungs as steam from a washtub, and cold besides. His thin coat was damp, his boots and pant legs saturated from wading through the tall dripping grass of the unmown Nickerson fields. His handsome face was twisted by anger. Anger at circumstances and his own weakness, at the miserable weather and his uncomfortable clothes, at the long mile to be rowed against the wind before he could sit down to his warm supper on New Erin. On his left, hidden under the fog, was Captain Sam's old wharf, broken in places, rotting in others, but serving to shelter his skiff. Rowing would warm him, but he shrank from the fog-greased planks and weeded spiles of the wharf, and from the damp thwart of the skiff.

He'd wasted his day, and his money. That was what really chilled him — his sense of failure that expanded from today's fiasco to include his whole life. He had never meant to become the man that he now (in the chill and the dampness) knew himself to be. What had happened to the young Dave and his resolve to change with marriage; of the husband who for a time had kept that resolve by virtue of his wife's clean strength and upholding trust? Bella! Zack was at sea; had there been a furtive movement behind the window when he had knocked at her door? Had his senses played him false when they signalled the presence, or recent presence, of another man? The suspicion that Bella might have deceived him, as she deceived Zack, brought a surge of anger that knotted his muscles. She had sworn there had never been anyone else. And with the first drink he had believed her. Oh, Bella was smart. She had the money and he had her easy promise, for what it was worth. Like fog the cold knowledge settled over him that Bella was too lazy, too indifferent and unscrupulous, ever to make a move or change her lot, so long as she had a roof over her head — and fools of men to hand her money.

Realization came like the clear ring of a bell-buoy. *I am the one who must leave. I must go back to sea. Away from women and their bedevilment. That's where I am a man, respected by my crew and by the fleet. Fighting the sea and the weather, not myself.* He ached for the feel of a pitching deck and the sounds of slatting canvas and running rigging, the lights of the anchored fleet, the galley's steaming tea. The women of Marblehead and Newfoundland? No more to him than the heavy mugs from which he drank their beer, and as smeared by the lips of other men. Bella, passionate but lazy, clinging and greedy—she had been the habit-forming draught which had betrayed him. *I wouldn't marry her; then why couldn't I have stayed away from her?*

The last of Bella's rum had worn away now. He wished he had stuck a bottle in his pocket; a drink would keep him warm until the oars' rhythm should push the blood throughout his body. *I must be getting old.* Pictures of Damie hobbling from bed to rocker, of the feeble men beside the shop stove, rose before his eyes. *Better to be swept from the deck by a king sea than to live and become like that.* He was filled again by his desire to be on the water.

Through a fog-flaw came a flicker of light from the outer shore. *Nabby Nolan's shanty.* Someone had told him, "Ye can allus git a drink from Nabby, if you'm hard put to it." He made no decision. He was shivering on the ridge of Grannie's Head; he was (still shivering) knocking at Nabby's door and watching a dim light behind a rimy pane, with the wind and the shore's rote at his back.

After the knock there was a long stillness, like a held breath, behind the flimsy, ill-fitting door.

"Who's there?" The voice quavered, but not with fear.

"Captain Malone."

A shriek and a string of epithets met the name; they were followed by orders to leave at once. Dave was abruptly filled with determination to be inside the miserable dwelling. "Open your door or I put my shoulder to it." One good thrust would suffice, and his voice was hard with purpose. He heard fumblings with latch and wooden button. When the door opened a crack, he seized the edge and drew it wide, then ducked beneath the lintel and stepped into the bare-walled, low-ceilinged room. Crooked fingers went up to screen a reeking tallow candle and a blurred figure moved back as he stepped in out of the wreathing fog. In the candlelight and its shadows, Nabby's hooked nose and hooked chin appeared to meet over her toothless mouth, and under a snarled pile of hair her eyes glittered up at him. *Cat's eyes.* Weren't witches supposed to be cats, or turn into cats, or something? He had laughed at the tales about Nabby Nolan, but now all his seaman's superstitions leaped to life. He wished himself anywhere else, even adrift in the cold fog, if away from the bent, round-shouldered figure with the baleful glare, but he stubbornly demanded, "Sell me a bottle, old woman. I need a drink before setting out for New Erin. Brandy, if you've got it. Rum."

"Cap'n Malone come t'call, eh?" The sour voice cackled. "Haven't ye got a merry laugh an' a clap on the back fer me? Like ye allus had fer my poor Waits'l?"

Dave involuntarily raised a fist. He could not endure reminders of Waitstill here in this evil-smelling, squalid room that had been his home. On that tumbled bed, dimly outlined in the corner, the injured man must have lain the long weeks following his skipper's blow, with this horrible creature the only one to care for him. She was glaring at her son's captain with such malevolence that Dave took a backward step. "Get me a drink," he reiterated and threw some coins upon the dirty table.

Muttering and half-sobbing Waitstill's name, Nabby was like a crazy thing, but she rummaged under the ragged blankets and passed Dave a stone gin bottle. "Here," she said, "and may it strangle ye." She watched him wipe mouth and bottle-top upon his wet sleeve, and drink. "Now git," she said. "An' the curse o' fire and water go with ye. May the water drownd ye and the fires o' . . ."

Dave laughed down at her jeeringly, feeling the gin chase away his chill and depression. "No water will drownd me," he told her. "You'm not the only witch in the world. An abler one than you told me long ago I'd never drownd."

"How could *she* know?" Nabby spat at him jealously.

He thrust his strong hand out to her. "She could read palms. That's how."

Nabby would not touch the out-thrust hand but she lifted the candle and peered down at the spread palm. She shifted the candle and looked again, and Dave laughed his silent, shaking laughter at her plain discomfiture. Her strange eyes were stranger yet when she lifted them, and she was abruptly in added haste to be rid of him. Warmed and enheartened by his drink, Dave felt the necessity of starting homeward. It would not do for him to be away from New Erin overnight, the remembered guilt of his December absence chided him. He picked up his bottle and Nabby flung open the door. As he went through it, she could not resist an envenomed dart. "Hasten home, you. Lest one o' these nights ye come from Bella's and find a better man than you in yer bed."

How had she guessed where he had been? And what was that she was hinting? He turned back savagely, but something evilly triumphant in her face halted him. This was not a shaft in the dark; real meaning lay behind the spiteful taunt. "What do you mean? What man? My wife . . ."

"Yer wife's a smart woman," Nabby interrupted. "She knows a real man from a sham. She's a right purty woman, too. Did ye think ye could run around an' leave her t'suck her thumb?" Nabby was not without decent instincts that warned her she was doing a great wrong in spilling the secret of the man who had befriended her and her son, but the doubt and fear plain on the shadowed face before her was too tempting. Again she revelled in the power her quick mind and sharp tongue had once given her over her neighbours. "Go ask yer good-lookin' cousin who I mean," she cackled, and slammed the door.

Not for an instant did Dave attempt to shrug off her insinuation. It struck home too surely and too strongly. He cursed his blindness, imagining himself the laughing-stock of Prince's Cove, of all the shore as far as the names of Malone and Redmond and Kendrick were known. There might be some excuse for Isles, who had been forced to stand aside while his girl had been taken from him; Isles had worn his love openly at the time, although he had practised deceit since. But Dave's anger at Adria was a withering flame. *Why, she's no better than I am!* He recalled her candid gaze, her open smile. "Lies. Lies," he panted aloud, climbing the ridge with long strides, almost running in his desire to be home and confronting his wife with her perfidy. But Nabby's dart punctured deeper than the surface pride in his masculinity, his power over women. At first he had wanted Adria because of an inner greed and desire for possession and, although possession had never entailed a yielded price, he had intended to be good to her. Since then there had been times when he loved her truly and unselfishly. That she had cheapened those times, and his picture of her as a faithful wife, was beyond endurance. If Adria had failed him, the world had become a ruin, a travesty of all he had believed it.

When he reached the head of Nickerson's wharf he was sweating. He wanted the oars in his hands, speeding the skiff in retribution towards New Erin, but he tipped the bottle and drank again. The boat's painter had tightened in the damp fog and approaching darkness hid the knot. He almost tore the rope free from the spile and dropped it towards the skiff, an indistinct blob on the black water several feet below him. He cursed the low tide when his ears told him the painter had slithered down the seaweeded timbers and fallen, not into the skiff but into the shallow water beside it. Then he turned and, grasping the slippery cap-log, swung his legs over the wharfside, calculating with half his mind what he must allow for wind and tide, while the other half tore at Nabby Nolan's taunt.

Back in the shanty Nabby reached under the bed's eelgrass mattress and found a bottle. A shake told her it contained little and she wished she had not sold her last full bottle to Cap'n Malone. Yet, looking back at the now unreal visit, she could not begrudge it. She drained what she had. *Why did he have to come tonight when the fog was all I could bear?* She shuddered, staring into the unknown with her mismatched eyes. She touched her shrunken chest and the certainty there. *And before winter my grave would have held Isles Kendrick's secret for him. I was the only one who suspicioned. And I promised myself wild horses would never drag it from me, after he was so good t'Waits'l. But I hated the other one so. I hated him.* She sat muttering and shaking her head, while the slap of water on rocks came from the tide line and the fog-breeze dripped about her cracked chimney, and above their nests in the swamp behind the desolate dwelling, the gulls shrieked and wailed and laughed their inhuman deriding laughter.

THIRTY-ONE

Isles stepped out into one of those mornings which compensate coastal dwellers for the dreary fogs and the raw winds off the sea. He faced the eastern sky, which dawn had tinted as exquisitely as the inside of a bleached shell, and the cove, lying equally motionless and translucent. The land was stirring under its thin sheets of mist and dew, the sea purled on the outer reefs and the tide rippled dreamily about the wharf timbers. From the spruce copse near the house, birds sang and twittered ecstatic matins, and smoke spiralled above chimneys like incense to the dawn. In the adjacent pasture a boy, alder hidden, had left a black path through the silvered grass and his "Co' boss! Co' boss!" drifted wide and clear. Mowers were already laying the dewy grass in pleated swathes and the scour and ring of whetstones against scythes echoed sweetly above the shore-lap, while the soft scents of cut grasses and blossoming land mingled intoxicatingly with the sharper tang from tide-stirred seaweeds, and from the brittle foam flowerets that burst without true fragrance and set no fruit.

Isles had spent a sleepless night with the problems aroused by Dave's afternoon confessions and the mounting need to see Adria again, if only from a distance. His response to the morning swelled into such poignant yearning that, for relief, he turned his eyes and his mind to the prosaic affairs of the coming day, and walked slowly down Ryder's wharf. Midway a pink, tide abandoned, leaned its slatternly sails towards the supporting wharfside, like a frowsy woman on the arm of an indifferent escort and, beyond the pink's scuffed side, green satin eelgrass lay in skeins upon the shallow water, swinging to the tide's hidden impulses. The flood would soon find them and untangled, each strand would stream in free and separate response to the enticing eddies. *I wish some tide would straighten out the snarl my life seems to have gotten into.*

Now that he had admitted his love and acknowledged Adria's, it became impossible, and less than honest, to continue as Dave's partner in the established business and to embark on new undertakings such as they had ambitiously, if tentatively, planned. Yet much of New Erin's livelihood now depended on the freighting business which Dave could not manage alone. The night's thrashings had brought no solution to his quandary and the morning light apparently was not going to clarify it, as he had hoped it might.

He turned and looked out the western entrance where his trap-boat should be appearing with the night's haul. In the dead calm, the men would be forced to use the small dories and tow the deep-laden boat, leaving the sloop to await a wind. He decided he would walk to Grannie's Head, as he sometimes did on such mornings, and watch the boats come up the bay, the oars flashing in the sunlight as they rose and fell in their patient and seemingly effortless strokes that nonetheless pulled the dories and the towed craft steadily homeward. He did not admit nor deny to himself that Grannie's Head afforded an excellent view of New Erin and the roof sheltering Adria.

He took the shore path along the margin of the cove, across the cluttered heads of wharves and over the stepping-stones where the sluggish Dreen left the marsh. Blue flag nodded, though no air stirred, and their cloying perfume drifted across the whaleboat, rotting on its side above tide line, and out to the merry little whirlpools playing about the weeded ribs of a schooner that had burned to the water's edge before Isles Kendrick had seen Prince's Cove. Every step of the shore road had become familiar and dear through the years. Although, for Adria, he would have forsaken it all, this morning each turn in the winding path, each indentation of the shoreline, welcomed him with special charm and beguiled his mind from its earlier hopeless turmoil.

He recognized that he and Adria were victims of no cruel and individual scourging by Fate. He had learned that tragedy was inherent in life and was not the outcome of man's wickedness and stupidity alone, but came also from the tyranny of circumstances and events; that the reasons for it lay beyond human comprehension. Life's success, he knew, lay in accepting its allotted griefs and injuries and going forward without vain repinings. In this Adria had proved herself worthy of emulation. He reminded himself that for many years he had made a worthwhile life and found, if not what the world calls happiness, then an inner security and a respect for the human spirit, including his own. This, despite the continuing emptiness that had followed his loss of Adria. The morning's beauty and peace assured him that what he had done, he could do again.

Near Captain Sam Nickerson's old boatshop a trio of men busied themselves with nets and corks. Isles recognized Little Obie's barrel shape and spar-like Bradford Sears. The third figure was Bradford's son, grown from a toddler to a fine young man in the fifteen years since Isles had come to the Cove. This reminded him that life was hurrying past him, that acceptance and endurance were all very fine, but life without fulfillment . . . He detoured inside the group, giving them only a swing of his arm in greeting; this was no morning for listening to Obie.

From the crest of Grannie's Head, he saw that the cove mirrored its shore as if it knew no other purpose. Adria had confessed at first that she found the inner water too shut-in, that she ached to push Narrah aside to watch the open bay with its splendour of rolling seas or its wide placidity. But the cove would charm her this morning. *Adria colours everything I see, or hear, or think. And why not, when she has been for so long the very beating of my heart?*

He looked towards New Erin's lighthouse where he and Adria had watched the *Clara Caie*. There was Nigh Hill, hiding the hollow where he had found her. Now, near the grassy mounds with their granite markers, Waitstill's empty grave was a ragged wound marring the peaceful burying-ground as the exhumation had marred Adria's life. *I must remember to tell her of the tiny clover plants I found already rooted in the raw muds of the grave, and which will in time cover the hillside's scar. She will see their message of healing, as I did.*

Contradicting this thought came anger at Dave and what his selfish dalliance had bred. Without further consideration his decision was made. He would break with Dave. Continued association would merely build up rancours and benefit no one. It was no real help to pay off Dave's strumpets; after Bella there would be others. It could not help Adria nor himself to keep the wound of their love raw with the rubbed salt of unavoidable (and secretly welcomed) encounters and the tragically barren meeting of glances. Let time deposit unhindered its scar tissues.

At the foot of the slope Nabby Nolan's shanty showed no sign of life, and the bay beyond lay empty of craft, but two dories were slowly edging into sight around Pilot's Point. The black line behind them was the trap-boat, deep with her silver catch. He found he had no true wish to watch their progress and turned about. On his one hand the sunlight poured into the broken fireplace and gaping cellar of the burnt Nickerson home, on the other it washed across the tipped spiles of the wharf and the tumbled rocks from the broken cribbing. A few yards beyond the end of the rotting wharf rode a skiff, with only a ripple near the submerged end of the dangling painter showing the tide's grip.

The hairs along his neck tingled and his breath, when it came again, rasped. Dave's skiff should not be drifting across the cove; it should be berthed on New Erin. With dread, Isles descended the slope towards the water inching in over the bared feet of the wharf-spiles. He soon saw the dark mound, like a rock awash where no rock should lie. He would have fled then, telling himself he had seen nothing and leaving discovery to another, but his legs carried him forward.

A rock, spewed from the broken cribbing, had lodged across an arm. There was a tear on one cheek as if a protruding nail had caught at the falling body, but the wound above the brow told Dave's end. The sea had cleansed the murdering rock, now indistinguishable from its innocent fellows. Body and rock had been covered and bared by the fulling and ebbing of one tide during the night. The picture of Dave lying there in the fog and water, while Prince's Cove—and New Erin—slept, was sad beyond bearing. This had been the end of Dave's resolution to terminate his involvement with Bella and to begin a better life. The end of his betrayals of Adria; but also the end of a skillful and courageous seaman, here in the flat-mud, with the once powerful body helpless in the slightest wash of the sea.

Isles saw again the handsome, companionable cousin of their early acquaintance; the merry host to the childish Sandy Claws; the exhausted hero with the rescued crew of the *Sapphire*. Had he contributed to this death by his love for Adria, secret and harmless though he had striven to keep it? He would never know with certainty. For the first and last time he felt less than accord with Adria. He would cherish her until Death claimed him, as it had Dave; he would find in her his heart's desire. But by her stubborn girlish blindness she had belittled them all: Dave, who could never match the image she had made of him and who would have been passably happy and successful if loved by a woman of his own sort; Isles, who had seen the lifting wings of love drop to become shackles; and Adria, whose sweet and generous nature had been worn by an unsuitable union. Shame swept him for such criticism of one who had been caught, as unknowingly as himself and Dave, in a snare laid for all three of them. Shame was replaced by a fine new strength that refreshed his spirit, so long wearied by denials and dilemmas. He would find courage and wisdom to make no false haste, no false delays, in this second chance. His thankfulness for the years he could see opening ahead was mixed with true sorrow for Dave, snatched from life in his young prime. But perhaps, since he had chosen to follow his baser and not his nobler nature, it was better that he leave the world now before all that men had liked and admired in him had died, and only his selfishness and his weaknesses were left. For the wages of sin *is* death, death to all that is best in a man. All this passed through Isles' mind so rapidly that Little Obie, watching from the boat-shop, discerned no pause in his stride as he splashed through the water's edge and bent above something at his feet.

Then Obie saw Isles raise his head and swing one arm in a summoning gesture. He hurried shoreward, for Isles Kendrick was lifting a water-soaked body. And a man needed help with such a burden.

"Cap'n Malone!" Obie's voice shook as he bared his head.

The two looked at each other across all that was left of the man who had wronged them both. "Ah," Little Obie said, and Isles would never have recognized the voice, "He's made Port. His stormy v'yages are over."

EPILOGUE

The rolling year had brought another July and another crystal morning. New Erin lay ringed by a glassy groundswell, too good-natured to do more than dimple above the covered ledges and playfully nudge the smaller pebbles, while its chuckle at tide line merely heightened the island's tranquillity. Beauty and peace were part of Adria's happiness as she reached the crest of Nigh Hill and looked down its green slope to the bright shore at its foot.

Isles was beaching his skiff. Something of the boy who had rowed to New Erin before The Storm was in his wave to her, and in the eagerness with which he climbed the hillside.

The woman waiting at the top was worth hurrying to—slender and erect, with grey eyes alight with love and all traces of pain or repression long since kissed from her lips. Isles could not have described her dress, nor the hat on her gleaming hair, nor the bright cloak she carried, but he knew they were exactly right for his wife on their wedding day. As he took her into his arms he also knew that the years of waiting had not been worthless if they had been necessary to form the present Adria and this moment.

It was some time before either could find eyes for the world about them. The sea, which had been trying on first the soft grey of low clouds and then the rich blue of the high sky, had finally chosen the blue and was flaunting it gaily. Down the bay several sprit-sailed fishing boats lazed towards the Rip. In a few hours the *Dauntless* would pass them, with Mr. and Mrs. Isles Kendrick watching them from the rail. For at last Captain Stoddart was to give Adria her promised trip to Boston. That it would also be a honeymoon for her and his friend had set him to scrubbing and painting until Isles swore he didn't recognize the schooner. "And the captain is still making things shipshape for us. Listen." From behind Narrah broken hammering rang like happy snatches of a partly remembered tune.

During the past months New Erin had echoed to its own hammering, as the lobster-canning factory on Short Wharf had taken shape. Though the house appeared unaltered, the shoreward wing had been renovated and refurnished. Adria was well content that Isles had chosen to live on New Erin, but she no longer felt the need of familiar walls, nor of the island as a refuge; wherever Isles was, there would be her home. When seasonal business demanded his presence in the Cove, she would be happy in Aunt Cilla's house. Thankful and Bella were both gone from the village and during the past year, at peace with herself, Adria had reached out to grasp tentative offers of friendship and to ease the shamed reaction many felt against the unthinking cruelty which had victimized her. She had sold Alethea's house, which had never been truly hers, and Isles had lifted from her shoulders all responsibility for New Erin and its people. All this was part of her present joy, though none of it was in her conscious mind.

Isles drew out his watch. His father's watch, which had marked the unfortunate tea-meeting. *How many memories we share! And who but Isles could put aside all their reproach and make them only precious.* He was smiling down into her eyes. "We must go, sweetheart. Mr. Stouten is waiting to marry us. Mother and Rhuanna and Vol were ready, even before I left, and the sloop carrying your mother and Serena must have tied up at Ryder's Wharf some time ago." With an echo of his youthful shyness, "Do you think I was silly to ask you to meet me here on Nigh Hill, instead of at the wharf? To want to row you myself in the little skiff?"

Adria clasped his hand to hold between them as they stepped forward. "You aren't alone in wishing to bring back the morning we met. I remember I said to you then, 'I'll walk to your skiff with you'."

Side by side, lovers and dear companions, they turned down the hill to the curved beach, where the clear tide lapped amongst the pebbles as if it had never known the turmoil of a tempest.

FORMAC FICTION TREASURES Also in the Series

Louis Arthur Cunningham
Fog Over Fundy
Fog Over Fundy traces the adventures of a young non-conformist French Canadian woman who returns from Europe to the Tantramar in New Brunswick to fulfill her duties on the family estate and her obligation to the "peasant" workers there.
ISBN 10: 0-88780-710-0 ISBN 13: 978-0-88780-710-7

By Frances Gillmor
Thumbcap Weir
Gid Wyn and his fiancée, Debbie MacQuarrie, are counting on getting her father's fishing weir when they get married in the spring; but there is one villager, Tony Luti, who thinks it's his weir and that it has been stolen from him. Luti sets out to destroy the young couple's dreams and his hatred gets greater with the passing months until one day, under cover of fog, he and his son take revenge.
ISBN 10: 0-88780-645-7 ISBN 13: 978-0-88780-645-2

By Evelyn Eaton
Restless are the Sails
Paul de Morpain, a prisoner-of-war in New England, overhears a plan to send an expedition against the French fortress at Louisbourg. He knows he must do whatever he can to warn the governor. It is 1744 — a dangerous time to attempt a 500-mile journey by sea and overland along dangerous forest trails.
ISBN 10: 0-88780-603-1 ISBN 13: 978-0-88780-603-2

Quietly My Captain Waits
This historical romance, set during the years of French-English struggle in New France, draws two lovers out of the shadows of history — Louise de Freneuse, married and widowed twice, and Pierre de Bonaventure, Fleet Captain in the French navy. Their almost impossible relationship helps them endure the day-to-day struggle in the fated settlement of Port Royal.
ISBN 10: 0-88780-544-2 ISBN 13: 978-0-88780-544-8

The Sea is So Wide
In the summer of 1755, Barbe Comeau offers her Annapolis Valley home as overnight shelter to an English officer and his surly companion. The Comeaus are unaware of the plans to confiscate the Acadian farms and send them all into exile. A few weeks later, the treachery unfolds and they are sent to an unknown land as pawns in the Anglo-French conflict.
ISBN 10: 0-88780-573-6 ISBN 13: 978-0-88780-573-8

By W. Albert Hickman
The Sacrifice of the Shannon
In the heart of Frederick Ashburn, sea captain and sportsman, there glows a secret fire of love for young Gertrude MacMichael. But her interests lie with Ashburn's fellow adventurer, the dashing and slightly mysterious Dave Wilson. From their hometown of Caribou (real-life Pictou) all three set out on a perilous journey to the ice fields in the Gulf of St. Lawrence to save a ship and its precious cargo — Gertrude's father. In almost constant danger, Wilson is willing to risk everything to bring the ship and crew to safety.
ISBN 10: 0-88780-542-6 ISBN 13: 978-0-88780-542-4

By Alice Jones (Alix John)
The Night Hawk
Set in Halifax during the American Civil War, a wealthy Southerner — beautiful, poised, intelligent and divorced — poses as a refugee in Halifax while using her social success to work undercover. The conviviality of the town's social elite, especially the British garrison officers is more than just a diversion when there is a war to be won.
ISBN 10: 0-88780-538-8 ISBN 13: 978-0-88780-538-7

A Privateer's Fortune
When Gilbert Clinch discovers a very valuable painting and statue in his deceased grandfather's attic, he begins to uncover some of his ancestor's secrets, including a will that allows Clinch to become a wealthy man, while at the same time disinheriting his cousins. His grandfather's business as a privateer and slave trader helped him amass wealth, power and prestige. Clinch has secrets of his own, including a

clandestine love affair. From Nova Scotia, to the art salons in Paris and finally the gentility of English country mansions, Clinch and his lover, Isabel Broderick, become entangled in a haunting legacy.
ISBN 10: 0-88780-572-8 ISBN 13: 978-0-88780-572-1

By Evelyn Richardson
Desired Haven
Mercy Nickerson's father returns from a voyage to the Caribbean with a young Irishman he has saved from a shipwreck. Mercy and Dan are instantly attracted to one another. Rather than go to Boston, Dan decides to stay and turn his ambition to the fishery and ship supply. But his desired haven becomes a more dangerous place than he intended when he turns to smuggling and his wife turns against him.
ISBN 10: 0-88780-675-9 ISBN 13: 978-0-88780-675-9

By Charles G.D. Roberts
The Forge in the Forest: An Acadian Romance
Jean de Mer, an "Acadian Ranger," returns, after three years' absence, to his lands on the shores of Minas Basin to find his son Marc in trouble with the Black Abbé — a French partisan leader. Marc is waiting to be tried as a spy. Together father and son make a daring escape but Marc is wounded and Jean must endure a perilous canoe journey with a young English woman to rescue her child from the Black Abbé.
ISBN 10: 0-88780-604-X ISBN 13: 978-0-88780-604-9

The Heart That Knows
She was abandoned just hours before her wedding. Helpless and shocked, she watched her 'husband' sail away, without so much as a word of explanation. When her fatherless son grows up he sets off to sea, determined not to return to his New Brunswick home until he has sought vengeance on the man who treated his mother so heartlessly.
ISBN 10: 0-88780-570-1 ISBN 13: 978-0-88780-570-7

By Margaret Marshall Saunders
Beautiful Joe
Cruelly mutilated by his master, Beautiful Joe, a mongrel dog, is at death's door when he finds himself in the loving care of Laura Morris.

A tale of tender devotion between dog and owner, this novel is the framework for the author's astute and timeless observations on farming methods, including animal care, and rural living. This Canadian classic, written by a woman once acclaimed as "Canada's most revered writer," has been popular with readers, including young adults, for almost a century.
ISBN 10: 0-88780-540-X ISBN 13: 978-0-88780-540-X

Rose of Acadia
One hundred and fifty years have passed since the Acadians were sent into exile; now, Vesper Nimmo, a Bostonian, sets out for Nova Scotia's French shore with the intention of carrying out his great-grandfather's wish to make amends with the descendants of Agapit LeNoir. Nimmo finds himself immersed in the Acadians' struggles to preserve their culture and language and meets Rose à Charlitte, the innkeeper where he makes his temporary home. Their romance is thwarted by her past; but he cannot leave.
ISBN 10: 0-88780-571-X ISBN 13: 978-0-88780-571-4

By Frederick William Wallace
Captain Salvation
Captain Salvation is a little-known novel of Maritimers at sea, now brought back into print in this new addition to Formac's Fiction Treasures collection. It is an exciting tale of a young reprobate who works his way up from able seaman to mate, skipper and then a ship owner. His strength and intelligence pull him through the violent life aboard ship. Finally, shipwrecked off Cape Horn, he has to face his demons.
ISBN 10: 0-88780-676-7 ISBN 13: 978-0-88780-676-6

Blue Water
Set in the early 1900s, Blue Water traces the adventures of "Shorty" Westhaver from boyhood to young manhood in the dangerous and often tragic world of the Grand Banks fishery.
ISBN 10: 0-88780-709-7 ISBN 13: 978-0-88780-709-1